Penguin Books
Mrs Eckdorf in O'Neill's Hot

William Trevor was born in Mitchelstown, Co. Cork, in 1928, and spent his childhood in provincial Ireland. He attended a number of Irish schools and later Trinity College, Dublin. Among other occupations, he has worked at those of teacher, church sculptor, and copywriter. His other books are *The Old Boys* (1964; Hawthornden Prize), *The Boarding-House* (1965), *The Love Department* (1966), *The Day We Got Drunk on Cake* (1967) – all these are in Penguins – and *Miss Gomez and the Brethren* (1971) and *The Ballroom Romance* (1972). He is also the author of a play, *The Elephant's Foot*, which was produced in 1965.

William Trevor lives in Devon, is married and has two young sons.

William Trevor

Mrs Eckdorf in O'Neill's Hotel

Penguin Books

Penguin Books Ltd, Harmondsworth,
Middlesex, England
Penguin Books Australia Ltd, Ringwood,
Victoria, Australia

First published by The Bodley Head 1969
Published in Penguin Books 1973

Made and printed in Great Britain by
Hunt Barnard Printing Ltd, Aylesbury, Bucks
Set in Linotype Granjon

For Jane

I

'I'm Ivy Eckdorf,' said Mrs Eckdorf as the aeroplane rose from the ground. 'How d'you do?'

The person beside her, a stoutly made red-cheeked English-man who happened at the time to be reading of unrest in Syria, lowered his evening newspaper and smiled at Mrs Eckdorf. He did not give his name, since he saw no cause to barter names with a stranger on an air-flight. He displayed further goodwill by nodding. He lifted his newspaper again.

'Now what are we going to take to drink?' said Mrs Eckdorf. She reached above her and turned on the little orange light that indicated a desire for attention. 'I loathe being up in the sky,' she confessed. 'Especially at night. Cognac for me,' she said when the hostess came. 'Now what for you, my dear?'

Amazed that he should be so addressed by a woman he did not know and thinking that he was clearly going to have to pay for her drink, the man asked for whisky. He glanced at Mrs Eckdorf and saw the face of a woman in her late forties, with blonde hair hanging from beneath a cream-coloured hat with a brim. She had eyes of so pale a shade of brown that they were almost yellow, and two reddened lips that were generously full and now were parted in a smile. There was a gap between her teeth, precisely in the centre of this mouth, a slight gap that an ice-cream wafer might just have passed through.

Mrs Eckdorf talked. She took the newspaper from the man's hands and neatly folded it. She placed it behind the flap of the rack in front of him while saying that she had been educated, if you could call it that, at St Monica's School for Girls, an academy at which she had had the misfortune to meet Miss Tample. Her own mother, Mrs Eckdorf said, had been a most dislikeable person, given to hysteria and lovers. Her father had disappeared one night, saying he was going out to post a letter and not ever returning: who could blame him, Mrs Eckdorf asked the man beside her, the circumstances being what they were? On the other hand, she added, he might have taken her with him.

'I turned to Miss Tample, having no one else to turn to,' continued Mrs Eckdorf, 'and she proved, quite monstrously, to be a snake in the grass. You know what I mean?'

'Well,' said the man.

'To this very day I'm haunted by the sordid propositions of Miss Tample. "Have cocoa, Ivy," she said to me. "Come up and have cocoa: you're looking peaky." An innocent girl, I followed her up those stairs. "Such fun," she said, handing me a mug of stuff with a skin on it. "Take off your tie," she said, "if you're feeling hot, Ivy." And as the hand of this vulturous woman went out to seize mine her sour breath struck my cheek.'

The man beside Mrs Eckdorf began to say something but Mrs Eckdorf gesticulated, indicating that she'd rather he didn't interrupt.

'Miss Tample,' she said, 'with her brown knitted cardigan and her support stockings, the soft moustache on her upper lip, two panting eyes behind spectacles – my God, you should have seen Miss Tample!'

She continued to speak of her life. She ordered further drinks. She was a photographer, she said: she had discovered the world of photography when she had gone to Germany, while still a girl. She had married two German businessmen, yet was herself entirely an English woman, having been born in London, in Maida Vale. 'I do not advise you,' she said, 'ever to marry a German.'

The man shook his head, at the same time stating that he was contentedly married already.

'The one who was my husband last,' said Mrs Eckdorf, 'gave me a taste for cognac. Hans-Otto Eckdorf.'

'Oh yes?'

'Indeed.' She paused, and then she said: 'That has been my life. A mother, a father who walked away. And then Miss Tample. And then two German businessmen. The only light in my life is my camera.'

'I see.'

'We are the victims of other people.'

'It's often so – '

'Hoerschelmann was my other husband. He had glasses and no moustache. Hans-Otto had a moustache of sorts. Hoerschelmann was sandy and fatter than Hans-Otto. Hans-Otto was dark.'

'I see.'

'You see me as a brash woman. Well, yes, I'm brash. I'm a brash, hard, sick kind of woman: I have no illusions about myself. My marriages failed for unfortunate reasons. I left England because of its unpleasant associations for me: soon I shall have to leave Germany too.'

In a different kind of conversational way, the man said he had never been to Germany. Mrs Eckdorf shook her head, seeming to imply that whether or not he had been to Germany was irrelevant.

'My last completely happy memories,' said Mrs Eckdorf, 'had to do with the dolls I had as a little girl. Can you imagine me as a little girl? Is it easy to imagine a woman of forty-six as a little girl at a dolls' tea-party? For all you know I might be drunk. Are you thinking that? If you're interested, what I'm saying is that despite a nicely groomed exterior I have a heart like anyone else.'

'Yes,' said the man. 'Of course.'

'When Hoerschelmann said he would have to divorce me I couldn't bear it. I walked around our apartment holding his shirts to my breast, weeping for hours and hours. Someone telephoned Hoerschelmann after the third day and told him that every morning after he left the apartment I wept noisily. He couldn't understand, because what he left behind was a nicely groomed woman who seemed also to be tough. It wasn't that I loved Hoerschelmann all that much, it was simply that his wishing to divorce me was another nail in the coffin of my life. In the end, naturally, I hated him. Have you been divorced?'

The man said he hadn't. He said he knew very little about divorce. He had married, he said, when he was twenty-two and had remained with the same wife since.

'On balance,' said Mrs Eckdorf, 'Hans-Otto was crueller. You understand why I have thrown myself into my work? I haven't had much luck with human relationships.'

'I'm sorry –'

'And still I have a needy heart. Let's talk about something else now.'

There was a pause. Then, as though reciting a practised piece, Mrs Eckdorf said:

'I flew this morning from Munich, which is the city where currently I live. About the city we're approaching I know extremely little.'

'It's a good business town these days,' the man informed her.

'A fair city,' murmured Mrs Eckdorf more romantically. 'In Dublin's fair city: that's a line in an old-fashioned song.'

'Yes.'

'Some cities are fairer than others. In my work I notice that.'

Mrs Eckdorf went on speaking, saying she knew as little about the inhabitants of the city they were approaching as she did about the city itself. She had read somewhere that they were litter-bugs and disputatious, but she didn't at all mind that. Revolution had taken place in the city, she knew, and was glad that it had: it showed spirit to rebel against *status quo*, it lent a certain pride to a people. She knew that the country of which the city was the capital was a land of legend and myth: she had seen a television programme about that, a programme that had shown old men talking and priests talking and children dancing in the stiff local manner. Vaguely at the time she had thought that she herself could have made more of it than the television people had, but it was not until years later, as a result of a meeting with a barman on an ocean liner, that she had been moved to think about the city again. This man, telling her much besides, had said he hadn't been attracted by the place. He had walked through it in the rain, apparently, seeking solace and finding it hard to come by. A motor-car, moving gently in the night-time traffic, had struck him as he crossed a street and the driver had smiled and waved, as though the contact created a friendship between them. The barman had wandered about until a man approached him outside a public house and offered to guide him to the solace he sought. He had walked with this man for a very long time, until they came to a person called Agnes Quin standing in a doorway, and the guide, whose name was Morrissey, had remained with them until they arrived at a yellow hotel.

'My work dictates the order of my life now,' Mrs Eckdorf said. 'I do what my work tells me to do.'

She continued to speak, talking about her work in such a passionate manner that the red-cheeked man came to the conclusion that she was a little odd. When she had said she was a photographer he had at once thought of photographs in an album and photographs in newspapers and on picture postcards, but it seemed she wasn't interested in this kind of photography at all. She said to him that her camera was an all-seeing eye. She was a merchant of truth, she said; she practised an art. She spoke of Marrakesh and some peasant family there with whom she had once lived for several months, absorbing the necessary background for a book of photographs that had eventually won for her a coveted award.

'A picture tells a story,' explained Mrs Eckdorf. 'The lines on an old face, broken teeth in a jaw, scars of a lifetime.' She paused in thought, as if viewing these images in her mind. 'An eye-patch where an eye should be,' she said. She had travelled the entire world, she added, seeking faces and the stories they told, laying bare the unvarnished truth.

Her companion inclined his head. 'It must be interesting,' he politely remarked, 'travelling about, doing that.'

'It is,' Mrs Eckdorf agreed, and went on speaking about the books of truthful photographs she produced: expensive volumes, beautifully bound. They were often to be discovered, she revealed, on the coffee-tables of the well-to-do.

'In this present instance I don't quite know what I'm after. I can't be sure. D'you understand that?'

'No,' said the man.

'I'm going now to photograph a tragedy that took place nearly thirty years ago.'

'I see.'

'If you'd care to listen to me, I'll tell you how all this has come about.'

The man sighed inwardly. He tried to smile at Mrs Eckdorf. She said:

'I had it from a barman on a ship.'

She reached up and again switched on the little orange light above them. A hostess came and Mrs Eckdorf ordered further drinks. She waited in silence until they came and then she thanked the hostess. She drew a street map from her handbag and opened it in front of her, asking her companion to hold one edge of it. With a red, shapely finger-nail she indicated an area of the sheet. 'Somewhere there,' she said. 'Near that place called Dolphin's Barn. Thaddeus Street.'

'Yes,' said the man, pretending to see the street she mentioned, in fact not bothering to seek it.

She folded the map and returned it to her handbag. It was a short street, she said, as he'd have noted, and a number of the houses that once had stood in it stood there no longer. 'That barman described it vividly,' she said. 'Corrugated iron hoardings with torn posters flapping in the breeze, a wasteland where children play among the rubble. Someone was going to build something but the money ran out: it's always happening down there in that city, apparently.'

Mrs Eckdorf closed her eyes, and her voice continued to describe Thaddeus Street. At one end stood the dingy yellow bulk of O'Neill's Hotel, once a flourishing commercial establishment, now forgotten more or less. Opposite there was a shop that sold groceries and next to that a turf accountant's. Two houses were empty and had fallen into disrepair, two others were occupied by several families, a fifth contained a priest. At the other end of the street stood a public house.

'The woman Agnes Quin pointed it all out to the visiting barman, as someone might proudly show off a local place of beauty. And then, or later, she told him about Mrs Sinnott, a woman of ninety-one who owns O'Neill's Hotel. It's now a disorderly house.'

The man fidgeted with his hands. He drank some whisky. He had been hoping on this journey to catch up on a little lost sleep. Mrs Eckdorf said:

'She's deaf and dumb, this woman. She sits there in an upstairs room high above Thaddeus Street, conversing with people by writing everything down in exercise-books. She knows nothing of what her hotel has become. Her son, Eugene, has let that happen, not caring apparently, or allowing it deliberately, I don't know which. She is a woman who was famous in her time because of her love of orphans and even still a few orphans hang about her, grown men and women actually. Agnes Quin's herself an orphan, and so is Morrissey and so is O'Shea, the hotel's solitary porter. They go to her and sit conversing by means of an exercise-book: in the silence of that room, I dare say, her goodness soothes them. It soothes Eugene, and Philomena the woman Eugene married, and Eugene's sister and his son and Eugene's brother-in-law. All of them make the journey to receive what she offers them and I have made this longer journey in order to photograph them all together on her birthday, which is the day after tomorrow, August 10th. Ideally they won't even know what's happening. Don't you think it's a beautiful thing?'

The man looked at Mrs Eckdorf in astonishment. She did not seem drunk, he thought. 'Beautiful?' he said.

'You've been to houses like that, I dare say,' Mrs Eckdorf said. 'Have you ever thought as you pleasured yourself that the house could also contain a person like Mrs Sinnott?'

The man protested vehemently, but Mrs Eckdorf explained that she knew about the desires of men and did not hold the desires of men in any way against them.

'The barman was moved. He thought it extraordinary that Agnes Quin should show him the houses of Thaddeus Street and tell him all about an elderly woman who was deaf and dumb, and about Eugene Sinnott who allowed her hotel to go to seed. What do you read into that?'

The man said he was not equipped to read anything into it. He repeated that he did not frequent the kind of house that Mrs Eckdorf was claiming this hotel to be. He would like, he said, to make that quite clear.

'The barman was curious also,' she said. 'He asked questions. Eugene and his mother live alone in the hotel now, with only O'Shea to tend them. Twenty-eight years ago Philomena left Eugene, taking from him their baby son. Twenty-eight years ago the daughter of the hotel ran away also, although the neighbours say she loved her mother's hotel. Why was all that?'

'Mrs Eckdorf, I've absolutely no idea. I've never even heard of all these people, or O'Neill's Hotel, or Thaddeus Street –'

'Agnes Quin pretended not to know either. She shook her head when the barman pressed her. "They all come together for the birthday," was all she'd say. August 10th. What happened once in O'Neill's Hotel?'

Tetchily, the man protested it was none of his business what had happened once in O'Neill's Hotel. Mrs Eckdorf said:

'Twenty-eight years ago a tragedy occurred, the results of which we see today.'

'You cannot know a thing like that.'

'When I close my eyes I can see the yellow hotel and Eugene Sinnott, a drunk according to Agnes Quin, a man destroyed. I think he's an amazing figure, like a tree that's dead. With a son somewhere, and Philomena his wife, and an old mother who watches over him.'

The man shook his head.

'Listen to me,' continued Mrs Eckdorf. 'This old woman sits alone, visited every day by a street-walker and by Morrissey. A priest comes also, climbing up the long stairs to bring her the sacrament.'

'Look here, I'm sorry: I find all this distasteful.'

'Distasteful? A priest climbing up –'

'I don't mean that.'

'Distasteful?' said Mrs Eckdorf again, speaking slowly, as though mentally examining the word for some meaning other than that usually implied by it. 'Distasteful?'

The red-cheeked man turned away from her and reached a hand out for the newspaper she had packed away. She seized the fingers of his hand and smiled at him. She spoke quietly. She said:

'I do not understand you.'

'I'd really rather read, Mrs Eckdorf.'

'When the barman was speaking, an intuition told me that the human story of O'Neill's Hotel was a story that must be told.'

The man said nothing. He lit a cigarette, hoping that his silence had a sourness about it. He imagined the kind of run-down place O'Neill's Hotel would be. He imagined a family that had fallen down in the world, a family apparently who'd had trouble in their lives for one reason or another. For profit, it seemed, this painted woman was about to photograph their decay.

'I have photographed tragedy before: I have followed every inch of a slaughterer's footsteps in Colorado, the path that less than a week before he crept along, into the humble room in which he dealt out death to an erring wife. I have recorded greed and depravity and pride and grief and poverty, yet this is the human story that I feel is closer to myself than any other I've yet pursued. I have a separate intuition about that.'

'I see.'

'You don't. Oh God, I must begin again. Listen to me – '

'It isn't necessary – '

'I live,' said Mrs Eckdorf, 'in a cinder-grey apartment in the Lipowskystrasse, in Munich. A month ago, on a German ship returning from Africa, I sat alone in the bar one night, chatting to the barman. "I'm a photographer," I said, for want of something better to say. "I photograph human stories of quality." And in the chat that followed the ship's barman told me of this hotel. He told me of that old woman there and of her love for orphans. He shivered in the hall of this hotel, passing through it. You see?'

'Yes, yes.'

Mrs Eckdorf lapsed into silence. The man reached for his newspaper and this time was not prevented from seizing it. He read again of unrest in Syria, but the words meant little as they came from the page. What was the matter with her? he wondered, and his thoughts went back to the first statements she'd made, about her misfortunes at a boarding-school and the trouble with her parents. She was one of those people who gossiped on and on so that you couldn't in the end separate fact from fantasy. Did a woman like that ever pause to think that other people, casually met, were not just listening machines? He did not at all care for her.

'Well,' said Mrs Eckdorf, 'what do you think of it all?'

He smiled at her and said nothing. His eyes returned to the printed message in front of him.

'Me,' she said, 'and all that?'

'Well –'

'You think I'm being half-baked when I say my professional intuitions can sense a tragedy in the past. You remind me,' said Mrs Eckdorf, 'of Hans-Otto. You probably think I'm a lunatic.'

'What I honestly think,' said the man quietly, 'is that no one has the right to go poking about in other people's lives in order to make money, or indeed for any other reason. There's such a thing as privacy.'

'We are all God's creatures,' replied Mrs Eckdorf equally quietly. 'We concern one another. That old woman there is the concern of Hans-Otto Eckdorf and he of her. Agnes Quin is your concern –'

'Agnes Quin is not my concern –'

'Oh yes. As I am too. As O'Shea, the hotel's solitary porter, is, and Eugene Sinnott and Philomena. Would you and I, if we spent a time together, come closer to one another's minds? Would we fall in love on the beaches of Tahiti? We do not take to one another, yet that could happen. We are all part of one another, my dear, and we must all know one another better.'

Listening to this, the red-cheeked man became angrier. He pretended to look through the window of the aeroplane at the darkness. He raised his left shoulder and edged himself around so that he was presenting most of his back to Mrs Eckdorf.

'Terrible things took place in O'Neill's Hotel,' cried Mrs Eckdorf shrilly, making sure that her voice carried to her companion. 'Call me what you will, but of that I'm certain. You're a man who goes to houses like O'Neill's Hotel and fails to spare a thought for the people there. Cherubim and Seraphim might –'

'I do not go to houses like O'Neill's Hotel,' shouted the man. 'You're talking a lot of damn rubbish.'

'No,' said Mrs Eckdorf.

'You've been sitting there talking rubbish to me about people I've never even heard of. I understand nothing of your conversation, Mrs Eckdorf.'

'Well, then, let me begin again. A barman on an ocean liner –'

'Will you please not speak to me!'

'A barman on an ocean liner met in that city below us a street-walker called Agnes Quin – '

'I have asked you to be quiet, Mrs Eckdorf. I have no wish to sit on an aeroplane quarrelling with a stranger.'

'There is something greater than just a skeleton in a cupboard there. There is something which, when known to other people – when seen in documentary form by other people – will help those other people: Hoerschelmann, Hans-Otto, people in Germany and England and in the United States of America, and Italy and France, and everywhere. Can you understand that? I'm quite a famous photographer.'

'My God!' murmured the man.

'What's the matter with you?'

'Nothing is the matter with me.'

'I believe you think it odd of a barman on a ship to confess to me that he had visited such a place: I thought it odd too, until afterwards I realized that when I mentioned human stories he couldn't help himself. He felt the presence of a human story. Intuitively, I felt the same. I can't make it clearer than that, I'm afraid.'

'I don't know you, Mrs Eckdorf, and I don't at all wish to know these facts you're telling me. For my part, I can't make it clearer than that, either.'

'I am advancing upon the lives of these people,' said Mrs Eckdorf loudly, 'so that others may benefit. Please don't forget that.'

'It's an unpleasant contemporary thing,' cried the man with sudden passion, 'this poking into people's privacy with cameras in the cause of truth. Films are made and earnest television programmes. I can well imagine your shiny books.'

'Morrissey,' said Mrs Eckdorf, 'and Agnes Quin. And Eugene Sinnott and Philomena. And the daughter who turned her back on that yellow hotel, and some man the daughter married. And Mrs Sinnott who neither hears nor speaks, about to become ninety-two. What are the lives of these people like? How are they the victims of other people, or of each other maybe? Has tragedy made them what they are? What would they say if they knew that a skilled photographer was flying in for the birthday of the woman who sits at the centre of them all? What happened once – '

'Shut up,' cried the man in a snarling voice and threatened then that if Mrs Eckdorf did not at once cease talking he'd make an official complaint.

'You're a smug, unimportant man,' said Mrs Eckdorf, and did not speak to him again. She applied lipstick to her mouth and powdered her cheeks. She hummed to herself, and after a time she addressed a passing hostess, enquiring about the weather. 'Is it good down there?' she asked. The hostess smiled at Mrs Eckdorf. Less than ten minutes ago the pilot had spoken to the passengers, telling them where they were and the weather that night in Dublin was cloudless. 'They're enjoying a heat-wave actually,' the hostess said to Mrs Eckdorf.

'Thank God for that,' said Mrs Eckdorf and added that, being a photographer, weather was her bread and butter. That night she would rest luxuriously: she would rest with a sleeping-pill, and tomorrow she would begin the day early.

2

The people towards whose lives Mrs Eckdorf was advancing awoke in their various resting places on the morning after Mrs Eckdorf's arrival in their city. O'Shea, the hotel-porter, was the first to do so. He was a tall man with a thin white face and below it a thin neck. His eyes were nervous, as though reflecting some inner anxiety, dark hair was light upon his head, his teeth protruded slightly. He left his bed in the moment that his eyes opened, and drew on to his spare body the faded uniform of his calling. A greyhound rose from a corner of his bedroom, stretching and wagging its tail.

On the way down the stairs of the hotel O'Shea met the source of Mrs Eckdorf's information in the person of Agnes Quin. He passed her by without a word, noting out of the corner of his eye an elderly man in the shadows behind her. The two waited as he descended. They saw his mournful figure reflected in a mirror that hung on heavily embossed, almost black wallpaper. Here and there on the staircase wall the paper had become dislodged in the warm summer of 1946, and O'Shea had fixed it in place with nails. Its edges curled inwards, revealing between long strips the paler plaster of the wall itself. The clumps of nails, placed at the top of the paper so that each piece might hang freely, had become rusty and were now unnoticeable on the dark, uneven surface.

In the pillared hall of the hotel, with its balding maroon carpet that extended up the stairs, eight chairs echoed a grandeur that once had been. They were tall, like thrones, their gilt so faded and worn that it looked in places like old yellow paint, their once-elegant velvet stained with droppings from glasses of alcohol. Behind this row of chairs, prone on the carpet, lay a man into whose rump O'Shea's boot was now driven with force. His eyes watched as the shrimpish form of his enemy Morrissey moved swiftly, without speech, across the hall and out of the hotel. O'Shea continued on his way to the kitchen, his greyhound loping behind him. Agnes Quin and her companion came down the stairs. Early morning in this house wasn't ever much different.

Mrs Sinnott awoke and her mind immediately filled: she saw scenes in Venice and the faces of her two children at different times in their lives, and the face of her husband who had been shot in 1911. *I am saying you should marry me*, he had written on a scrap of paper, a scrap she still possessed, for she had never believed that she would receive a message like that. She had shaken her head at the time, smiling at the fair face of this man who once had written that his name was Leo.

She remembered then that the day following this one would be her ninety-second birthday and she wondered how long she would go on living, or if she would live through the present day. Often her heart murmured and she felt a pain, which was, she knew, to be expected at her age. She was frail in appearance, but did not give the impression of delicate health; there was a strength about the way she moved, although she moved slowly as if conserving energy. Her face was thin and as sharp as an axe, with neat grey hair which soon she would attend to for the day ahead, pinning it up at her dressing-table, peering at her reflection with black eyes like currants. She would lie on a bit, she thought, as every morning she thought: she would take her time. She would wonder and remember in the silence, looking straight ahead of her at an azure wall.

In the room beneath, Eugene Sinnott, a man of fifty-eight, opened his eyes and at once closed them again, blaspheming quietly. There was sunlight in the bedroom. He felt its presence on his face and on the backs of his hands, which lay outside the sheet that covered him: again, he reflected, he had omitted to draw down the blinds the night before. The warmth made him uneasy, as did the reddish, unsatisfactory darkness he had induced by dropping the lids over his eyes against the glare.

The night before, at four minutes to midnight, he had stood in the centre of the room, thinking of nothing, unbuttoning the jacket of his black suit and then unbuttoning his waistcoat, seizing his braces and drawing them free of his shoulders, stepping from his trousers and then removing his shoes. He had walked to the door to extinguish the light and had entered his bed in his underclothes. One day in 1948 O'Shea had said to him that his three pairs of pyjamas were now beyond repair and he had nodded his head, deciding that it was not necessary to replace them.

Eugene, on this sunny morning, remembered his dreams. He stretched out his left hand and found a packet of Sweet Afton and a box of matches on the table beside his bed. He lit a cigarette and saw himself as he had seen himself while he dreamed: a man with a plump face that was patterned with exploded veins, a man with a cigarette in the centre of his mouth standing in Riordan's Excelsior Bar, bald-headed except for a ridge of sandy hair at the back of his neck and tufts of it near his ears. He saw a man in clothes that were marked with cigarette burns, who weighed sixteen stone and measured five foot eleven, whose forehead glistened with a skin of perspiration, whose eyes were pale blue. He had been standing at the bar when Morrissey had entered and announced that Eddie Trump was dead. 'He dropped dead,' he said, 'when he was opening a bottle.' Morrissey had extracted from a paper bag a bottle of pale wine that had a corkscrew stuck in its cork. Eugene had taken it and had read on the label: *Niersteiner Domtal*. 'It came over on the wireless,' said Morrissey. 'He died in Washington Zoo.'

At that moment O'Shea entered the bar and said that Eugene was urgently required in the hotel. He reported that a circus trainer was standing in the hall, requiring rooms and warm stabling for his animals. 'It's like the old days,' said O'Shea, excitedly seizing Eugene by the shoulder. 'Those circuses pay through the nose.' Eugene had handed the bottle of hock to Mrs Dargan and against his will had accompanied O'Shea from the bar. They had walked the length of Thaddeus Street in a drizzle, but when they arrived at O'Neill's Hotel there was no sign of a circus trainer.

There had been another dream in which he had observed himself slowly descending the stairs of the hotel. O'Shea, waiting for him in the hall, had said there was something wrong with one of the cisterns. He had seen himself later, walking in Dalkey, climbing over rocks and seaweed; he had paddled in the sea, surprising himself by doing that. A dog had come up to him, a black animal of indeterminate breed, and Father Hennessey had appeared in the distance, on the cliffs. Father Hennessey had called down that he wanted to see him some time, and then had turned and walked away.

Eugene drew smoke into his lungs: he coughed with the cigarette still in his mouth, causing ash to fall on the sheet and on his vest. As far as he could remember, he had experienced no other dreams. With his eyes still closed, he drove his mind back into the night, searching for some particle that he might have overlooked, but he could discover nothing.

Dreams were important to him, as they were to his friend Eddie Trump, the barman in the Excelsior Bar, for both men had profited from racing tips that their dreaming over the years had revealed. Eugene had first won eight pounds, in 1955, on a horse called Persian Gulf, having dreamed the night before that he was flying on a carpet. Eddie Trump had done even better with the outsider Pin Money, Kevin Moloney up, having dreamed that he'd been holding in his hand two sixpenny-pieces. Their dreams often misled the two men, but they put this down to their lack of skill in interpretation, and regularly pointed out to one another that all that was necessary was practice. It was Morrissey who had first reminded them that dreams were a known source of racing information, a reminder that they had now forgotten but which Morrissey remembered.

Eugene crushed the butt of his cigarette into a green ashtray that contained a number of other butts. He left his bed and stood for a moment on the brown rug that lay beside it, his arms hanging loosely by his sides, his eyes fixed on a picture of the Virgin Mary that hung between the two windows. He remembered the picture being placed there at the instruction of his mother, a long time ago now, when he was seven or eight. The room had just been redecorated: his mother had chosen a brown wallpaper with small flowers on it and a frieze to match it, and pale buff paint. Modern spring blinds had been installed, the same blinds, discoloured by the sun, that he had forgotten to draw the night before. The floor had been re-stained and the two brown rugs had replaced badly worn linoleum. His mother had carried to his freshened room the framed image of the Virgin, and one of the workmen had driven a nail into the wall between the two windows and had placed the cord of the picture on it.

Eugene withdrew his gaze from the soft face he had known for so long. He dressed himself slowly, not thinking about the face, but remembering instead Morrissey saying that Eddie Trump was dead. He wondered if it would upset Eddie Trump to hear the dream retailed and he attempted to estimate how he would feel himself if someone in Riordan's public house related the same thing about himself. He placed a foot on the edge of a white-painted table that bore a china jug in a basin; he tied the laces of his shoes. In a mirror that hung on the wall above the white table he could see reflected the bed he had slept in and the table beside it. Into this room, some time between the distant past and now, he had brought his wife. She had paused at the door and then had walked forward, while he, not quite sure of what he should do, had opened a window. The narrow bed that had been there then had been dismantled and exchanged for the large bed in his mother's room, which was something she herself had suggested. He remembered her standing above O'Shea while he toiled with a pair of pliers and a wrench, endeavouring to unbolt various parts. *It was a bed I bought in Roche's Stores*, she had written. *You were born in it, Eugene. And Enid too.*

Lightly whistling a popular tune of the past, Eugene lifted from a chair near the white table a shirt-collar, a striped tie, and two collar-studs. Later in the morning, after he had shaved himself, he would put on both collar and tie, for those additions to his dress were ones that he did not ever care to be without when he emerged from his mother's hotel and stepped into Thaddeus Street to begin his day.

Far away from Thaddeus Street, in the suburb of Terenure, Mrs Sinnott's daughter, who fifty-one years ago had been christened Enid Mary and was now Mrs Gregan, listened to her husband's voice talking about tomatoes. She looked away from him, hearing him say that there was a fortune to be made on the side. Tomatoes, he said, were always in demand.

His mouth consumed food, his eyes behind his spectacles were fixed on his knife and fork. Soon, still speaking, he would rise from the table and leave the room. She'd hear him whistling and when the whistling ceased she'd guess that he had paused to light his pipe. His footsteps would thump on the stairs, a slow and heavy tread, going up and down several times.

'You know what I mean, Enid?' he said, rising from the table.

She said she did. She cut a piece of toast, trying to think about a recipe for Frangipan Tart. Two eggs, she said to herself, one and a half ounces of sugar, one and a half ounces of butter, half a pint of cream, half a pint of milk, a quarter of an ounce of flour, one bay leaf, lemon rind, nutmeg, short-crust . . . Upstairs he banged the lavatory door so that she felt the reverberation. Mix the flour smoothly, she thought, with a little milk. Simmer the remaining milk with the bay leaf, lemon rind and a pinch of nutmeg.

He stood before her in his soft, fawn mackintosh coat, bicycle-clips gripping his ankles, a brown hat on his head. He was head of the Home and Personal Effects Department of an insurance company, a department into which he had taken Eugene's son, Timothy John, feeling it to be his duty, since Timothy John didn't appear to know what to do with himself.

'Good-bye so,' he said, speaking through smoke, his pipe in his mouth.

He went away, and she watched from the window, drawn to the window, as she was at his departure every morning. He wheeled his bicycle down the short path. His fingers touched the front tyre and then the back one, checking the pressures. He knocked his pipe out and then slowly, with the bicycle leaning against his body, filled it again with tobacco. He cupped his hands around the bowl, firing the tobacco in his own particular manner, employing a method, so he had told her, that he had perfected himself.

In another suburb, in Booterstown, Philomena, wife of

Eugene and daughter-in-law of Mrs Sinnott, fried rashers and eggs in the kitchen of a bungalow. In contrast to Mrs Gregan, who was tall and grey and square-faced, Philomena was a tiny woman, with hair that was as black as ever it had been and with chestnut-brown eyes in an olive face.

'Don't forget now,' Philomena said to her son, for whom she was cooking the food, 'you have to go to the dentist.'

He, shaved and cleanly-attired, sat waiting at the kitchen table: Timothy John, twenty-eight, whose face, set in a narrow head unlike either of his parents', at once suggested his timid nature. The day would be the same as other days, he reflected as he waited, except that an electric drill would grind into one of his teeth.

She placed a warm plate containing eggs and rashers before him.

'Have you thought of a birthday present?' she said.

'I'll get a tray-cloth.'

'That's nice. Eat up now. Don't be late.'

'I won't be late, Mother.'

She smiled and he tried to smile back, ashamed of not being able to stop thinking about the probing of instruments and the sudden striking of a nerve, and ashamed as well of being afraid to tell her that for too many years he had found her love oppressive.

'I'll bring her the gooseberry jam and maybe something else as well,' she said. 'She'll like the jam we made.'

'She's fond of gooseberry.'

'She is,' said Philomena.

They'd made the jam together. At the kitchen table he had prepared the fruit for her, one evening a month ago, while she had drawn from him the details of his day. 'We'll save a few pots for your grandmother's birthday,' she'd said at the time. 'She's fond of gooseberry.'

'You'll get a tray-cloth in Arnott's,' she said now. 'You'll probably get it in your lunch-time.'

He nodded. He saw her looking at the clock on the window-sill.

'Don't be late for the dentist now,' she said again.

She smiled as he rose from the table. 'Don't forget to give your teeth a good wash,' she said.

O'Shea bought five herrings at a stall not far from the canal. He was a familiar sight in the neighbourhood of Thaddeus Street and beyond it, a man who was the same age as Eugene Sinnott and who wore on all occasions his uniform: epaulettes on a blue jacket, gold-coloured buttons, gold braid stretching the length of cherry-red trousers. His greyhound was always a pace or two behind him, and often as they walked O'Shea would speak to his pet, although he rarely turned his head to do so. In the evenings he polished the buttons of his uniform and placed, at night, the cherry-red trousers beneath his mattress in order to gain a crease for the following day.

'You gave me stale ones last week,' O'Shea complained to the elderly woman who was selling him the fish. 'We were sorry to see that.'

He spoke sadly. He listened to the protestations of the fish-seller, nodding when he heard her say that the herrings she had sold him last week were the freshest that had ever passed through her hands. He nodded, not because he agreed but because he accepted that the elderly fish-woman believed what she was saying. She had been hood-winked by a wholesaler: she could not be blamed for her simplicity.

'It's all right,' he said.

'Ah, I only have the freshest. What use is a fish to you if it's in a bad condition, sir?'

'No use at all.'

'Is Mrs Sinnott fit?'

'Mrs Sinnott will be ninety-two tomorrow.'

'Isn't she a great woman? There's not many women like that these days, sir. There's not many that spend a lifetime in silence and would be smiling at ninety-two.'

She put in an extra small herring for which, she said, she would make no charge in honour of Mrs Sinnott's approaching birthday. 'She's never heard the song of a bird,' she said, and O'Shea agreed that this was so. 'God bless the poor soul,' said the fish-seller.

For her birthday O'Shea had purchased, a month ago, a small ivory-white image of the Virgin Mary. Wrapped in tissue paper, it was in a small cardboard box that he often opened. He imagined her opening it herself, tomorrow afternoon in the kitchen with everyone around her, and looking at him, to thank him. It would be there in her room always, to remind her of his affection and his gratitude. *I did not know my parents at all*, he had written for her forty-four years ago, having been sent to her hotel from the orphanage which was his home. She had smiled at him and agreed that he might come and work for her, running errands and helping in the kitchen. In those days she took an interest in everything: when a man complained about a maggot in the bacon he was eating she tasted the meat herself to set the man at ease.

'She had an ear for everything in your mind,' O'Shea said to his dog, 'even though she never heard you.' He spoke in an emotional voice, causing the greyhound to wag its tail vigorously and to rub its head against his legs. It was a dog that had walked into the back-yard of the hotel seven years ago and had remained since, rarely leaving O'Shea's side.

The two hurried on, through streets that many said wouldn't be the same without their regular presence. The ivory-white statue, he thought, would stand among all the other sacred pieces he had given her on her birthday over the years, for it had always seemed suitable that he should offer her gifts of this nature. For the last three years her son had given her a pencil-sharpener, on each occasion requesting O'Shea to buy it for him. It saddened O'Shea that Eugene Sinnott should devote so little of his energy and imagination to the selection of a gift: he had pointed out that in Mrs Sinnott's room there were now many pencil-sharpeners, of different shapes and in different colours, all of which were adequate for the purpose for which they'd been designed. A pair of scissors, he considered, or a bowl for flowers would have been more suitable than the little red pencil-sharpener, made of plastic, that last year Eugene had selected out of the half dozen he had brought back to the hotel for Eugene's perusal. 'He chose the worst,' the man had said when O'Shea returned with the others, and O'Shea had felt ashamed.

He would fry her the nicest of the herrings, and butter a little bread for her and make tea in the small tin tea-pot that was offered only to her. He would write down a few details about the people he had seen that morning. One day, he knew, he would go up the stairs with her breakfast tray and find her gazing ahead of her without any sight left in her eyes, without warmth in her body. And what would happen then? Her wish was that he should remain in the hotel, in charge of her son, a man who drank too much, whose only other interest was betting on horses and greyhounds and the retailing of his dreams. The hotel was in its present state because Eugene Sinnott, whose duty it was, could not be bothered to run it on efficient lines. He lived on his mother's money, on money accumulated at a time when O'Neill's Hotel had always been full of commercial travellers going to and fro. Fifteen years ago O'Shea had stood in the hall turning men away courteously, as she had taught him. It was her wish, he believed, that before or after her death the hotel should regain its lost glory even if a miracle had to happen. Her father had founded it: in her mind, O'Shea believed, it was a memorial to him, a man she had honoured and loved. Yet it was not her nature to complain, but rather to live in hope. It was not her nature to write, for her son to see, a message that questioned the poor state of her property today. 'Have glasses of sherry destroyed him?' said O'Shea aloud. 'Is there no cure at all?'

The dog made a noise and the two strode on, O'Shea moving swiftly on the pavement, his body bent, his motion like that of a hurrying crab's. It was quiet, that warm morning in the neighbourhood that O'Shea and the dog passed through. Few voices were raised in Bond Street or Pim Street or in the streets near them, in Morning Star Road or Rosary Road. In greengrocers' shops unshaven men in their shirt-sleeves and waistcoats sat with a morning newspaper. Cats slept in doorways, children eyed through sweet-shop windows boxes of liquorice pipes and pink money-balls, women sniffed at fish.

The area reflected the impression of Thaddeus Street. There was waste ground, where weeds and rough grass grew among bricks and rusting tins, and old prams lay discarded on a litter of paper. Tall houses here and there rose on their own, lonely edifices in cement, exposed by demolition and yet untouched by it. Humbler red-brick dwellings filled quiet roads, their gardens neat, a few with coloured elves reclining.

In Dolphin's Barn that quiet morning a patient in the New Coombe Maternity Hospital gave birth to identical twins in so quiet and matter-of-fact a manner that all but one who tended her were amazed. 'I have seen it before,' said the one who was not, an Indian doctor from Deogiri. 'Fine weather and poverty keep the pregnant silent.' The nurses glanced at one another, doubting the theory, for they knew that the man from Deogiri was keen on joking. In Reuben Street a widow said to her priest that her life had been hard. 'But you are grateful for the life?' the priest urged, and the woman, consumed by an illness, said she was grateful. A child sent out by her mother to purchase sugar in a nearby shop observed the hunched form of the hotel porter moving swiftly towards her with a greyhound. She noted that the man was murmuring and she stared with interest at the sorrowfully moving lips. She had noticed this figure a few times before but always at a greater distance, the coloured uniform tending to draw attention from afar.

'Hullo,' said the child to O'Shea, smiling at him with a mouth that was bare of teeth.

O'Shea stopped and the greyhound stopped. He regarded the child, feeling nervous, knowing that the children of the district were given to mockery.

'What do you want?' he demanded.

'I was sent out to get sugar, mister. I like the clothes you have. Are they special clothes, mister?'

'I'm the porter at O'Neill's Hotel.'

'I seen you on Tuesday, turning the corner of Cork Street.'

In the distance, hunched in a doorway, smoking a cigarette, O'Shea saw Morrissey. Pretending otherwise, he was with some interest observing O'Shea's encounter with the toothless child.

'Can a girl be a porter?'

O'Shea shook his head. The child said that when she was bigger she'd like to wear a uniform like this, which was why she'd asked the question. She liked the colours. She asked if she could touch it.

29

He saw Morrissey watching intently while the child stepped forward and touched him.

'It's nice,' she said.

It meant something, he thought, that this child had come up to him. He was aware of wanting to talk to her about the hotel as once it had been, how he had stood in the hall waiting for people to arrive, how he had carried suitcases and advised about bus routes, how he had done good work and understood his place in the world. The child touched his uniform a second time, and he knew then that he must not speak in that manner and that he must not speak of himself.

'Maybe you'd work in an hotel in some other way,' he said. 'Maybe you'd be a maid. You'd have a little uniform to be a maid.'

'Maybe I would, mister.'

The child began to go away. 'Excuse me,' said O'Shea, calling after her. He looked down at the child, trying to smile and then finding the effort beyond him. It was difficult to say some things, especially to a child who was strange to you, especially when you weren't used to the company of children. He believed he had to speak because when the child had touched him he had felt the urge of his duty and he had also been aware of the precise form of the statement he had to make.

'Mister?' said the child.

'Don't ever go into a church without a covering on your head. D'you understand that? No girl or woman should ever enter a church without the head is covered.'

He walked away, not waiting for the child's response. Morrissey would be wondering what had occurred between the child and himself. He had never spoken to Morrissey, but he knew the kind of person he was. Morrissey was always on the streets, stopping people and trying to talk to them. He would probably stop the child and ask her what had been said to her, and when she told him he wouldn't understand. Not if he sat and thought about it for two years, O'Shea reflected, would Morrissey understand that a child had been sent to a hotel-porter so that she could be given a necessary command. Morrissey took advantage of Mrs Sinnott, writing down rubbish in her books, wasting good paper. Morrissey crept into the hotel at night, he brought Agnes Quin there, he passed water in the back-yard, on a little flower-bed that O'Shea had made himself.

He stopped and prayed, with his eyes tightly closed. He prayed that the child whose name he did not know would not pass the doorway where Morrissey was standing and so be exposed to the evil that came from him. He prayed that in return for performing his duty by the child he would be granted that favour. When he opened his eyes he felt it had been said to him that all he'd asked had been decided anyway, that the child was being well watched over. He turned and saw the child running on the pavement, far away from where Morrissey stood.

If he could see the cut of himself, Morrissey was thinking, the tall eejit. It was scandalous that a man like that should be allowed on the streets, tramping about with an old dog, bothering people. He'd often thought of the old dog lying in the back-yard, with its interior thrown up on the flower-bed. It was totally scandalous that a man like O'Shea was alive at all, let alone in a position to raise his boot to a fellow human being. *Morrissey is passing nights in the hall*, he had read in O'Shea's handwriting in one of the old woman's exercise-books. If O'Shea complained to Eugene he'd be asked what harm could it do, a homeless man lodging for a little while in the hall until he settled himself out? Eugene wouldn't care a damn if the national army laid itself down in the hall, and why in the name of God should he? 'O'Shea's a jealous man,' he had taken the opportunity of saying to Eugene. 'Jealousy has him cantankerous.' One of these nights he'd walk up the stairs and enter a bedroom like a civilized human being: was it right that a whole hotel was sitting there while a human being could be homeless through no fault of his own?

He imagined O'Shea asking Eugene to explain to him how a man could get into the hotel at night when it was locked, and Eugene shrugging his shoulders and telling O'Shea not to be annoying him. O'Shea knew that a key had been borrowed out of Eugene's pocket and that Morrissey had gone down to Wool-worth's to have another one cut. O'Shea had guessed that this was the only explanation, only O'Shea wouldn't say it outright because he wasn't made like that. O'Shea'd be afraid that Eugene would say no one could borrow a key out of his pocket without his knowledge. He'd be afraid Eugene would challenge him and then he'd have to say that anyone could borrow a key from a drunk man in Riordan's public house, which was a statement that might cause Eugene to give O'Shea a blow on the face.

Morrissey touched his body where the porter's boot had earlier struck it. It was extraordinary, any man doing a thing like that for no reason whatsoever, and not doing it once but regularly and without ever speaking a word. He remembered the first time he'd seen O'Shea, the first time he'd entered the hotel. He'd said hullo to him and O'Shea had turned his head and gone off in another direction. Morrissey had been thinking at the time that a porter in an hotel was a man with whom he might exchange a civil word and might on later occasions hold other conversations. He'd been thinking generously, anxious to please a person who was a stranger to him, addressing him with good intentions. It was extraordinary that any human being could be so entangled inside himself, and so cantankerous that he couldn't bring himself to issue a single word but could only raise his boot. Another man would have taken a knife to O'Shea by now, but Morrissey knew that if he lifted a knife he would have the misfortune to be observed by some woman looking in through a window, just as if he poisoned the old dog they'd put him in gaol for ten years, saying he intended the poison for a human being.

Morrissey was singularly small, a man in his mid-thirties who had once been compared to a ferret. He had a thin trap of a mouth and greased black hair that he perpetually attended, directing it back from his forehead with a clogged comb. He was dressed now, as invariably he was, in flannel trousers and the jacket of a blue striped suit over a blue pullover, and a shirt that was buttoned to the neck but did not have a tie in its collar.

A few weeks ago he'd been asked to vacate his lodgings owing to a failure to pay the rent regularly, and his life had since become complicated in detail. Late at night, long after O'Shea had gone to bed – for the porter retired at nine o'clock – Morrissey shaved himself in the hotel kitchen. He washed his hands and face and rubbed oil into his hair, afterwards hiding his meagre toilet equipment behind one of the two kitchen dressers. The remainder of his clothes and belongings were in a canvas bag in the left-luggage department of Connolly Station, in custody until he had again established himself permanently.

Loitering in the doorway and thinking about the difficulties in his life and the nature of O'Shea, Morrissey watched a horse and dray bearing sacks of coal go by, its bell jangling loudly. He watched the driver seize a piece of coal and hurl it at a mongrel dog that was running wildly about, barking at the legs of the horse. The coal struck the animal on the back and Morrissey saluted the driver, wagging his head in approbation of the action. It would have been good, he thought, if the dog had been O'Shea's greyhound and if the lump of coal had destroyed it: he imagined the greyhound dead on the street and O'Shea lifting the carcass, crying out in distress, and the coalman kicking O'Shea on the jaw. He laughed and spat on the pavement and went on his way. He walked towards no particular destination, until suddenly he thought that he'd go down to Woolworth's and see if he could take a little brooch or a jewel off one of the counters, as a gift for the old woman's birthday.

On that same morning of Friday, August 9th, a man from Liverpool, a salesman of cardboard, rose from his breakfast table in another Dublin hotel and whistled briefly through his teeth. He was a man who wore rimless spectacles and had fair, balding hair and a small mouth. His name was Mr Smedley and, like Mrs Sinnott and all her regular visitors, he did not at that time know the woman called Ivy Eckdorf. Yet Mr Smedley, before he left this city, was to know her and was to remember her with vividness for the remainder of his life. He crossed the floor of the hotel breakfast-room, wondering about the city that was as strange to him as it was to Mrs Eckdorf, and wondering what, apart from business, it held for him.

Mrs Sinnott, having risen and completed all her preparations for the day, now dressed in black, felt tired as she settled herself into the chair by the window to await the arrival of O'Shea with her breakfast. Around her, on azure wallpaper that had once been richly coloured and now was bleached to nondescript, hung in profusion small religious emblems, the gifts of O'Shea over many years. Among them, and dominant, a painted copy of the Virgin in Baldovinetti's Annunciation had seventy years ago come from another source, from her mother. In a corner, a dressing-table made to fit the corner held her father's gifts: an oval looking-glass that was silver-framed, and brushes with silver backs, and a smaller glass that matched the brushes in its silver decoration. Her husband, killed in revolutionary action, looked down from a wooden frame, fair-moustached and stern, with softness in his eyes.

Mrs Sinnott sighed a little and closed her own eyes, returning for a moment to the past, to orchestras playing silently in the Piazza San Marco. She watched the violinists, feeling through the excitement of their movement a reflection of the reality. People danced among the pigeons. *A long way from Thaddeus Street,* her father wrote on the back of a cigarette packet. He showed her the message, leaning towards her and smiling.

She walked on the Zattere al Gesuati. She stood in the Cathedral. *That is by Bellini,* her mother wrote in the Church of the Glorious St Mary of Friars, her mother who was herself a Venetian. The face of the Child in the Triptych came into her mind and then faded away. She opened her eyes and looked down from her chair into Thaddeus Street. A youth threw open the peeling door of the turf accountant's, a woman hurried by.

She looked away, regarding instead the eight piles of red

exercise-books that were stacked beneath the deep window-sills on either side of her, against the blue-papered wall. There was a ninth one, a smaller pile that was set a little to one side and contained her conversations with Father Hennessey. Although she understood deaf and dumb language and had once taught it to her husband and to both her children, she no longer employed it. There was an urgency about the sign language that seemed like impatience, and reading other people's moving lips had never appealed to her. She preferred the written messages because as the pencil moved slowly over the paper she imagined that for her visitors the room was as silent almost as it was for her: she drew her visitors into her tranquillity and she imagined they appreciated it.

The day before, Father Hennessey had spent an hour with her, showing her what he had written concerning the legend of St Attracta, about which he was composing a book. It was said that this hot-tempered saint had received the veil from St Patrick and had divided the waters of Lough Gara and had harnessed deer with her hair. *We must skim the truth from pretty myth*, Father Hennessey had written for her benefit alone. *There is plenty of truth in St Attracta.*

She took an exercise-book from one of the piles and read, in the handwriting of Morrissey: *If you are thinking of a holiday, August is the best. Make no decisions this forenoon. Avoid tension in the p.m.* Morrissey had sat there contentedly copying the information out of a magazine. He had opened the magazine at a moment when he imagined she wasn't noticing him and had placed it close to him, assuming it to be hidden from her view. *Venus in Cancer*, Morrissey had written. *The holiday to suit you best will be one with evening entertainments.*

Her son, her daughter, her grandson, her son's wife, her daughter's husband, her priest, her last three orphans: all her visitors were there in the red exercise-books, and their lives were continuing now in their different ways. The troubles and mistakes that were reflected in the pages of the exercise-books were haunting again those whom they possessed, for her visitors, like everyone else, had lives in which there was, with all the rest, failure and sorrow and regret. She thought of them one by one, and imagined them beginning a new day, struggling against the difficulties of existence, which she no longer was required to do.

'Dinner in the diner, nothing could be finer,' cried a voice from the wireless of Mrs Sinnott's daughter. In her house in Terenure, while O'Shea was entering O'Neill's Hotel with five herrings, Mrs Gregan was listening to music on her kitchen wireless and washing the dishes from which she and her husband had eaten their breakfast. She was thinking of the Society of St Vincent de Paul, a charity for which she did much work. Sums of money ran through her head, a figure that had been recently reached, another figure that must be reached before the end of the year.

The telephone sounded in the hall and Mrs Gregan turned the wireless off, her wet fingers fumbling on the bakelite knob. The sums of money, the figure reached and the one that had to be reached, disintegrated in her mind. She moved to answer the summons, instinctively knowing it would be from her husband. She saw that he had left his gum-boots by the hallstand, which specifically and repeatedly she had asked him not to do. There was a portion of black pipe-dottel, she saw, on the linoleum she had polished yesterday. 'Hullo, hullo,' said his voice on the telephone. Faintly she could hear the clicking of typewriter keys and the murmur of conversation.

'Is that you, Enid?' he said.

His breath was heavy on the mouth-piece of the receiver. In her mind she saw his face, the folds of red flesh, the grey hair brushed straight back from his forehead, the spectacles with black frames.

'Yes,' she said.

'It's Desmond here, Enid.'

'Yes.'

He lowered his voice. 'I was thinking,' he said, 'about the tomatoes.'

'Desmond, I'm busy with the dishes now –'

'Will you go into a butcher's – can you hear me, Enid?'

'Yes.'

'Will you go into a butcher's and make arrangements for

congealed blood? Ask the cost of a gallon of congealed blood every week as a regular order. Explain it's for the cultivation of tomatoes and we won't be requiring it till later on. Enid?'

'Yes.'

'Could you compare the price of a gallon in one place with the price in another? The type of blood is immaterial, tell the man. D'you understand that? It can come from any animal whatsoever, only a pig might be best if he gives you a choice.'

He had bought a small plot of ground a few miles from where they lived and he had just erected on it two glass-houses in which he proposed to cultivate tomatoes for profit. He had come back one evening and asked her if she'd ever noticed tomatoes laid out in the shops. 'A full chip when you go by in the morning,' he'd said, 'and an empty one when you come home at night.' The plot of land had been paid for out of capital left to her by her father, as had the shed he had built in the garden and the concreting of the yard. Earlier in her marriage to Mr Gregan she had once or twice protested at his way of appropriating her money, but he had pointed out that it was essential to invest money in a sensible manner rather than to purchase clothes with it, or household luxuries that would wear out quickly. He had a way of speaking about such matters over a period of several weeks, making his point after tea every evening when they sat down by the fire. 'A garment can let you down,' he would say. 'A fur coat taken off the back of some misfortunate animal could be eaten by our friend Master Moth and then where'd you be? Or you'd have it stolen off your arm by some brigand when you were out walking in the Botanic Gardens. You'd be paying out good money on insurance with an expensive garment, whereas a concreted yard requires no insurance whatsoever. Once it's down it's in place for ever. A concreted yard is an improvement to any property.' He would go on until it was time for the News and when the News was over he would continue. She might ask him if he'd mind not sitting by the fire in his socks in case anyone came to the door, but he usually didn't hear when she referred to his personal habits. He never appeared to notice her anger, or her sarcasm. He went his way, but somehow she found it difficult to go hers.

He had explained to her once that a brooch she had seen in a shop in Nassau Street would be of little use to her since there would never be an occasion in her life when she could wear it. 'The insurance on that,' he had said, 'would be four pound a year.' When she questioned that figure he replied that he had been in the insurance business for the full span of his adult life and if he didn't know what he was talking about it was a queer thing. On another occasion she had bought a little antique chair and when she'd shown it to him he hadn't said a word. He had waited until she was occupied in the bathroom and then he had lifted it into his car and the next day he returned it to the dealer from whom she had bought it. The wrangle over whether or not this man should repay the full amount of money went on for four months, with letters piling up on the mantelpiece and a nightly report from Mr Gregan about the difficulty he was experiencing. 'You made a terrible boob over that,' he said to her. 'The old chair wasn't worth twopence, Enid.' On the day he received the full amount from the antique dealer he said all was well that ended well, except that he was nineteen shillings down due to expenditure on postage stamps. He took off his shoes and cleaned the mud from them with the poker, while she sat there asking him not to.

'Any type of stuff from a slaughterhouse,' he said on the telephone, 'and you could collect it once a week when you're out on your shopping.'

She didn't reply. She remembered him saying to her, thirty years ago, that she had the nicest hands he'd ever seen on a woman. He had suddenly put his lips on her lips one night in Chapelizod. 'There was never a woman like you,' he said.

'Are you listening to me, Enid?'

The day before she had purchased the ingredients for a Basque omelette, a recipe she'd been planning to attempt for some time. She had turned on the wireless in her kitchen and had sliced a green pepper, which she then fried in pork fat. She had chopped other peppers, crushed garlic, and diced ham. She had simmered the mixture, waiting until she heard his key in the door before beating the eggs. He shouted out at once, complaining that he'd telephoned several times and hadn't received an answer. 'I was out buying peppers and garlic,' she said. 'I have a delicious dish for you.' But when later she placed the *pipérade* before her husband he poked at it with his fork and said he'd rather have a couple of pieces of fried bread with marmalade on them. 'Taste it,' she urged. 'It's called the *Pipérade du Pays Basque*. It's one of the great dishes of the world.' But he had replied that he'd rather not taste stuff like that. Was she trying to poison him? he asked with a rolling laugh, pushing the plate away and again mentioning fried bread. Later he talked about the plans he had for the cultivation of tomatoes. There was first-class profit in tomatoes, he said, as witness the financial standing of certain greengrocers.

'Are you all right?' his voice demanded on the telephone. 'What's troubling you?'

She wanted to say that he'd left his gum-boots by the hall-stand and a piece of filth on the clean floor. She wanted to say that she made simple requests of him and he took no notice. She wanted to remind him that those same hands now were being ordered to carry pailfuls of animal's blood about the streets of Dublin.

'Desmond,' she said.

There was a silence from him. In the background a man laughed, cups rattled on saucers. She might go on for ever, she thought, remembering things, looking at him and listening to his voice. He had gone to sleep once, four years ago, with his pipe carelessly thrown down on a little table that had belonged to an aunt of hers. The hot bowl had left a mark on the surface, causing her to complain more bitterly than before. She recalled the occasion vividly because it was one of the few times he had appeared to notice that she was upset. 'Leave it to Bobs,' he had said, and when later she was out on St Vincent de Paul work he had attempted to remove the mark by scratching at it with a screwdriver.

'Desmond,' she said again.

'Are you there? Did you take in what I said, Enid?'

'Desmond, d'you remember the time your pipe burnt the table?'

'What's that?'

'You went to sleep and your pipe burnt a mark at the table. Four years ago.'

'I can hardly hear you.'

'You understood that I was upset. Desmond, I'm upset now.'

'What's that?'

'I'm upset by things, Desmond.'

The palm of her hand, gripping the receiver, was warm with sweat. She could feel her mouth trembling as she spoke. She would cry, she thought. In a moment she would become hysterical.

'What's eating you?' her husband said.

'You understood that time, Desmond. I'm upset because you don't listen to me when I ask you not to sit in your socks. I'm upset – '

'Is it the time of the month?'

'Oh God, haven't I told you?' she cried. 'Haven't I told you every day for the past six weeks that I've got to a certain stage in a woman's life? I've told you I'd be touchy. All women are touchy now. I keep seeing you, Desmond, in my mind's eye. I keep knowing the next thing you're going to say. Desmond?'

'Look, I have to get back to the desk – '

'I was washing the dishes and the wireless was on. I was going through figures in my head and the next thing was the telephone rang. I knew it'd be you, Desmond. When you were talking I thought of the time you put up the garden shed and the time you said a concreted yard was there for ever, and the day you took the chair back. D'you remember in Chapelizod when you said I had the nicest hands you'd ever seen? You're asking me to carry buckets of blood, Desmond. You're telling me to go into a butcher's – '

'I can't hear a damn word you're saying. Are you sick, girl?'

In the hall she shook her head. She held back her sobs. His voice questioned her again, and she said again that she was upset. She said she was fifty-one years of age and had borne no children. She said that for some reason she couldn't bear the thought of his growing tomatoes in his field. She said that for some reason she couldn't bear the thought of seeing him on his bicycle.

'Enid –'

'The car never leaves the garage, Desmond. I thought we'd
go out –'

'Can you hear me, Enid? If you're feeling under par why
don't you go and get yourself a bottle of stout? There's nothing
to beat a half pint of stout drunk slowly and leisurely –'

'You left your gum-boots by the hallstand and a piece of filth
on the clean floor.'

She put the receiver down, knowing he would be glad of that,
knowing that he wouldn't ring up again to make sure she was
all right. A few weeks after she'd left the hotel they had stood
in the hall of his mother's house, smiling at one another, with
the day of their wedding established in their minds. She wept
as she stood now, thinking of the dishes in the sink, not understanding anything.

At his desk, in his private glass-partitioned office of the Home
and Personal Effects Department, Mr Gregan went over the
order of events. He had left his house, bidding her good-bye.
She had been at that moment in perfectly good form, having
cooked the breakfast. He had mounted his cycle and made the
journey to Westmoreland Street in record time. In the large outer
office he had noted the absence of his nephew, Timothy John,
and on enquiry had been reminded that his nephew that morning
was paying a visit to a dentist. While taking off his coat he had
made a mental note to have a word with his nephew about that.
He had attended to a number of enquiries and complaints, he
had dictated three letters. He had sent the girl off to type them
and then, suddenly remembering that he'd read about slaughter-
house blood as a tip-top fertilizer for tomatoes, he had telephoned
through to his wife.

It was an extraordinary thing, he reflected, that she had told
him all of a sudden that she had borne no children. She could
hardly imagine he was unaware of that. Completely out of the
blue she'd told him she was touchy, adding that she was fifty-one
years of age and that the car never left the garage. Relighting his
pipe, Mr Gregan frowned. Never in their whole married life had
they quarrelled. Never once had they stood opposite one another

shouting abuse and insults, as a reading of the law reports suggested other couples did. Through hard work he had risen to a certain position in the insurance company, he had supplied the house they lived in with comforts and conveniences. Other couples attacked one another, not just with words but with household property and with their fists: he had never shown signs of violence, or indeed of ill-temper, he had never used to her words or implications that were slanderous. And yet all of a sudden, without warning or stated reason, she was going on about his gum-boots. Any man could forget to put a pair of gum-boots in the correct place, just as any man might leave a pipe on an old table that was in poor condition anyway. She'd made a fuss right enough at the time, but hadn't he repaired the damage as soon as she drew his attention to it?

Was she blaming him because she had borne no children? Was she suggesting in some peculiar way that he hadn't been capable of causing children to be born to her? For a moment, and in amazement, he saw his wife in her mother's room in the hotel, looking through the conversations he had had over a period with Mrs Sinnott. Slowly he shook his head: she would not do that, nor would Mrs Sinnott ever permit such a thing in her presence. Privacy was privacy, it would be like listening at a door.

He dismissed the thought completely, but his mind, having arrived in the room of his mother-in-law, lingered there. He had first visited her on his own only a few years ago, to borrow money for an artificial pond he was hoping to sink in the garden. He had sat with her, scribbling out a chattering conversation until quite unexpectedly he had said to himself that the old woman was lonely. The family visited her, as did one or two waifs and strays, but he felt as he sat there that somehow she appreciated more than he'd ever have guessed this visit from another person. *I'll drop in again*, he had written.

It was easy to get away during the day when affairs were quiet in the department. *'I'm sorry we couldn't give you grandchildren,* he had written, and from that moment he had written about nothing else except the longing he had, and had always had, for children of his own. He wrote of the years going by and the disappointment growing. He wrote of the house as it might have been, with other people in it, growing up and going to school. He wrote about his own childhood, telling her in detail of his life at that time and the things he had done. She had always been interested, she had always been anxious to learn more. It was a subject he felt he could not broach with his wife, since he felt that their failure in this way was something that should not ever be mentioned between them. Nor was it something he could talk about to a casual acquaintance or a colleague in the office: it was easier with an old woman in a quiet room, and it was easier not having actually to speak the words.

Mr Gregan put down his pipe and took from a drawer in his desk a tube of fruit-gums. He ate one, for his mouth felt hot and bitter from an excess of tobacco smoke. Should he telephone her again? he wondered. There was no doubt about it, if she'd only relax herself for five minutes and go down the road for a bottle of stout she'd feel improved. He tried to see her in his mind's eye leaving their house, making certain the door was secure behind her, and then entering one of the bars in Terenure. 'A bottle of stout when you're ready,' he tried to make her say, but he shook his head over his efforts. He himself, when a bit of difficulty arose in the Department, would take himself across the road to the Pearl Bar or up to the College Mooney. Twenty minutes with a glass in front of you and you felt as right as ninepence again, able to tackle anything, able even to think of the disappointments in your life without entering depression. In this day and age there was nothing whatsoever to prevent the wife of an insurance man from going into a public house in the middle of the morning in order to relax her mind. He wondered if he'd made it clear what he'd meant, or if she'd listened to him properly. She had a way of not listening when he was talking to her, which he found a bit irritating, but nothing of course for a mild-tempered man to write home about.

He picked up the telephone and asked for his home number, thinking that he'd explain it further and point out to her that there was no reason at all why she shouldn't do something she'd never done before. He'd remind her that when the barman brought her the stout she should pay him at once and drink it slowly; he'd tell her to bring a newspaper in with her so that she'd have something to do. He listened to the ringing at the other end and he remembered her suddenly, standing in the hall of his mother's house on the night they'd fixed the date of the wedding, a few weeks after she'd left the hotel because of the bit of trouble there'd been. 'We'll have six children,' he'd said. 'Five boys and a girl.' He thought of the two glass-houses that were standing empty in the field he'd bought, and he saw himself in the fullness of time picking orange tomatoes from healthy plants and bringing them back to her, charging her nothing for as many pounds as she wanted. In the fullness of time he would erect other glass-houses until the field was full of them. He would spend his days there, with a couple of assistants, young lads who'd share his interest. He would cease to work in an office, which was something he had always wished to do, although he doubted that she knew it. The telephone in his house went on ringing, until in the end he replaced the receiver, still thinking of the glass-houses as one day they would be.

Carrying his tie and his collar and his two shirt-studs, Eugene passed through the hall and entered a passage that led to the kitchen, and then entered the kitchen itself. It was a huge cavernous place with a mass of hooks suspended from dark ceiling-beams: once it had been the hub of everything. Beneath barred windows three sinks were separated by draining-boards that stretched beyond them to either wall. Copper pans and kettles had once upon a time thronged shelves near by, but the shelves were empty now: a man had come one day and had offered Eugene a good price for the copper-ware, which Eugene, in O'Shea's absence, had accepted. The dressers were still full of red-and-white crockery: plates piled high, gravy boats, cups and saucers, dishes and serving bowls. Old bills on lengths of wire hung from cup-hooks; thick cookery books, neatly arranged by O'Shea, lined the lower shelves. A long wooden table of proportions that matched those of the kitchen itself stood on the flagged floor, with chairs all around it. A kettle murmured over the fire in the old-fashioned range, a clock ticked loudly on the mantel-shelf, registering a quarter to ten.

Eugene placed his tie and his shirt-collar, with the two collar-studs, on the edge of the table. He sat down beside them and picked up a morning newspaper that O'Shea had earlier been reading. He perused it with care for twenty minutes, sitting at the table with the pages spread out before him. Malacca was tipped to win at Harold's Cross, rumours about Yellow Printer's limitations were denied. Ginger Bomb had won at Bath, and Spinning Top, Two Seater, Priority, Pettyless and Primstep at Pontefract. Courageous was tipped for the double at Lingfield. The strike of three thousand semi-skilled and unskilled Dublin Corporation employees had entered its fourth day. A man had been sentenced to three months' imprisonment for stealing from a handbag. At Brighton the £35 filly Qalibashi had won at twenty to one, Whisky Poker was selected for the three o'clock at Redcar, and Whisky Noggin for the three thirty. Privy Seal would win at Ascot.

He read slowly, and then he folded the paper, ready for O'Shea to carry upstairs with Mrs Sinnott's breakfast. He sat considering a few of the facts he had absorbed, listening to the ticking in the clock. Within a couple of minutes his head dropped on to his chest and he returned to sleep. He snored softly; he dreamed he was standing in Riordan's public house.

'It's a fine day,' said O'Shea's voice in Eugene's dream, and he opened his eyes to find that O'Shea was crossing the kitchen with a commodity wrapped in a newspaper. The greyhound followed him, its nose close to the flags of the floor, as though sniffing the trail of a mouse.

'I think they're fresh this week,' O'Shea said. He put the herrings on one of the draining-boards and loosened the paper that wrapped them.

'I had several dreams,' said Eugene.

'Have you seen your mother?'

Eugene nodded and continued to nod. He enquired as to the nature of the fish and received a reply. He said:

'I dreamed that Eddie Trump was dead, passed out after uncorking a bottle.'

O'Shea, Eugene knew, never dreamed. He didn't know what it was to fall asleep and enter a world of fantastic happenings.

45

He was incapable, which was why he was resentful; he was jealous of those who had the knack.

O'Shea cut the heads and the tails off the herrings. He slit them open beneath a running tap and cleared the offal from their stomachs. Behind him, he could hear Eugene muttering to the greyhound, making a clicking sound to attract its attention. He finished gutting the last of the fish and for a moment, while the noise behind him continued, he glanced through the window into a yard that was half in sunshine and half in shadow. Horses had once been stabled there, brewery drays had rolled over the cobbles to deliver porter in barrels. It was peaceful in the yard now: an old cat, owned by nobody, slept near a dustbin in the gathering August heat; no birds sang in the hornbeam tree.

'D'you remember the time,' said Eugene, 'that Jack Tyler fell over the banisters?'

He took a matchbox from his left-hand trouser pocket. He selected a match and poked it into a tooth at the back of his mouth. *How are you feeling today?* he had written and she had nodded over the words, implying that she felt well. He had written down the dreams he'd had because she always displayed an interest. When he won something from a tip he'd received he always reported it, which pleased her too. He had stood for a moment with his tie and his collar and his studs, and then he had come away.

'Have you thought about a birthday gift at all?' O'Shea said.

Eugene took the match from his mouth. He examined a grey shred on the end of it. He said he thought it must be a particle of mutton.

'You've not forgotten, Mr Sinnott?'

'No, no.'

He took the shred of food from the end of the match and returned the match to its box. He sighed and closed his eyes.

O'Shea dried the herrings on a cloth and took a frying-pan from a shelf beneath the sink he had been working at. He placed the pan on the range. He took a jar of fat from one of the dressers; he cut a piece from it and allowed it to drop on to the warm pan.

'Jack Tyler was alive till a while back,' said Eugene, 'and

then he died with his boots on. One Saturday at Leopardstown.'

The herrings sizzled on the pan. Forty-four years ago, when he had walked into O'Neill's Hotel for the first time, he had seen Eugene Sinnott in the hall, a youth of fourteen like himself. 'Is Mrs Sinnott about?' he had said to him, and Eugene Sinnott had replied that she was in the dining-room and had then agreed to lead him to her.

'I showed you the little Virgin I got,' said O'Shea. 'What kind of a gift did you think of? Will I buy something for you, Mr Sinnott?'

'We could do worse than a pencil-sharpener.'

O'Shea turned from the range. He looked at Eugene sitting there, his two hands concentrated on the lighting of a cigarette. In a quiet voice he reminded him that for three years now he had given his mother a pencil-sharpener for her birthday. He reminded him that last year he had pointed out that another pencil-sharpener wasn't necessary. Mrs Sinnott had plenty of pencil-sharpeners, he said. She'd had plenty, he said, even when Eugene had begun to give her extra ones. If there was one object in the world that she didn't need it was another pencil-sharpener.

'They get blunt,' said Eugene.

'Mr Sinnott, they do not get blunt.'

'The people that come to see her do a lot of writing. She has exercise-books full of it – '

'I have seen the exercise-books, Mr Sinnott.'

'Get her a new little sharpener. Spend up to four shillings.'

He placed two florins on the table. A coloured pencil-sharpener, he said, a gay colour that would cheer her up.

'Don't stint it, O'Shea. Don't get shoddy goods for the sake of a coin or two. I'm obliged to you now, O'Shea.'

'She asked me to get her a scissors in April. I said to you last year a pair of scissors might have suited her. You didn't listen, Mr Sinnott.'

'There's a sharpener I saw one time done out in the shape of a globe. It had a coloured map of the world on it and you opened it down the equator to get out the shavings. Could you find one of those, d'you think?'

'Would you not think a little bowl for flowers, Mr Sinnott? Or a picture she could hang on the wall?'

'You've always a better idea,' shouted Eugene in sudden anger. 'You're a servant in this house, O'Shea. Will you do what you're told? Will you get on with it, for Christ's sake? A bloody pencil-sharpener.'

O'Shea turned away, unable to pursue the conversation. He gathered the plates and cups and placed them on the table. He set places for both of them. He laid Mrs Sinnott's tray.

O'Shea annoyed him sometimes, Eugene thought, with all his old talk. He was always in the sulks, going on about something when there was no need to at all. You might be talking to the wall when you were talking to O'Shea for all the notice he took. He looked at him and said:

'Did you dream, O'Shea?'

O'Shea didn't reply. He poured some of the water from the kettle into two tea-pots. He buttered bread for Mrs Sinnott.

'I had a dream I was paddling in the sea at Dalkey and Father Hennessey was up on the cliff and a black dog came up to sniff me. I had another dream that you were on about the condition of a cistern.'

O'Shea placed Mrs Sinnott's herring on a warmed plate and moved towards the door, carrying the tray.

'There was another thing too,' said Eugene. 'You came into Riordan's and said there was a circus man back at the hotel. You were talking through your hat.'

'She's up there in her room,' said O'Shea quietly, 'and her house is being used for immoral purposes.'

'You're talking out of turn, O'Shea.'

'Who'll change the sheets after Agnes Quin?'

He left the kitchen and Eugene Sinnott remained where he was, awaiting the porter's return. Had his mother dreamed? he wondered. What sort of a dream, he wondered, would a deaf woman of ninety-one have?

In the bungalow I see myself, Philomena had written. *I am sitting alone, there is no more work to do. In the early morning I am thinking of him and he is in another house. He has forgotten me then.*

On the morning of August 9th, a long time after composing these sentences, Philomena, in the Church of the Assumption in Booterstown, prayed for Mrs Sinnott, and for herself, and for the happiness of her son. She sat for a moment thinking of her son, seeing his face clearly. Clothes he wore came into her mind: two navy-blue suits, shirts and socks that she washed and repaired, ties she had bought for him. When he was sixteen she had bought him a safety razor and six blades in a chemist's. They had gone together to the pantomime every year in the Gaiety Theatre. She had watched him play with his Meccano sets. Every Sunday they still walked together on Sandymount Strand, she a slight figure in her grey coat and the hat they had bought for her one autumn together, he tall and thin, straight as a die.

'Oh God, don't let it happen,' she whispered. 'Oh God, I know it's a sin to ask You. It's only that I love him.'

It was more than a month since the Saturday morning in Lipton's when he hadn't heard what she was saying to him. 'Will we buy a bit of porksteak for the dinner?' she'd said, looking at the porksteak on the counter. She had felt the absence of his reply and glanced up quickly: his eyes were fixed on a girl who was cutting cheese, staring at the girl's neck, bare beneath her white overall. His eyes moved while she watched, to the hands that were slicing through the cheese with a length of wire. They moved again, to the girl's face. The girl was coarse, she had thought: a fat girl, with black wiry hair and cold-looking red hands. 'Will we have porksteak for the dinner?' she had said more loudly to him, pulling at his sleeve, and he had turned to her, smiling, saying that porksteak would be lovely.

Often since, when they had passed the shop, she'd seen him glancing through the window. She imagined him in the morning, going to work, hanging about to catch a glimpse of the girl. She imagined him walking into the bungalow and saying that he was thinking of getting married. 'Wait a second,' he'd say, and then he'd go away and return with the girl, whom he'd left standing in the garden. 'Isn't she lovely?' he'd say.

'Oh God, forgive me,' she whispered. She saw the girl walking with him, she saw them sitting in a cinema. The lips of the girl kissed her cheek as a daughter might; she felt herself flinching. 'Oh dear sweet Jesus,' she said.

The bungalow would be the same except that he would not be there and his clothes would be gone and his room would be like a graveyard. It had happened so easily, like a leaf falling from a tree, like the sun disappearing: they had stood in Lipton's together and it had happened as they stood there. Ever since she had felt the presence of the girl in his thoughts; she had felt his desire for her, although she knew he did not suspect that she was aware of it. She had thought they would go on together in the bungalow, eating together and talking about the day he had spent; she had thought he'd decided that that was how he wished his life to be, that he wanted nothing else. But already, even though she was sure he hadn't yet got to know the shopgirl, she felt that she was sharing him, and if it wasn't this girl who would walk into the bungalow and kiss her on the cheek it would be some other.

He's all I've got, she had written in Mrs Sinnott's room, ashamed to write more, or to confess that she was jealous in anticipation. But Mrs Sinnott knew. God gave and took away the words in Mrs Sinnott's eyes: life was not easy. 'Isn't she lovely?' said the voice of Timothy John again, and his face smiled at her, and she saw again the cold red hands slicing mouse-trap cheese.

Thirty-four years ago she had come to O'Neill's Hotel from West Cork, sent there by an uncle who had arranged the matter by letter with Mrs Sinnott. Her mother had just been admitted to the hospital in Clonakilty, her father a year previously had driven a hook into his hand and, failing to consider the wound, had died of blood-poisoning. 'She will hardly come out, Philomena,' her uncle had said to her, unable to hold back his tears. 'The nuns will be good to her.' She had wept too, thinking of her mother in the hospital bed, her mother who hated even to sit down. 'Clonakilty, God help us!' people used to say, making a joke about the town. Her mother would die there, and she would die quite quickly because of her loathing of being enclosed. *I'm sorry, Philomena*, Mrs Sinnott had written. *You've had bad fortune*.

She had stood in the dining-room of the hotel with two cardboard suitcases in her hands, holding them until Mrs Sinnott indicated that she should place them on the floor. She had come from Clonakilty by bus and then, with difficulty, had found her way to Thaddeus Street.

You'll be tired, Mrs Sinnott had written.

She shook her head.

Mrs Sinnott had been helping to clear the tables after the six o'clock meal. She sat down and indicated that Philomena should sit down also. Between them there was a pile of plates, the top one marked with traces of egg-yolk, knives and forks arranged on it in two sections.

I would have to train you, Philomena, Mrs Sinnott wrote. *What age are you now?*

Fifteen.

It was an excitement, spelling out a conversation, communicating in this formal way and watching Mrs Sinnott's face as she read the replies she received. Mrs Sinnott was never in a hurry. She carried an exercise-book and a pencil in the pocket of her apron, but even with that facility she didn't wish to communicate much. It surprised Philomena that she didn't read people's lips, but afterwards she thought that perhaps she preferred not to know everything that was going on about her. There was a tranquillity about her face that might have come from the silence that held her: she made her condition seem almost a blessing.

There is a nice room and of course all board. Mrs Sinnott referred to wages, explaining that they would be slight at first but would increase as time went by. She was responsible, she wrote, for insurance stamps.

Thank you, Mrs Sinnott.

Mrs Sinnott had pointed through the open door to a youth in uniform who stood in the hall, indicating that he would show Philomena to her room. She picked up the pile of plates. O'Shea led Philomena away.

Her mother died a month later. She returned by bus to Clonakilty, where her uncle had met her and said at once that he would pay for the funeral. The coffin was taken to the big, ugly cemetery in which her father was buried also, and when she went back to O'Neill's Hotel the other girls were kind to her and a man who used to put his arm around her tiny body didn't do that for a week or two. She wrote every Sunday to her uncle, who had explained to her that he wouldn't be able to reply because writing letters to people was a burden for him. Having written regularly for two years and having spent a week's holiday on his small farm, she ceased the correspondence and did not ever see him again.

O'Neill's Hotel had became her home. She made the beds of the travellers who stayed there, she carried trays of food from the kitchen to the dining-room, she helped to wash sheets. She never lost her shyness, and when the other girls recommended a film that was showing, or told her to look out for some local youth at Mass, she rarely heeded them. 'You'll make a great wife one day,' a man in the meal business said to her once. 'If I hadn't one myself I'd bring you back to Roscommon tonight.' She laughed, imagining being married to the big, bluff good-hearted meal merchant, but she knew that she'd like to be married to someone, to be in love, and to have children. In the hotel her birthday was celebrated on its day, as everyone else's was. Everyone gave her presents, as Mrs Sinnott had ordained that they must.

At night in the kitchen they would sit playing rummy, which Mrs Sinnott had taught them all. On winter evenings the fire in the range would glow and murmur, occasionally stoked by old Kathleen Devinish who had been in the hotel longer than Mrs Sinnott herself, who used to tell stories about Mr O'Neill, Mrs Sinnott's father, a wild man, apparently, yet one with a head for business, a man who had married an Italian. Kathleen Devinish was almost eighty when Philomena first came to O'Neill's: she still cooked and controlled the work in the kitchen; she was content, she often said, and added always that God had been good to her. Sweets were passed around when they played rummy, and cocoa was taken by everyone before going to bed at eleven o'clock. 'Is O'Shea hungry?' someone would say and O'Shea, his face full of happiness after the pleasant evening, would say he could eat a cream cracker. Eugene Sinnott always laughed then and his sister joined with him, but they, too, ate cream crackers and butter when they were placed on the table. Eugene always won at rummy; O'Shea was a loser.

During the first Christmas that Philomena spent in the hotel she wondered why, since no one was staying there over the holiday, the other maids and O'Shea weren't permitted to return to their families, as she herself would have wished to had her parents been alive. It was then that she realized that the people whom Mrs Sinnott employed were all, like herself, orphans. Kathleen Devinish told her. 'She's a woman that loves orphans,' she said. 'She likes to make things up to people.' On Christmas Day they had dinner in the kitchen at half-past four in the afternoon and there were presents for everyone, and wine with the food. People from the neighbourhood came in at moments during the day to celebrate the occasion with a glass or two. Keogh the grocer came with a confection in the form of a yule log with a robin redbreast sitting on chocolate icing, and a calendar for the year ahead. Priests who were friends of Mrs Sinnott's came, and Mr Riordan from the public house at the corner, and a coal merchant called Lynch, who always brought his wife and left behind him a bottle of Winter's Tale sherry. In the evening while they talked or played cards an old man who had once held the position that O'Shea held came to the hotel by the back door and was given a drink. He was deaf and did not say much, but his advent was looked forward to as a small tradition and there was disappointment the year he did not come, although all had known he would not. On Christmas evening, before they went to bed, Mrs Sinnott would make signs to remind her two children of their father, without whose love they would not exist. She asked that neither family nor servants should fail between this Christmas and the next to remember him and to pray for his continued peace.

It would all, Philomena had thought then, go on for ever. As Mrs Sinnott aged, her son and daughter would take on increasingly the running of the hotel, but nothing much would change since there was no need for it. Eugene and his sister did not quarrel, although he went out more than she did and came less and less to the kitchen in the evenings to play cards. His mother regarded him with a kindly eye and had not been known to upbraid him for the late hours he was beginning to keep, or the occasional tipsiness that a few had noticed in him. 'He reminds me of O'Neill,' Kathleen Devinish said. 'He'll settle himself down.' His sister was the younger of the two; but she, it was said, would be a steadying influence when they held the reins between them.

He had smiled at her across the table on his mother's birthday, the day of their troubles, when he'd come in and said that Southern Dandy had won at a hundred to eight. She had seen his eyes looking at her face, and then his lips had parted slightly and she had wondered why he had done an amazing thing like walking out of the hotel and going to the races on his mother's birthday. She had seen his sister glancing at him, as though deciding that the next day she would speak to him about his lapse.

'Help me, dear Jesus,' Philomena prayed in the Church of the Assumption. 'Forgive me this weakness.'

She would buy her a crocheted shawl to give to her with the gooseberry jam: doing that would make her feel better. She rose from her knees, genuflected in the aisle, took holy water, blessed herself, and stepped from the empty church into the heat of the morning.

When he was a sleeping infant, a tomcat had attacked Timothy John in his pram; when he was a child he had once been tied to a tree by a gang of girls and unfortunately forgotten. His nature seeming to attract such attentions, he had learned from an early time to tread nervously, not confident of much. This morning, even though the dentist had been less than gentle over the drilling of his tooth, he had feared to protest in case the dentist would take against him for being a nuisance. His hands had gripped one another as he sat there, the heel of his right shoe pressed painfully into the other ankle. 'She may have to come out,' the dentist had said. 'We'll do the best we can.' Small instruments scraped, the drill tunnelled deeper. The dentist talked of a race-meeting he proposed attending the following day, while fear of greater pain became the essence of his patient. 'Come back if there's trouble,' the dentist said.

In the bus Timothy John thought about other matters. He

thought of his mother and of the tray-cloth he intended to buy during the lunchtime for his grandmother's birthday. 'Have you fallen in love with me?' a voice said to him in his mind, and his repaired tooth gave a slight jump, as though a part of him did not care to hear that voice. Hastily, he turned his thoughts in another direction: he reflected upon the work he did. It was, so his uncle had said ten years ago when welcoming Timothy John to the Home and Personal Effects Department, interesting work. It was varied work, Mr Gregan had also pointed out. Before ever a decision had been reached as to whether or not Timothy John should join the business, Mr Gregan had spoken in detail about the work that he himself had performed over many years. He had spoken of the varying size of the claims that an employee would be dealing with and if necessary investigating. Some old woman in Irishtown, Mr Gregan pointed out, would be putting in a claim for the loss of two tea-towels, while a different class of person would be speaking on the telephone about a bracelet that had had, apparently, a faulty clasp. 'Now it is a question,' Mr Gregan had repeated, 'of being capable of knowing the line to adopt with each and every type of person. A trained employee, Timothy John, can tell a lot from handwriting, the loops and the sloping, that kind of thing. And of course your same trained employee can tell a lot from a voice on the telephone. In this day and age,' Mr Gregan had with sincerity added, 'a surprising number of people are criminals under the skin.'

Timothy John travelled all over the city, examining furniture that had been damaged by fire and trying to discover if the claimant was a criminal under the skin. 'You want to watch their eyes the whole time,' Mr Gregan had advised him. 'They'd put a match to anything. "There's a smell of paraffin" is the first thing you say when you enter a house. Examine the burnt object and say the smell of paraffin would knock you down. Take a little compass or a whistle or something from your pocket and pass it over the damaged area. I used always carry a compass with me in order to explain to them it's a meter for seeing if there's traces of paraffin. Keep playing around with the compass and keep watching their two eyes. If you don't make a boob of it they'll tell you the gospel truth within thirty seconds.' There were people, said Mr Gregan, who'd kindle a fire in an upholstered chair and scorch the flesh off their arms so that they could show you that they'd been trying to put it out. 'Lift up the arm,' said Mr Gregan. 'Put the arm to your nose and tell them it smells of paraffin.'

Although the work was as varied as Mr Gregan had said it would be, with much colourful uncovering of attempts to hood-wink an honest insurance company, Timothy John had for many years felt that he was not cut out for the Home and Personal Effects Department, since he had a shy manner with claimants and found it difficult to establish the truth. He bought a pocket compass, but when he passed it over the burnt area of a hearthrug or an armchair and reported that traces of paraffin were present, he was invariably asked to explain how a compass could register this information since compasses were designed for another purpose. At length, he enquired of Mr Gregan if the experience gained in the Motor Department was in any way worth obtaining, but Mr Gregan replied that the Motor Department did not go in for insurance in any real sense at all, although he did not elucidate this statement. 'I will be retiring myself,' he pointed out, 'one day in the not too distant future.' He had looked at Timothy John as he spoke those words, implying a hint of what might be: everyone in the Home and Personal Effects Department would move up a step if everyone's work continued to be satisfactory, and Timothy John might find himself at least within reach of the position that his uncle now held. 'The Motor Department,' Mr Gregan added, 'is for the fly-by-night class, just as the Life Office is for our friend the morbid mind. I welcome loyalty,' he added, looking closely at Timothy John's face and into his eyes, as if seeking to establish, once and for all, criminality under the skin. Beneath this scru-tiny, Timothy John agreed to remain in the Home and Personal Effects Department, and a few weeks later when Mr Gregan asked him if he was happy he endeavoured not to hesitate before replying that he was. 'That's a very good thing, boy,' Mr Gregan had said, regarding his nephew through his spectacles and the smoke from his pipe. 'It would give me pleasure to live to see you where you should be, in full charge of the Home and Personal side. There's no reason why you shouldn't be, if you watch the claims and don't make any more boobs.'

Mr Gregan himself was well known in the Department for his boobs. He had stepped from boob to boob in a miraculous way and to his own great surprise had found himself one day in charge of everyone else. Timothy John, though fearing him greatly, felt sorry whenever he heard the clerks in the outer office disparaging him. It seemed to Timothy John to be pure justice that a man who had suffered because his soul had never been absorbed by the work should be rewarded in this way, but when he thought about it he was obliged to agree with the opinion of others: that the position his uncle held was due to some kind of error. He felt his uncle believed that too, or at least believed that it was his talk rather than his performance that had achieved the position for him. His uncle could be convincing when he told his stories about taking a compass from his pocket, but Timothy John suspected that the true climax of such stories was similar to his own experience. In his uncle's eyes when he said he'd like to see Timothy John in full charge of the Home and Personal Effects Department there was a glazed reflection of his own failure, and the wish that a nephew of his should in some way make up for it.

At one period of his childhood, regularly every week on Saturday afternoons, Timothy John used to visit his aunt and uncle in order to help Mr Gregan in the garden. By chance on one of these occasions, it came out that Timothy John was being mildly but persistently bullied at school. 'We'll fix that,' said Mr Gregan in a businesslike way. He bought two pairs of boxing-gloves and tried to teach his nephew to defend himself, but the sight of Mr Gregan's large hands encased in his gloves caused Timothy John to feel sick in the stomach. In the end, after a smartish attack of Mr Gregan's had opened a cut on his mouth, it was suggested by the doctor who came to stitch the wound that the weekly contest was doing more harm than good. His uncle had looked at him with reproach and although Timothy John felt sorry that he had let him down, especially after he'd bought the two pairs of gloves, it was fear of the man and of what he might next suggest that possessed him more acutely. There was the same reproach when his uncle held out some claim in the office and said that as far as he could see Timothy John had made a boob. It was unlikely, he knew, that his uncle would ever give him another crack on the mouth, but the memory of the stitches going into his lip naggingly remained. And it was difficult to explain that a boob was hard to avoid when some man was swearing that his claim was genuine in all respects and was threatening violence, or when a husband and wife were allied in their story, one supporting the other in a network of small details. The husband and wife might speak quite gently, putting their case with reason and clarity, but in no time at all Timothey John would grow afraid of them, and not be able to remember afterwards what it was they had said.

As he stepped from the bus, he guessed that his uncle would approach him in the outer office and remark on the time of day, even though the evening before he had told him he would be late on account of having to pay a visit to the dentist. His uncle had a way of forgetting what had been carefully told to him, and he was constantly on guard lest it should seem that he was guilty of favouritism towards a member of the family. He would ask him, Timothy John knew, to make up the hour that had been spent, and Timothy John would naturally agree.

On the bus and on the street this brief consideration of his work and his uncle had successfully kept other matters out of his mind, but as he ascended the rubber-clad stairs of the insurance company his tooth seemed quiet and he was unable to control the leaping of his thoughts. 'Why are you always looking in at me?' she had said to him. 'Have you fallen in love with me?'

She had been there, at the door of Lipton's one morning, waiting for him to pass, and he had felt a warm flush creeping all over his neck and face as she spoke. 'What's your name?' she asked, and when he told her she said that hers was Daisy 'Daisy Tulip they call me,' she said. She had laughed in a casual way, as though every day of her life men looked through the shop window at her, as though every day she lay in wait for another of them in order to ask questions. 'I'll be seeing you,' she said. He had walked on, his face flushed and grave above his blue suit and unwrinkled shirt. She was beautiful, he had thought, and ever since he had been thinking the same. The work he did, the people he saw, his uncle's reproaches and his mother's little face made little sense now when he thought about her. There was a passion in him that made even his fear of speaking to her again seem strangely slight. *Her name is Daisy Tulip*, he had written. He laughed to think of it, a name like that, a made-up name that suited her.

4

In St Stephen's Green that morning the woman called Ivy
Eckdorf took a photograph of a floating duck. She wore the
same cream-coloured hat that she had worn in the aeroplane,
and was dressed otherwise in a suit of pale linen over a cream-
coloured blouse with buttons of pearl. Her finger-nails were
lengthy, meticulously painted to match the shade of her mouth;
her stockings were fine, the colour of honey; her flat-heeled
shoes had soft wicker-work uppers and soles of a flexible
leather. She carried a commodious cream-coloured handbag and
about her neck, suspended by a thin length of plastic, hung the
camera with which she had photographed the duck. It was an
instrument of Japanese manufacture, a Mamiya.

'How charming!' murmured Mrs Eckdorf, referring to the
duck and to other ducks that floated on the water in the park.
'What a truly attractive city!'

A man going by, a projectionist in a cinema, had an obscene
thought about Mrs Eckdorf when he saw her standing there,
for she was a beautiful woman in her tall, angular way. She
saw the man glancing at her and she guessed that in his mind
he had already placed her on a bed and was unfastening her
clothes. She smiled at him, quite pleased that he had paid her
the compliment. 'You naughty chap!' she cried, and noted scar-
let embarrassment spreading all over the man's face. He hurried
on, and Mrs Eckdorf lifted her camera and photographed his
retreating back.

An old woman spoke to her, asking for alms, her hand held
slightly out. She said she would pray for Mrs Eckdorf, who
told her to stand back a bit, which the woman did, imagining
that money would follow. 'There are social services to see to
you,' said Mrs Eckdorf, smiling more. She photographed the

woman, explaining to her that her face would now travel all over the world. She spoke harshly when the beggar woman again asked for alms. 'Get off to hell,' she ordered angrily.

The woman went, and Mrs Eckdorf consulted her map. She saw the way to Thaddeus Street lay along York Street, over Aungier Street, past St Patrick's Cathedral, along the Coombe and then on and on. She did not much care for the look of this route. An instinct told her that a more roundabout one would provide greater interest. She turned her back on York Street and set off in another direction, towards the river.

Twenty minutes later, in Bachelors' Walk, she encountered two card-sharpers, one of whom carried a large cardboard box which bore the legend *Kellogg's Cornflakes The Sunshine Breakfast*. He was a red-haired man, tall and heavily constructed, with evasive eyes. His companion was smaller and excessively dirty. She photographed them and then moved on, only to find herself pursued by the men, who demanded money with menaces, claiming that she had offered them money in return for permission to take their photographs. They reminded her that they had specially performed their trick on the cardboard box and had risked observation by the plain-clothes police. All that, they said, they'd done to oblige her.

Mrs Eckdorf balanced her camera on the wall that ran above the river. She photographed two nuns crossing the Metal Bridge.

'Local interest,' she explained. 'There's local interest everywhere.'

'We're working men,' said the smaller man.

'You're local interest to me,' murmured Mrs Eckdorf, again setting her sights on the nuns.

'Excuse me, missus,' began the red-haired man in a threatening way, edging closer to Mrs Eckdorf, his shoulder actually touching her clothes.

'Buzz off,' said Mrs Eckdorf snappishly, thinking it was extraordinary the way people in this city were always asking for money.

'You promised us,' shouted the red-haired man. He took her elbow in his left hand. He raised the cardboard box slightly in the air. 'You said a consideration, missus.'

Mrs Eckdorf stared into the eyes of the man and spoke while doing so. She told him to release her elbow and to stand well back.

'I'm a professional photographer,' she said. 'I cannot possibly go paying out cash for every piece of local interest I find. You must see that.'

'I see nothing,' cried the red-haired man. 'We risked arrest standing up there, exposed for you –'

'There's a Superintendent in uniform,' said Mrs Eckdorf quietly, 'on the other side of the street.'

She waved at the Superintendent, who was strolling along, tapping the calf of his right leg with a cane. He was in the company of two members of his force, a pair of dignified Civic Guards immaculately turned out. She lifted her camera and photographed the three of them. Then she trained her lens on the backs of the card-sharpers, who were sidling urgently away.

Having waved again at the Superintendent, she continued on her journey. She passed by the humped metal bridge and strode along Ormond Quay, occasionally snapping the shutter of her camera at people or vistas that took her fancy. She thought, as she walked past empty shops and hoardings that advertised the services of a hypnotist, that Hans-Otto's face was a face she should never have expected understanding from. In the apartment she still occupied in the Lipowskystrasse she had spoken frankly to Hans-Otto one evening four years ago: she had sat with him for several hours in the fading light, telling him the things about herself that he apparently had been unaware of when he married her. She remembered now the bony face of Hans-Otto, with its very dark jowl seeming to shine in the gloom, while she said she couldn't understand any man marrying a woman without knowing by instinct her nature. He had lifted a glass of cognac to his lips. '*Du hast mich betrogen,*' he said, and she had instantly denied that she had betrayed him. But Hans-Otto shouted at her then to keep her lies to herself, he refused to listen to reason or explanations: he had appeared suddenly to be a jungle beast with cognac in its hand, storming about the place, issuing threats and accusations.

Mrs Eckdorf photographed a seagull swooping over the river. She glanced about it at the sky and said to herself that the weather was set for the day: the light-blue sky was empty of clouds, the haze that earlier had obscured the sun was gone. She took a pair of dark glasses from her handbag and placed them before her eyes. Hans-Otto had asked for a divorce. Hans-Otto had said that in any case he was tired of her.

A year before, he had wept when she'd told in court of how Hoerschelmann had hit her: how he had lifted a small table from the carpet and had struck out powerfully with it, how fortunately she had managed to escape the brunt of its weight. She told of how on another occasion she believed he had put some kind of drug in a plate of *Nierensuppe* she was eating, causing an illness that had brought her close to death.

Now she lived alone in the apartment in the Lipowskystrasse and wondered often if it would be forever her home. In her bedroom, the low, square bed had a cinder-grey bedspread on it. Everywhere, throughout the apartment, there was steel furniture with grey cushions or trimming on it, and cinder-grey carpeting stretched from wall to wall of every room. There were light-fittings that were of steel also, the woodwork was unpainted but had been gently dyed to reflect the motif of steel and cinder. In her studio, which looked out over the Theresienwiese, her favourite photographs, blown up to great dimensions and each behind a sheet of plastic, hung from metal rods that swivelled ingeniously from a central fixture. There were more than a hundred of them, the cream of many thousands, all of people from the cities and villages of four continents, people laughing or weeping, people in agony or smiling, people awkwardly posing or caught unawares. In this studio she wished to perform the remainder of the work she had begun. To this room, with its fathomless grey walls and serene calm, she wished to return from Bahia Blanca or Bingerville or Halmahera, or wherever it was she felt called upon to attend with her Mamiya. In this room, all of a sudden on that evening four years ago, Hans-Otto Eckdorf had said that she was mad.

'*Du Schwein!*' cried Mrs Eckdorf at the corner of Capel Street. '*Gott im Himmel, du knöchernes deutsches Schwein!*'

People looked at her, pedestrians and cyclists, surprised that a well-dressed woman in dark glasses and a hat was standing on the pavement speaking emotionally in a foreign language. A garda on point duty cast a glance in her direction and was reassured when she smiled at him.

She crossed the river, recalling another statement that Hans-Otto had made that evening: that the facts of her previous marriage were not as ever she had claimed. She it was, he pronounced in a gritty voice, speaking both in English and in German, who had lifted the table from the floor. She it was who had struck Hoerschelmann with it, breaking a small bone in his shoulder. She had torn the flesh of Hoerschelmann's face, she had put sleeping drugs in his *Nierensuppe* lest he should be a nuisance to her at night. '*Du bist das grausamste Weib, das jemals gelebt hat!*' Hans-Otto Eckdorf, a manufacturer of typewriters, shouted at her that evening fours years ago; and then, to make certain she understood, he repeated the accusation in slow, lugubrious English: 'You are the cruellest woman that ever lived.' Hoerschelmann, he bitterly added, had agreed to any story she cared to invent in order to be rapidly rid of her; Hoerschelmann had willingly paid alimony, and he himself would willingly do the same.

In Merchant's Quay she placed her camera on the river wall and prepared herself to photograph, across the width of water, the Courts of Justice. She took the picture and said to herself then that she must be close to O'Neill's Hotel. 'Thaddeus Street? Am I near it?' she asked a youth who had come to watch her at work. 'Ah, you're not,' he said, and then directed her. She smiled at him and walked on.

Why should she care about either of them? Was it not more important that she should dip with her camera into the souls of people than that she should bleakly please two German businessmen? They had come to her, demanding her, paying her compliments that were grotesque in their lavishness, pressing upon her adoration and passion. Yet between the moment of their warmest desire and the moment when they rejected her she had not altered. She was the same woman, thinking the same thoughts. She remembered suddenly the man she had sat next to on the plane and how he had not understood at all when she'd tried to explain that only human understanding could save the world in the long run. He had not been equipped to understand that mysteries had no right to exist because mysteries interfered with human understanding and with truth. How could Hoerschelmann or Hans-Otto have sympathy and love for the man on the plane, or how could the man on the plane have sympathy and love for them, if they all appeared as mysterious and private figures? Her book about the old Sicilian priest, Tomaso Leoni, who had lost his faith, had brought her several thousand letters from all over the world, in many languages. Yet the story of Tomaso Leoni, told almost entirely in photographs, had been an extraordinarily personal one: there were few who could have shared the experiences of the old priest, the spiritual suffering that the lines on his face revealed, the loss and the emptiness in his life, and the agony that his peasant parishioners had suffered also. But thousands of hands had picked up pens and written to say that she had caused them to feel a nagging sorrow, to say she had caused them to understand the torment of all those strangers.

'We must know one another,' murmured Mrs Eckdorf, not smiling as she spoke. 'Only that makes sense.'

She walked on, noting tall houses that overlooked the river, where gracious living must once have thrived: sacking hung often where windows should have been, and people lived behind it. In other houses lace curtains trailed, grey and seeming damp. It was a city that was keen on curtains of lace, she'd noticed, and venetian blinds, and gangling television aerials that made a pattern in the sky.

All about her children ran, ragged and shrill, for ever begging. She saw advertisements for Crested Ten, which seemed to her too beautiful and strange a title to represent a kind of whiskey. She had seen, somewhere, the Machusla Ballroom and could not forget those two words strung together either, nor Sweet Afton Cigarettes, which had blinked at her from a neon sign. In St Stephen's Green the air had been fresh like country air, but now a cloying smell, as though from creatures already dead, came from the river; and from some houses came the smell of poverty. *We are fighting still* were words she read, chalked on a boarded doorway.

'Thaddeus Street?' she said.

She listened and continued on her way. She left the river behind her and turned to her left, up St Augustine Street. The shutter of her camera opened and closed repeatedly, she smiled politely at those who paused to examine her. She said to herself that she would return when there was fog, for already in her mind she could see the scene and its people on a day that was gloomier than this one. She saw the forms of men and women huddled in their clothes against a penetration of weather, she imagined buildings and patches of wasteland in a grey wash that would come out gorgeously in black and white.

'Do you get much fog at all?' she enquired of a middle-aged man carrying a basket.

'Stuff in the air,' explained Mrs Eckdorf when he did not reply. 'Like thick mist.'

The man looked at her, still not speaking.

'Fog,' said Mrs Eckdorf. 'You know.'

'I know what fog is,' said the man. 'What about it?'

'Do you get much?'

The man walked on, pushing past Mrs Eckdorf, striking her knee with his basket. She turned to take a photograph of him and at that moment he also turned and told her to leave him alone.

'I don't mean now,' cried Mrs Eckdorf, suddenly aware that there was a misunderstanding. 'I mean in winter, sir. Fog in winter.'

A woman with curlers in her hair, wheeling a pram containing a small chest of drawers, spoke to the man, whom she addressed as Mr Greevy. He said that Mrs Eckdorf was drunk.

'No, no,' cried Mrs Eckdorf, drawing back her lips and tinkling with professional laughter. 'No, no, no, no. I was asking about fog,' she said to the woman. 'I like the effect in my photographs.'

'Fog,' said the woman.

'I'm a photographer,' said Mrs Eckdorf. 'My name is Ivy Eckdorf.'

'There is no fog at all this time of the year,' said the woman with the pram.

'That is what I'm saying,' agreed Mrs Eckdorf, trying to smile at the woman and at Mr Greevy, although neither of them was smiling at her. 'What I am saying is that I would like to return at the time of year when the fogs come.'

She had moved closer to them. 'What awfully nice cloth!' she said, feeling the lapel of Mr Greevy's serge jacket. He was about to protest and then he changed his mind. He eyed Mrs Eckdorf's handbag and her camera and her pale linen clothes. He removed his hat and held it in his hand, in the same hand that already held the basket.

'Are you a tourist?' the woman asked.

'No, no. I'm here after local interest. I'm here to take photographs and I'd like to take some more, quite honestly, when the fogs descend. If they descend, which is what I am asking you. I'm not myself German, if that's what worries you. I was born in England.'

'We don't get much fog,' said the woman. 'Ah, well, we do the odd time, coming up off the river, only it doesn't last long.'

'We would get a night of it,' said Mr Greevy in a notably altered manner, 'and then again we wouldn't see a sign of it for the winter. It comes and goes, the fog we have.'

'We had it around Christmas. It came off the river two days before Christmas and we had it for a week. D'you remember that?' the woman said to Mr Greevy, and he nodded his head.

'I have the wife in hospital,' he said, addressing himself directly to Mrs Eckdorf, 'with broken knees.'

'God, isn't that shocking!' cried the woman with the pram. 'Is she bad, Mr Greevy?'

'She's not so hot at all. She came down off a ladder,' Mr Greevy said to Mrs Eckdorf, 'when she was repairing a ceiling. I'm off work myself for the last three years.'

'Stand just as you are, the two of you,' requested Mrs Eckdorf. She stepped back and lifted her camera.

'Any assistance I was offered,' said Mr Greevy, 'I would take.'

The Mamiya performed, Mrs Eckdorf smiled. 'It must look

magnificent,' she said, sweeping her arm about her. 'The fog like a halo on everything.'

The woman left her pram beside Mr Greevy and came close to Mrs Eckdorf in order to whisper in her ear. Mr Greevy turned his head away.

'A decenter man never walked the streets,' said the woman. 'A few bob would see him right for a day or two.'

'My dear, I'm as penurious as any of you,' murmured Mrs Eckdorf.

She touched the woman on the shoulder and walked briskly off. It was marvellous, she thought, when they asked you for money: she had seen them, all over the world, becoming completely natural when the thought of money entered their minds, which was the moment to give the Mamiya its head. When everyone became respectable and well-to-do, Mrs Eckdorf reflected, there would be no more local interest, and the loss would be more considerable than anyone had ever dreamed it could be.

Behind her she could hear the voices of Mr Greevy and the woman, both employing obscene language in their abuse of her. She wondered about the couple and about the card-sharpers in Bachelors' Walk and the elderly woman who had begged in St Stephen's Green. Occasionally, having entered into conversation with a person on a street, she managed to return to the house of the person in order to learn more, in order to steep herself in the background before calling again on her camera. Although interesting, none of the persons she had encountered that morning had seemed to her to justify the effort of deeper investigation that a return to the home involved. Mrs Eckdorf saw in the distance the modern building of the Coombe Maternity Hospital, where twins that morning had been safely delivered. She passed along Marrowbone Lane, moving close to Thaddeus Street.

The two men ate their breakfast in silence. When he had finished his, Eugene rose and took a shaving-brush and a razor from one of the window-sills and placed them ready on the draining-board. He had poured himself three cups of tea, he had eaten with pleasure his share of the herrings and a few slices of bread. On his plate lay bones and roe. 'Well, they were fresh today,' he remarked. 'As fresh as a daisy, O'Shea.'

As he crossed to the range with an empty cup in order to get hot water from the kettle, he saw that O'Shea was apparently in a sulk, staring at the brown tea-pot. O'Shea always ate the roe and the bones of herrings: his plate was empty now, seeming almost as if it had been washed and dried because O'Shea had wiped it repeatedly with pieces of buttered bread. That is the difference between us, thought Eugene: he is a neat and tidy man, he does not enjoy a drink, nor the company of others, he takes life hard, he cannot have dreams at night. O'Shea would spend the whole day brushing the carpet on the stairs of the hotel, raising a dust that settled elsewhere. He would clean the red and green panes in the glass of the entrance doors; he would spend five minutes rubbing at the pan he had fried the herrings on. Eugene sighed, shaking his head slightly. He poured boiling water into the cup and returned with it to the sink. He surveyed his face in a small mirror that hung from a nail between the windows. 'We've run out of shaving soap,' he said.

'She could be dead for all you care, Mr Sinnott.'

Eugene, used to the suddenness of this, replied quickly.

'My mother is not dead,' he said.

'She was in a room one time where a fly was on the window-pane. She signalled to me to let the creature out.'

Eugene laughed, and O'Shea felt tears coming to his eyes. This man understood nothing, he remarked to himself, and he prayed quietly, in his mind, without moving his lips. Make him gentle like his mother, he asked. He would happily do all that was required of him, he promised, if only this man would not be as he was.

'Someone else,' said O'Shea, 'would have told me to take the fly's life. That is the difference with her.'

Eugene dipped his shaving-brush into the hot water and tried to entice a lather from a piece of kitchen soap. He shaved for a time in silence. Then he said:

'Did you see Yellow Printer is drawn for trap four? Trap four is a big handicap in a Derby final.'

'Mr Sinnott, she has no use for another pencil-sharpener. When I was up with her breakfast I counted fourteen pencil-sharpeners.'

'I know what you mean.' He shaved again. He said he felt better. O'Shea began to speak but Eugene interrupted him. He said:

'Johnny Basset says the Printer is in tip-top fettle. Did you ever think of racing your man there?' He pointed his razor at the greyhound. He laughed, scraped foam and bristle from his neck. He rinsed the razor under the tap.

'Mr Sinnott, would you not reconsider?'

Eugene removed the blade and dried it on a towel. He wiped his face and put away his shaving things. Then he crossed the room to where O'Shea was standing.

'Does it matter a damn?' he said. 'A sharpener with a globe on it, O'Shea, so that she can travel about on it: what's wrong with that? Is she the Queen Mother, O'Shea, that you're making a fuss? Is this joint Buckingham Palace? She'll be ninety-two years of age.'

'Mr Sinnott –'

'Four or five people a year, O'Shea, come into this place. O'Neill's Hotel has had its day, can't you understand that? She's a woman who never heard a human voice.'

'She's your mother, Mr Sinnott.'

'She is.'

'The hotel was famous once. The hotel was thronged from top to bottom – '

'Things have changed, O'Shea. The area's not what it was.'

'You don't care, Mr Sinnott. You're down in Riordan's drinking sherry – '

'I am, O'Shea.'

Mechanically, Eugene offered O'Shea a cigarette but O'Shea didn't take one. *Is it a sin that they go to Mass with nothing on their heads?* he had written. *What's wrong with the world, Mrs Sinnott?*

'Why wouldn't I drink sherry?' enquired Eugene. 'I have the one life only.'

He put on his collar and tie, and as he completed the task a voice called out in O'Neill's Hotel, demanding instant attention.

The two men, although not in the mood for this, looked at one another. The voice continued. O'Shea quietly opened the door and they listened, standing together in the kitchen passage.

'Mein Herz ist voller Liebe für alle Menschen,' cried Mrs Eckdorf. *'Ist jemand da?'*

'It's not real,' said O'Shea in a whisper. 'There's some ghostly thing in the hall.' But Eugene said the voice did not come from a ghost but from a person who was possessed of a distressed mind. 'A female lunatic,' he said.

'Wer ist es?' cried Mrs Eckdorf, and Eugene repeated his opinion. O'Shea shook his head. He began to say something, and then paused. They remained as they stood, listening to the silence until they heard Mrs Eckdorf's voice again, more quietly bringing to them words from a German song.

'My God!' murmured O'Shea. He looked at Eugene, trying to catch his eye and finding himself instead staring at the yellow distemper of the passage wall.

'Es ist ein Ros' entsprungen,' sang Mrs Eckdorf, lending the words a morose harmony of her own. *'Es ist ein Ros' entsprungen.'*

In a brown suit, with a watch-chain running across his stomach from one pocket of his waistcoat to another, Mr Smedley had that morning, while Mrs Eckdorf dawdled, hurried through the city streets from one business appointment to another. Now, finding time between one engagement and the next, he paused in a public house and dropped into an enquiring conversation with its barman, being anxious to establish, even at this early hour, the extent and availability of the city's fleshly pleasures. The barman, having listened to his queries, offered no reply.

'You know the kind of thing I mean,' urged Mr Smedley with a smile. 'I'm a man of vigour.'

'Keep talk of that nature to yourself, please,' replied the barman unpleasantly. 'We make do with our wives in this town.'

5

The Excelsior Bar of Riordan's public house was a dimly lit place, with walls that had been painted pink by the late Mr Riordan in pursuit of his belief that inebriation was pleasanter if induced in an atmosphere of rosiness, which was something he had read in a trade magazine. In front of the dark upholstered seating that lined these walls, tables were spaced so that a customer could be alone, a little away from the other customers, in order to meditate or doze. There was matting on the floor that absorbed the sound of footsteps, and there was no television set.

Mr Riordan, having served behind his own bar for sixty-two years, had become increasingly interested in the process of inebriation. He enjoyed observing his customers becoming more like themselves; he said it was a joyful thing, and even on mornings when the back lavatory was not a pleasant place to enter Mr Riordan had not shifted from his principles, the chief of which was that only in intoxication were people truly happy. He had given the Excelsior Bar its name in 1933, having been reading in a trade magazine about the cocktail bars of Manhattan, which seemed to him to be curiously and aptly titled. After his death the house had fallen into the hands of his son-in-law, Edward Trump, who had made few changes. He had kept the Excelsior Bar as a small and quiet place that few people entered, a greater number being alienated by all that Mr Riordan had hoped would attract them. It was mainly Eugene Sinnott, Morrissey, Agnes Quin, and a woman called Mrs Dargan, who enjoyed the pink haze of the Excelsior Bar these days: they welcomed a place they could call their own, with the sound of music coming lightly from the television in the public bar and the opportunity for peaceful conversation.

On the morning of August 9th Morrissey and Agnes Quin were alone in the bar. Like Morrissey, Agnes Quin was dark-haired, but a person of greater proportions than Morrissey, a foot taller, loose-limbed and fleshy, with hair to her shoulders. She was more smartly turned out than he: small silver-coloured ear-rings pierced her ears, her shoes were smart but comfortable, chosen for walking like Mrs Eckdorf's had been. She wore, this morning, a purple dress and carried a patent-leather handbag. Her face was free of make-up. Her puffed, bruised-looking lips hid teeth that were discoloured and large. Her blue eyes were cautious, constantly on the watch.

'I got her this,' said Morrissey, taking from his pocket a brooch in the shape of a spider. A green piece of glass formed the body, the legs were of gold-coloured wire. It was attached to a square of cardboard on which a price had been heavily marked.

'Two pounds ten,' said Agnes Quin.

'You wouldn't stint yourself,' said Morrissey. 'You'd do the best you could on an old woman's birthday.'

'I'm giving her a cup I saw.'

'A cup, Agnes?'

'A special one she could have for herself. I saw it in a window on the Quays.'

'A gold cup is it?'

'A cup with flowers on it. With a saucer.'

'Isn't that a peculiar thing to give, Agnes? The legs on that spider are gold, so the man said. That's a jewel in the middle.'

He ran his comb through his hair. He looked at the comb after he'd done that and made a dissatisfied noise with his lips. 'Give us two more bottles,' he called out. He rose and approached the bar. 'Isn't that a grand day for you, Eddie?' he said.

'There's rain on the way,' said Eddie Trump, passing over the bottled stout and receiving payment. 'It was on the wireless: a deluge from the West.'

'I hate rain,' said Morrissey, thinking that business was diffi-cult in the rain, especially heavy rain. Hanging about the streets, following men into public houses and trying when you were dripping wet to talk to them about their desires wasn't as pleasant

73

as it might be. Rain put a damper on things, as Morrissey had often observed.

'Eugene's late this morning,' remarked Eddie Trump, a big lugubrious man in an apron. Morrissey, receiving his change, agreed that this was so. He returned to Agnes Quin and poured them each a further glass of stout. When he'd finished he took his comb from his pocket and showed it to her. 'Is that dandruff?' he said.

She shook her head, saying it was more likely grit from the air.

'It's a filthy old town.' Morrissey returned the comb to his pocket. He made a noise in his nose. He said:

'Isn't it a great brooch I got her?'

'Great.'

The nuns had given her the name Agnes Quin. Sister Tracy, old and forgetful about what should be said and what withheld, had told her that a man had come to the convent in the middle of one night and had banged about, shouting for the Reverend Mother, who rose from her bed to see him. 'Will you look after that thing?' he had said, handing her a living baby. They had attempted to restrain the man, they had pointed out that the facilities at the convent could not be so unorthodoxly used. 'You're there for the homeless, aren't you?' the man had replied. 'What's an orphan-house for?' He pushed his way from the convent, and when, years later, it became known that Sister Tracy had passed the story on to the child who was presumably his daughter, this elderly forgetful nun wept when she was reprimanded. 'It's not an easy life, Agnes,' the Reverend Mother had said soon after that. 'It must fill you completely; you must be surer about this than you have ever been sure of anything before.' She had been sure: she had seen herself clearly in the ascetic habit, a calm novice, compassionate and gentle. She had said so to her Reverend Mother, but her Reverend Mother had quietly replied that all that might not be enough. And then one day the convent orphanage was visited by a woman who was often spoken of, a kindly friend of the orphanage, a woman known to love orphans for their own sake, a Mrs Sinnott. *It is a beautiful thing*, Mrs Sinnott had written, *but it is hard too, as Reverend Mother has warned you. If you do not in the end have the vocation come out and see us: O'Neill's Hotel in Thaddeus Street.* Agnes promised that she would, but a number of years later, on her fifteenth birthday, when she mentioned her desire to do so, that same Reverend Mother shook her head. Hadn't she noticed, she asked, that Mrs Sinnott had not been to see them for a long time now? O'Neill's Hotel, she said, had fallen on sad times: no longer were there positions there for young orphan girls. She smiled. 'You've been lucky,' she said. 'We've found you a place in Ringsend.'

Agnes left the convent the following Sunday evening, knowing that the nuns and the orphans were praying for her and would continue to do so. She went to work for the Englishes, living with them above their hardware shop, looking smart, so Mrs English said, in a green overall that Mrs English herself, having put on weight, had no longer a use for. She learned to sell nails of different lengths, and bolts and screws for metal or wood, and paraffin oil and cup-hooks, quite soon becoming swift at the task. 'She's taken to it like a duck to water,' Mrs English said, and Mr English agreed.

At that time she used to go for walks with a boy who whispered often that he loved her, until one night, behind the Electricity Works, he had taken liberties with her unresisting body and afterwards had whispered nothing more at all. He had walked home beside her in silence and she had felt him thinking that he had performed a dirty action. After that, he wasn't on the lookout for her as he had been in the past, to suggest walks together to Poolbeg Lighthouse. She confessed the sin and accepted the penance, with the face of the boy still vivid in her mind, and his hands seeming to caress her body while the priest's voice murmured. A little while later, unable to restrain herself, she went to the shoe-shop where he worked. He was going to marry a girl from Tallagh, he said, and she wondered if he had said to himself that night behind the Electricity Works that in spite of love he could not marry her because she had not resisted, because she hadn't thought to say that what he demanded was a sin. He knelt before her in the shoe-shop, removing old shoes from her feet and placing on them new ones. The back of his waistcoat was black and shiny and there were rubber bands on his arms to protect his shirt-cuffs from the footwear of the customers. He pressed the leather of the shoes to discover where her toes were. He was happier doing that, she thought, than doing what he had done before. 'Ah God, you look great in them,' he said, and she went away with the shoes on her feet and her old ones in a paper bag.

She was courted next by a man called Doyle, whom she met in the Crystal Ballroom. He had said he had money and the expectation of more as a clerk with responsibility: he was securely employed in the offices of a firm that manufactured lemonade and he hinted that there was a tinned-meat business, down near Baltinglass, that would come his way any day now. It became a custom between them to go once a week to the cinema, and as soon as they took their seats the lemonade clerk would spread his waterproof coat over their knees and a few minutes later Agnes would feel one of his roughened hands creeping about beneath her clothes. Once or twice, while his fingers struggled with some difficulty in her garments, she had glanced at him, but always his full attention appeared to be on the screen. He would even give a laugh at some amusing incident in the film, and occasionally he turned to her with a roar of delight and asked her if she'd ever heard anything better. When they had tea and a grill after the film he talked only about inheriting the Baltinglass meat business. 'I wonder will I ever marry?' he now and again mused, as though in the company of his mother, of whom he spoke a lot, or with a stranger. He ate heartily on these occasions, usually asking the waitress to bring a further supply of rashers.

Every Tuesday she went out with him, and when he left her at night – a street or two away from the hardware shop because, he explained, he didn't want the Englishes to see him – she would walk slowly home, thinking of what life would be like with this man who might one day suggest that they should share it as a man and wife. He had said that since his childhood he had had a wish to live in Drumcondra, and she imagined that: the two of them in a house in Drumcondra and Doyle returning one day and saying he had received his inheritance, that the meat business in Baltinglass was his at last. But often she saw him in a different mood and somehow it seemed more real. A letter would arrive to say that the meat business was bankrupt and would be a debt to inherit, and he would buckle himself into his waterproof coat and go out without eating anything and later return unruly and intoxicated. She imagined repairing his clothes and lifting from a floor his soiled shirts, his socks and his under-garments. She saw him on a chair removing his boots. She heard him whistling and then he looked up to tell her more about his mother, who had died ten years ago. The slight smell he gave off would occasionally enter her nostrils as she walked away from him, back to the Englishes' shop. As she smelt it, she could see a whole life clearly: Doyle and herself, Doyle assaulting her in silence in a bed, and eight of Doyle's children. She imagined his naked body.

'Excuse me, girl,' a man said to her one night in Ringsend, after Doyle had left her. 'D'you know where South Lotts Road is?'

There was a strawberry mark on the man's face, stretching from the centre of his left cheek to his forehead, enclosing his left eye. He wore glasses with pale rims. He was smiling at her.

'Near Bath Avenue?' he said interrogatively. 'Or am I walking in the incorrect direction?' He was a middle-aged man, small and stout, wearing dark clothes: before she noticed his tie she took him to be a priest.

'Over the bridge,' she said. 'Turn left, round by the greyhound track.'

'Would you take a drink at all?'

'Pardon?'

'Would you join me in a glass of refreshment?'

She watched a drizzle falling on his features, as she had watched it five minutes ago falling on the features of the lemonade clerk. Doyle had stood by a street-light, saying there was a good thing on at the Capitol next week and that they'd meet outside the cinema at half-past six. 'You're getting wet,' she had said. He had lifted his hand to his forehead to wipe the damp from it. He agreed that he was getting wet, and went away.

'It's a poor night,' the man with the strawberry mark observed. 'A glass of refreshment sets you up.'

He spoke with a soft accent, as if he came from a long way away; there was nothing nasal about his voice; he was not a Dublin man.

'Ah, no,' she said. 'No, no. It's very good of you. Thank you very much.'

She remembered, years afterwards, how she had said to herself that he was not a Dublin man since he didn't have the nasal sound. She had thought of Cavan or Leitrim without quite knowing what men from those parts spoke like, guessing in her mind. Looking back, she felt that she had known that something was happening, that her brain was piecing together facts in her life while the man spoke to her and as she thanked him for his offer. Seeing the incident from a distance, it seemed that as they stood in the drizzle Sister Tracy was speaking about the advent of her father at the convent, and that Doyle's fingers were on her flesh.

'What harm'll it do you?' said the man with the strawberry mark. His left hand had taken her arm. He was smiling at her more than before, his face with the drizzle on it was turned towards her the way it never occurred to Doyle to turn his. 'A ginger ale,' said the man, 'and a small drop in it. That could cheer the two of us up, you know.'

She smiled back at him, beginning to shake her head and then not shaking it at all.

'There's a place called Phelan's I saw,' he said. 'It'll do us rightly.'

She had known as she walked with him what was going to happen and she had been seized in those moments with a sudden bitterness. Faces appeared before her as she kept up with him in the rain: the faces of her customers in the hardware shop, of the Englishes, the face of the Reverend Mother and the face of Doyle. She had stood while the green overall was fitted on her body, with love she had given her body to a salesman of shoes who had loved her then too. She felt she could have stabbed their faces now. She could have watched them burn.

'It does you good,' he said in the bar, and she nodded. It was near to closing time, she reminded him: he should fetch them a couple more. He went away to do so, laughing delightedly.

He put his arm around her as they walked from the public house. He led her towards the sea, along the dockside near Thorncastle Street. 'Ah God, it was great meeting you,' he said. He pressed her body with his arm and drew her into the shadows among timber crates. He smiled at her again. She reached out her hand to touch the skin of his face, asking him for money.

Thirteen years later, in the Excelsior Bar, Agnes Quin drained the stout from her glass. 'A small Power's,' she said, calling out to Eddie Trump. 'Take something yourself, Eddie.'

'She'll be ninety-two,' said Morrissey.

She rose and went to get her drink. She had never in her life bought a drink for Morrissey, nor had any of the other women as far as she knew. She remembered hearing Beulah Flynn discussing the point with Mrs Dargan and Mrs Kite one time. Morrissey relied on them for his living; to buy him drinks would be an absurdity, they had said.

'Is it an expensive cup, Agnes?' he asked her now.

She shook her head.

'You saw what I gave for the spider.'

A long time ago, walking one day in the neighbourhood of Dolphin's Barn, she had met him. He had spoken about O'Neill's Hotel in Thaddeus Street and she had remembered Mrs Sinnott, who had visited the convent. 'She can't be bothered with visitors,' Morrissey had hastily said. 'She likes to sit there alone.' She had walked to the street and had seen Mrs Sinnott at the window of her room, and then she had gone into the hotel.

Morrissey stood up and combed his hair again. 'I'll go over now,' he said. 'I'll be seeing you, Agnes.'

She watched him going away, pushing open the swing door so that the sunlight blazed in the rosy bar for a moment, revealing evidence of neglect. She thought of his hand writing down for the old woman sentences from Old Moore's Almanac and sentences from the works of John Pendragon, and the old woman's pretended interest. She would give him sixpence before he left her.

'How're you, Agnes?' exclaimed Mrs Dargan, laboriously entering the bar. 'Will you draw me a stout, Eddie?'

She was a middle-aged widow of great bulk, attired almost always in a tightly belted black coat and a headscarf with horses on it. Her round, pale face was harshly marked with lipstick and eye-shadow; her hair beneath the headscarf was the colour of an orange. At all times of the year, summer and winter alike, her plump legs rose from black, fur-lined boots.

'I'm dead tired,' she said to Agnes Quin.

She went on talking and Agnes listened, thinking, as often she did, how different her life was from the life of Olivia de Havilland. She had seen the Hollywood actress for the first time nineteen years ago, when she was eleven, playing the part of a pleasant person in *Gone With The Wind*. She had since seen her in other roles, giving performances that had always been moving. Regularly she wondered what it would be like to be Olivia de Havilland, to have riches all around you, to lie in sunshine whenever you felt the need, to eat food in a bath, covered with foam. She imagined changing places with Olivia de Havilland and often, when she lay wakeful, she saw Olivia de Havilland in a fur coat strolling around the streets of Dublin, extracting money from men or talking men around to an arrangement that suited her better than it suited them. 'Have you had something to eat?' Agnes had said to a man the night before, adding that there was a shop that stayed open late, where she could buy pieces of chicken and a few biscuits for both of them. They had walked together, agreeing on the way that as well as food a little more to drink would be pleasant also. The man gave her ten shillings with which to obtain the chicken and the biscuits. 'There's a place I can get a bottle,' she said. 'Crested Ten's the strongest.' She accepted more money and asked the man to wait for her while she went down an alley to the back-door of a public house, at which, she said, she was well known. She walked through the darkness, away from the man, past the public house and out into another street. She went on walking until she caught sight of Morrissey, in conversation with the elderly man with whom she later entered O'Neill's Hotel. She had afterwards imagined Olivia de Havilland being spoken to by Morrissey and then falling into step with his elderly companion.

'Morrissey fecked a spider out of Woolworth's,' she said to Mrs Dargan. 'A brooch for Mrs Sinnott's birthday.'

'Jays, he's a shocking twister,' said Mrs Dargan.

'He rubbed off the price and wrote on two pounds ten. Ninepence those spiders are.'

Mrs Dargan laughed, rolls of flesh shifting and wobbling on her neck. If Morrissey's mother had known him, she said, she'd have drowned him in a bucket.

Agnes agreed, thinking again of Olivia de Havilland and of other women in Hollywood whose luxurious lives she found pleasanter to consider than her own. *Why can't I forget it?* she had written. *Why would it make a difference, a man handing you in?*

In another bar Mr Smedley spoke. He spoke less directly than he had spoken before, having come to the conclusion that the barmen in this city were given to touchiness. The best ploy, he decided, would be to gain a barman's confidence by means of interesting conversation and then, in a man-to-man way, to reveal what was on his mind.

'I'm a salesman of cardboard,' Mr Smedley said agreeably. 'I go all over the globe.'

The barman who had served him, now busy with bottles, made no reply.

'I sell to factories,' revealed Mr Smedley. 'Have you a carton handy? A cardboard carton?'

'What for?'

Mr Smedley smiled. He offered the barman a cigarette, which the barman took and placed behind his ear.

'The sheeting I sell,' explained Mr Smedley, 'is turned into boxes and cartons. After that it's stamped with a name and a sales message. Hand me up that thing there.'

The barman handed him a battered carton that once had contained packets of potato crisps. Mr Smedley felt it. He bent a piece of it between his fingers. He asked the barman if he might tear it slightly, and the barman replied that as far as he was concerned Mr Smedley could do what he liked with the carton. He could eat the carton, the barman suggested, if he wished to do this. Mr Smedley shook his head. He tore a piece of the cardboard away and lifted it to his nose. He handed the piece and the carton back to the barman.

'That's not of our manufacture,' he said. 'That's cardboard of very poor quality.'

'It does its stuff.'

'You're a man of the world,' replied Mr Smedley. 'Listen to me.'

He told the barman that he had traded in cardboard in five continents. He had spent time in the company of West Indian women as well as Australian, American, and Chinese women, and the women of the Philippine Islands. He had spent time in the company of women from every European country and the outlying European islands. He was only wondering, he added, what the facilities were for a man of vigour in this present city.

After a pause, during which he examined Mr Smedley's face, the barman requested him to leave his bar.

6

'Are you O'Neill?' Mrs Eckdorf asked in the hall of O'Neill's Hotel, her left hand playing with the dark glasses she had just taken off.

'I am Eugene Sinnott,' said Eugene. 'O'Neill is dead.'

'How charming that sounds, the way you put it!' cried Mrs Eckdorf, trying not to regard too closely this person who spoke to her. 'And who is that man?'

She smiled in the direction of O'Shea, who stood some yards behind Eugene, remembering the position from the past.

'O'Shea,' said Eugene. 'Hall-porter and boots.' He gave a laugh to indicate that he spoke humorously. He took the remains of a cigarette from his mouth. He threw it on to the ground and lit another.

'And I am Mrs Eckdorf. Ivy Eckdorf from Munich in Germany, a photographer. May I perhaps sit down?'

'Sit down, of course, why wouldn't you? Can O'Shea get you a drop of something?'

'My dear, nothing at all. I saw from the sign outside that here was an hotel and in I came. What a charming dog that man has!'

O'Shea stepped forward and said that if Mrs Eckdorf wished to stay in the hotel it could easily be arranged. The hotel, he added, was not full at present, although once upon a time, on an August day, you wouldn't have been able to get a room in O'Neill's for love or money. 'I am fascinated,' said Mrs Eckdorf, her glance moving from Eugene to O'Shea and over the maroon carpet and the tall thronelike chairs and the wallpaper that was kept in place with nails. Coloured sunlight streamed through the red and green panels of the entrance doors, on the air there remained a trace of the powerful scent of Agnes Quin. She hoped her manner was right, for it was essential that it should be. She wondered what her mother would think to see her now, standing in a place like this, saying in her professional way that she was fascinated.

'Breakfast from eight a.m. onwards,' said O'Shea. 'Luncheon in the dining-room, a meat tea at half-past six. Special arrangements can be made – '

'You've got the wrong end of the stick,' interrupted Eugene. 'The lady hasn't come to stay.'

'And why shouldn't I stay?' cried Mrs Eckdorf, jumping up and taking Eugene by the arm. 'Mr Sinnott, I'm not of German stock myself if that's what's worrying you. I was born in a place called Maida Vale. In London.'

'I don't imagine – ' began Eugene.

'My dear, you don't have to. You don't imagine it's my sort of place? Well, there you're happily wrong. I cannot stand plush. I walked the streets of your charming city and met with beauty and delights. You find the real people of a city only if you go out and look for them. What can you expect if you sit on your bottom in a cocktail lounge? Reality is the grail I seek, Mr Sinnott, and I see that I have found it again.' She gestured expansively at the whole area of the hall and at Eugene and O'Shea standing in it. 'Could you,' she said to O'Shea, 'telephone through for my bags and baggage?'

'There's no phone here,' Eugene said quickly.

'I can ring through from the box outside,' said O'Shea. 'No trouble in the world, Mrs Eckdorf.'

'Look here,' said Eugene, but already Mrs Eckdorf was giving O'Shea the name of the hotel where her luggage was. 'Let them put the bags in a cab,' she commanded, 'and the bill with them.'

'No trouble at all,' said O'Shea again.

'Now listen,' said Eugene, stepping in front of O'Shea. 'Listen, Mrs Eckdorf, this is a bad time to stay here. Tomorrow there's an occasion here, a lot of people coming, a family thing. It'd be awkward with a stranger about.'

'Mr Sinnott, I'm like a mouse.'

'Added to which, there's only myself and O'Shea. There's no

cook in the kitchen or anything like that. The dining-room hasn't been entered since we had a farmer from Monaghan here two months ago, a man O'Shea found wandering – '

'Oh God, I love your way of talking,' cried Mrs Eckdorf. 'All the time this morning I've met only the nicest and now it's best of all. Any old bed will do, and a meat tea I adore.'

Eugene stared at Mrs Eckdorf and while he was occupied in doing that, transfixed by the uttering of these odd words, O'Shea slipped from the hall. He was smiling, Eugene saw. The sorrow had for a moment gone from O'Shea's face. It was as though the advent of this smart woman made up for all the empty years: O'Shea had returned to the past he worshipped.

'After all,' said Mrs Eckdorf, 'I'll be paying good money. Look at it like that, why don't you?'

'It's ridiculous, Mrs Eckdorf. A place like this – '

'Mr Sinnott, I've explained.'

She smiled. She was always smiling, he thought. Ever since she had come into the hotel she had been smiling and laughing, and speaking in a shrill voice that seemed itself to be full of smiles and laughter. He watched her mouth. He could see the tip of her tongue between slightly parted teeth. She spoke again. She said:

'I live in the Lipowskystrasse. I've an apartment done out in a cinder-grey. Mr Sinnott, can you imagine that?'

'Mrs Eckdorf – '

'But I'm happier here. I'm happy in this hall listening to you. I wish to stay, Mr Sinnott: I like your old hotel.'

'Very well,' he said after a longish pause. 'O'Shea will be back in a minute. I have to be on my way.'

'I could eat you to your bones, Mr Sinnott! I'd like to talk and talk with you: I could listen for ever.'

'I'm not here much actually.'

'Mr Sinnott, you have gentle eyes.'

He went away, and as he passed through the entrance doors she photographed his back, although she was aware that, not having re-set the Mamiya for the poor light of the hall, the photograph would be one for her record file only. He had stood there, not quite the extraordinary figure she had imagined, but

85

a character at least who was not uninteresting. His eyes had not seemed to see her properly, and while he spoke a cigarette had shifted from one corner of his mouth to the other. She had noticed his hands shaking; she could see that he was indeed an inebriate and she felt excited by that thought, and excited too by the bizarre-looking porter who had gone to telephone for her baggage. She imagined the Sinnott man returning to the hotel later that day, lurching from side to side, mouthing words that did not make sense. She saw an image of him, with the porter supporting him all the way up the shabby stairs: she saw it in colour, the porter's uniform glowing against a matt background.

Mrs Eckdorf rose and strode about the hall, her professional eye alighting on details of form and colour. She narrowed her eyes, seeing everything at first in black and white and then in pastel shades. Something jumped in her stomach, telling her that the urge which had brought her in was a more fruitful one than she had ever realized. She felt she was standing on the done-for court of some done-for monarchy; bodies might once have strewn this hall; the air was heavy with people weeping.

As she walked about, more slowly now, she knew instinctively that this would be a greater work than her study in Marrakesh, where she had lived with the Haziti family, recording a story of incest. She had caught some bug and had been laid up for days in the little raggy bed they gave her and which had afterwards appeared on the dust-jacket of her book. When she returned to Munich she discovered that she had lost a stone and a half, which did not surprise her since most of the food supplied in the Haziti household was inedible. She was used to such hardships, though: she had suffered in a similar manner in Sicily, on the Ganges, in Lesotho, Afghanistan, and in the home of a nail-maker in Peru. It had never not been worth it.

Mrs Eckdorf sat down again. That porter was taking his time, she thought. She closed her eyes and fell asleep.

Give attention to wardrobe and cage-birds, wrote Morrissey. *Venus moves forward in Aries.*

She remembered the herrings that O'Shea had carried to her

earlier. She had always enjoyed herrings when they were fresh. The best way to cook them, she remembered, was to hold them in boiling water like the fishermen themselves did.

She had taught Enid to stuff herrings and to pot them. You baked herrings with cloves and mace for an hour and a half in a slow oven, or you could bake them with mustard butter. Enid had written one time that she'd stuffed herrings with shrimps, but her husband hadn't liked them done that way. She remembered Enid as a child in the kitchen, beating eggs in a bowl and Kathleen Devinish showing her how to make bread. O'Shea simply fried the herrings and that was enjoyable too, fish with a crisp skin. Dublin herrings were supposed to be particularly tasty, Ardglass herrings were famous. A herring that wasn't fresh was a different commodity and had a different taste. Kathleen Devinish had claimed that gently boiled herring flesh could be fed to babies at birth. *Herring-bone*, her father had somewhere written.

A moment ago she had seen Eugene moving slowly down Thaddeus Street, as he did every morning at that time. A little before that, O'Shea had walked urgently from the hotel accompanied by his dog. It was pleasant that O'Shea had a pet; a pet was company. She saw weathered bricks in a zig-zag pattern: was it in Italy? The sun was on them, sunshine that was soft and reddish like the bricks, the sunshine of a late evening.

She had had pets herself, two cats she'd been given by old Mr Riordan. They used to follow her everywhere like O'Shea's greyhound followed him, they used to sit with her in the dining-room. It was a long time ago now.

She saw O'Shea hurrying back, seeming more cheerful than usual. His body was not bent in despondency, his swift motion was like that of a man on stilts, as though he employed elements within himself that had fallen into desuetude.

The sun is square to Saturn, wrote Morrissey, *Uranus and Jupiter in your fourth house. Buy no new clothing*.

Her father's finger pointed and she looked at the zig-zag brickwork. *Herring-bone*, he had written. Leo had promised, she suddenly remembered, that he'd teach her to fish in the Dodder.

For the last two weeks of this month, continued Morrissey, *prefer easy mountaineering to water-sports*.

The pencil and the exercise-book were violently snatched from his hands. Exclaiming a protest, he looked up to see that the sombre hotel-porter had silently entered the room. There was something that might have been a smile on the lips of this man who had never addressed him.

A visitor has come from Germany, reported O'Shea. *A woman dressed in white*.

She had seen a woman in Thaddeus Street and had wondered about her. *They are at war with Germany*, someone once had written for her: she had not been much interested.

O'Shea began to leave the room, having dropped the exercise-book at Morrissey's feet. Morrissey picked it up and heard for the first time in his life the porter speaking to him. He turned his head and saw O'Shea standing by the door, not looking at him but looking at a corner of the room.

'If you pass water again on my flower-bed,' said the voice of O'Shea, 'I will hit you with a knife.'

The door closed. Morrissey stared at it for a moment and then stared at the page in his exercise-book that O'Shea had spoiled with his large, ungainly handwriting. He tore the page out and began to write, continuing his advice about the last two weeks of the month. It was a time, he noted, for hair-trimming and scalp treatments. He wrote that down, keeping the magazine from which he culled the information out of Mrs Sinnott's sight. His sixpence was waiting for him on the dressing-table, where a similar coin always was. O'Shea had stood in a bank and the teller had counted out sixpences and put them in a little bag for O'Shea to carry away. It pleased Morrissey that O'Shea was obliged to go to that trouble so that this small payment might daily be made. If O'Shea caused any injury to him because of the flower-bed he would receive compensation in the courts and O'Shea would suffer a gaol sentence, which was the best thing that could happen to him. Ridiculous, the man coming into the room like a thunderstorm and writing down that a woman from Germany had come into the hotel. Who could be interested in that?

Having left the room, O'Shea decided that he would make up a bed for Mrs Eckdorf and then go out and buy fish for her luncheon and for Mrs Sinnott's, a piece of plaice or a fresh mackerel. The family would come for the birthday, and he would tell them a visitor from Germany was staying in the hotel. They might see her on the stairs or the hall, they would turn to one another and say that a new era was beginning.

Ten minutes ago he had entered the hall from Thaddeus Street to discover that Mrs Eckdorf, sitting on one of the tall chairs, had dropped into a doze. Her mouth was open, her eyelids, carrying long curled lashes, were down, like blinds, over her eyes. The greyhound had sniffed her legs and the handbag that lay on the floor beside them, not causing her to wake. Her arms were drooped over the arms of the chair, the palms of her hands facing upwards, the fingers splayed. Looking at her, O'Shea had recalled the coarseness of Agnes Quin. Once in the early morning he had seen her combing her hair as she came down the stairs. She had pulled at it, forcing the comb through the matted strands and speaking to him with her mouth full of hairpins. 'You're looking great, O'Shea,' she had said, showing darkened teeth.

Hurrying now, he passed the room where she had spent the night and through the open door saw the bedclothes strewn all over the floor. He closed the sight away and mounted to the next landing, where he took two sheets and a pillow-case from a large wall-cupboard. With these in his arms, he entered a room that faced Thaddeus Street, the room that Enid Gregan had occupied during her girlhood. He opened the window to clear the air of the smell of fust. Across the street he saw in white writing on the windows of Keogh's grocery information about a reduction in the price of butter. Sunlight glared from the stucco of the houses, a dog slept on the pavement. He wondered if Mrs Eckdorf would look out of the window at all, or even lean out, and be seen by the people passing below in Thaddeus Street. It was certain, in any case, that people would see the taxi-cab arriving with her luggage. 'She preferred O'Neill's,' he would say to anyone who asked him. 'The quiet homeliness of it.' He had suggested to Eugene Sinnott one time that it would be a good idea to have cards printed with a message on them, something like: *O'Neill's Hotel, Thaddeus Street. Best for Meals and Service*. 'I could pass them out on the street,' he'd said, but Eugene Sinnott had replied that the whole operation would be costly and a waste of time.

O'Shea moved from the window and proceeded to make the bed. He wondered if there might be dampness in the blankets, for it was more than two years since anyone had slept in the room. Mrs Sinnott had always been anxious that no one should be put in a damp bed. There were hot-water jars in the kitchen, he remembered; he would fill a couple and put them between the sheets.

As he completed his preparations, covering the grey striped pillow with the pillow-case, smoothing and tucking in the sheets, O'Shea felt a tremor of unusual excitement 'Stay there,' he said to his dog, and abruptly he left the room and crossed the landing. In the hall below he could see the figure of Mrs Eckdorf on the tall chair, her legs crossed, the camera about her neck, her handbag still on the floor. He gazed down at her, at her pale hat and all her pale clothes: she was not at all like Mrs Sinnott, he thought, without knowing why he had thought that. 'That is beauty,' said O'Shea, whispering to himself, still looking down at the sleeping woman. 'That is the most beautiful woman who has ever sat in our hall.' He returned to the bedroom and completed the making of the bed. For a moment he placed the palm of his hand on the pillow where her head would rest and then his hand went between the two sheets and lay where she would lie. He felt a ticking in his stomach that never in his life had he felt before, he felt his heart gathering speed, his mouth seemed dry of saliva. 'I have waited,' said O'Shea. As he stood with his right hand between the sheets of the bed that the photographer was to occupy, there came into his mind an image of himself and Mrs Eckdorf in the kitchen of the hotel, she occupying the chair of Eugene Sinnott. O'Shea did not understand that, but the image was none the less there. 'Something funny is happening,' he said aloud, withdrawing his hand and smoothing the surface of the bed. His dog came near to him and whimpered. He would ask her if she'd rather have plaice or mackerel, he'd buy peas and small potatoes, and eggs for her tea. He would cook everything carefully, he would heat the plates.

It was quiet in the room except for the continued low whimpering of the greyhound. O'Shea gestured at it to be silent. He had a sudden urge to take off his uniform and enter the bed himself so that the warmth of his naked body would air it for her, so that she would lie on sheets that he had lain on. 'My God Almighty,' said O'Shea, his face reddening, sweat breaking out on the calves of his legs.

He stood for several minutes until normality returned to him, and then he left the bedroom and descended to the kitchen, tiptoeing past Mrs Eckdorf in the hall. He put some water on to heat. He took from a cupboard two brown hot-water jars and placed them on the edge of the table. He swept the floor, he put coal into the range, he drew away the ashes and emptied them in the yard. When he returned to the kitchen, Mrs Eckdorf was standing in the doorway.

He said that he had made a bed up for her and was about to air it. She interrupted him, questioning him about Eugene Sinnott and the hotel. She suggested with a laugh that Eugene Sinnott had struck her as a chap who enjoyed raising his elbow. He enjoyed sherry and cigarettes, O'Shea replied; he hadn't touched food in the middle of the day for twenty years.

'You look after him.' She smiled at O'Shea, her eyes fixed on his until he felt he had to look away.

'I look after both of them,' he said.

'Both, O'Shea?'

'His mother is ninety-one. She never had hearing or speech. I carry her food up. I make her bed and clean her room.'

Mrs Eckdorf said that was kind of him. She had noticed when first she saw him that there was kindness in his face. She could quite imagine it, she added: his kind face bent over an elderly person's bed, his hands smoothing the sheets.

'I thought a mackerel for your luncheon,' O'Shea said quickly. 'Or a bit of plaice. With parsnips and potatoes, and rhubarb afterward. Which would you prefer, Mrs Eckdorf, of those two fish?'

She smiled again, not answering the question. She touched his left hand with the tips of her fingers. Then she moved away, towards the two windows.

'You have a hornbeam tree in your yard.'

'And a little flower-bed that I made myself.'

He poured boiling water into the earthenware jars, banging the corks safely home with his hand.

'An interesting tree, the hornbeam,' she said. She turned to look at him again, standing with her right hand resting on the side of her camera, which was still suspended from her neck. Her eyes were yellow, he said to himself, which was a colour he had never seen in the eyes of a woman or a man before. He could see the tip of her tongue between her upper and lower teeth.

'I like this place,' she said. 'I like this whole hotel.'

She walked about the kitchen, picking up knives and spoons and plates. She looked at them and put them down again. 'What is happening tomorrow?' she enquired. 'Mr Sinnott said something was happening.'

He told her, adding nothing to the information she already possessed.

'How fascinating,' she remarked when he had finished speaking. 'A family birthday.'

'I put up a paper-chain, like you have at Christmas.'

'A paper-chain,' said Mrs Eckdorf softly. 'And the family chats about the year that's been. Is that it?'

'They don't say much.'

'Show me the whole hotel, O'Shea. I'm interested in it.'

He nodded, thinking slowly, trying to come to a conclusion. She was here for a reason: he'd felt it the moment he first heard her voice, he'd felt it when he imagined her sitting with him in the kitchen, and he had felt it ever since. He was staring at the soap with which Eugene Sinnott had shaved himself that morning; he would like to draw her attention to this soap, to the fact that the inheritor of the hotel shaved himself with kitchen soap. He had this desire, to discuss the soap with her, but felt he should not. He'd have liked to repeat the conversation that had taken place that morning in the kitchen between himself and Eugene Sinnott, explaining to her that for the past three years Eugene Sinnott had insisted on giving his mother a pencil-sharpener for her birthday and was again insisting on it, that he had gone on about a greyhound race instead of devoting thought to the question of the birthday present. He'd have liked to explain that the hotel was not always as she saw it now, that once upon a time actors and commercial travellers had spent comfortable nights in it and had eaten well-cooked food in the dining-room. He wanted to explain that it was all of a pattern, Agnes Quin and Morrissey and the empty rooms and Eugene Sinnott caring about nothing except sherry and the dreams he had, and the racing of animals. Was it a sin, he wanted to ask her, for a woman or a girl not to cover her head at Mass? She wore a hat herself; it was the first thing he noticed.

Mrs Eckdorf coughed to arouse the porter from the reverie he had entered. She'd noticed that a piece of soap beside the sink had caught his eye. He continued to stare at it. Loudly she asked the name of the dog, which was looking up at her, its head cocked to one side. O'Shea did not reply.

In the silence he heard his own voice speaking to him: his lips, he knew, were not moving, no sound disturbed the stillness in the kitchen. 'She has come to buy the hotel,' his voice said in private to him, and then repeated it again. People were going about, a man in a shop had told him, buying properties that no one had thought of putting up for sale. No one had ever thought of putting O'Neill's Hotel up for sale, but wasn't it the only thing that could happen now? Meticulously, O'Shea considered the facts as they were: an old woman whose heartfelt desire was that her father's hotel should be as once it had been, Eugene Sinnott given up to sherry, he himself waiting. He had said prayers, he had wished, he had willed, he had written that one day O'Neill's Hotel would rise like a phoenix-bird. Being too old now to make demands and it being foreign to her nature to seem a nuisance, she had passed her heartfelt desire from her soul to his, so that her desire might become his duty. God is looking after us, he thought: she would have said that He had never failed them.

'The dog,' said Mrs Eckdorf. 'What is the name of your dog?'

O'Shea's eyes moved from the piece of green soap. He spoke slowly, saying that the dog had no name. He explained that the dog had wandered into the hotel yard one evening six years ago and that neither her nor Eugene Sinnott had been able to think of a name for it.

'My God,' murmured Mrs Eckdorf quietly.

Her face was like a pearl, he thought. He moved towards the door with the greyhound behind him. 'I will show you the room I have for you,' he said. 'And I will show you everything else.'

They crossed the hall and entered the dining-room, a low-ceilinged room with a central table and smaller tables arranged around it. A mirror stretched the length of the mantelpiece, reflecting the sideboard opposite and cane chairs and bottles of sauce on a dumb waiter. There was an unpleasant smell, she noticed, of stale food and of cats.

'They don't have the birthday party here?' she said, and O'Shea replied that the birthday party was always held in the kitchen since that was what Mrs Sinnott wished. He closed the door. They went upstairs.

On the first-floor landing, above a leather sofa that sagged untidily, there was a mirror that was larger than the mirror in the dining-room. In this they were reflected: she with her hat still in place, smiling slightly, her legs in their finely meshed stockings seeming slight and slender, he towering behind, bent within his uniform, the top button open to ease his neck, the greyhound's head at his knees. She saw this picture of them and stopped. He was staring like a man caught up with religion: a Christ could get away with eyes like that. The red and blue and gold of his clothes ran into the whiteness of her suit, their move-ments were confused in the reflection. The camera rose, her fingers made fast adjustments, the shutter snapped.

'This is his,' O'Shea said.

She peered into Eugene Sinnott's bedroom and saw the sacred picture on flowered wallpaper and the bed unmade.

'Thank you,' she said.

He attempted to lead her past the room in which Agnes Quin

had spent part of the night, but Mrs Eckdorf was insistent. An ornamental candlestick had been knocked from the dressing-table, a sheet was torn.

'Disorder,' she murmured. 'Disorder everywhere.'

She heard him whispering to himself that he would rather that two wolves had spent the night there. His eyes were fixed as absorbedly on the fallen candlestick as they had been on the soap in the kitchen.

'I would love to meet Mrs Sinnott,' she said, fearing that he was again about to become entranced. 'Shall we?'

'I will show you the ledgers of the hotel in the past.'

He led the way and they mounted to attics that were full of empty stout bottles and trunks and suitcases. Ledgers were stacked against a wall; there were stuffed birds, their glass domes broken, and cardboard boxes containing knives and forks. 'I hid those,' said O'Shea, 'in case Mr Sinnott would sell them.' There were mildewed sacks which O'Shea said contained cups and saucers, which he had placed there for safety's sake also. Mice had eaten the labels on the stout bottles and nibbled their way through stacks of receipts. The floor was littered with shredded paper and with droppings. 'Look at this,' said O'Shea, opening a ledger and pointing at lines of figures. 'February, 1933.'

'Why was it?' asked Mrs Eckdorf. 'Why is it, O'Shea, that the hotel has fallen down like this?'

He shook his head. Mr Sinnott was always drinking, he said, and then the words came flooding out of him like a torrent joyfully released. All he had wished to say to her in the kitchen came now. He told her about his life with Eugene Sinnott and his mother, he said that the disordered room downstairs would have to be scrubbed with Vim before any decent traveller could spend a night there, he mentioned the soap in the kitchen with which Eugene Sinnott had shaved himself, and the cigarette-butts that Eugene Sinnott scattered all over the hotel. He went to bed himself, he said, at nine o'clock every night, knowing that later Eugene Sinnott would return to the hotel in a state of drunkenness, and that Morrissey would come to sleep in the hall and would admit Agnes Quin and a stranger.

He spoke at length about Mrs Sinnott and the red exercise-books that were full of conversations. He mentioned the day he had arrived in O'Neill's Hotel and how Eugene Sinnott had shown him where the dining-room was. He mentioned the fly she had asked him to open the window for. He talked about the birthday party, about Eugene Sinnott's wife and his son, and his sister and his sister's husband. He spoke again of Morrissey and Agnes Quin, who came to Mrs Sinnott's room in order to take what they could from her. 'He's a kind of devil,' he cried emotionally. 'He passes water on the flowers I have.'

His eyes, inflamed with passion, saw her standing before him and it seemed to him that she was touched with light, as though her body had a flickering shroud about it, as religious figures have in pictures. She would not ever fail to wear a hat, he thought, and then he said things he had not meant to say; he gave up his secrets to the vision that was smiling at him. 'You have come to buy the hotel,' he said in the end.

'Buy?' said Mrs Eckdorf.

'You have come to buy O'Neill's Hotel.'

Slowly she nodded her head. He had guessed, she said. He was right: she had come to buy the hotel.

'It will be like it was.'

'What happened to change it all, O'Shea?'

'He is only interested in animals racing. I will bring you to Mrs Sinnott now.'

She wished to press her question but considered it inadvisable: she had had experience of chaps like this suddenly shutting up like clams. She looked at him: he has adenoids, she thought; that man, as well as everything else, is far from healthy. She saw him in black and white, a shot from low down, his white face in profile against shadows. He reminded her of a garage hand she had once noticed in Georgia, repairing a bicycle wheel by a petrol-pump on the roadside. She had obtained a photograph of the man: she remembered his hands on the spokes of the wheel and the bulk of the petrol-pump looming beside him, to the right of her picture.

'You have come to buy the hotel,' he said again, and she felt she almost loved him for giving her the role she had to play.

'How nice you look,' she said, 'up here in your uniform.'

Blood came into his face; he shuffled his feet, playing with the grit on the boarded floor. He wished she might remain there for the remainder of his life and that he might remain where he was also, the two of them standing in the gloom of an attic: two strangers, each thinking the other nice.

'I'm dying to meet Mrs Sinnott,' she said.

'A photographer from Germany,' said Eugene, 'as mad as a hatter.'

There was no speech in the Excelsior Bar for a moment, while Eugene's tidings of the events in his hotel were absorbed by Mrs Dargan and Agnes Quin. Then Mrs Dargan said it was disgraceful the people who were about these days. She warned Eugene to be careful in case the woman didn't pay up when the time came.

'She said she could eat me,' said Eugene, standing in the centre of the bar with a glass of medium dry sherry in his hand. 'She paid a compliment about O'Shea's old animal.'

'I heard of that kind of thing,' said Agnes Quin. 'They go into a hotel, Eugene, and the next thing is they owe you sixty pounds.'

'They leave suitcases behind them,' said Mrs Dargan, 'full of cement blocks.'

There was further conversation about dishonest conduct in hotels. Eddie Trump related an anecdote concerning a man he'd heard of who had managed to spend two years in a hotel without ever paying the bill. Mrs Dargan remarked that it would terrify you, the activities people got up to these days.

'I had a dream last night,' said Eugene. 'I want to tell you, Eddie.'

'I had a dream myself,' said Eddie Trump, 'that I was teaching Geometry in a school. I had two triangles chalked up on a blackboard and I was trying to prove to the lads that the sides of one were equal to the sides of the other. I was making a whole-sale bollocks of it.'

'Geometry,' repeated Eugene. 'There was a horse called Geometry about fifteen years ago.'

Reaching for a bottle, Eddie Trump laughed.

'There's a thing called Mark Ruler at Lingfield,' said Eugene. 'E. Davies up. You'd use a ruler drawing triangles, Eddie.'

Eddie Trump looked doubtful. 'It could be,' he said.

'Or the three-thirty Handicap at Ascot. R. Fawdon on Resolved. Isn't that a word you have in Geometry?'

'I don't think there's a thing in it, Eugene. I spent an unprofitable night.'

'I had a dream you dropped dead, Eddie.'

The barman, a glass tilted in his left hand to receive the beer he was pouring from a bottle in his right, wagged his head slowly. Mrs Dargan sighed. In a whispering voice she remarked to Agnes Quin that this bar was an impossible place, the way people were constantly relating the dreams they had. She gave it as her opinion that there were more dreams related in Riordan's public house than anywhere else in Europe; she'd take a bet on that, she offered, only it could never be proved.

'The death was given out on the wireless, Eddie. You died in Washington Zoo.'

'I was never in that place.'

'Keep well away from it,' advised Mrs Dargan.

'Was it heart?' Agnes Quin enquired. 'Did they give the cause on the wireless, Eugene?'

'He was eaten by an elephant,' said Mrs Dargan. 'An elephant thought Eddie was a bun.'

Eugene said that that wasn't so. No details had been related concerning the manner of the fatality except that at the time a bottle was being uncorked.

'There was a relevance in it,' he said, 'because the bottle was of Germanic origin. There was a second relevance because O'Shea came in the door there and said a circus man was looking for accommodation. D'you see what I mean?'

Eddie Trump shook his head.

'I do not, Eugene.'

'Your woman above in the hotel has a touch of the sawdust about her.'

'Is that what she is?' said Agnes Quin. 'Out of Duffy's Circus or something?'

'Ah no, no.' Eugene paused, swaying his body back and forth, his eyes screwed up against the smoke from his cigarette, ash falling on to his waistcoat. 'You could see her on the back of a horse going round in the ring. She's that type of woman.'

'Is that so?' said Eddie Trump.

'She has a big red mouth like a clown would have. D'you mind me referring to the death, Eddie?'

Eddie Trump said he didn't mind at all. It was interesting certainly, he said, a woman like that coming into O'Neill's Hotel.

Eugene handed round his packet of cigarettes.

'*Niersteiner Domtal* was on the label of the bottle,' he said. 'Have you heard of it, Eddie?'

'I have of course. A great old wine.'

'Keep well away from it,' advised Mrs Dargan.

'What's the woman want?' Agnes Quin asked, and Eugene replied that he didn't know. She came into the hotel, he said, saying she was looking for a grail. He repeated the details of his dream, drawing attention to the fact that O'Shea had said the circus man required warm stabling for his animals.

'She has definitely no animals with her,' he reported, and he went on talking, telling about the dream in which he'd been paddling in the sea at Dalkey. 'A dog came up and sniffed me,' he said, and then, reminded of the event by his reference to a dog, he mentioned the forthcoming Greyhound Derby. 'I saw on the paper,' he said, 'that it'll be the greatest race ever run on Irish soil.'

Mrs Dargan was thinking that she had a touch of indigestion. Eddie Trump wiped the counter with a grey cloth. Eugene began to cough. He gripped the bar with the right hand to steady himself. She'd take two Rennies later on, Mrs Dargan thought, and then she wondered if she could return to a post she'd once had, plucking chickens for a butcher.

'The wife,' said Eddie Trump, 'dreamed she was picking marigolds.'

There was a silence for a moment in the Excelsior Bar. Eugene drained his glass and edged it towards Eddie Trump. He drew smoke into his lungs and slowly released it, watching it curling in the air. He received his glass and paid for its contents. Speaking slowly, he said:

'Would you see anything in it if I said she had yellow eyes?'

'Yellow?' repeated Mrs Dargan.

'Would you see anything in it if you think of the dog coming up to sniff me and the mention of the circus man in the hotel and then your woman coming in and admiring O'Shea's old animal?'

Plucking chickens was no joke, Mrs Dargan thought, but it was better in a lot of ways than having to listen to this kind of talk. Eddie Trump could make nothing of it either, she noticed. She shook her head and Eddie Trump shook his.

'A woman with yellow eyes,' said Eugene, 'and the emphasis on the dogs. A woman saying she was English born and bred. D'you see what I mean?'

'I do not, Eugene,' said Eddie Trump.

'*Niersteiner Domtal* on a printed label. Printed words on a label. D'you see?'

'No, Eugene.'

'Trap four in the Derby.'

There was a pause. Eddie Trump drank deeply from his glass of beer. He drew a hand across his mouth. He said that as far as he remembered trap four was scheduled to contain Russian Gun.

'I read he's good,' said Mrs Dargan. 'Is Russian Gun the tip, Eugene?'

Eugene said it wasn't. Russian Gun, he corrected them, would perform from trap six, which was a good trap to run from. 'Trap four,' he said, 'is a big handicap, but if there's a dog to beat the animal in it I'll put two half-notes on that counter tomorrow night.'

'Is it Yellow Printer?' said Mrs Dargan. 'Is that the tip, Eugene?'

'An English animal, born and bred, trained by Johnny Bassett, kennelled out at McKenna's in Cabinteely.'

'A great old dog,' said Eddie Trump.

'Replenish that,' said Eugene, pushing forward his glass again.

'Bedad, it's extraordinary.' Eddie Trump wiped his hands on

the cloth with which he had wiped the counter. It was extraordinary, he said, the way things were, that a woman would travel from Germany and end up by being a tip for a dog-race.

'If you could see her,' said Eugene, 'you'd say it's all she's fit for.'

They laughed in the Excelsior Bar, the others imagining what the woman looked like from Eugene's description. Mrs Dargan experienced another pang of indigestion. Agnes forgot about Mrs Eckdorf and imagined herself walking down a Hollywood boulevard on the arm of a thin man who had once been an admired criminal and was now reformed, an owner of night-clubs. Counting out Eugene's change, Eddie Trump said that it was an ill wind that blew no good. It was an extraordinary thing, he repeated, and added that he couldn't wait to take a gander at her himself, this woman with yellow eyes.

7

Had Morrissey known that Mr Smedley was anxiously making himself agreeable to the city's barmen so that he might question them concerning the city's pleasures, he would have said that the failure of their paths to cross was typical of the sourness of life. Morrissey was in one place, Mr Smedley was in another. They were not aware on this warm morning of one another's existence, yet as Mr Smedley sought between business appointments to make arrangements for the evening Morrissey sought to oblige a man with just such requirements. Had he known of Mr Smedley's travail, he would have said that the absurdity of the situation was only to be expected of a gross and unjust society.

Morrissey held his fellow men in poor opinion, and had always done so. In his view the world was populated mainly by the hypocritical, by rogues who were untrustworthy even in roguery, by the cruel and the foolish. He had believed as a child that if he turned his back on his enemies they would damage him from behind, and in this he had frequently been proved right. His nature was dominated by suspicion, a quality that broke out in his eyes and was apparent for all to see. Change given him by shop-keepers or publicans he counted meticulously, the mathematics involved coming loudly from his lips. A man in a tobacconist's had once said to him, having watched this small ceremony, that he had never made a mistake with change: it was something you get used to, the man said, you became quick and accurate over the years. Morrissey, whose manner was occasionally direct, replied that he had suspected the man not of carelessness but of dishonesty. There were a lot of dishonest people in the world: you had to steer a course through them.

In a way, Morrissey's view reflected that of Mr Gregan, whom he had first met one Christmas Eve a long time ago now. Mr Gregan, on his way home from the insurance company, had called in at O'Neill's Hotel with two Christmas presents for Mrs Sinnott. He had been pumping up the back tyre of his bicycle in Thaddeus Street, and Morrissey, unaware then that the cyclist was the son-in-law of Mrs Sinnott, had dropped into a seasonal conversation with him. After he had suggested that if Mr Gregan was in need of a certain kind of company he could oblige him in the matter, they had gone together to a public house on the Quays, where Morrissey had introduced Mr Gregan to Mrs Kite. 'I'll not bother,' Mr Gregan had whispered to Morrissey when he saw her sitting there, but he had remained none the less and had taken several Christmas drinks with them. Speaking in a professional way, as a man of the business world, Mr Gregan said that a lot of people were criminals under the skin. It was an expression that pleased Morrissey greatly. He repeated it more than once, saying he understood its meaning perfectly. He was sorry when Mr Gregan put on his bicycle-clips again and went away.

The next time the two met was in Mrs Sinnott's room a month or so later. Morrissey was about to go, Mr Gregan had just arrived for a lunchtime conversation. Eagerly, Morrissey saluted the insurance man who had spoken so sensibly, but to his astonishment received a curt reply. The man who had talked so long and so agreeably on Christmas Eve appeared to be embarrassed by the memory of that, and on future encounters Mr Gregan was no more forthcoming. 'We think the same way,' Mr Gregan had said on Christmas Eve, 'although we come from two different classes. We've a lot in common.' Morrissey often now heard the voice of Mr Gregan in conversation with O'Shea or Eugene Sinnott, relating pleasantly the improvements he was making to his property. Yet because of the embarrassment, because of the small fact that once upon a time he had wheeled his bicycle in the direction of Mrs Kite at Morrissey's instigation, there could apparently be no further relationship between them. In the end, Morrissey came to believe that Mr Gregan was as bad as anyone else, an untrustworthy and hypocritical man.

Having left Mrs Sinnott's room on this Friday morning,

Morrissey stood now, at fifteen minutes past twelve, in McBride's public house in Thomas Street. He stood alone, drinking a small quantity of whiskey. He was talking to himself in his mind, his voice saying that neither Agnes Quin nor Beulah Flynn was a female you could trust. You would go out of your way to oblige women like that and they wouldn't hand you the price of a small one. Mrs Dargan was little better: only the night before he had spoken about Mrs Dargan to a man he'd met on Eden Quay, but when he had led the man up to her she had refused to have anything to do with him. Afterwards he had seen them together, Mrs Dargan getting into the man's motor-car. He had obliged both of them by bringing them together, he had acted in good faith. Yet both had turned their backs on him, both had plotted in order that he should be deprived of his just fee. It amazed Morrissey that these two people, who had never before laid eyes on one another, should have succeeded during the brief moment of the initial encounter in passing to one another the suggestion that they should act deceitfully. 'She's a bit touchy,' he had said as they walked away from the bar in which he had led the man up to Mrs Dargan. 'Nothing personal at all, mister.' He had suggested that if the man came with him he would introduce him to a more agreeable woman, but the man said he'd had enough for one night and had gone away quickly. What he'd done, Morrissey guessed, was to return to the bar as soon as Morrissey was out of sight. He could imagine the two of them laughing.

Beulah Flynn owed him a pound. Mrs Kite, the char-woman, had suddenly become unco-operative. It amazed him that money borrowed should not be paid back and that a woman like Mrs Kite should take it upon herself to talk about a conscience at her time of life. In a just and straightforward world he wouldn't be expected to associate with such women in the first place, nor would he be obliged to go along to O'Neill's Hotel in order to earn money by being a help to an elderly person in need of human company. It was Morrissey's belief that the world, far from being just and straightforward, was disgraceful no matter how you regarded it, an opinion that had been strengthened by his association, many years ago now, with a woman called Miss Lambe.

Reading a magazine one day, he had come across a small advertisement. *This cultured lady*, it had said, *would like to hear from kindly widowers interested in astrology.* He had written at once, and in time a reply had arrived from the North of England, from Miss Lambe, who worked in a boarding-house in Wigan. She it was who in the subsequent correspondence had introduced him to the stars. She it was who had sent him, free of charge, paper-backed books on the subject. *I see to the domestic side here*, she had written. *The house is owned by Mr and Mrs Crosbie. We have nine residents.* He had written to say he was a widowed lung specialist, forming the letters of his words carefully, checking the spelling in a dictionary he had managed to take from a bookshop. Her letters to him incorporated lessons on how to read the Tarot and one day, she promised, they would meet and go together to consult the famous shadow-reader, Bhagawan Soaham. She related details of her life, of the troubles she now and again experienced with the domestic staff and with Mrs Crosbie, who was a difficult woman. *I envy you not having mundane problems*, she had written. *I envy you the useful work you do. Lung disease is a terrible affliction.* In the books she sent him he read about Aquarius and Taurus and Virgo. Being born beneath the sign of Gemini himself, as she was too, he learnt that he must take care when crossing roads and when close to sharp instruments. *When Uranus and Jupiter are in your house of true love*, Miss Lambe had written, *you may enter a happy life. We must both take care when Venus makes a square aspect to Neptune.* She sent him her photograph and he saw a blurred image of a woman in a coat, standing in a garden. He cut from a magazine a picture of a man in evening dress and sent it to her, saying it had been taken at a lung specialists' conference and was the only reproduction of himself he possessed. *I've put it in a frame*, she wrote, *that used to have a picture of Bhagawan Soaham in it.* At heart he wasn't much interested in prophecies, or in shadow-readers or palmists, but he continued to peruse the paper-backed books and the magazines she sent him, and always he opened her letters with eagerness. He took from a bookstall some torn copies of Old Moore's Almanac and posted them to her, which pleased her enormously, for she had never studied this seer before. He told her about his childhood and how he had battled his way through his studies in order to become a lung specialist. *All that is in your horoscope*, she wrote. *You are a remarkable man.* He thought that one day he would write to her, quite out of the blue, and say that in performing an operation on a person's lungs he had committed a fatal error due to lack of sleep. He would say he had been struck from the medical register because of this error and was now without money or standing. *Could I come to Wigan?* he would write. *Would there be humble work for me in the boarding-house?* In his mind's eye he saw them working together in the kitchen of the house and one day, perhaps, they would marry one another and when the Crosbies died they would receive the boarding-house as a reward for all their years of servitude. He wouldn't object if she wished to talk constantly about the stars or insisted on visits to shadow-readers. They would be happy in their companionship, they would develop a relationship and understand one another's needs.

Unfortunately for Morrissey, none of that came about. What happened instead was that Mrs Crosbie died and two months later Miss Lambe wrote: *An extraordinary event has occurred. Last Friday in the evening Mr Crosbie came down to the kitchen and said he admired me. I did not know that Mr Crosbie was a Gemini too. We will marry in October, with Uranus and Jupiter in our house of true love.* That was the end of it. The correspondence dwindled, and it was at that time of his life that Morrissey first began to visit O'Neill's Hotel and the Excelsior Bar.

He had often seen Mrs Sinnott at the window of her room and one day, imagining that she smiled at him and knowing that she cared in a special way for the parentless, he entered the hotel. He held with her, in a new exercise-book she handed him, their first conversation. He told her the story of his life, he told her about Miss Lambe, he wrote down prophecies from the paper-backed books because she seemed to be interested.

Later, in the Excelsior Bar, he interested Eddie Trump and Eugene Sinnott in their dreams. Miss Lambe had reported many of her dreams to him and he had read in one of the magazines she sent him that many famous people derived benefits from racing tips received while they slept. He had repeated the information in the Excelsior Bar, reading the piece from the magazine, and ever since that day, eleven years ago now, the discussion of dreams had become a conversational topic between Eddie Trump and Eugene. But Morrissey, not being interested in sporting matters, had been forgotten in all that. He had listened while the dreams of the gamblers were daily related, he had observed the excitement in their faces when a tip was discovered. A whole new pattern had developed in the lives of these two men, a pattern that could be traced back to his own instigation, yet at no time did anyone in the Excelsior Bar say that if it hadn't been for him their lives would be less rich. He had subsequently stated in the bar that Old Moore's Almanac was also a source of gambling advice and that lucky racing colours could be established by the reading of a detailed horoscope, but the two men had laughed at that, telling him not to be ridiculous. He had given them something all those years ago, free of charge, and they were incapable of showing gratitude. He had obliged them as he had endeavoured to oblige Mr Gregan in the matter of Mrs Kite. He had listened to Mr Gregan talking for two hours, he had helped him to wheel his bicycle, yet Mr Gregan, too, had shrugged away all gratitude.

In the bar where he stood alone Morrissey sighed, thinking that it was always the same: no one could be trusted: to expect good of a person was to build the foundations of disappointment.

A soldier entered the bar and ordered a glass of Celebration Ale. 'Will Privy Seal win?' he enquired and Morrissey replied that it would, definitely. You'd think he'd have something better to say, he thought, examining the soldier's pimpled face. In every public house it was the same. In every public house there were men coming up to you and attempting to talk to you about sporting events. In Morrissey's view such events were a waste of time and energy, being organized by untrustworthy people for the purpose of extracting money from simple-minded onlookers like this spotted soldier.

He noted that the soldier's tunic was smartly buttoned in the regulation manner and that there was a smell of violets coming from his hair. He wondered what it would be like to have the soldier as a friend. He looked at him again and for a moment he imagined that the soldier had come into the bar and that each had greeted the other in a comradely way. 'That damn old Sergeant Farrell,' the soldier might have said, and might have gone on to tell the latest ignominies he had suffered at the hands of his superior. Morrissey might have nodded in sympathy and might later have related the ignominies he had himself endured since the evening before, the last time the two comrades had conversed. Except for Miss Lambe, Morrissey had never had a friend. He had been scorned as a companion in the institution where he had spent his childhood, he had appealed to few in the world outside it. He was aware that Agnes Quin did not much care for him, nor, he guessed, did Beulah Flynn or Mrs Dargan or Mrs Kite. In all the world only Mrs Sinnott was a person he could consider as a friend, and Mrs Sinnott was a woman in her ninety-second year. He had often seen two companions walking together on the street, sometimes talking, sometimes respecting a silence that was an understood thing between them. He imagined games of cards or draughts that might continue for a few hours between two friends who shared this interest. Once he had met a man who told him he was a collector of postage stamps and had over a thousand stuck down in albums. The man promised that the following day he would bring the albums to the public house where they had met, but although Morrissey said that he had often considered collecting stamps himself and was greatly interested in the subject, he had never seen that man again.

'Lester Piggott up,' said the soldier. 'I think he'll walk it.'

'He is good certainly,' agreed Morrissey.

'Sandy Barclay beat him two weeks back.'

Morrissey nodded. He was thinking that the smell of violets coming from the soldier's hair suggested that he was out to attract females, and he wondered if he'd be interested in meeting one of the four he was in a position to offer. Since it was his business to do so, he would bring the idea up, and if the suggestion was declined there was no reason why he and the soldier shouldn't continue to have a talk together.

'On Secret Ray,' said the soldier, 'which Sandy is riding again today. Isn't the weather great?'

'I was saying that to the wife,' replied Morrissey, taking from the inside pocket of his jacket a photograph of Beulah Flynn. 'I wonder you can stand it in the uniform.'

'You get used to anything. Is that your wife?'

'Isn't she a great-looking woman?'

'God, she is. She's bigger than yourself.'

Morrissey nudged the soldier with his elbow. He winked at him. 'Would you like to meet that woman?' he said.

'Your wife?'

'Would you like to meet her?'

'Is she coming in here?'

'Not at all. Would you like to have carnal knowledge of that woman?'

The soldier, a trooper who was by nature and inclination a simple man, registered surprise. He looked at the photograph that Morrissey was still holding in his right hand and then he shifted his eyes to Morrissey's countenance.

'What did you say?' he asked, suddenly struck by the notion that he had not heard properly, that this small man had said something different.

'I could fix you up with that woman,' said Morrissey, 'if you were at all interested.'

'Your wife?'

'As a matter of fact, she's no one's wife at all, that one. I was misleading you there: I'm an unmarried man.'

Morrissey mentioned a sum of money. He said that Beulah Flynn was beautiful in all departments: men had gone to their graves for love of her, only she was down on her luck now, which was why he was at liberty to place her on offer to a stranger.

'I'm a Catholic, mister,' said the soldier. 'I have Catholic morals.'

Even though it meant a loss of possible earnings, Morrissey was always pleased when he received such a reply. With business out of the way, he felt free to engage in a purely friendly associ- ation. 'Isn't that a great woman for you?' he had remarked to the stamp-collector, displaying the photograph of Beulah Flynn, and when the stamp-collector had shown no interest and had registered a similar lack of excitement about photographs of Agnes Quin, Mrs Dargan and Mrs Kite, Morrissey had ordered two drinks and had listened for a long time to information about stamps. He had attempted to establish with the man when his birthday was, being keen to offer him in return a reading from the stars. It was then that the man had gone away.

'We'll say no more,' said Morrissey to the soldier. He replaced the photograph in his pocket.

'I'm not in need of any of that,' muttered the soldier. 'I wouldn't touch a woman of that nature.'

'I was only codding you. Will we go and sit down?'

The soldier shook his head, but Morrissey, having bought further drinks, in the end succeeded in persuading him that the attempted retailing of Beulah Flynn had not been in earnest. When eventually he carried two full glasses to a table in a corner the soldier followed him.

'I have these little books with me,' said Morrissey, taking his paper-backed volumes from several pockets, 'that tell us about the universe. Do you know when your birthday is?'

The soldier said his birthday was February the twenty-third, and Morrissey said February the twenty-third came under Pisces, the sign of the fish. 'You're in with a decent crowd,' he said. He read from one of his books. He said:

'*Be alert now for any chance to improve your appearance. Courtesy will help you.*'

'What's that mean?'

'*Saturn is in your house of earnings and income.* What it means about appearance could be a reference to the skin. D'you mind me mentioning that to you?'

'What?'

'You have a few little spots on your face. What it means is that this is a good time to try and fix them with an ointment. You can get stuff that you could apply before you go to bed in the barracks. In a day or two those few spots could have vanished for good.'

The fingers of the soldier's left hand touched his chin, moving slowly from one blemish to the next.

'Don't worry them,' said Morrissey. 'Go into a chemist's before the end of the month and ask the man for a tube of something. Explain the whole thing to him, how you have a friend who has a knowledge of the signs. Tell him it's a favourable time for dealing with the little ailment.'

The soldier drank hard at his Celebration Ale, wondering why this man was giving him advice about his face.

'There's some good ointments these days,' Morrissey said, 'for a condition like that.'

'I think it's the razor I have.'

Morrissey shook his head. 'Excuse me,' he said. He put his eyes close to the soldier's chin. 'That's a nervous complaint,' he said.

'Ah, no, no –'

'That's easily curable with an ointment. Only the root of the trouble is mental. Have you much on your mind?'

The soldier said he hadn't a worry in the world. He was free and easy, he said. He slept like a top. He continued to speak about the ease with which he slept and then, abruptly changing the subject, he referred again to horse-racing. Ignoring the reference, Morrissey said:

'Did you wonder what it meant when it said Saturn was in your house of earnings and income? Did you understand that?'

'Ah, no, no –'

'It means there'll be opportunities this month for gain.'

'Money?'

'For an individual born on February the twenty-third there'll be good opportunities,' said Morrissey, '*through mines, metals, steel, elderly persons, publishing, advertising, law, dentistry and established firms.* What d'you think of that?'

The soldier said you wouldn't know what to think.

'I have studied the whole thing,' explained Morrissey. 'The writings of John Pendragon, Old Moore, whatever you like. I could teach you the subject inside out. I could give you an aptitude analysis. I could teach you to read the Tarot.'

'The Tarot?'

'The subject's a hobby I have, to tell you the truth, like another person might make a hobby out of another subject. There's people going about that don't use their minds at all. Would you agree with that?'

The soldier moved his head back and forth, indicating either a negative or an affirmative reply. Morrissey said:

'Would you care for me to teach you? The Tarot?'

'Ah, no, no –'

'Why not?'

'I'm not interested in that thing, mister. They'd have a bit of a laugh up at the barracks –'

'The undereducated would laugh, definitely they would.'

Morrissey picked up their glasses and went to the bar with them, thinking to himself that he didn't know why he bothered with soldiers who weren't equipped to hold a conversation except about sporting events. The soldier could drink the beer all right, there was no question about that. He could lap up beer he didn't pay for and all he could think to say was they'd have a laugh up at the barracks. It was an extraordinary crowd of men who were defending the country these days. He returned to the soldier and found that he had taken a small mirror from his tunic and was examining his face in it, putting pressure on one or two of the pimples.

'I'd leave them alone,' said Morrissey. 'You'll heal nothing that way.'

The soldier returned the mirror to his pocket. He took the glass from Morrissey and drank from it. Morrissey said:

'Are your parents alive?'

'Ah, they are of course –'

'I'm parentless myself. I was brought up in an institution.'

'Is that a fact?'

'I was given no advantages. There was a time when I used steal little things out of Woolworth's. I used go down to Henry Street and take the stuff off the counters.'

'I never did that.'

'I had a hard life.'

'It wasn't easy for me, mister.'

'If you have a hard life you have to use your mind the entire time. You have to outwit everyone. If you're a parentless person you're on your own from the first.'

'It's unfortunate to be like that.'

'Is there anyone gives a damn?'

'It's bad, certainly.'

'Listen to me. There is no crime that doesn't come into your head to tempt you. If there's a crime committed they look round for a victim like myself who never lifted a finger.'

'I thought you went into Woolworth's –'

'Is there a child living that didn't take things out of Woolworth's?' demanded Morrissey loudly. 'Isn't it their own damn fault for spreading the goods out to tempt you?'

The soldier said he'd have to be going, but in his anger Morrissey didn't appear to hear him.

'I took forty packets of seeds,' he said, 'on a Saturday morning. I threw them into the river.'

'Cherrio then.'

'Where're you going?'

'I have to be back at the barracks.'

'Wait a minute now, I have something to show you.'

When he put his hand in his pocket the soldier said immediately that he wasn't interested in photographs of women. 'It's not a woman at all,' explained Morrissey, holding out the spider that he had acquired for Mrs Sinnott's birthday present. 'Isn't that a great thing?' he said.

'A spider,' said the soldier.

'It's for the birthday of an old female. Mrs Sinnott over in Thaddeus Street. Ninety-two tomorrow.'

'Is that a fact?'

'She's a deaf and dumb woman: you go in to see her and you have to write everything down. Isn't it a great spider?'

'Ah, it is.'

'That's a jewel in the middle, and gold legs. That spider's worth a fair bit. It's written on there.'

The soldier nodded.

'You do what you can,' Morrissey continued, 'to cheer up the elderly. Mrs Sinnott takes an interest in my own subject. I write prophecies down for her and she pays me a little fee. D'you think she'll like the spider?'

'Ah, she will of course.'

'There's a terrible old scut called O'Shea who's a total damn nuisance to her. O'Shea buys her a holy thing every year that she has no use for whatsoever. D'you know what I mean?'

'I'll be seeing you, mister – '

'O'Shea's a long string of misery in a porter's uniform. Maybe you saw him around? With a fat old greyhound?'

'No, no – '

'He's not fit to be tinned. D'you like the little spider?'

'It's nice certainly.'

Morrissey returned the spider to his pocket, and the soldier again said that he'd have to be going.

'Listen,' said Morrissey quickly. 'Do you play cards at all?'

'Ah, I don't – '

'I don't myself. No cards of any kind was allowed in the institution. I often think I'd like to go to a whist drive if I could play the game. Or Twenty-One. There's a female I know, a woman I do a bit of business with called Mrs Kite. She plays a lot of Twenty-One. A very deceitful woman, as a matter of fact.'

'Is that so?' said the soldier, rising to his feet.

'I was thinking,' said Morrissey, rising also, 'that maybe if we palled up you could teach me the rules of some card games. Do you mind me saying that to you?'

'I don't know any rules – '

'Will we have one more drink? It won't take us a minute.'

'Cherrio now, mister.'

Morrissey put his hand on the sleeve of the soldier's uniform and when the soldier tried to ease himself away he found that the hand was not released. The hand held the green material of the tunic while Morrissey talked in a rapid voice, saying he had a rough way of putting things because of the circumstances of his upbringing. He asked the soldier if he knew what he meant. He said he was sorry to have offended him, he repeated that two more drinks wouldn't take up more than a minute of their time.

'You didn't ever offend me, mister.'

'Did you mind me saying that about your face?'

'Excuse me, mister.'

Morrissey did not remove his hand. Once again a person was going to turn his back on him. He would ask the soldier if he intended to return some time to this bar and the soldier would say he'd be back the following day, telling a lie in order to get away. He had pretended an interest in what Morrissey was saying in order to get drinks out of him, which he had succeeded in doing.

'Will you be here again?' Morrissey asked.

'I'll be in tomorrow, mister.'

'That's a bloody lie –'

'Excuse me.'

Still gripping the sleeve of his uniform, Morrissey looked up at the soldier's face. He stared into his eyes. 'You cadged drinks off me,' he said, 'and now you're telling me lies.'

'Leave go my clothes, mister.'

'I told you personal things. I told you things in confidence –'

'You told me a lot of damn rubbish. I can't be wasting my time listening to that stuff.'

'You listened when the drinks were there. You said you were interested.'

'I did not ever –'

'You displayed an interest.'

'I did not display an interest in any words you said. I couldn't understand you talking about things in my houses and going on about my face. My face is my own business.'

'You're a bloody liar. You're a bloody disgrace to the army.'

'Go back to your institution, mister. Go and tell someone else about metals and dentistry. Let go my clothes.'

'Will we have another drink?'

'I will not have a drink with you,' shouted the soldier. 'If you were the last object on the face of the earth I wouldn't take a drink with you. This man tried to sell me women,' he shouted in a louder voice, attracting the attention of the drinkers at the bar. 'This man is selling his wife.'

The barman glanced towards the source of the interruption

and saw that the annoyed soldier was being held by the sleeve of his tunic. 'Keep him quiet,' he said to Morrissey, imagining that the hand on the tunic was there as a restraint against an outbreak of violence. 'Keep him quiet or get him out of here.'

'This man steals stuff out of Woolworth's,' shouted the soldier.

'You'd need two tons of ointment on to get those boils off your face,' Morrissey said quietly. 'You're a completely untrustworthy man. You haven't the brains of an insect.'

He released his hold and the soldier marched away, his face the colour of an open beetroot. Morrissey turned to two men who were standing near by.

'That fellow's a Communist,' he said.

He finished his drink and he drank what remained of the soldier's Celebration Ale. It was always the same: everywhere there were the hard-hearted who pretended an interest, who began a conversation and then, their cadging over, walked away. Was it just and fair that he should spend his nights lying down on the floor of the hall in O'Neill's Hotel while Agnes Quin, an immoral woman, was permitted to occupy a bed and while O'Shea, a half-wit, should occupy a bed also? Was it just and fair that as a child he had been unable to turn his back on his enemies without receiving punishment he in no way merited? Was it just and fair that the woman in Wigan had betrayed him utterly?

In Old Moore's Almanac it had been written that men with yellow faces would be flying over Paris by the turn of the century: Morrissey trusted it would be sooner and that the yellow-faced men would fly onwards from Paris to this city in which there was only injustice, stupidity and hypocrisy. He imagined Beulah Flynn, Mrs Dargan, Mrs Kite and Agnes Quin transported for life to the bamboo fields, where they would suffer side by side with O'Shea and the stamp-collector, Mr Gregan, Eugene Sinnott, Eddie Trump, the spotted soldier, and everyone else who had ever walked away from him. He trusted that the woman in Wigan, now Mrs Crosbie, would be sought out by the men from the East and imprisoned and tortured. He trusted that she and all the others would be made to suffer every ignominy that the human mind had yet devised.

He left the bar and strode out into the sunshine of the afternoon with bitterness only in his heart.

'Are you busy tonight?' Mr Smedley enquired of a waitress. 'I'm
a stranger in the town. Shall we go to a dance?'

The waitress, placing a plate of buns on the table in front of
him, quietly declined this offer. It was nice of him to ask her,
she said.

'I've plenty of cash,' said Mr Smedley. 'I'm a well-off man
from the Liverpool area.'

'Ah no, sir, no,' replied the waitress.

Sighing, Mr Smedley cut a bun.

8

At one o'clock that day, while Eugene Sinnott was lighting a cigarette in Riordan's Excelsior Bar, his son entered Bewley's Café in Westmoreland Street, where he ordered cod and chips. He touched with his tongue his newly repaired tooth, reflecting that it seemed sorer now than it had been an hour ago.

'It's fine weather,' a man sitting opposite him said. Timothy John nodded. He opened a newspaper and read, as his father had read some hours before, that the strike of the city's semi-skilled and unskilled Corporation workers had entered its fifth day. The strike of three hundred firemen, he noted, had also entered its fifth day. The Irish Post Office Engineering Union, on behalf of four thousand five hundred members, had served strike notice on the Minister for Posts and Telegraphs. The Minister for Social Welfare had declared open a new cinema in Middle Abbey Street. Drought was reported in Cork.

'Excuse me, sir,' said the man sitting opposite him, and Timothy John put down the newspaper and listened to the man asking him if he was a writer. 'I was hit by a Christian Brother,' said the man, 'in the industrial school I was at one time. I have a story to tell, sir, which is why I am saying that to you. I need a writer to write it down.' Timothy John said he was employed in an insurance company. 'I seen plays on the television,' said the man, 'that is nothing at all compared with what I could tell you, sir. I was hit on the eye, sir.'

In the bungalow in Booterstown, Philomena made tea. In Terenure Mrs Gregan bought lozenges from a chemist. In his office Mr Gregan ate sandwiches that his wife had that morning prepared for him, and said to himself that they were dry today. He thought of her and then he thought of the field with the glass-houses in it, and of green tomatoes turning orange in the sun.

'You couldn't forget a thing like that,' said the man in Bewley's. 'A Christian Brother lifting his fist, sir.' He rose and went away, saying that his eye had never recovered.

Timothy John ate, keeping the food on the left side of his mouth, away from the tenderness. He went over in his mind various insurance matters that had come before him that morning; he said to himself that after he had eaten his lunch and had a few cups of tea he'd buy the tray-cloth for his grandmother and then he'd go down and look at the books in Webb's bookshop. He felt a sudden, brief sensation in his tooth, a different kind of pain from the soreness that had remained after the dentist had drilled it. He held his mouth open for a moment to see if the dart of pain would occur again. When it didn't he chewed cautiously, reassuring himself, pointing out to himself that there was always a bit of unease after a visit to the dentist. His eye fell again on the newspaper. Barmen in Dundalk, he read, were planning to strike on Monday week in support of a claim for an increase of four pounds a week and other benefits. In Wexford a new oratory had been released by a bishop. In Sligo the water shortage was critical. Rain was on the way.

All over Dublin that lunchtime people from offices and shops took advantage of the sunshine; children, tired of the good weather, waited for the cinemas to open. Youths in open shirts crept over the grass in St Stephen's Green, causing the girls they crept upon to shriek. The card-sharpers whose photograph Mrs Eckdorf had taken spent part of their gains in a bread-shop in Mary Street, and the twins that had been that morning born in the Coombe Maternity Hospital passed their first midday asleep and in health. The Indian doctor who had delivered them stood in the Municipal Art Gallery regarding the face of Lady Gregory as represented by the Italian artist Mancini. 'God give me patience,' said the manager of the hotel where Mrs Eckdorf had been staying. He had just been told that in his absence the luggage of Mrs Eckdorf had been forwarded to an hotel in Dolphin's Barn. 'Are you half-witted?' he noisily demanded of the untrained clerk who was responsible for the action, and the clerk replied that a clear message had been received from the lady, and that for his part he had done his best. 'You said to be always civil, sir,' he reminded the manager, who replied by depriving him of his position.

In Reuben Street the woman who had said to her priest that she was not ungrateful for the life she'd been given was measured by local undertakers. In a public house in York Street the old woman who had begged from Mrs Eckdorf poured the dregs from glasses into a can and thanked the publican for allowing her to do so. The cinema projectionist whom Mrs Eckdorf had called a naughty chap hummed to himself in the projection room of one of the cinemas which children were preparing to enter.

It was a day in Dublin as any other, except that, being a Friday, less meat was consumed than on other days. The sun glittered on the water of the river, seagulls stood quietly on walls and parapets. At half past one the banks were open for business again, later the public houses closed for their quiet hour.

With careful, unhurried gait, Eugene Sinnott walked along Thaddeus Street towards his mother's hotel, finding the sunlight a burden on his eyes. The street was peaceful as he moved along it: Keogh's the grocery was closed for the lunch-hour, there was no sound from the turf accountant's, no excited voice on the radio reported the progress of a race while men stood still and listened. The tall stucco houses revealed no sign of life, although life continued within them. On corrugated iron there were tattered rags of posters, their colours glaring in the sunshine. On the yellow wash of O'Neill's Hotel its title in white stared out between two rows of windows, and shone again on the paned glass of the entrance doors.

Eugene entered the hotel and mounted the stairs to his room. He opened the wardrobe, drank briefly from a bottle that lay inside, and stretched himself on his bed. With the blinds still raised and the room full of sunshine, he closed his eyes and slept.

Two flights below, in the kitchen, O'Shea filled a third hot-water jar, being newly concerned about dampness in the bed he had prepared for Mrs Eckdorf, while miles away Mrs Eckdorf walked in a cemetery. She had left the hotel in order to consider and to eat. For lunch she had taken oysters and steak, and then she had asked to be driven to a cemetery, where she could wander among the stones and devote herself to thought. She did so, strolling slowly about and turning in her mind the pages of the book she planned.

Its form had not crystallized, and yet it seemed apparent to her how in essence it should be. Through her own two eyes she saw this city while searching in it for a house she'd heard of. She walked along the quaysides: what she saw was there on paper, for others also to see, one page following the next. She walked towards a mystery that fascinated her imagination, even though she had not known and did not know its nature. *I was told an ordinary story*, she might well write, *and sensed a human tragedy that was shot with beauty, I knew not how*. The fruit of the Mamiya and her talent would set the background for the disorder in O'Neill's Hotel: the faces of card-sharpers and alms-gatherers, children and animals, seagulls on an oily river, spindly aerials rising high from façades of a lost splendour, old milk bottles on a window ledge. And in the hotel itself, as she herself moved closer to the heart of things, so too would those who turned her pages.

In the room where the old woman sat she had seen the man called Morrissey, crouched by the window, copying words from a magazine. The old woman stared through the window, looking down, at the few who passed below. On either side of her were the exercise-books, and hanging on the walls a mass of cheap-looking religious mementoes that the porter, so he proudly claimed, had bought for her himself. As they entered, Morrissey had ceased to write and had looked at them instead. In a moment Mrs Sinnott turned her head too, sensing another presence, and Mrs Eckdorf saw the black eyes like currants and a face that was thin and frail and yet had a wiriness about it. Her hair was neatly kept in place, a cameo brooch gleamed whitely at her neck, on the black material of an old-fashioned dress.

The camera had not ceased to work in this room that was so different from the other rooms in O'Neill's Hotel. Tourists took photographs, Mrs Eckdorf's smile suggested, and Mrs Sinnott showed no surprise, even if Morrissey did. O'Shea was used to her camera by now.

I have come to stay in your hotel, she had written on the open page that Morrissey had been writing on. *I love your city*.

Mrs Sinnott made no sign. She turned her head again and surveyed the street below, and Mrs Eckdorf felt that to this ancient woman it was a natural thing that a person such as she should come on a hot day to stay in a house that had known more gracious times. *Tragedy haunts the steps of your stairs*, she had wished to write but knew she could not. *There is tragedy in your hall and in your kitchen. What happened once?*

The pages of her book ceased there, with the woman's face, itself most photogenic, and the question mark. The pages would continue with the birthday party itself, when all the family came to the kitchen: Eugene and Philomena and their son, Mrs Sinnott's daughter, who once had run away, the daughter's husband, and O'Shea. Morrissey and Agnes Quin fed on the tragedy that had happened: there would have been no place in the hotel for either of them had the hotel not lost its virtue. Eugene Sinnott, had he not been seedy, would never have permitted the presence of such flotsam in his mother's room; and no ordinary establishment could tolerate the one stretched out in the hall by night, and the other using beds for profit. *What happened?* she would ask, and write the question down. *What happened once to make them all what they are today?*

She would write it down that she in Munich, a thousand miles away, had felt her intuitions working; that she in Munich, on slight evidence, had visualized these people and sensed their hidden tragedy. While the birthday in the kitchen continued she would show from their faces how they carried with them the past. She would tell the documentary truth that only the probing of a camera, enriched by compassion and perception, could supply. She would supply it because she knew that the truth about the lives of people must continue day by day to be told, in one way or another, on the screens of cinemas and television sets, in newspapers and magazines, or in books like hers that incorporated beauty too: truth was the parent of understanding and love.

She remembered old Father Tomaso, who had lost his faith. For weeks she had lived among his congregation in her search for the facts she had in the end established: that the man could accept no God at the end of his life, that he remained on nevertheless as his people's pastor, and that they in their love for him allowed him his position, believing that before he died all would again be well. She had suspected it all but no one would admit it, until one night she cracked the old priest and the story was quickly told. She remembered the faces of the small community, the fear on the faces in case there should be repercussions from the Church authorities if the matter was made public. 'We'll go to hell, we'll burn,' a woman had shouted in the Sicilian dialect. There was a photograph, towards the middle of the book, that caught the woman's simple agony and beneath it the passionate words she'd uttered. Eyes all over the world gazed now upon the woman's face and upon the atheistic priest conducting the Mass and offering the sacrament, continuing his life as always it had been, working in the fields with his flock, eating his plain food. He and his parishioners had asked her often to go away, but she had always smiled and said she would not. 'For the truth will set you free,' she had reminded them, quoting St Matthew. And in the end she had been proved right, for it was right, she knew, that the fears and faithfulness of poverty-dogged peasants should be seen and understood on the coffee-tables of the rich.

Hans-Otto had grasped none of that because Hans-Otto had no sense of humanity or of art. Hans-Otto used to go on and on about a man in Copenhagen whom she had photographed with his wife's spittle foaming on his chin. These two Danes had quarrelled in a rifle range in the Tivoli as she and Hans-Otto, newly married then, had walked by. 'It does not concern you,' Hans-Otto had muttered in dreary irritation, hardly listening when she tried to explain that everyone was the concern of everyone else. He had lost patience completely when she'd said that by catching the spittle on the man's face, seconds after its ejection from the wife's mouth, she had created a rare photograph. To Hans-Otto the idea of art was an electric typewriter.

Looking at her pictures of Eugene Sinnott in O'Neill's Hotel, Hans-Otto would not be able to use his imagination because he did not possess that attribute. Hans-Otto would not sensitively see what was there on paper even: he would be unable to visualize Eugene Sinnott as he might have been, a fortunate and happy man, the prosperous inheritor of O'Neill's Hotel, a man who wore tailored suits and gave without protest to charity.

'Who wants to know all that?' Hans-Otto had demanded, looking through the book she'd done on Jasper Grider, and she had been obliged to remind him that already the book was an extravagant success. But he had continued to make a fuss and in the end she had wept beneath his scorn, vividly recalling every painful step she had taken along the path that Jasper Grider had earlier moved with the murder weapon in Yikesville, Colorado – blow by blow, past the hens that the erring wife had five minutes ago fed, past the eucalyptus tree, through the back porch where fuchsias grew in pots, into the kitchen and up the stairs: the book of that journey included some of the most beautiful and some of the most evocative photographs she had ever taken, even though it didn't contain a single human being. It did however have the Grider mongrel dog, for the Grider mongrel dog had at the time, apparently, bounded ahead of its master, and it was this that had made the book what it was and had given it its truth and its pathos.

On thick photogravure grey-tinted paper she told this story that Hans-Otto had jealously claimed no one wanted to hear. Hoerschelmann at least had been able to accept the facts of her artistry, understanding, or at least claiming to understand, that it was necessary for her to go to extreme lengths in order to achieve success. Both Hans-Otto and Hoerschelmann had married again: they'd married German puddings, she'd heard, whose idea of life was to prepare applestrudels and to breed indifferent children.

'Why didn't you say?' O'Shea had cried on the landing outside the old woman's door. 'Why didn't you write it down in the book?'

'Write what?' she'd said.

He looked at her, amazed. 'That you have come to buy the hotel.' His words came strangely to her, for she had for the moment forgotten. She smiled at him, appreciating again the simplicity of the notion that she had come to the city to purchase an hotel. It was a prosperous tourist city, people had said to her: was it not plausible to wish to share in that prosperity?

'I must talk to the family first,' she'd said. 'It is a family thing to sell an hotel that has always been in a family. I feel it's a courtesy to talk to the family before worrying Mrs Sinnott: there may be objections.'

O'Shea had nodded. That was kind of her, he'd said; everyone would appreciate that.

She would talk to Philomena, the wife of Eugene, and to the daughter who had run away, and to Mrs Sinnott's grandson, the child of Philomena. In casual conversation the truth would slip through, the past would reveal itself in a natural way. When they came to the kitchen for the ninety-second birthday she would have all the facts in her mind and she would know then what her camera must seek, so that others might benefit.

She walked in the cemetery among old cyprus trees and the grey graves of people who had died too long ago to be remembered. *Sacred Heart of Jesus have mercy on the soul of Thomas Rinkle*, she read. No wreaths cheered these old, old resting places, no flowers in jam-pots; no women knelt. The dead live on for a time, she thought, and then they die. Her mother's body was ashes now. Her father's continued to breathe, she knew not where and did not care. Miss Tample, the mathematics mistress whose lips had quivered too close to hers, was dead – or so she hoped – and blazing for ever in the pyre she had in her lifetime established. Mrs Eckdorf shivered in the sunshine. She returned to the car that awaited her and read from a scrap of paper the address of the daughter who had run away, written for her by O'Shea in his ungainly hand.

'Are there women to be had in this town?' Mr Smedley asked, addressing a man who was standing at a street corner, offering him a cigarette.

'Women, sir?'

'I'm free tonight: I wouldn't mind meeting up with a girl or two.'

'Aren't there women all over the place?' said the man, gesturing about him.

Mr Smedley explained what he meant. He was a business-man who had travelled the globe in the pursuit of trade. He had been in the company of women in five continents. He was a man of vigour who didn't mind spending a bob or two.

'Whores,' said the man.

Mr Smedley laughed, but the man, unamused, informed him that no such persons were permitted to exist in this city of god-liness and decency. He walked away from Mr Smedley, spitting to the ground the cigarette he had just accepted.

'Charming,' said Mr Smedley, and went on to consider that of all the cities he had ever visited this one was the most unfriendly, the most unenterprising, the rudest, the ugliest, and the stupidest. There was litter everywhere, he noticed, and poorly-clad children, and a piety in the eyes of the people that wasn't at all to his liking. It was not a city, decided Mr Smedley, that he would ever wish to return to. He'd end up in a dance-hall, he supposed, pick-ing up stunted wall-flowers in the hope that they were starved of what he had to offer.

In Thaddeus Street Father Hennessey wrote about St Attracta. *How can we reconcile the wild figure of Lough Gara with the humble nun? Why is there a tendency to turn our women into furies?* He put down his pen and rubbed his eyes. He rose wincing from his bureau, for he suffered from arthritic joints. He walked about the room to loosen them, an old thin man, gnarled like a nut.

His mind was full of the saint he'd been writing about. The more he wrote the more he was assailed with doubts as to whether or not she had ever even existed. The truth about any saint, he reflected, was particularly difficult to establish: saints went to people's hearts, they became decorated with legend, as statues of Our Lady were decorated with glass jewellery in Italian churches. There was no harm in that, except that the decoration too often obscured the reality, and even then one couldn't condemn because it was a form of worship.

Of all the myths relating to saints the one associated with St Cosmas and St Damien fascinated Father Hennessey most. Often he considered these two moneyless doctors who had defied death by water, fire and crucifixion before eventually being beheaded, and who were reputed, long after their death, to have returned to their church in Rome in order to perform a miracle. A man with a diseased leg, having fallen asleep, awoke to find that the doctor saints had replaced his bad leg with one from a dead Negro, so that he now possessed legs of different colours. How this tale had come about and been developed in that particular way interested Father Hennessey greatly, as did many of the supposed activities of St Attracta, and the image of St Clare supping with St Francis in Portiuncula, and St Helen in possession of the Cross. Had St Verena taught the peasants of Solothurn personal cleanliness? Had St Fiacre ordered Anne of Austria, Queen of France, to pray outside his door, being unwilling to permit women into his presence? Had green appeared on a withered tree when the coffin of St Zenobius touched it? Had St Catherine not suffered on the wheel?

Father Hennessey paused by the window of his room. He made a chink in the net curtains and peered through it: the street was empty except for Agnes Quin on her way to O'Neill's Hotel. He raised his eyes and saw over a long distance the seated form of Mrs Sinnott, close to her window. She was always there, looking down into the street or asleep, and he thought again that it must be extraordinary to live in so silent a world. Was the red of the exercise-books more radiant in compensation? Did the faded blue of her bedroom walls seem charged with a beauty that others missed? Was Thaddeus Street magnificent that she regarded it so humbly?

He watched Agnes Quin moving slowly away from him and he thought that she was extraordinary too. He had offered to find work for her, he had said that any help he could give she'd be welcome to, but she had shaken her head. What would a woman like that think? he wondered.

Father Hennessey returned to his bureau, but when he picked up his pen he found he was unable to write. His mind functioned in another direction. He visualized the figure of Agnes Quin mounting through the gloom the stairs of O'Neill's Hotel and entering the room of Mrs Sinnott. He visualized the two women sitting there, one closer to the window than the other, one asleep perhaps and the other awake. Did they ever think of him? Did they ever consider, two different kinds of women, that he had failed in his duty to both of them, that he had failed to understand them and could think of them now only as extraordinary? Did they share the thought that he was more at ease with dead saints than with the ordinary living?

Such thoughts, and the hotel itself, occasionally depressed him. It depressed him that Mrs Sinnott sat in her crowded room while all that had been created in the past fell down around her. It was harsh that that should happen, and he did not know how to explain it to her. *Venice is heaven*, she had written for him, as though she expected when the moment came to find herself in that watery city again, hearing the sounds that had escaped her in her lifetime. She had looked at him, wishing maybe to see his seal of approval on her anticipation, and again he was unable to contribute anything.

Tomorrow, the feast day of St Laurence of Rome, he would visit the kitchen of the hotel, timing his arrival so as to catch only the end of the birthday, since he was not a member of the family. He found it awkward in the kitchen: sometimes he entered to find that only Mr Gregan was talking and that no one was apparently listening to him. 'The hard man,' Mr Gregan always said to him. 'We're having a whale of a time.' He would smile at Mr Gregan and his eyes would pass over Eugene and Philomena and he would feel his limitations like a pain inside him.

Increasingly the hotel had an effect on him, as though it stood there to challenge him, as though it, and more especially the people associated with it, offered him some chance that he was unable to seize. O'Shea, eccentric in his uniform, his greyhound at his heels, came out of O'Neill's Hotel every morning. At night Eugene Sinnott, in another world, returned to it. Morrissey misled an elderly woman with nonsense; he took money from her, as probably did Agnes Quin. 'As a child I wanted to be a nun,' Agnes Quin had said, and would say no more.

Father Hennessey picked up his fountain-pen but instead of St Attracta he discovered St Laurence in his mind. St Laurence had died laughing, some said. St Laurence, burning on his gridiron, had asked to be turned over, saying he was underdone on the other side. St Laurence, patron of washerwomen and schoolboys, martyr and wit: did it matter, really, how he had died? Did it matter if St Attracta had taken the veil from St Patrick or had lived a century later?

Father Hennessey shivered, thinking of the people of O'Neill's Hotel: if the mysteries of the saints didn't matter there was the implication in his mind that the mysteries of the ordinary living did, and should instead be solved. He had been given every chance, he knew the people of the hotel well: he it was who had married Eugene and Philomena and had baptized Timothy John. He had known O'Shea for the greater part of his life. He had known the parents of Mrs Sinnott and her husband too. And yet he could solve no living mysteries, nor indeed the mysteries of the dead he had been acquainted with: for an elderly priest who had done his best in other ways, his reward to himself was the documented lives of his chosen saints. What would God, wondered Father Hennessey, say to him about that?

That morning he had passed Mrs Eckdorf in Thaddeus Street without paying her any attention. At the time he had been absorbed in his thoughts; he had noticed a whiteness going by him and had devoted no consideration to the matter. The whiteness might have emanated from the overalls of a workman for all he knew, or from sheets carried on a person's arm. He had not thought to himself that a stranger was abroad in Thaddeus Street, and when later that day O'Shea was to describe the clothes of Mrs Eckdorf to him he did not connect the whiteness he had vaguely noticed with the visitor who had come to the hotel.

At half-past three on that warm Friday afternoon, while he wondered what God would one day say to him, Father Hennessey was unaware that Mrs Eckdorf existed. At that moment he could not have guessed, nor would he have accepted even as a possibility, that he would come to believe that God might one day wish to hear him speak only about the advent of a stranger in his parish.

Mrs Sinnott opened her eyes and discovered that Agnes Quin was in the room with her. Just perceptibly, she gestured towards her visitors' chair. Agnes sat down, Mrs Sinnott's eyelids dropped again. It was nice to sleep in the afternoon, to doze when there was somebody with you. She remembered that her father had given her a bracelet and she'd lost it. Leo had given her the cameo brooch as they walked by the Dodder; he'd teach her to fish, he said, but he never had. She slept again.

Lower down in the hotel O'Shea dusted Mrs Eckdorf's room and opened one of the windows slightly. She was the kind of woman, he was thinking, who probably didn't eat any lunch at all and had forgotten to tell him that.

'Ridiculous,' said Eugene Sinnott, as he raised himself from his bed. 'Ridiculous,' he said, thinking of the woman in white who had come into the hotel that morning, announcing her search for a grail. A moment ago, lying for some minutes after sleep, he'd been wondering if by chance he had dreamed the encounter. He had recalled O'Shea standing in the background while the stranger uttered her remarks; he had recalled O'Shea's movement from the hall to a telephone booth from which he might phone for the stranger's luggage. It was then, as this particular detail returned to his mind, that he realized that the arrival of the woman called Ivy Eckdorf had been no fantasy. He recalled that in the Excelsior Bar they had discussed the advent of the photographer, concluding that as far as they were concerned she represented a tip for the Greyhound Derby. Yet, that being so, why didn't she now go on her way? What was to be gained, either from her point of view or theirs, by her continued presence in the hotel?

Eugene stood beside his bed, thinking about her. Her face

with its smile and the pale eyes came easily back to him. It was entirely O'Shea's fault that she was still here. O'Shea had made it seem the most natural thing in the world that a person of that appearance should lodge for a night or two in an hotel that offered neither service nor comfort. There was something wrong, he slowly thought; there was some reason why this Mrs Eckdorf had demanded attention and a room; there was some reason she had failed to reveal. He patted his suit, trying to smooth the creases it had suffered during his siesta. Still concerned with Mrs Eckdorf, he left his room.

In the hall O'Shea was brushing the carpet. On one of the chairs there was a white enamel basin containing water and a cloth. These were the preparations for the washing of the glass panes in the doors of the hotel: Eugene had seen them often before in the afternoon. What was the point of it? he thought again.

'O'Shea.'

'We need a new carpet, Mr Sinnott.'

'Why is that woman here?'

'I spoke to you myself about Agnes Quin, Mr Sinnott. I said this morning – '

'I mean Mrs Eckdorf.'

'Mrs Eckdorf is staying here. Her luggage arrived.'

'Why is she staying here?'

'She chose O'Neill's for quietness. She liked the feel of the place. It'll not do, Mr Sinnott, that Agnes Quin and Morrissey come in at night when Mrs Eckdorf –'

'Why did she come here?'

'She's anxious to buy O'Neill's, Mr Sinnott. She's going to buy it and set it going again.'

Having imparted that information, O'Shea continued with the brushing of the carpet. Eugene watched him, his face without an expression, his left hand coaxing open a packet of cigarettes. He lit one, still regarding O'Shea as he laboured. Then, dropping the used match on to the floor, he began to laugh. He laughed loudly, increasing the volume of the noise until O'Shea took notice of it.

'What's the matter, Mr Sinnott?'

'I'm thinking of her nibs.'

'It's the best thing that could happen,' said O'Shea, not pausing in the brushing.

'It's a lot of old cod,' said Eugene.

Whistling unmelodiously, he stepped from the hotel into Thaddeus Street. There, his whistling abruptly ceased and the signs of laughter that his face had retained at once disappeared. His brain worked swiftly and uneasily. His mother was old; she was quite capable of doing a foolish thing without knowing why she was doing it. She would not be guided; she might easily get it into her mind that the future of the hotel could be better ensured in hands other than his, even though it meant allowing the hotel to pass out of the family. She might in some senile way consider it wise to take what could be acquired for the hotel; she might consider it more satisfactory to distribute money at her death instead of leaving behind an hotel that had ceased to function. She would make her own mind up and no one would be able to influence her once she'd done it. Where would he live? What kind of life would there be for him without the empty hotel and his walking every day up and down Thaddeus Street?

It did not occur to Eugene that O'Shea might be mistaken or that the photographer who had come had been making a joke. It seemed to him to be not at all unlikely that a person with money should seek to purchase a property that was not for sale. Foreigners were buying up a lot of property, he had heard: they came as foreigners had come before, upsetting the natives. He'd now be obliged to think about the whole matter, the fact that a peculiar woman had made this statement to O'Shea, and he'd have to consider in detail its import and possible consequences. He hadn't time, he said to himself, to be devoting his mind to such affairs, but simply because the woman had made a nuisance of herself he'd have to do it, and if necessary he'd have to argue with her and request her not to annoy his mother. Why couldn't she go back to where she came from and allow the people of Thaddeus Street to continue as they were meant to?

A man spoke to him, and Eugene replied. They conversed for

a moment together and then Eugene walked on, feeling relaxed after an exchange of views on the capabilities of certain greyhounds. He'd think about the other matter later, after he'd cleared his mind with two or three glasses of sherry.

In the exercise-books Agnes had never told how her livelihood came to her, guessing that somehow Mrs Sinnott must know but might not care to see it written. The books were full of talk about films she had seen and suppositions about the lives of Hollywood actresses, in particular the life of Olivia de Havilland. In her thoughts there was the feeling that the women of Hollywood had made their lives what they were, that many had clambered to their pinnacles from beginnings as grim as her own. Whole cinemas of people watched their shadows now, and wept and loved them. They could lift their fingers and the world would come to them, longing to look upon their real faces. Often she imagined a woman among them who had precisely shared her own first moments on earth, receiving from the two who had caused her existence only the gift of rejection. In desperate compensation, this woman created herself again, making of herself a creature in glamorous armour who knew more easily who she was.

Agnes recognized now the source of the desire she'd had as a child: the habit of a novice was an armour, too. Glamour bred love of a kind; no one did not respect a nun. Behind the Electricity Works she had received again, from the boy she'd loved, the same gift of rejection that her parents had lavished on her. Doyle had wanted her in his way, but what was Doyle's wanting of her compared with the wanting of one man after another, men with passion in their eyes and hands, who for a time wanted her more than life itself, more than wives and children, more than they wanted the God who, too, had turned her away?

A lot of years had passed since she, that first night, had asked a man for money. *How can it matter so much?* she had written once upon a time. *Why would it make a difference, a man handing you in?* Now, so much having happened, she knew it didn't matter as greatly as it had. She had turned away while men took off their clothes, looking back again to see a corpulent body or one that was stony with bones. Men seemed different naked, or different to her because in her presence they were different, with all their spirit turned to flesh. A man had once unstrapped a leg, another's back was in a metal harness. A man from Belgium, so he said, had made an odd request. A man in black, his collar gone, had asked only to look upon her body. An Englishman had shown her photographs of a wife and children, Janet eight and Jeremy four. 'I love you,' men had said. A man had kissed her hair with pure affection, as a friend might kiss her. A man had plugged a razor in and shaved himself before coming to her. A man had poisoned her with biting. Men had sought her toes, others the crook of her elbow. A man had tried to kill her, another had had a convulsion. Some made her retain her clothes, her shoes and scarf as well. 'I love you,' men had said. 'I want you,' men had cried. A man had given her a stick to strike him with. 'As God is my witness,' men had cried. 'I love you,' men had said.

But now their wanting of her palled. Men waited now while with their money she bought whiskey and biscuits and did not bother to return to hear them speak to her. She had nothing more to write down in the exercise-books: she came to the silent room while the old woman slept, to be there when she woke, to offer the company that any human being on earth could give, to take no more away.

And yet she knew a time was near when men no longer would pause beside her. No man passed her by now as men passed Mrs Dargan and even Beulah Flynn, and Mrs Kite had long since learned to live with that. Compensation could be thieved away by time: would she age in night-time doorways, would she die as she'd been born?

In the shop on the Quays she had bought the china cup that she'd mentioned to Morrissey. Tomorrow she would bring it to the hotel. She would hand it to the old woman whose silent sympathy had helped her a little in her life. Now she needed help that couldn't come from comfort, but from within herself: she must do what she had to do, as she had done in another way before, and for that she had courage to find.

Mrs Sinnott awoke. She turned her head, seeing her visitor, acknowledging her again in her economic way, not smiling.

Leave me money when you die, Agnes might write, explaining that she could buy a sweet-shop with money left to her, that money left to her could mean the turning of a new leaf. She had often thought of writing that, of making it apparent to Mrs Sinnott that with enough money to help her along she could be a happy person for the remainder of her life. She had never written it because she knew that Mrs Sinnott would take no notice. In matters of money, Mrs Sinnott had a sense of family: what she had would pass to Eugene and Eugene would spend it on sherry and cigarettes and the placing of bets. Over ten years he would probably spend in that way the asking price of a small sweet-shop.

Tomorrow she would hand her the cup and she would pick up an exercise-book and write in it, wishing her a happy birthday and saying only that she was moving away from the area and would not be back in Thaddeus Street ever again. It seemed easy when she considered it like that, giving a present, writing down two ordinary sentences. She had at one time saved the money she earned, willing it to accumulate quickly so that when the moment came, when men began to pass her by, she would look and see that she had enough for a small business. Beulah Flynn had done the same, and she hadn't succeeded either. Sweets and chocolate would be different from the nails she'd sold in the hardware shop; sweets and chocolate, and cigarettes, maybe, in their gay packets, and Easter eggs and fruit. She had planned it on wakeful nights. She had seen herself dressing a small window, building a castle with Black Magic. She knew it would never be.

Mrs Sinnott looked down on Thaddeus Street. She remembered Agnes as a child standing in the convent, not pretty then. Why could she not stretch out a hand and touch the hand of this one who was unhappy and need not be? She was useless in her old age. They came and wrote her messages, they cheered her up with company. All she could do was to give them nods, and smiles when she felt she could smile, which wasn't all that often these days. It was good of Agnes Quin to come and sit with her, and of Morrissey to try and please her in his own particular way. Often she wondered what it meant, the information he wrote down, but who could know what everything meant, or indeed who would want to?

Agnes Quin stood up, and Mrs Sinnott nodded her gratitude. She watched the street again and in a moment saw her visitor walking away from the hotel. She wondered what the end of her would be. She was an immoral woman: repeatedly she committed mortal sin and yet she had stood that day with innocence in her face, a child who wished for another kind of life and had not been granted that.

Her mind became blank while Agnes Quin walked in Thaddeus Street. She tried to go on thinking about her but could not, and then, abruptly, her father's handwriting emerged from the blackness, black ink on yellow paper. *He was shot*, a message said.

In Venice she'd seen a funeral, gondolas blackly ribboned. The coffin floating away had made her shiver for some reason. She'd seen it exactly as it was, she'd thought: for those who watched it was as it was for her, silent on the water.

In the hotel, after their wedding, she had felt the noise around her. His friends had lifted up their glasses: she hated his friends when he was dead. She hated their saddened faces at his funeral. They had carried his coffin in a ceremonial way: he had died for their cause; if they had all not come together he would not have died at all.

Of all her visitors, she'd pray the most for Agnes Quin. Of all the orphan children she'd known, Agnes had taken her orphan state to heart the most. And yet she probably wasn't an orphan at all: were dead parents easier to live with than two people somewhere, still walking around? She gave them nothing, she thought again: her visitors came, they loved her because they were sorry for her. They wrote about themselves, they confided troubles because they knew she liked to feel a privileged person. It was their love for her that comforted them. She was useless in her old age; she didn't deserve the attention they gave her, she couldn't even smile when she didn't feel like it any more. Was it because of her affliction that she had known the warmth of love, from both her parents and from her husband too? Everyone, always, had been gentle with her, as all her visitors were today, and O'Shea and Eugene. Who was that woman, she wondered, who had come that morning?

Her father had been born in a year more famous for death than for birth, in 1846. The house was prosperous then, an ordinary house in Thaddeus Street, not far from the canal. Then there had been no wastelands, no smaller houses all around, no shops. There were fields and gardens, a mill that took in local people. Her father, selling land and losing money, had turned his house into a small hotel, urged towards that by his Venetian wife. *Hoteliers*, he had written. *They are all hoteliers, Italians.*

It was her mother who had made the hotel a place of grandeur, as Italians always do, or so her father said. How had he met a Venetian? She had often pondered, and had never known.

She wondered if she'd live to see her birthday through: a month ago she'd sensed the worrying of a doctor. She thought again about Agnes Quin, and then about all her visitors. Their faces appeared in her mind: her son, her daughter, her grandson, her son-in-law, Philomena, O'Shea, Morrissey, Agnes Quin. Father Hennessey, who was another kind of visitor, smiled at her too; her husband smiled; in Venice she walked with both her parents. She would sleep, she thought: it was nice to doze in the sunshine, by her window.

Father Hennessey left his house and walked slowly down Thaddeus Street. Ahead of him two children stalked a cat. 'Leave it alone,' he said.

At that moment in the Home and Personal Effects Department Timothy John put his arms around the naked body of Daisy Tulip. *We've had no luck here this year*, a letter in front of him stated. *First a death and now the hearthrug gone up like a cinder. His mother made that rug for us, God help the woman.* His hands traversed the plump body of Daisy Tulip, her voice murmured at him with an eagerness in it. He touched her two blue eyes with his lips, he put his cheek against her hair, which was what he had so urgently wanted to do the first time he saw her, that morning in Lipton's. 'Stay with me always,' whispered Daisy Tulip, and he felt as she spoke a sudden sharp pain in his tooth. *I never failed to pay the premiums*, stated the sloping handwriting of the letter. *Trusting to hear from you.* The tooth ached again, and he thought of his mother, waiting for him in the bungalow, with his tea ready to be cooked and she herself ready to hear from him all that had happened during his day. 'Stay with me always,' whispered Daisy Tulip.

The children in Thaddeus Street, having obeyed their priest, watched the cat they'd been interested in. It sloped off, its body close to the houses, blinking sleepily. 'You could skin a cat,' one child remarked to the other, and the other said that first you'd have to kill a cat, which might, he suggested, be neither easy nor pleasant.

Eugene Sinnott, alone in the Excelsior Bar, glanced through its window and observed the moving cat and the children standing. Cats were animals he feared, and he recalled uncomfortably his mother's cats and remembered too the tomcat that had jumped on to his son's pram on a day as sunny as this one, in the backyard of the hotel. He turned away from the window, thinking that a week later, quite suddenly one morning, Philomena had left the hotel, being advised to do so by his mother.

In Terenure, while Eugene remembered that, the doorbell of the Gregans' house rang and Mrs Gregan answered it. That, said Mrs Eckdorf to herself, is the daughter who ran away.

'I'm Ivy Eckdorf,' said Mrs Eckdorf. 'Mrs Gregan, how do you do?'

She held out her right hand and Mrs Gregan accepted it.

'May I perhaps come in?' suggested Mrs Eckdorf. 'I'm staying in your mother's hotel, Mrs Gregan. I thought I'd come and see you.'

'In O'Neill's?' said Mrs Gregan, amazed.

Mrs Eckdorf nodded. She stepped into the hall. She glanced around her, thinking that she did not at all care for the decor. It was odd this thing of people having no taste. She said:

'I'd like to take up two minutes of your time, Mrs Gregan. I'm interested in buying O'Neill's Hotel.'

'Come in,' said Mrs Gregan, leading the way to a small sitting-room. She gestured towards an armchair with a chintz cover on it. Mrs Eckdorf sat down.

The conversation that developed between the two women did not greatly please Mrs Eckdorf, although she attempted repeatedly to lead it in a profitable direction. It was interesting, Mrs Gregan said, the notion that someone wanted to buy the hotel: it would clearly be an excellent thing if the hotel passed out of the family at this stage, since no one much stayed there any more. She had often thought it absurd that the big old house should stand there in decay, but she added that her mother was attached to it for family reasons and would probably not for a minute consider its sale.

'You lived there, of course?' Mrs Eckdorf said, and Mrs Gregan agreed that she had lived in the hotel as a child and as a girl. More than that, in spite of pressure, Mrs Gregan didn't seem interested in saying, and talked instead of recipes. She insisted on making tea for Mrs Eckdorf and giving her macaroons. 'Delicious,' said Mrs Eckdorf and was at once obliged to eat another one, although in fact she didn't at all care for the taste. She spoke in what she hoped was a natural manner about O'Neill's Hotel in the past, making the point that in a city that increasingly attracted tourists there was no reason why it should not again enjoy prosperity.

'I'm sure,' replied Mrs Gregan. 'Now look, I'm just going to write this out for you.' It was nice having a visitor unexpectedly. She scribbled down a recipe for moussaka, which Mrs Eckdorf accepted, thinking how odd it was that this woman should imagine she'd ever go to all the trouble of buying minced raw meat and cheese and onions and tomatoes and blend them together in a dish. She sat on the chintz-covered chair, listening to Mrs Gregan's voice telling her about other food and offering her instructions for its making. Her husband, Mrs Gregan said, enjoyed some dishes and did not enjoy others, being conservative about food. Coffee cake he liked, she said, and told Mrs Eckdorf how best to make a coffee cake. No hint or disturbance in the woman's demeanour suggested that any mystery surrounded O'Neill's Hotel.

'It's odd to see it quite so poorly,' Mrs Eckdorf remarked with a laugh.

A shame, Mrs Gregan agreed, which was why it would be a good thing if someone bought it up. There would be no objections from the members of the family, she was sure, but she reminded Mrs Eckdorf that her mother had never known another home and didn't much notice the increasing decrepitude of the hotel, since she so rarely descended from her room. She would tomorrow, of course, on her birthday.

It was when she mentioned her husband in terms of the food he cared for or did not care for that Mrs Gregan displayed traces of emotion. Her existence with Gregan, Mrs Eckdorf deduced, was proving something of a disappointment. 'It's that time in my life,' Mrs Gregan said apropos of absolutely nothing, holding out the plate of macaroons.

Mrs Eckdorf rose, shaking her head at the offered sustenance. Her figure would protest, she said, and anyway she must be off.

She asked Mrs Gregan for the address of her sister-in-law, Philomena, and for the address of the insurance firm where her husband and her nephew worked: she wouldn't bother her husband, she promised, but she'd like to have a courteous word with Eugene Sinnott's son in order to put him in the picture. She didn't want any member of the family to think that she was going behind the family's back: the elderly were often irresponsible and she was giving the family the chance to offer a full programme of advice to Mrs Sinnott before Mrs Sinnott made up her mind.

'You fry the mince and the onions first,' reminded Mrs Gregan before her visitor left.

She might have been talking to a stone wall, Mrs Eckdorf thought, as the taxi-cab moved her away. She sympathized with the square-faced woman in the matter of her marriage, but she hadn't trekked all that way just to hear what some anonymous husband ate and did not eat. She tore up the recipe for moussaka and threw the pieces out of the taxi window.

As she was carried along, she felt uneasy, as though something, somewhere, was wrong. She frowned, feeling the beginning of a bewilderment, and then she shook her head, conscious again of the leaping of her intuitions.

The taxi brought her to a bungalow that was set among other bungalows in a short road that was a cul-de-sac. The driver got out and stepped around the car to open the car door for her. He returned to his seat and opened a newspaper that already he had thoroughly read.

'How d'you do?' Mrs Eckdorf said, standing on the doorstep of the bungalow, regarding with interest the small face of Eugene Sinnott's small wife. 'I'm Mrs Eckdorf. I've been sent round by Mrs Gregan. Your sister-in-law,' she added, 'in Terenure.'

'Enid?'

'I'm thinking of buying O'Neill's Hotel.'

'What?'

'Yes,' said Mrs Eckdorf, smiling and crossing the threshold. She closed the door behind her. 'How awfully nice,' she said. Why couldn't they just paint their places out if they weren't able to select suitable wallpapers? The ceiling of the hall pressed uncomfortably down: that could quite easily be corrected by the use of a light shade of paint instead of the heavily patterned paper that someone had seen fit to stick on it. She longed to tell the woman, but felt that a conversation about decoration would hamper progress as gravely as the conversation about Mrs Gregan's culinary pursuits had.

She was led to another small sitting-room. 'So very nice,' she said.

'It really has nothing to do with me, Mrs Eckdorf –'

'Your son will one day inherit O'Neill's. I'm saying I wish to purchase it. In which case it would not be there for anyone to inherit.'

'You must talk to Timothy John –'

'I would like to talk to you first, my dear.'

'I know nothing –'

'You are Eugene Sinnott's wife, am I right in that?'

'Mrs Eckdorf –'

'Mr Sinnott said that while everyone else might agree, you might not. The old hotel, he said, has memories for you, as it

141

has for him. You might wish to see it one day in the hands of your son.'

The flesh of the little woman's face, Mrs Eckdorf noticed, seemed suddenly to have whitened. That was the colour they should have done the hall ceiling. She longed to photograph this whiteness but she felt she had better not: it would hardly be the thing for a woman who said she wanted to buy an hotel to pick up a camera and suddenly to take photographs in a bungalow.

'You do not mind,' she said, 'my reference to your husband?'

'No, no.'

'I ask because of the estrangement. Sometimes there is a difficulty. Men are terrible, I always say. I've been married myself.'

She watched the face closely and wondered if she saw a trembling of the lips.

'I found your husband a charmer,' she said.

'I can't imagine my husband saying a thing like that. I think you may have misheard, Mrs Eckdorf.'

Mrs Eckdorf smiled. She had been on the point of saying that of course she had misheard and that it was stupid of her, of adding that she was always mishearing things. She had been on the point, but at the very last moment she had drawn the words back from her lips, although they were actually shaped to issue them. Something was happening in the room, and what was happening, said Mrs Eckdorf to herself, was that a journey was being made down memory lane. She felt excited. She nodded to encourage Philomena.

'It has memories for me, yes,' said Philomena. She began to say something else and did not say it. She picked up a framed photograph and handed it to Mrs Eckdorf. 'That is Timothy John,' she said. 'My son.'

What happened next was that, to Mrs Eckdorf's irritation, Philomena talked about her son. Just as Mrs Gregan had chosen her husband and his eating habits as a conversational topic so this smaller woman saw fit to choose a narrow-headed youth, whose age was twenty-eight but who might be taken, from his mother's way of speaking, to be a person still in childhood.

'He was born in the hotel,' Philomena said, and did not mention the hotel again until Mrs Eckdorf brought the subject up. She went through the early years, the years at school, the fondness of her son for mathematics, his distaste for French.

'He's nervous, of course,' said Philomena. She added that his uncle had been kind to him. He had felt at one time that he was not cut out for the department of the insurance company in which he currently worked; he had thought about the Motor Department but had been dissuaded. He was settling down now, finding his feet quite well.

Mrs Eckdorf remembered the red exercise-books in which all these people had written and continued to write. Was this the kind of stuff? Chatter about a son finding his feet? Recipes for moussaka? Wandering down memory lane for this little thing clearly meant a walk hand in hand with a golden boy. Could it truly be that the first thing the woman thought of when O'Neill's Hotel was mentioned was that the birth of her narrow-headed son had taken place there? Philomena talked about an ailment he had had when he was nine.

'It's a shame to see it,' said Mrs Eckdorf. 'It could be a nice enough hotel.'

Philomena, interrupted, said that at one time O'Neill's had certainly been a nice enough hotel.

'Yes?'

Philomena nodded. Years ago when first she arrived there the hotel had been a busy pleasant place. She told Mrs Eckdorf of her position then. It had been a home, she said.

'And now?' urged Mrs Eckdorf.

'Now?'

'Whatever happened in the meanwhile?'

She listened while Philomena informed her of what she already knew: that Mrs Sinnott was old. 'My husband takes no interest in it,' said Philomena, 'and never has.'

'You prefer it here?'

'Well, yes,' said Philomena, sounding surprised.

She showed Mrs Eckdorf three albums of photographs, saying as she turned the pages that she knew Mrs Eckdorf would be interested, since she carried a camera herself. The photographs had not been taken by her, she admitted, but by her brother-in-law, Mr Gregan. She herself had not ever owned a camera.

Timothy John appeared in a variety of stances, wearing different clothes as the years went by. Most of the photographs had been taken in a garden which was, Philomena explained, the garden attached to the Gregans' house in Terenure. She pointed at trees and shrubs and said that Mrs Eckdorf had probably seen them when she had called on Enid Gregan. She liked Enid Gregan, she said in passing, and then she laughed over a picture of her son at the age of three, wearing only a white hat. Mr Gregan had amusingly placed his pipe in the child's mouth, which added a surrealist note to the simple composition. He was fond of children, this tiny woman told Mrs Eckdorf: he had always been keen to play with her son.

In the bungalow, as in the house in Terenure, no clue was dropped. Mrs Gregan had seemed to be a person consumed by disappointment who sought a release by cooking things, only to be disappointed again. Philomena was eaten up by love. And yet Mrs Eckdorf was sure that her face had perceptibly whitened when she'd said that the hotel might have memories for her. You do not go white, she thought, if the memories are happy ones, of a child being born and lovingly cared for. Angrily, she wondered if all these people were not being honest. Was O'Shea's bizarre talk deliberately employed in order to fog the issue? Had Mrs Gregan spoken about food and Philomena about her son because they deliberately refused to allow their minds to return to certain events? Why had this woman left her husband?

'I've got her a shawl for her birthday,' said Philomena, taking a black crocheted piece from a paper bag.

'How very nice.'

Philomena spread it out on the sofa, and then returned it to its paper bag. She wasn't wrapping it up in its special birthday paper, she explained, because she wanted to show it to Timothy John when he came home. As well as the shawl, she added, she'd be giving her mother-in-law some pots of gooseberry jam.

'You get the feeling that something might once have happened there,' said Mrs Eckdorf with a needling irritation in her voice.

'Happened?'

'I mean in O'Neill's Hotel.'

A man called Jack Tyler, Philomena said, had fallen over the banisters one night and hadn't felt a thing. She recalled other incidents, none of which interested Mrs Eckdorf at all. She began to talk about her son again. Mrs Eckdorf said:

'It can't by the sound of things have lasted long.'

'What?'

'Your marriage to Eugene Sinnott.'

'It lasted a year, Mrs Eckdorf.'

'So Timothy –'

'Timothy John was three months when Mrs Sinnott said that she had made a mistake: Eugene and I should not ever have married.'

Mrs Eckdorf laughed in an attempt at casualness.

'Wasn't it you and Eugene, my dear, who'd made that little mistake, not Mrs Sinnott?'

'It would be difficult to explain to you.'

Mrs Eckdorf spoke again, and was unable to keep a hint of enthusiasm from her voice as she questioned further.

But Philomena, unmoved in any way at all, replied with finality. 'The situation was impossible,' she said.

'But how could Mrs Sinnott have made the mistake? I mean –'

'It's a private thing, Mrs Eckdorf; a family thing.'

Morrissey, loitering about the streets, watched for men who had finished their day's work and might be interested in what he had to offer. 'Excuse me, sir,' he said to a man whom at a much later hour, a month or so ago, he had introduced to Mrs Kite. 'What's the trouble?' the man demanded, and Morrissey showed him his photograph of Mrs Kite, asking the man if he remembered her. The face of Mrs Kite was scrutinized. The man frowned and shook his head. 'Some kind of charity case?' he suggested.

He walked on, and when Morrissey ran after him to explain he said he had never seen either Morrissey or the woman in the photograph before. 'In Queen Street,' Morrissey reminded him. 'You were driving a blue Cortina, sir: would you be interested in meeting that female again at all?'

The man told Morrissey to get off the streets. With his right index finger extended, he gestured peremptorily and when Morrissey did not move he drove his finger powerfully into Morrissey's stomach. 'You low bastard,' he said.

Morrissey made no reply. For a moment he believed that the surface of his stomach had been punctured, giving him grounds for legal action. But when he looked at the finger he saw that it was bloodless. The man repeated his insults and walked away.

My God, thought Morrissey, does he own the town? Is he the damn Lord Mayor? Well within living memory, this violent man had opened the door of a blue Cortina and had beckoned to Morrissey in Queen Street. 'Any chance of a mott at all?' he had enquired, his face jovial in anticipation. He had offered Morrissey a cigarette, which Morrissey had taken. 'Isn't that a great-looking woman?' Morrissey had said, displaying the photograph of Mrs Kite, and the man had agreed that she was.

They had gone together to the street where Mrs Kite was usually to be found. The man had paid him six shillings and had driven off with Mrs Kite in the front of the car beside him.

Meditating on this new evidence of hypocrisy, Morrissey continued in his search for lone men. His eyes darted swiftly about the faces that moved by him, most of them a little higher than his own. The men were hurrying, or engaged in the rapid purchase of an evening newspaper. One of them dropped a penny without noticing: Morrissey watched it roll and bent down to claim it. As he put it in a pocket and glanced again around him, he saw Mrs Eckdorf.

Morrissey had been surprised when O'Shea had written that a woman from Germany had come to stay in the hotel and later had led her into Mrs Sinnott's room. It was unusual for anyone to lodge in the hotel; and it was more unusual that the person referred to should be a well-dressed female with a hat. She was moving along now, he noticed, at a fairish pace, looking for something. Since at this unprofitable time of day little could be lost by the action, he dropped into step behind her, thinking about her and wondering if a time would ever come when he could offer to those in need a woman such as this.

Unaware that she had excited attention, Mrs Eckdorf advanced in a rage. Her taxi-driver, a species of idiot, had delivered her at the wrong insurance company. Taking the man at his word, she had hurried up the steps of a prosperous building and had asked to see, most urgently, the son of Eugene and Philomena Sinnott. She had wasted a quarter of an hour insisting and arguing with a receptionist, who appeared to be of the same order as the taxi-man. She had then been told that the insurance company she sought was a rival concern that lay fifty yards along the street. People bumped into her as she searched for it. She swore at them, thinking that as a result of all this rubbishy carry-on the narrow-headed son would have left his office and would by now be seated on a bus.

It was not, however, the frustration of having been delivered to the wrong insurance company that so angered Mrs Eckdorf: it was the feeling that she was in the wrong city. For the first time in her professional life she felt she had made a mistake.

Absurdity had landed her where she was: her instinct for a human story, which had never before been wrong, had deluded her utterly. In the taxi-cab that had carried her from the bungalow she had felt, suddenly and frantically, that she was cracking up, that all of the ugliness in her life, Hoerschelmann and Hans-Otto Eckdorf, had without warning defeated her, that the loud-mouthed barman on the ship had played some unpleasant joke. She was in a city she did not wish to be in, having flown by night, risking her life. She had consorted with beggars and card-sharpers, and had ridiculously moved into a disgusting hotel. She had listened to the obsessions of two women who were as ordinary as the pavement she stepped on. She had wasted her time with a preposterous hall-porter, she had said to an inebriate that he had gentle eyes.

Morrissey, several yards behind Mrs Eckdorf, was surprised when suddenly she screamed. People stopped and looked at her. A woman went to her and attempted to seize her hand, but Mrs Eckdorf pushed the woman roughly away. In a shrieking voice she cried that she had felt the presence of people weeping. Was this the end of a woman's life, that a farce should drift her into madness?

Her voice shrilled, mentioning the names of people: a priest who had lost his belief in God, a murderer somewhere, a family of people who were incestuous. She would tear the truth from a narrow-headed youth, she cried, for how could it not be true? She would break the narrow-headed youth across her knees, for how could all her intuitions have failed her? And then Mrs Eckdorf walked on, quite calmly, as though her outburst had not occurred. She turned into a building, while Morrissey, intrigued that this female who was so strangely staying in O'Neill's Hotel should have behaved with even greater strangeness, decided to continue his pursuit of her.

'A nut,' a man said to him. 'There's a lot about these days.'

Morrissey indicated his agreement. He cast a glance over the man, who appeared to be loitering. Excusing himself politely, he enquired of the man if he would care for the company of a female, making it plain that he did not refer to the female who had just behaved dramatically. The man reacted unpleasantly, issuing oaths and threats. A girl came up to him as Morrissey moved away, and he heard the pair of them laughing. 'It's a terrible old town,' said the girl's voice amusedly. 'You wouldn't be safe!' He saw himself turning suddenly and going back to them. In the same polite voice he said the man had misheard him, that what he had said was that two million Chinamen had landed in Wicklow and were approaching the city in buses. 'They'll not leave a female intact,' he said, watching the merriment drain from the girl's eyes.

Not far away, on the second floor of the building that Mrs Eckdorf had entered, another enemy of Morrissey's laughed also. In the Home and Personal Effects Department, Mr Gregan, lighting his pipe preparatory to leaving the office for the night, recalled what his wife had earlier announced to him about the absence of children in their house in Terenure. He had been mulling the matter over during the course of the day and it seemed to him now to be not unamusing that any woman should inform her husband on the telephone that they were a childless couple. He would mention the matter to Gorman, he decided, when they stopped for a bottle of stout on the way home. Gorman, who was apparently married to a woman without any kind of brain at all, would certainly appreciate it and would probably relate a similar experience he'd had himself. Gorman often said that you could be trying for ever before you'd understand the ways of women, and in that opinion it appeared to Mr Gregan that Gorman was definitely right.

'Good night, boy,' Mr Gregan said, passing Timothy John's desk in the outer office. 'You're making up that hour or two, are you?'

'There's not much to do, Uncle. Would I wait until an evening when we were busy?'

'A week well spent, boy. Sit where you are and make up your time.'

Typists obscured their machines beneath black covers, clerks put their pens away and cleared their desks. Everyone in the Home and Personal Effects Department said good night to Mr Gregan, many adding wishes for the weekend. Mr Gregan spoke again to his nephew, in a more confidential voice. 'Sit where you are,' he counselled, 'in case they're thinking there's favour-itism. Slip out when they've gone. I'll be with you,' he said to Gorman, who was standing by the door. He put a match to his pipe. 'A week well spent,' he repeated.

Timothy John waited. He heard his uncle's voice continuing on the stairs, saying to Gorman that the week had been well spent and adding that it was a difficult thing to have a relative in a department because everyone was watching for favouritism. 'He didn't get in till all hours this morning,' his uncle said, 'and not a damn word to say for himself.'

Timothy John put away his pen and cleared his desk. He left the empty department, wondering if the day would ever come when he'd be the head of it and do no actual work. Did his uncle ever get bored sitting in the private office that was partitioned off with glass and ply-board, eating tubes of gums and smoking his pipe? Whenever he went in there to see him about some matter his uncle would tell him to mind the step, which was a joke because there was no step to mind. 'Have you made a boob?' his uncle would say when he saw him coming, and Timothy John would always feel frightened then. When his uncle retired, Gorman would be chief and when Gorman retired the position would fall to the employee with the best record, which he hoped would be himself. He'd be a man of fifty-two by then. He walked down the stairs, concentrating on the idea of being fifty-two and in a position of authority, trying not to think of Daisy Tulip with her clothes off. 'Are you Timothy John Sinnott?' a woman asked, approaching him from the shadows of the hall.

Morrissey, standing outside on the steps, close against a green entrance door which was partly open, overheard that question and was interested in it. He had observed Mrs Eckdorf hovering in the gloom of the hall and he heard her now suggest that she should be taken to the offices of the insurance company for the purpose of conversation; he heard some stumbling reply from her companion. He allowed them to begin their ascent before he pushed the green door inwards.

The hall was square and had a concrete floor. Two bicycles, seeming as if they had not been used for a considerable time, leaned against a green wall. Morrissey had seen other bicycles being wheeled from the hall and down the steps. It had whetted his interest to see Mr Gregan with the same bicycle that he had pushed that day in the direction of Mrs Kite. Why, wondered Morrissey as he observed that, was the woman from the hotel visiting Gregan's place of work?

The hall contained a wooden table on which lay an assortment of unclaimed letters, many of them now dirtied by dust. Morrissey passed them by and mounted the stairs. He could hear the voice of Mrs Eckdorf above him and the murmuring of Timothy John Sinnott, a person he had never met. Narrow corridors ran from the first-floor landing, glass doors were marked with titles, all the walls were painted green. Morrissey continued his pursuit past that landing, to the second floor. There, cautiously poised for flight, he listened outside an open door, standing to one side.

He heard Mrs Eckdorf repeating her reasons for being in O'Neill's Hotel. To his surprise, he heard her relate her desire to buy the place. She said that old Mrs Sinnott would soon pass beyond the care of a porter, which was something that she had pointed out to the porter himself. And then, in a peculiar way, the woman who had had an outburst on the street spoke about Eugene Sinnott.

'Do you realize,' she said, 'that a man like your father could easily set fire to that place?'

He might be lying in bed, she explained, and his cigarette might drop on to the blankets. Fires in hotels were always starting like that, dry old blankets going up like nobody's business. She'd seen it happen.

Morrissey listened with care. No comment came from Eugene Sinnott's son. Then the woman said:

'Your father's given up to drink and decadence. Why is that?'

'My father drinks a bit, certainly he does.'

'Why is it?'

'My father lives his own life, Mrs Eckdorf.'

'Why doesn't he live in the bungalow?'

'My mother and my father parted. A long time ago now.'

'Where would he live? If the hotel changed hands, what

about your father? Would he live in a stables some place, a character like that?'

'Look now, Mrs Eckdorf –'

'What happened once?'

'I'm afraid I don't follow you at all, Mrs Eckdorf. I have to get home, you know. I don't know what you mean –'

'The man we're talking about is your father. You would not exist were it not for your father. No one can exist without a father, or a mother either.'

'I know, Mrs Eckdorf.'

'Can't you think of your father, for God's sake?' cried out Mrs Eckdorf's voice, startling Morrissey as he stood there. 'Think of his existence while you live your luxurious life. Your grandmother bought that bungalow for you. Your grandmother has kindly supported you all these years.'

'My grandmother –'

'Honour thy father. That's a holy commandment.'

Morrissey heard Eugene Sinnott's son protesting again that he didn't understand. He heard the female say that O'Neill's Hotel was the haunt of street-walkers. 'O'Shea is in the dumps,' she said. 'Agnes Quin by the sound of her is a bag of nails. D'you see what I mean?'

'No.'

'Your father rises up in the morning, he returns to bed at night. He hasn't had a midday meal for twenty years. His days are passed in a public house. Why is that?'

'I don't know, Mrs Eckdorf.'

'Of course you do. Why is it now?'

Morrissey heard the youth reply that he couldn't make out what any of this had to do with Mrs Eckdorf's proposal to purchase the hotel. He said again that his father lived his own life.

'Go home,' said Mrs Eckdorf. 'If you will not help me, you will not.'

It seemed to Morrissey as he listened that the female might be weeping. Her voice was sorrowful, certainly, reminding him of Mrs Kite's voice one night after a man had turned nasty in Loftus Lane.

'It's only that I don't understand.'

'Leave me alone.'

'I can't leave you here, Mrs Eckdorf.'

No reply came from Mrs Eckdorf and a moment later Morrissey heard footsteps approaching. He moved quickly away and opened a door marked 'Motor Department'. He heard the footsteps descending the stairs, and remained where he was. What had happened, as far as he could see, was that the female had been left weeping in an office because Eugene Sinnott's son couldn't understand her and the reason he couldn't understand her, Morrissey estimated, was because she was not in her right mind. He recalled that she had openly referred to madness in a public street, mentioning a murderer. In a totally unbalanced manner, she had taken photographs with a camera in Mrs Sinnott's bedroom.

In his empirical way, Morrissey deduced that a woman had landed in the city he knew so well and had entered a state of confusion. She had become involved with an hotel and with a family, and through them at the moment she was acting out her condition. It might be a common thing of the times that a person should arrive in a strange city and there, in the twilight of sanity, seek to achieve some goal or other because her condition ordered it. It could be that in many cases all it took was a new set of surroundings and situations to tip a person head over heels.

He continued to think about her and about the fact that in her fantasy she wished to buy an hotel that on her own admission was a haunt of street-walkers. Did she, he wondered, desire to meet the clients of such people? Did she wish to buy a run-down hotel so that when such clients arrived she could herself entertain them, or at least select from among them those she desired? Was that the way her madness took her? She was of good stock by the sound of her, but he had read of more amazing things than a female like that turning round and placing herself for her own pleasure at the disposal of males. Females often moved in this direction, it seemed, when their minds were affected: after all, if Beulah Flynn had been in full possession of her mental faculties she'd hardly have given up a position in a sewing-machine factory for the unreliable earnings of the thoroughfares. This female had frightened the breeches off young Sinnott, but, as Beulah Flynn nightly proved, there was no reason at all why a woman who wasn't in full possession of herself should be an object of terror to a more mature type of man. There was no reason at all, if she had cash to play about with, why a disused hotel shouldn't be transformed by someone like himself into a pleasure garden for her desires. Nor was there any reason to suppose that she mightn't be induced to permit Agnes Quin, Beulah Flynn, Mrs Dargan and Mrs Kite to occupy rooms in the hotel on a permanent basis since they were, in the reverse way, in the same line of business.

While Morrissey speculated thus, Mrs Eckdorf sat grimly in the large outer office of the Home and Personal Effects Department, possessed by a failure she could not accept. The son of Eugene and Philomena had betrayed as little sign as Mrs Gregan or Philomena had, or as O'Shea or Eugene himself had. He had mouthed a few clichés and then he had gone away, causing her to feel again that at the end of her grey rainbow there was only ordinariness. On paper, it seemed that Eugene Sinnott and Philomena simply hadn't made a go of it, that Philomena had decided she didn't like his boozy face: she had taken her child and gone away to a bungalow, for which his mother paid because she had an inordinate sense of family. And yet why had Philomena said that it was Mrs Sinnott who had made the mistake? How could Mrs Sinnott have been responsible for a mistake made by two other people? She did not herself claim that her mother had made a mistake when the memory of Hoerschelmann came into her mind, or the memory of Hans-Otto. She it was who made the mistakes, as had Hoerschelmann and Hans-Otto: how could it be otherwise?

A charwoman came into the office with a pail of water and a mop. She spoke to Mrs Eckdorf about the weather.

'Yes,' replied Mrs Eckdorf, still recalling the voice of Philomena saying that it was Mrs Sinnott who had made a mistake. She looked around her at desks and typewriters and steel filing-cabinets, and calendars on green walls. She entered Mr Gregan's private office and looked at it too: a cheerless place, she considered, in which to spend one's days.

'Missus,' said a voice beside her.

Mrs Eckdorf looked and saw the ferret-faced individual who

had that morning been in the old woman's room: Morrissey the procurer. He was speaking in the rapid voice of a person telling lies: he said that he had come to see Mr Gregan about an insurance matter but had unfortunately missed Mr Gregan. It was a coincidence, he remarked, finding her instead; he reminded her that they had met that morning.

'I'd like to talk to you,' said Mrs Eckdorf.

'We could take a drink together,' Morrissey suggested. 'The only thing is, I'm short of cash.' They might talk together for an hour or so, he thought, during which time he would place in her deranged mind the notion that if she bought up the hotel he could guarantee her a succession of well-dressed visitors. He would take it easy with her: he would employ guile and flattery.

'Could you leave us alone?' Mrs Eckdorf said to the charwoman.

'I have work —' began the charwoman.

'I'm the wife of the owner of this place,' Mrs Eckdorf announced. 'I must ask you to go.'

Morrissey eyed the charwoman, wondering what her circumstances were and if she'd care to exchange her life of drudgery for something more glamorous. Mrs Kite had washed out offices, he reflected, before he'd discovered her.

'I think you can be of help to me,' Mrs Eckdorf said to Morrissey. 'I'm trying to establish one or two facts.'

'Of course I can be of help to you, missus —'

'When will I do the room out?' asked the charwoman. 'Will you be here long, ma'am?'

'You'll be discharged this instant minute,' cried Mrs Eckdorf. 'Go away at once.'

The charwoman left. Morrissey wagged his head, greatly admiring this display of imperiousness. It was very good the way the female had said she was the owner's wife. He began to laugh.

'You're a dishonest, fraudulent tramp,' said Mrs Eckdorf. 'I know a lot about you, Morrissey, that I could pass on to the police. I'm about to ask certain questions. If there's any trouble about the answers I shall do my duty.'

Morrissey's mouth, which had slackened so that it might give vent to his amusement, remained so. Nervously the fingers of his right hand played with the teeth of the comb in his pocket. He closed his mouth and then opened it again. He said in a nonchalant voice, designed to humour her:

'I'm not a tramp, as a matter of fact.'

'I don't care what you are. I am standing here with the whip hand. Do you understand that? I'm extremely angry. I'll stand no nonsense of any kind whatsoever. You're a procurer and a criminal.'

'There's no evidence about procuring, missus –'

'There is sworn evidence from a ship's barman that you procured for him a woman called Agnes Quin. There is sworn evidence that you approached this man, of hitherto impeccable morals, and enticed him from outside a public house to where Agnes Quin was standing in a doorway. There is sworn evidence that you led the couple to O'Neill's Hotel in Thaddeus Street. There is sworn evidence that you received from that man, as you have received from countless others, a sum of money.'

'Are you interested in that type of thing at all? I could have male visitors in O'Neill's Hotel at every hour of the day and night. It could be a great place altogether.'

'It's no business of mine what it could be. Sit down in that chair.'

Morrissey sat down at a desk that bore a covered typewriter. 'Are you buying O'Neill's Hotel?' he asked quietly. 'It's a good purchase. It has a right position out there.'

'I want to know what happened in O'Neill's Hotel to cause Eugene Sinnott's wife to leave him.'

'What?'

'Did you or did you not hear what I said? Are you deaf?'

'I heard you, missus.'

'Eugene Sinnott's wife left him twenty-eight years ago. I've asked you a question, Morrissey.'

'I was seven years of age twenty-eight years ago. I was inside an institution. I wouldn't know what happened.'

'For God's sake, you must know. You go into that hotel every day of your life.'

Morrissey took his comb from his pocket and ran it through

his hair. He agreed with Mrs Eckdorf that he went to the hotel every day. He had business there, he explained. He spoke cheerfully, as though Mrs Eckdorf's questions about occurrences twenty-eight years ago did not at all surprise him. He smiled at her.

'You sit with Mrs Sinnott,' cried Mrs Eckdorf. 'You delude her with dishonest talk – '

'Ah no, no. Ah, I don't do that at all.'

'Hasn't she ever hinted to you what happened? Hasn't she ever given you a reason why that woman left her husband?'

'It's all in the past, missus. Why would we be worrying about the past if you have it planned to buy up the hotel? It's the future,' explained Morrissey carefully, 'that's the interesting period now. D'you understand me? I could have males going up and down the stairs. I could arrange anything you asked me. D'you see, missus?'

Mrs Eckdorf did not hear Morrissey saying that. She was standing, while he remained seated at the desk. Beside her, on another desk, there was a heavy ebony ruler. This she now seized.

Hoerschelmann was making the point to her that she should have told him before their marriage more about herself. He quite understood that she was a woman of talent, he said: he appreciated her art and he understood her desire to pursue the truth so that everyone, everywhere, should know more about one another. It was she herself, Hoerschelmann was saying in his loud voice: it was she herself he wished to discuss, it was she herself they should have discussed a long time before.

His voice was full of insult; his teeth were exposed in a snarling kind of way, the whole lower part of his face was sneering at her, his eyes were half-closed.

'For Jesus' sake!' cried Morrissey. His right hand was pressed to the side of his head, where the ebony ruler had struck him. Pin-pricks of white light were dancing before his eyes, pain occupied his whole head, causing tears.

'I could not buy a house,' Mrs Eckdorf said, 'and live in a house in which an unfortunate occurrence had taken place. That is why I'm questioning you.'

He could feel a lump rising. She might have damaged his brain with a blow like that; she could have knocked an eye from his head. He watched her while she pursued her conversation as if nothing untoward had happened, just as when she'd shrieked on the street she'd walked on, unknowing, a moment later.

'No one mentioned unfortunate happenings in O'Neill's Hotel?' she said. 'Not Agnes Quin?'

Still watching her with care, Morrissey replied that Agnes Quin didn't ever have much to say for herself. She was a very close female, he said slowly, a deceitful woman.

'Is she?'

He tried to nod. She had returned the ruler to the desk beside her. She was standing there now as though she'd never touched it.

'Tell me about yourself, Morrissey.'

His hand went to the side of his head again. She was no damn use to him if she was in so poor a condition that she'd strike a person without knowing it. And yet being in a bad way like that would mean she'd be unfit from now on for a normal life. Again he reflected that what had happened was that this female had come to the city on some business and had rapidly entered a state of confusion: it was up to anyone who could to make the most of that, since that was the law of the world. If he could press her on to buy the old hotel and to set herself up there, she might improve in herself. She'd asked him about himself a moment ago, she'd shown a civilized interest in another human being: it would be looking a gift horse in the mouth not to make an effort to oblige the female. The pain in his head had decreased and the pin-pricks of light had vanished. He touched the lump again and assured himself that it would go down in time.

'Would we go on to a bar?' he suggested. 'I don't feel happy here, with the char hanging around. I could wet my whistle in a bar without difficulty.' He laughed. He combed his hair again.

'We might see what's to be had here,' said Mrs Eckdorf. 'It might be a mistake to go to a bar since you are short of money.

I have very little myself. Mr Gregan may have a drop put by.'

She opened the glass door of Mr Gregan's private office and looked about it. Morrissey watched her while she investigated a cupboard full of stationery.

'So this is where Gregan's employed?' he said. He could have taken a hatchet to the place, he thought. Acting swiftly and surreptitiously, he lifted a pile of papers from the desk and dropped them into the wastepaper basket. He put a paper-knife and a rubber into his pocket. Mrs Eckdorf hunted in the drawers of the desk, shaking her head over the absence of bottles.

'The char would drink anything,' Morrissey explained. 'Nothing could be left unlocked. You can trust no one.'

Mrs Eckdorf discovered Mr Gregan's tube of fruit gums. She took one and handed the package to Morrissey.

'There's not much I can tell you about myself,' said Morrissey. 'I fought my way up in the world and now I have descended again. I was a lung specialist one time until I committed an error due to lack of sleep. A small thing like that can fix you for life. I was engaged at the time to a female in the North of England who was the housekeeper in a boarding-house. She let me down with a bump when she heard the news.'

'How horrid for you,' murmured Mrs Eckdorf. They were all the same, the people that Mrs Sinnott had mothered. They came from the empty life of institutions and then they made things up. Was that why Mrs Sinnott had surrounded herself with them, so that she might be amused by their fantastic stories? O'Shea, she had noticed, was entirely given up to superstition. This animal-like creature, who was far from clean, was passing himself off as a lung specialist without batting an eye. Did Agnes Quin suggest tragedy to the strangers she shared her bed with in order to live, in some strange vicarious way, a life that wasn't her own?

'Where would I find Agnes Quin?'

He opened the stationery cupboard, pretending to continue the search for bottles of alcohol. 'What's this?' he said, withdrawing a corked earthenware jar.

'Ink,' said Mrs Eckdorf. 'Where would Agnes Quin be?'

'You wouldn't want to be bothering with a female like that, missus.'

He removed the cork from the jar of ink and put the jar on its side on top of a pile of unused foolscap paper. The ink would spread, soaking into the paper and spreading to other areas of the cupboard: it might do ten pounds' worth of damage. He closed the cupboard door. He said:

'I could be of use to you in the hotel. You could sit in a nice room there and not worry about anything. I could bring you up visitors: wouldn't you like that?' He smiled at Mrs Eckdorf, endeavouring to imply his meaning. She said:

'Where can I find Agnes Quin?'

'There's a half-witted man on the premises at the moment that we could get rid of. A terrible old scut called O'Shea – '

'I've asked you something, Morrissey.'

On Mr Gregan's desk there was a paper-weight in the shape of a castle. He noticed that her hand had moved close to it. Sulkily, he said:

'In Riordan's Excelsior Bar, in Thaddeus Street. I could give her any message – '

'I must be going now. I've enjoyed our chat, Morrissey.'

'Will we meet again? I could show you round the town if you'd like me to. Will we maybe have a drink some time?'

She said that maybe they would. He seemed to wish to hold her unnecessarily in conversation: she wondered why. He said:

'If you have the money for it, you couldn't do better than O'Neill's. There's lots of quiet rooms, ideal for entertaining. Companionship is a great thing.'

'Yes.'

'What d'you think of that little thing?' He took the spider from his pocket and held it out to her. 'Isn't it a grand brooch? I got it for Mrs Sinnott's birthday.'

'Charming.'

'That's a jewel in the middle.'

'And gold legs. No wonder you're short of cash.'

'I'm fond of the elderly, missus.'

She walked quickly from Mr Gregan's office, sensing that this small man was about to become a bore. In the outer office he went on talking about the spider and Mrs Sinnott. When she didn't reply he said:

'Will you be O.K. now?'

'O.K.?'

'Would you like me to stop with you for a while?'

'That's quite unnecessary, Morrissey.'

'The heat can affect the best,' said Morrissey agreeably. 'I think you thought you were conversing with some other person when you mentioned one or two things. I never knew a ship's barman in my life.'

'I'm not insane,' said Mrs Eckdorf, smiling tightly, 'if you're implying that.'

He was walking beside her. He turned to her to say that he was implying nothing of the kind. Something happened in the air, close to his eyes. Pain shot through his head again and the light that was all around him turned to darkness.

O'Shea stood pensive in the kitchen, his right hand resting on the table, the other touching the head of his greyhound. He had hung up the paper-chain. He had bought from Keogh's the same food that every year they ate: cake and biscuits, nuts, fruit, several kinds of jam. Riordan's would send over a bottle of Gilbey's port in the morning, a traditional gift.

As he stood, he was not thinking of the birthday party. He was watching Mrs Eckdorf poking among the old pictures in the attic, as briefly she had done. She was slightly bent, her arms reaching down, her feet in turn touching the picture-frames to move them this way or that. When she walked towards him, glass splintered on the boarded floor. Her mouth opened in speech. He could see her teeth and the little gap between the two in the front.

O'Shea moved suddenly, causing the greyhound to give a little jump. He led the way from the kitchen, across the hall and out into Thaddeus Street. Rapidly he crossed the street and then strode on. He rang the bell at the door of Father Hennessey's house.

'Another good day,' a woman who was passing by on the pavement said to him. He nodded his head.

'You could not be unhappy on a day like that,' said the woman.

The evening was warm, although by now the sunlight slanted less powerfully over Thaddeus Street. Soon the shadows would lengthen dramatically in an amber light: the weather had been predictable for more than a week.

'Is Father Hennessey in?' O'Shea enquired of the priest's housekeeper. There was a smell of polish and mulligatawny soup. Brown flowers gleamed from the linoleum. On a table there was a painted statue of the Virgin, on the faded wallpaper a red light burned beneath the Holy Child.

'Come on up,' commanded the housekeeper. Her eyes were on the greyhound as she spoke, but she did not say that the dog should wait in Thaddeus Street. She had said that once about another dog, and Father Hennessey had been angry.

'Is there anything wrong?' Father Hennessey asked, turning his head as O'Shea entered the room. He was seated at his bureau, and when O'Shea replied that nothing was actually wrong in the sense that something should urgently be set right, the priest requested that he be allowed to finish what he was writing.

'Do of course, Father,' O'Shea urged, considering it decent of Father Hennessey to seek permission of an hotel-porter.

'It's a lovely evening,' murmured the priest as he wrote. 'Well now?' He turned to face his visitor.

'A person has arrived who wants to buy the hotel, Father.'

Father Hennessey, who had been winking at the dog, straightened his body too hurriedly. He hit his leg with the palm of his hand, annoyed by the pain that had occurred there. 'Buy it?' he said. 'O'Neill's?'

'A woman from Germany, Father. A Mrs Eckdorf. I asked her, Father.'

Father Hennessey turned his back. He went to the window and separated the lace curtains. Across Thaddeus Street he could just perceive the form of Mrs Sinnott sitting at her window. With his back still to O'Shea, he said that Mrs Sinnott would not sell her hotel.

'I find it difficult to care for her, Father, these days. You said to me once that a time would come when we'd have to let her go to the nuns.'

'I don't understand you, O'Shea.'

'She wants the hotel brought back to what it was, Father. That's in her heart all the time. How can I do it, with Eugene Sinnott dropping cigarette-butts all over the place and Agnes Quin and Morrissey –'

'Who is this woman that's come?'

'She's staying in O'Neill's. She came this morning, Father. I am only thinking of Mrs Sinnott's wishes, Father.'

Father Hennessey shook his head. He looked at O'Shea's face, trying to fathom something from it. O'Shea had been known to let his imagination run away with him before: in his longing for the hotel to clamber to its feet again he was capable of fantasy.

'You are good and faithful, O'Shea. Bless you now.'

'Father –'

'I think you've made a little error.'

Father Hennessey patted the greyhound and winked again at it, which was something he had discovered the dog liked.

'She stood in the attic, Father, and a light came out of her. There was a glow on her white clothes. It was a sign to me, Father, of the way things must be. She has gone out now to speak to the rest of the family.'

'Was she lighting a cigarette in the attic?'

'It wasn't that, Father.'

'I don't understand you at all, O'Shea.'

'Our Lady sent down that little light so that I could see it. The Queen of Heaven –'

'O'Shea –'

'I thought it out ever since.'

'What you're saying is silly, O'Shea.'

'Mrs Sinnott has reached the time when she must go into expert care, Father. Eugene Sinnott must be sent into a home for drunks. It is the Queen of Heaven interpreting the wishes in Mrs Sinnott's heart.'

'The imagination is God-given, O'Shea. It is a powerful possession –'

'Mrs Sinnott is too kind to order her son into a home for drunks, she's too kind to order out Agnes Quin and Morrissey. Our Lady looked down and saw the way things are. She took charge of everything, so that the wishes in Mrs Sinnott's heart could be fulfilled, so that the hotel of her father could rise like a phoenix-bird. People could come again, Father, and go up and down the stairs the way they used to, men from the provincial breweries, actors and families, businessmen from the North. Morrissey passed water on a flower-bed I made. It's a sin to do that, Father, on top of living flowers. Agnes Quin had an elderly man with her — '

'O'Shea — '

'There's girls at Mass uncovered, Father. Is that a sin, Father?'

Father Hennessey shook his head. He would prefer, he said, that the girls wore hats or scarves as a sign of respect, but in his view the failure to cover the head on the part of girls and women did not constitute a sin. O'Shea, staring at the open books on the bureau, did not acknowledge the opinion.

'There's disorder everywhere,' he said. 'I heard Mrs Eckdorf say that today. There's disorder on the streets and in the hotel.'

'We mustn't worry too much — '

'The nuns are more expert than myself when it comes to looking after an elderly woman who has neither hearing nor speech. I can't manage her, Father, which is the thing that's being recognized.'

Thinking to arrest his visitor's progress from reality, Father Hennessey said:

'You would miss Mrs Sinnott, O'Shea.'

'Mrs Eckdorf is there now.'

'You would miss Mrs Sinnott.'

O'Shea shook his head. Mrs Sinnott was a good woman, he said, and he reminded Father Hennessey of the time there had been a fly on a window-pane and she had asked him to open the window for it. She was a good woman, he said, who had never harmed a living creature, but the time had now come when the disorder must cease, since that was her own wish as well as the wish of God.

'Go back and rest yourself,' advised Father Hennessey. He was about to add that O'Shea should say a prayer or two, but in the circumstances he decided against it, thinking that he'd say the necessary prayers himself. 'Rest yourself, O'Shea, and try to remember that the imagination is a powerful possession.'

The words sounded weak: unhelpful and inadequate in the circumstances. Father Hennessey sighed.

'I came to tell you,' said O'Shea, 'so that you could speak to the nuns about what has happened, so that they'd be prepared for her. After her birthday. I wouldn't say before. And Eugene Sinnott –'

'We'll think about it all, O'Shea.'

'I believe we are meant to act fast.'

'We mustn't be hasty. I think there's no hurry.'

'I thought I would tell you so that you could do something at once. I spent the afternoon thinking, ever since I was up in the attic with her.'

'Don't worry,' Father Hennessey said. 'Go along now, like a good man. Good-bye, O'Shea.'

He has got out of touch, O'Shea thought: the greater world is passing that old man by while he sits there writing about the saints in Thaddeus Street.

'Thank you,' he said to the housekeeper, who was waiting at the foot of the stairs. She opened the hall-door so that he and the greyhound might pass from the house. 'It has been good weather,' she said.

'We are lucky,' said O'Shea.

He walked away, along a street that was now coloured by the setting of the sun. It was a bad thing that Father Hennessey had allowed himself to get so badly out of touch with the way the world was. They needed a younger man, who would have more of a grasp of things and would act more quickly. Father Hennessey, in his old-fashioned way, found it hard to understand that someone would come from Germany to buy property, yet that was the way the world was going.

He entered the hall of the hotel and stood for a moment, as earlier he had stood in the kitchen. Why had he felt as he had about the bed she was to sleep in? Why had he left her bedroom to look down upon her as she slept in the hall?

A bell rattled in the kitchen passage, which meant that Mrs Sinnott had worked her bell-pull. Slowly O'Shea mounted the stairs.

He stood beside her while she rose from her chair, refusing his aid. She left the room and when she returned she nodded her thanks at him: she liked to have him there, near by, in case she fell on the journey. He had cared for her lovingly, he thought, but the nuns would care for her with expertise, which was more important in the circumstances.

Outside her room, he stood in meditation again. He watched the nuns as they aided her downstairs, two kinds nuns who listened to what she was saying. Father Hennessey waited in the hall, nodding at her when she handed him a note that said she knew it was the best thing for everyone. She passed from the hotel in the care of the nuns, with Father Hennessey falling in behind them, making of it a little procession. In Thaddeus Street people stood to say good-bye to her and handed the nuns bunches of flowers. Keogh the grocer was there with a honey-comb. Eddie Trump stood by in his Sunday suit. 'There has been no loyalty like the loyalty of O'Shea,' someone fondly re-marked. Mrs Sinnott stepped into a motor-car, and when the car had drawn off all the people turned to O'Shea and nodded their heads at him. A few shook hands with him. The old fish-seller was there, and the child who hadn't any teeth, both of them looking serious. The fish-seller put into his hands a pair of trout, the child gave him sweets. The people went away and O'Shea still waited, standing on the steps of the hotel with Father Hennessey. 'Have you sent for the police?' the old priest said to him, and he nodded, not trusting himself to speak. While they watched, two officers came marching up Thaddeus Street. 'Mr O'Shea?' one said, and he said yes, and he and Father Hennessey stood aside so that the officers might enter the building. They emerged a moment later with Morrissey and Agnes Quin under close arrest. They led them down Thaddeus Street, the captives aware that they must accept their fate and showing no resistance or resentment. 'They will be grateful to you, O'Shea,' remarked Father Hennessey. 'They will begin a new life when they're released.' Eugene Sinnott left Riordan's public house and took up a position in the middle of Thaddeus Street. He walked towards the hotel, while people from the windows of shops and houses observed him. 'They are seeing that for the last time,' said Father Hennessey, and when Eugene Sinnott was close enough he told him that Mrs Sinnott, having been placed in the care of nuns, had agreed that the hotel should be immediately disposed of, since her son was incapable of taking charge of it. It was proposed that Eugene Sinnott should enter the care of those who had expertise in the business of handling drunks. O'Shea was a loyal man, Father Hennessey said, but he could not be expected to continue to attend to a person whose only wish was to fill the capacity of his body with alcoholic refreshment. O'Shea had done his duty over the years: the time had now come for his reward, which had been sent down by Our Lady, Queen of Heaven. Eugene Sinnott bowed his head. He turned to O'Shea and apologized. 'God bless you,' he said. The three men entered the hotel and beheld on the stairs the figure of Mrs Eckdorf. 'Come to me,' she said, and O'Shea stepped shyly forward and stood there by her side. 'It will be a fine hotel again,' she said. 'People will talk about the service and the comfort.'

The greyhound licked O'Shea's hand on the landing outside Mrs Sinnott's door. Together they made their way down the stairs and entered the room he had prepared for the guest. Her white luggage was neatly stacked. A shaft of waning sunlight touched the thorns of Christ in a sacred picture above the mantelpiece. The greyhound's small head jerked to one side as the eyes within it followed O'Shea's slow motion towards the bed. He felt beneath the covers for the hot-water jars, murmuring aloud that they had lost a little of their heat and would again require to be filled.

II

Twilight dwindled into darkness. In a dance-hall Mr Smedley unhappily danced. People on the city streets moved less swiftly than they had in the busier time of the day. Couples in love strolled the dry suburban roads, or window-gazed, or sat in cinemas or lounge-bars. By a bus-shelter in Rathfarnham a hospital nurse waited in vain for the man she was to meet, and in the end wept. On her way home from a meeting of the Society of St Vincent de Paul, Mrs Gregan saw her standing there. She wondered why the girl, unknown to her, was tearful by a bus-shelter and then forgot about her, having other matters to consider. She had not seen her husband on his return from work. She had left him a salad and some brawn she'd specially made, knowing that he liked brawn. Her spirits had risen during the course of the day: she wanted to apologize to him now for being so emotional on the telephone and to tell him about the woman who had called to see her, and to tell him what had been decided at the charity meeting.

'I need a new pair of gum-boots,' he remarked as she entered their sitting-room.

He listened then while she told him that a person called Mrs Eckdorf had come to the house that afternoon. She related all that had taken place between them, she raised her voice when he seemed about to sleep in his armchair. She'd given Mrs Eckdorf a recipe for moussaka, she said, and the address of three estate agents, since there was little chance that her mother would be willing to part with her property. She described Mrs Eckdorf's appearance. She apologized for her touchiness on the telephone, explaining that she was at a certain period of her life, that touchiness often accompanied that time with women.

'Eckdorf?' said Mr Gregan.

It was funny her coming like that, she said, and yet she had enjoyed her visit. It had bucked her up a little, a new face on an ordinary afternoon, a breath of fresh air.

'Eckdorf?' repeated Mr Gregan. 'That's a most peculiar name.'

With a laugh, he suggested that his wife might possibly have imagined the whole thing: why would a woman want to buy a property that wasn't for sale? And why would she come to see a person who was not the owner of the property?

Mrs Gregan began to feel low again. 'She ate macaroons,' she said. 'She sat there, Desmond, in the chair you're sitting in.'

'Eckdorf?' he said for the third time, and repeated also that it was a most peculiar name.

Mrs Gregan made tea for both of them. While she did so, he shouted from the sitting-room to the kitchen, telling her that new gum-boots would be necessary for work up in the field, especially when the weather worsened. He was silent then, and when she carried in the tea and biscuits he said that he'd been sitting quietly because he'd been thinking about this woman who had called. He asked her if she was certain she hadn't had a little dream, and when she again assured him she hadn't he said they'd better telephone through to Philomena to find out what she'd made of this Mrs Eckdorf.

She stood beside him in the hall while he dialled. She should have left him a note about the visitors, he said, and not wait to pass on information like this at a late hour in the evening.

In the bungalow Philomena said that Mrs Eckdorf had called on her also and had called on Timothy John in the office. She had discussed the visitor with Timothy John, who had reported that he'd been completely foxed by her manner and her conversation.

'Is he there?' demanded Mr Gregan. 'Can I speak to the boy if he's available?'

Timothy John related to his uncle what had taken place in the offices of the insurance company, how Mrs Eckdorf had been hanging around the downstairs hall and had asked for a word with him, how they had ascended the stairs together. He did not repeat what Mrs Eckdorf had said about his father because it would have embarrassed him to repeat any of that: he simply said that Mrs Eckdorf had not made herself clear.

'It's most peculiar,' said Mr Gregan. 'That's most peculiar, boy.'

In the house in Terenure and in the bungalow the conversation about Mrs Eckdorf continued after the two telephones had been replaced. Mrs Gregan, who had not at the time thought it out-of-the-way that she had had this tea-time caller, frowned over the visit now. Her husband pointed out that it was strange that Mrs Eckdorf had hung about the downstairs hall of the insurance company, waiting for Timothy John instead of going up. 'I think I must have passed her there,' Mr Gregan said, 'and didn't notice.' Philomena asked her son what it was that Mrs Eckdorf had said and he repeated that he hadn't understood a word that came from her. In the house in Terenure and in the bungalow bewilderment increased. Who in their senses, they said to one another, would want O'Neill's Hotel, tucked away in Thaddeus Street, a house whose day was done? She had frightened Timothy John, but he did not say so. His tooth ached while he listened to his mother's wondering voice.

Morrissey was far away, but had he been present in the house or in the bungalow he could have quickly explained, producing physical evidence, that what had happened was that a woman from Germany, who had nothing to do with any of them, had succumbed to aberration in their city. He could have displayed the lump on the side of his head that had been inflicted with a black ruler, and could have told of how he had felt another blow and had returned to consciousness to find himself stretched on the floor, receiving attention from a charwoman. The Sinnott family and O'Shea, and himself and Agnes Quin, were all being drawn into a stranger's lunacy for no reason whatsoever. Morrissey, who by now felt strongly about Mrs Eckdorf, would have reminded them that nothing Mrs Eckdorf had said made sense, that in particular she had talked to him crazily about a ship's barman.

Having been restored to consciousness by the presence of a wet floorcloth on his forehead, Morrissey had immediately and finally decided that the female with the camera was too far affected to be of any possible use to him. An association with her would clearly lead to death: and was it not typical that the rosy future he had planned – he himself in charge of a mildly unhinged woman who now owned an hotel and was desirous of male visitors – should have evaporated almost as soon as it had appeared? In the bungalow and in the house in Terenure Morrissey would not have mentioned this envisaged future, but he would have mentioned everything else, and he would have asked those present to feel the injuries on his head. As it was, neither Mr Gregan nor his wife, nor Philomena nor her son, said to one another that the explanation of Mrs Eckdorf lay within her own mind and her own life. They did not say that what had happened and was continuing to happen was that an agitated woman, drawn towards them in an eccentric way, had now entered a state of further agitation in which, her distress being what it was, she felt the need to involve people she did not know.

Eating creole *jambalaya*, Mrs Eckdorf recalled in total detail her conversation with the ship's barman. The ship had been steaming away from Benguela, she had been sitting on a high stool. She'd bought the man a number of drinks, for he had displayed an interest in her work. She'd told him about her books and about some of her methods. In return he'd told her about one or two places he'd been to. 'A bawdy-house?' she'd asked. 'I'd love to do a bawdy-house.'

She had imagined, as she spoke, women and girls dressed in chiffon, their hair most intricately arrayed or flowing casually to their shoulders, some with their suspenders revealed. She had imagined these attractively painted birds of paradise moving soundlessly and slowly across a hall that was, she now realized, not unlike the hall of O'Neill's Hotel. She had seen the creatures standing idly about, in the hall and on the stairs, doing nothing whatsoever, or examining their lips in the gilt mirrors that hung here and there.

'The only bawdy-house I was ever in,' the barman had confessed, 'was a curious place.' After which, he had told her everything else.

She felt almost at peace, eating creole *jambalaya*: she felt calm enough to sit there with the wool pulled away from her eyes, accepting the doubts that were nibbling at her, recalling that conversation with an accuracy that was necessary now. He had remembered the names of Morrissey and Agnes Quin, and of the street and the hotel. The names had stuck in his memory, she recalled his saying, because of the curiousness of everything. And he'd remembered Agnes Quin telling him that the respectable side of the family came back annually for the old woman's birthday.

'Some tragedy,' she had murmured, handing the barman more money.

As she ate, she heard her voice murmuring the two words. She saw the barman pouring from a bottle, treating both of them to an extra measure of cognac. It was sad, he had said: he'd felt a sadness as he passed through the hall the next morning, sensing what once it had been like.

'Some tragedy,' she had murmured again, and she recalled that she had closed her eyes and had imagined the hotel and the people, and that when she had opened them the barman was looking puzzled.

'Tragedy?' he had said.

They had gone on drinking, until in the end he, too, had spoken about the tragedy that her intuitions had felt; but she knew now, and would admit it to herself, that it was she who had used the word first. All the barman had done was to visit a bawdy-house and to remember it for her. She had sensed the tragedy all by herself, thousands of miles away: she had put her finger on what appeared to be the truth.

The waiter came with *crêpes au mocha*, and for a moment as he approached she imagined that he was encased in the form of Hans-Otto Eckdorf. She half-rose from her chair, smiling at Hans-Otto, about to tell him she'd remembered in time that it was she and not the ship's barman who had felt the tragedy. Then, very suddenly, she saw that the figure was the figure of a waiter. He placed the *crêpes* in front of her; she forgot that passing confusion.

The barman had not been sensitive. He'd been quite an ordinary servitor who carried with him a number of anecdotes, a man who could not have felt what she had felt, who had said only that the hotel was curious and sad. She was glad she had thought about it and had established the accuracy. The barman had not really been an ally.

She rose and left the restaurant. She asked a taxi-driver to take her to Riordan's Excelsior Bar, in Thaddeus Street. 'Masterpieces do not grow on trees,' she once had pronounced, 'which is something you would know little about, Hans-Otto Eckdorf. You're too coarse-grained, Hans-Otto, to know a thing like that.'

She would be calm now, she resolved in the taxi, for she felt that she had not been calm enough today. She felt exhausted, as though that day she had worn one part of herself entirely out. Her professional side kept going, like one engine of a machine when its twin has died: a photographer now would continue for the time being, until the rest of her was recharged, until something happened to recharge the person that she was. She yawned in the taxi-cab, wanting to sleep. Had she hit Hoerschelmann with the edge of the small table or had Hoerschelmann hit her? She couldn't remember. She remembered speaking about it in court, but she didn't know why the consideration came to bother her now: how could it matter? Hans-Otto had said she had driven a fork into his hand. He had walked about with bandages on, looking at her with grim reproach: he had cut his hand trying to open a tin of fish, of that she was certain.

The taxi stopped. She left it, moving as in a tired, familiar dream. She paid the man, and then there seemed to be a vacuum in her mind, until in the same tired dream she bought for Agnes Quin yellow Chartreuse and sherry for Eugene Sinnott. She stood with them in the Excelsior Bar while they told her nothing at all. No hint, no clue dropped from their lips; the woman seemed preoccupied, the man spoke nonsensically about a greyhound that was not the greyhound in the hotel. For a while it seemed to Mrs Eckdorf that he likened her to the animal he spoke of, reminding her that the dog, like herself, had been born and bred in England. While Agnes Quin sat silent and morose, he talked about dreams he had had, dreams that featured circus people and German wine and the death of the barman who was serving them with all they drank. The barman mentioned a dream too, in which he had apparently been instructing a class of boys.

The eyes of Eugene Sinnott appeared sightless as he bent over her, refusing to sit down. He covered her clothes with ash from his cigarettes. He said that the barman was to be buried on Tuesday morning after Nuptial Mass in the Pro-Cathedral. He swayed back and forth.

'Tell me about the hotel,' she whispered wearily to Agnes Quin, but Agnes Quin only shrugged her shoulders, and soon afterwards left the bar.

'O'Shea says you're buying us up,' Eugene Sinnott remarked, as though the matter didn't much concern him. The barman enquired what she intended to do with the property. Was she planning to manufacture radio-sets? he wanted to know, and added that such manufacture was common among German industrialists who had bought land or property in the country. She denied that she was German. 'English,' said Eugene Sinnott, nodding knowledgeably at her.

A woman of immense size who gave her name as Mrs Dargan entered the bar and shook her hand, saying she was pleased to meet her. 'You're in the circus business,' she said, and went on to say that she herself was considering a return to a trade she had once pursued, the plucking of chickens. 'I pursue an unmentionable one now,' said Mrs Dargan, nudging Mrs Eckdorf and giving a squelching laugh.

She tried to ask Mrs Dargan questions about the hotel, but Mrs Dargan, like everyone else, told her nothing of value.

'D'you like this city?' enquired the barman, bringing her a drink she hadn't asked for and standing there boldly, with his hand out for payment.

'She's buying us out,' said Eugene Sinnott to Mrs Dargan.

She paid for the drink she hadn't ordered. She was tired and must go, she said.

'You're a tip for the Greyhound Derby,' said Mrs Dargan, and the laughter in the bar began all over again.

She walked into the hotel and felt in the hall that people weeping would soon appear. She mounted the stairs, and then mounted again, going past the room that the tall porter had allocated to her. She listened outside the door of the deaf old woman, and then went in.

There was moonlight on the sleeping face of Mrs Sinnott. The deaf have extra senses, she thought, proceeding quietly. She lifted each stack of exercise-books to the landing. She closed the door. Making many journeys, she carried the exercise-books to her room.

In time she heard the footsteps of Eugene Sinnott mounting to his room, and thought she heard his voice speaking to himself. She listened, and then continued her task.

For several hours she read the conversations, while far away Mr and Mrs Gregan slept in their two beds, and Philomena slept in the bungalow and Timothy John's tooth nagged. The thought of the tooth coming out, its deep roots grinding on bone as they were wrenched away, sickened him. He tried to think of business matters, but the words that Mrs Eckdorf had spoken and the face of Daisy Tulip were there in the room with him, as persistent as the pain. 'He hasn't eaten a midday meal for twenty years,' said Mrs Eckdorf. 'His days are passed in a public house.' The eyes of Daisy Tulip laughed at him. 'It isn't my real name,' she said. 'I won't tell you my real name.' O'Shea slept, as did Eugene now. Agnes Quin packed her clothes into a suitcase, having found at last the strength for her resolution. 'Have you a match on you?' a man said to Morrissey, and added conversationally that his name was Smedley.

While Mrs Eckdorf read what he had written about his other dreams, Eugene dreamed again. Animals had entered his body and were unpleasantly devouring it. They were tearing away his stomach; he was powerless to stop them because he could not move. He thought he could hear them making the sound of cats, and the teeth on his flesh felt like feline teeth. He was in a room lying down, in his own bed. He couldn't sit up because he knew if he did the cats would snarl among his entrails. In his dream he imagined their faces, eyes gleaming through the blood that saturated their fur, their teeth bared for a new attack, the cats of his mother.

Outside, Thaddeus Street was white with moonlight; everywhere the night was still and warm. In the Coombe Maternity Hospital the mother of the twins lay awake, worrying about the financial aspect of the birth. In the convent where Agnes Quin had been handed in other orphans slept, a novice prayed for guidance, an old nun prayed also. A man, passing the window of English's hardware shop in Ringsend, paused to examine the wares displayed: tools for plasterers, wooden planes, oil-burners, clothes-pegs, several kinds of saws. In Reuben Street the bed of the woman who had died was empty. In Thaddeus Street Father Hennessey sat at his bureau. In a room high above the Excelsior Bar Eddie Trump put his arms around the daughter of Mr Riordan, whose belief had been that only in inebriation are people truly happy.

Mrs Eckdorf read of their lives. In the red exercise-books the handwriting of Mrs Sinnott occurred hardly at all. Her part of the conversation had been a nodding or a shaking of her head, a hand stretched out, some other gesture in this simple communication. Mrs Eckdorf read about Doyle the lemonade clerk, and Miss Lamb in Wigan, and about the worries of O'Shea. Once, she read, a few years ago, Eugene had altered the routine of his day: he had walked past Riordan's Excelsior Bar one morning and had continued to walk until he found himself in the centre of the city. There, he had entered a steak bar in a tall new building and had ordered a steak, being hungry after the undue exertion. He had felt dazed, he reported; the city had changed since the time he had known it better. Thaddeus Street was pleasanter.

She read of the upbringing of Timothy John and of the gratitude that his mother felt for all that Mrs Sinnott was doing for both of them in a practical way. She read on, meeting Daisy Tulip.

Father Hennessey, a visitor who was less involved than all the others, wrote of the legends that had developed around the lives of certain saints, a St Attracta in particular.

I have come from nowhere, wrote Agnes Quin. *I can't make out how I'm meant to be. What shall I do?* cried Agnes Quin, but Mrs Sinnott did not reply.

I made a ragoût, murmured Mrs Gregan. *I had to eat it all myself.*

In a tireless, sloping hand her husband reported a vision: produce ripening in the sun, young men and himself working all together in long glass-houses. *I have never cared for office life*, Mr Gregan revealed. *I have never been successful in it.*

Morrissey wrote with difficulty, O'Shea in his sprawling way. Philomena's hand was light upon the page, suggesting humility.

I pray, she said. *I cannot help myself. I know I have no right to pray for that. It will happen: what can I do?*

Her son wrote badly, as though fearful of marking the page at all. Mrs Eckdorf had to peer.

I have brought you fudge, whispered Timothy John, *and now I want to tell you.*

A man who was a stamp-collector, said Morrissey. *I obliged him by listening. When I looked up he was gone.*

O'Neill's, cried O'Shea. *O'Neill's will be famous again because I feel it inside me. People will come.*

Toytown, said Eugene Sinnott. *L. Johnson up.*

Around her, the red volumes lay scattered and confused, the conversation of Agnes Quin interlaced with that of Mr Gregan, Morrissey breaking off abruptly. O'Shea's lines were open for all to see, every one was higgledy-piggledy because Mrs Eckdorf had snatched the exercise-books from this pile or that and had thrown them carelessly from her. Her eyes were like lead in her head. She read and read, wading into the lives of all these people and yet discovering nothing of what she sought. A mother and a son, a husband and a wife, a ne'er-do-well who drank, a porter affected by religion, a strumpet obsessed by her conception, a procurer to whom no one would offer friendship: they spoke about themselves only, or about the hardships they encountered at the hands of others.

'There is nothing,' said Mrs Eckdorf.

She left the exercise-books and left her bedroom. Moonlight lit the landing and part of the staircase. She listened. There was a movement in the hall, so light it might have been that of a small nocturnal animal. She looked over the banister and saw below her the shadow of Morrissey. He was preparing his resting place behind the tall gilt chairs, having shaved himself in the kitchen and gone to the backyard, and eaten some bread he'd found. Through gloom that was only here and there relieved by moonlight, the precise activity of Morrissey was difficult for Mrs Eckdorf to discern: she guessed at it, remembering the voice of O'Shea as it had spoken in the exercise-books. O'Shea had not ever said that Agnes Quin conducted business on the premises of the hotel. He had not said that while Mrs Sinnott slept the hotel of her father was becoming, through the fecklessness of her son, a house of common disorder. Mrs Sinnott was protected, as was her human due.

She ascended to the top of the hotel, to a door that the porter had sixteen hours previously indicated as the door of his bedroom. Without knocking, she entered and turned on the light. Sacred effigies hung about, an evening newspaper lay on the floor. The greyhound came moaning from a corner. O'Shea wakened at once.

He saw her standing at the foot of his bed, with his greyhound beside her. The camera that had before hung from her neck was not there now. She was hungry, he thought: she had come for food. Her clothes were still the same pale clothes, her hat was still on her head.

'You must be ravenous,' he said.

'O'Shea, it's half-past three.'

'If you'll take a seat in the dining-room, I'll be down at once.'

'O'Shea,' she softly said, 'what happened in this hotel?'

'What?'

'I've read every page of those exercise-books.'

He stared at her and continued to stare. He said:

'Those are private conversations. Those are the conversations that people have with Mrs Sinnott.'

'Yes. And I have read them.'

'You said you were buying the hotel.'

She stretched out a hand and touched the flesh of his hand. She could not help thinking that his pyjamas did not seem clean. She said:

'An event took place in this hotel.'

He did not reply. The greyhound jumped on to the bed beside him. She said:

'This old hotel will again be famous, which is the heartfelt wish of Mrs Sinnott. People will come to Thaddeus Street and you will carry upstairs their baggage. There was a time, O'Shea, when a fly buzzed on a window-pane: another woman would have asked you to destroy that fly. It is her wish that the hotel of her father, whom she loved, should again hold up its head, as a living memorial to that man, and to her Venetian mother also, and to her husband who died for his country. Her husband married her, although she has neither voice nor hearing; he married her for her goodness and her beauty. She would like to honour him, he who might have run this fine hotel as well as her beloved father had.'

'He would have done,' cried O'Shea. 'He would have.'

'O'Shea, what was the hotel like once?'

She closed her eyes, listening to him, seeing a vision of the hotel as it had been, according to what he described. There must have been a heavy atmosphere there, she thought, as she had noticed in the middle-class, old-fashioned hotels of Germany. The chairs that stood in the hall had a solidity that might have been oppressive. Upstairs on the second landing there was a huge leather sofa flanked by leather chairs, all in poor condition now, but not beyond reclaiming. The great mirror on the stairway and the one in the dining-room, the sideboards and the dumb waiter, must all have added to the weightiness. She imagined the carefully kept floors, linoleum daily polished, carpets brushed, the sacred pictures on the bedroom walls, the painted statues here and there on tables, everywhere clean. And at the centre of it all the woman who was kind to orphans and kept her house in order.

'O'Shea, what happened once in the hall of the hotel?'

He shook his head. The only thing he could remember that was of note, he said, was that a bookmaker called Jack Tyler had once fallen over the banisters and landed in the hall and had not been hurt. He had not been sober at the time. Only that morning Mr Sinnott had mentioned Jack Tyler, recalling that the bookmaker had died a few years ago, at Leopardstown. Mrs Eckdorf interrupted him. She told him to think, and when he had thought for a time he said that the only other out-of-the-way occurrence that had taken place in the hall was that once, in the middle of the night, Eugene Sinnott and his sister had quarrelled. When she questioned him, he replied that that had taken place a long time ago now, on the night of one of Mrs Sinnott's birthdays.

'What happened, O'Shea?'

He was silent for a while, and then he said that Eugene was late for her birthday that day. He had come into the kitchen saying he had been to Baldoyle, where Southern Dandy had won at a hundred to eight. She had a great keenness for birthdays, O'Shea said: everyone's birthday was celebrated in turn: her own, her son's, her daughter's, and the birthdays of all she employed. She loved ceremonies and games and watching people talk, and giving people special things to eat, and giving people presents.

'He sat down,' said O'Shea, 'and laughed. "Southern Dandy," he said. You could smell his breath even though he was smoking a cigarette.'

He had sat down and his mother had made the best of things. The cake and all the teatime food she liked were brought to the table: barm brack, Jacob's Mikado biscuits, egg sandwiches. Eugene didn't take much, a piece of birthday cake or so, a cup of tea. Kathleen Devinish cleared away the plates, the cards were dealt and port was offered. O'Shea remembered the evening coming to an end in a quiet way. Eugene had said he was tired; his mother smiled at him. Her daughter and the maids had said good night to her, and Kathleen Devinish had said the same. O'Shea himself had not said good night, since he would see her in the hall as she passed through it on her way upstairs; which she did a minute or so later, with her two cats.

'Yes,' said Mrs Eckdorf.

The next thing that happened, as far as O'Shea was concerned, was that he was wakened by a screaming in the hotel. Having listened and heard nothing more, he had drawn an overcoat about him and had left his room. No one else had apparently been roused. He passed down the stairs and saw from the first-floor landing the figure of Eugene sitting on one of the tall chairs in the hall, with a glass in his hand and a bottle on the floor beside him. It was the first time that anyone had sat like that, drinking in the hall of O'Neill's Hotel, although now

Eugene Sinnott often sat in that same chair, with a bottle and a glass.

As he watched, Eugene's sister had passed him without acknowledging his presence, without, so O'Shea's impression had been, even seeing him. She had descended the stairs and had struck the face of her brother with a small brass ornament. 'You have torn the soul of God,' she cried, saying that over and over again. Her brother did not move.

O'Shea's voice continued or ceased, Mrs Eckdorf was not sure which. The scene repeated itself in her mind. 'You have torn the soul of God,' cried the square-faced woman with whom she had that afternoon eaten macaroons, insistent in her accusation, yet gaining from her brother no response.

Mrs Eckdorf nodded. She said:

'And then, O'Shea?'

Eugene's sister left the hotel the next morning and did not return to live there. She married, O'Shea said, not long afterwards: she married Mr Gregan.

She married a man, Mrs Eckdorf corrected, for whom she had little love: it was not enough to say that she married Mr Gregan. Soon after that, she added, Eugene himself married one of the maids, an orphaned girl called Philomena, and then one day Philomena took her baby from the hotel.

'Well, yes,' said O'Shea.

'Why did they quarrel on the night of the birthday, O'Shea?'

O'Shea replied that it must have been that there'd been a family disagreement between them. It was none of his business, he said. He'd gone back to bed, thinking that.

'O'Shea, you can be honest with me.'

She said that she was tired by now. She said that only her professional side was conducting this enquiry. What did Eugene Sinnott think that afternoon when he was late for the birthday, twenty-eight years ago? With steady emphasis she asked that question and others too. O'Shea spoke in reply.

She watched his mouth opening and closing. She heard the words he uttered, and then it seemed to her that her questions were being answered anyway, without his help, by the intuitions that had set her on this journey. She closed her eyes so as not to see the moving lips, since it was not necessary to see them.

The small woman who had showed her pictures of her son sat in the kitchen of the hotel, desired across the birthday table by Eugene Sinnott, who was flushed with race-course drink. He felt rebellious, returning late to the heaviness of the hotel. He looked at his mother sitting silently there, not passing judgement, a woman famed for her goodness to orphaned children, a serene person who kept as pets two cats, although the exercise-books revealed, years later, that Eugene had always had a fear of cats. He hated her for a moment; he hated for a moment all the traditions of the hotel, all the reverence for her dead husband and for her father and her Venetian mother. He felt overshadowed by those two dead men who so often occupied his mother's thoughts, as though in some way they accused him. He desired the small maid, with her black hair and her olive face; he desired her in the same moment that he hated his mother.

'Would I make a cup of tea?' said the voice of O'Shea, coming into the birthday scene. He went on talking, speaking of buttered bread and mackerel, and then his voice faded away.

In her ears she heard screaming and knew that it came, not from the square-faced woman, but from the maid. She saw Eugene going down the stairs, and his sister, alarmed by the screaming, going to Philomena. She saw O'Shea standing, confused, on the landing, and then she saw Eugene's face while his sister cried at him that he had torn the soul of God. She had gone from the hotel, and Mrs Sinnott, being told the facts, decreed that her son must stand in marriage by the ravaged girl. And Timothy John was born.

'It would be a private matter,' said O'Shea, 'what they quarrelled about that time in the hall. I left it as it was.'

And yet, thought Mrs Eckdorf, they all come back: they sit together once a year on an old woman's birthday, looking at one another as though nothing had ever happened, the sister thinking now of the man she'd married in order to escape the hotel that once she'd loved, Philomena thinking of her son, and Eugene Sinnott of race-course revelations in his nightly dreams.

'And they forgive,' said Mrs Eckdorf.

She asked O'Shea to get up and help her sort out the exercise-books and to return them to Mrs Sinnott's room. He put an overcoat on over his pyjamas and in his bare feet accompanied her to her bedroom. He felt bewildered by Mrs Eckdorf. The ebullience that had accompanied her earlier had turned itself inside out: he could hardly hear what she said when she spoke, for a humbleness came from her that had not come before. She had sat in silence, seeming unaware that he was in the room with her; several times she had spoken mysteriously. Why had she taken the exercise-books from Mrs Sinnott's room? Why had she read them?

As he helped her to sort them out, he asked her. She paused in what she was doing and looked at him closely, without smiling.

'Forgiveness,' she said.

He carried the books back to where they belonged, and when he had carried them all he said good night to her. She did not smile, but looked again closely at his face. She spoke in a whisper: she said she felt a love for Mrs Sinnott, and not for Mrs Sinnott alone but for all the people of the exercise-books. The goodness of Mrs Sinnott, she whispered, had taught her family to forgive: the sympathy she offered made all forgiving easy.

She spoke to him of other people, of her own mother and of some other woman, and of men. The beauty of a woman's goodness continuing while an hotel decayed should not go unnoticed in a world that needed goodness. That was one thing, she gently said: there was a greater thing. And while O'Shea's bare feet were cold on the linoleum of her room, and while he did not mind the coldness, she told him.

She whispered and sometimes her whispering ceased and she stood still, saying nothing. Words came, when they came at all, in broken sentences. He wanted to interrupt her, to tell her that he knew now that she had read the exercise-books because she had been told to do that. She loved the people of the exercise-books, she had said; she loved Mrs Sinnott, whose place she would take. He wanted to tell her he had seen her that morning

183

with a light coming out of her clothes, but when he attempted to speak she restrained him.

Tears moistened her cheeks as the voice that was intermittent for O'Shea continued in her mind consistently. It said that as a child she had imagined a bearded face glancing from behind a cloud and had prayed to the face before going to sleep. It said she had laughed one day at the bearded face, that she had ceased to pray. At St Monica's School for Girls she had laughed at Elsie Timson, who read the Book of Common Prayer in bed. She had flushed Elsie Timson's *What Jesus Said* down the lavatory. She saw in this early morning that she had been punished ever since. She had been punished by her disgraceful mother, by the predatory Miss Tample, and the bitter failure of her marriages.

O'Shea went, because having told him that, she signalled that he should.

She stood alone then, in the centre of her bedroom, thinking that she had come in arrogance and treachery, the woman her life had made her. Yet without knowing a thing about it, she had come so that she, too, might learn forgiveness. She would display now for all the hard world to see a human story that was her own story also: she would tell how she had felt her intuitions working and how, through the example of the people of the exercise-books and the goodness of Mrs Sinnott, she had herself been given the strength to forgive those whose victim she had been, for she believed that strength was now being offered to her. The pages of her book would turn, leading strangers through a city to O'Neill's Hotel, where they would see the image of a woman who once had wakened to find herself assaulted accepting a biscuit from the plate that her assailant offered her. They would see the child who had been born in crime, and beside him the father whose crime had brought that life about. They would see the sister smile across the icing of a birthday cake at the brother who had driven her to dreariness. On azure-tinted photogravure paper she would show the working of a forgotten God.

12

The early mist of that morning did not presage heat. It turned to rain, which the people of Dublin, waking to this unwelcome advent, deplored in their different ways. It fell on the swollen face of Timothy John as he descended the steps of his dentist's house, but Timothy John did not mind: he had left the tooth behind. There was an aching in his jaw, but he knew that with time that pain would fade away. He had felt sick when he saw the needle of the hypodermic, thinking that he wouldn't be able to open his mouth, that the muscles would contract of their own will and hold his two jaws tightly clamped. But when the moment came the muscles obeyed him: he felt the needle plunging into his gum and plunging again and then again. 'The weather's gone,' the dentist said while waiting for the anaesthetic to take effect. 'You'll feel me pressing,' he had warned. 'Don't worry about that at all.' The tooth had come out with stabbing agony, during which he longed for death.

But now, in the rain, he was joyful as he walked. He bought fudge in a shop and saw the confectioner eyeing his face. 'I've had a terrible molar out,' he said. He thought of Daisy Tulip.

In Dublin the rain fell heavily that morning. Turf in public parks became soft underfoot and the unpainted wood of hoardings changed colour and soon could absorb no more. Water spilt from chutes, gutters ran, puddles were everywhere. Raindrops spattered on all the formal water of the Garden of Remembrance in Parnell Square and on the water in old horse-troughs, and on horses themselves standing drenched between the shafts of tourist jaunting-cars. Statues glistened: washed of their summer dust, gesturing figures seemed less jaded in their stance, eyes stared out with a liveliness. Rain ran on Robert Emmet and Henry Grattan, on Thomas Davis, on O'Connnell with his guardian angels, and gentle Father Mathew, apostle of temperance. It dribbled from the moustached countenance of Lord Ardilaun and fell on Lecky and on William Conyngham, and on the empty pedestal of the Earl of Eglinton and Winton. It damped the heads of Mangan and Tom Kettle and the Countess Markievicz, it polished to a shine the copper-green planes of a tribute to Yeats. Moore and Burke, Wolfe Tone and Charles Stewart Parnell, Goldsmith and ghostly Provost Salmon: dead men of Ireland were that morning invigorated.

Timothy John clambered to the upper deck of a bus. He thought about his father, his mind inspired in that direction by the memory of the woman who had talked to him yesterday. In the bungalow they never discussed his father, which was understandable. The marriage had been a mistake, a fact that had quickly manifested itself, apparently: he himself was all that had come out of it, the only real reminder that it had ever occurred. He found it impossible to imagine a life in which his father played a part: he couldn't see his father in the bungalow, sprawled out on a chair, smoking cigarettes while he and his mother made jam. Nor could he easily visualize the three of them together in the hotel. His father lived a lonely life, he often thought, doing no work, going on from day to day, seeming to have neither a past nor a future, and seeming not to care. Yet, as the woman had implied, if his father didn't exist he would not exist himself, nor would his mother's life be what it was. It was best to live apart, he thought, when a mistake had been made; it would have been impossible if his grandmother hadn't helped, which was why, no doubt, all three of them felt a debt to her.

He watched the rain trickling on the window of the bus. His mother had been excited last night, talking about the woman who said she wanted to buy the hotel. They'd find something out today, she'd concluded, when they went there for the birthday; but when he'd seen her that morning all the excitement had vanished, dissipated by her concern for his toothache. She would be waiting for him when he got back, with aspirins and consolation, and breakfast, he supposed. With her face vivid in his mind, he got off the bus, although he was still a distance from his destination. For ever, he thought, he would climb the stairs of these cream-and-blue city buses, going to and from the insurance company, returning always to the bungalow and her folded hands. He walked slowly, hearing her saying that it was foolish to walk in the rain after a tooth had been taken out. People were always telling him things and advising him; always, it seemed, he stood still, listening and then agreeing. He would have preferred the Motor Department, he felt sure of it. He should have said more firmly to his uncle that he wished to be transferred, he should have said to his mother that he had fallen in love with a girl in Lipton's.

Ahead of him he saw a telephone-box and for a moment he thought he would step into it and dial his uncle's number and tell him, while he still had the courage, that on Monday morning he would seek a transfer to the Motor Department, and tell him too that he had just had a molar out.

He passed the telephone-box, although it was empty and inviting. He walked more quickly now. It was ridiculous of the woman to go on about the way his father spent his day. His father was a man who had no interest in him, whose hand, as far as he could remember, he had never shaken. He had a life of his own to live, as his mother had too. It was difficult enough without bringing his father into it.

Forcing himself not to slow his pace, he walked ahead, seeing the shops and knowing that in one of them she'd be standing in her overall. Her nakedness haunted him again with familiar suddenness: her bosom rose and fell, her hands hung by her sides, her thighs were as white as paper. He caressed her back through the wool of a red jumper. Her breath was warm on his face.

In the shop she saw him coming and was surprised. She smiled at him, putting pieces of cheese for display on grease-proof paper. He saw her wondering about his swollen face, which was flushed by now and wet as well.

'I've had a molar out,' he said. His stomach heaved over, not at the memory of the tooth coming out, but at the thought of her body again, seeing it with that familiar suddenness. His hands felt clammy. They touched her body, warm like that. He wanted to talk to her forever. He wanted to carry her breakfast in bed. He wanted to see her sitting in an armchair. He wanted her hands to cook him food. He wanted to tend her in illness, to hold out medicine to her on a spoon, to smooth a pillow for her, to forbid her to exert herself. He wanted to hear her voice telling him who she was, speaking of her childhood and of her father and her mother. He wanted to hold her body to his and for both of them to die in the same instant.

'You're a hard case,' she said.

Stumbling over the words, he asked her if she'd come for a walk some time, or maybe to the pictures. She laughed at him and said that maybe she would.

He turned away, unable to say anything else, and in the moment that he did so his uncle, three miles away, said that he had lain awake since half-past five worrying about this would-be purchaser of the hotel. As well as that, he reported that the rain depressed him, since he'd been looking forward to a good morning's work in his field. She should have telephoned him immediately, he reprimanded his wife, when the woman had arrived. It was incredible that this person had apparently talked to every member of the family except himself; it was incredible that no one had put her in the picture as to the part he had endeavoured to play in the family over the years. He asked Mrs Gregan if she had not explained, and Mrs Gregan looked up from a newspaper and shook her head, not knowing what he was talking about. As far as she was concerned, all the conversational value had by now been squeezed from the fact that a strange woman had appeared among them: time would sort that matter out. 'Did you not say,' pursued Mr Gregan, 'that with your brother the way he is, it has fallen on myself to give a lead in family matters? Did you not explain the interest we have in Timothy John, how I kept a fatherly eye on him?' He reminded her of the number of times he had visited the hotel to give her mother a piece of advice that might be necessary. She cleared away the breakfast dishes, hearing his voice repeating that he felt depressed.

The rain which washed the statues and soaked Timothy John and lowered the spirits of Mr Gregan did not, that morning, rattle on the white mackintosh that Mrs Eckdorf had packed in Munich. The coat was still in a suitcase and Mrs Eckdorf, who appreciated the effect of rain on a city almost as much as fog, sat careless of it in Mrs Sinnott's azure bedroom, to which earlier she had carried a breakfast tray. Receiving it from O'Shea in the kitchen, she had said that she herself would not eat again until she felt more completely at peace with herself. Eugene Sinnott, engaged with a newspaper at the kitchen table, had looked up when she had said that, but had passed no comment. In the eyes of O'Shea there was understanding. She remembered the coloured figure of O'Shea mingling with her own white clothes in the great mirror on the first landing, and O'Shea saying that for the birthday he put up a paper-chain.

She had carried the tray upstairs. She had placed it by Mrs Sinnott's side, on the table in the window, and from that moment on, all that morning, Mrs Eckdorf remained in the company of the woman who that day was ninety-two. She remained in the room while Agnes Quin delivered, as a birthday present, a cup. She did not say anything: she watched the street-woman writing a message and watched Mrs Sinnott reading it and then kissing the cheek of Agnes Quin. It was the first time that Mrs Eckdorf had seen her express emotion.

When Agnes Quin had gone Mrs Eckdorf left the chair by the bed and sat in the visitors' chair. She read the message that Agnes Quin had written: *I am taking up a job that the Holy Rosary Sisters offered me at nine o'clock this morning. I could have worked in a kitchen in Harcourt Street but I chose the Sisters because they might be nicer to work for. It's a job polishing and cleaning up.*

Mrs Eckdorf closed the exercise-book. This woman had wished to be a nun, and life had swung her round to clearing the floors that nuns' feet dirtied. That was not a bad thing, Mrs Eckdorf said to herself: the creature had found her place and would fill it happily now, freed maybe of introspection. She leaned forward and saw in Thaddeus Street the figure of Agnes Quin quickly striding. Mrs Sinnott regarded that figure, too. We are thinking the same, Mrs Eckdorf thought. *Do you mind my sitting with you?* she wrote at the back of the book that

Agnes Quin had used. *Say if you mind, Mrs Sinnott, and I'll go away.*

Mrs Sinnott shook her head.

I want to photograph your birthday, Mrs Eckdorf wrote. *Will you mind if I do that?*

Again Mrs Sinnott shook her head. Why should she mind? It was good of the woman to sit with her; it would be nice to have pictures to look at afterwards. The woman was keen on photographs, she thought, as she had thought yesterday when O'Shea had first brought her to the bedroom.

In her mind Mrs Eckdorf saw her own handwriting on the green lines of an exercise-book: *I came here telling lies. I said I would buy the hotel. I said your son had gentle eyes and I did not mean it. I was cruel to O'Shea. I told lies to Philomena and to your daughter Enid Gregan. I frightened your grandson with ridiculous talk, I was impatient with Morrissey and Agnes Quin. Yet I am worthy of none of them. I should have kissed the shoes of Agnes Quin when she came in with a cup for you, I should offer to anoint the feet of Morrissey. I read the exercise-books. I plundered them like a thief. I love you, Mrs Sinnott.*

She could not yet write that, any more than she could write about her husbands and her mother and Miss Tample. She could not yet explain how it was that her mother and Miss Tample and her husbands were part of the same horror in her life, that one led to another. *God is in this hotel,* she might have written and did not, and did not write either, although she wished to: *He is hard to find in other hotels. In the Trader Vic Bar of the London Hilton God does not always seem to be present, although of course He must be. God has made you a special servant, Mrs Sinnott, like Joan of Arc and Bernadette.*

Morrissey came to the room, and Mrs Eckdorf left the visitors' chair and sat on a chair by the bedside. He looked at her nervously, and she remembered that the day before, in the office of the insurance company, she had been rude to him. She crinkled up her face, seeking to offer humility.

Morrissey kept his eyes on her. He nodded very slightly. He moved the position of the chair he was about to sit on so that his back was not presented to her.

'Forgive my rudeness,' she hoarsely said.

She saw him glance towards the dressing-table on which, earlier, Mrs Sinnott had placed a sixpenny piece, having taken it from a small drawer. He took from his pocket the spider, which he had wrapped in a piece of brown paper. He handed it to Mrs Sinnott, who removed the paper and then removed the spider from the cardboard to which it was attached. She fastened the ornament to the material of her black dress.

The silence in the room was intense. It was almost eerie, Mrs Eckdorf thought, this giving and receiving without a word. Earlier, Eugene Sinnott had stood briefly by his mother, wishing her good morning without saying anything. *I dreamed about your cats*, he had written. *O'Shea stabbed me in Dawson Street.* Mrs Eckdorf had read that because, like Agnes Quin, he had left the exercise-book open. *You had a cat called Polly*, he had written. *There's a horse called Polly Bellino today.*

It was funny taking photographs at a birthday tea in a kitchen, Mrs Sinnott thought, instead of at a picnic, under a tree somewhere. Had the woman made a mistake? Did she imagine they were all going out on a picnic? No one could go on a picnic on a day like this.

The door opened and O'Shea came in, carrying Mrs Eckdorf's white hat. Morrissey applied himself to a perusal of his astrological volumes.

'I was tidying up the room,' O'Shea said, holding out the hat.

She took it and smiled a little at him. He didn't go away. He said:

'You would not forget it if you were going out to Mass.'

She shook her head and slowly placed the hat upon it.

Under the impression that her continued presence in the room had to do with her desire to purchase the hotel, O'Shea then explained to Mrs Eckdorf that often when some suggestion was put to Mrs Sinnott she didn't take any notice. Mrs Eckdorf might write down a message to the effect that she was interested in the property and Mrs Sinnott might neither nod nor shake her head. It might be necessary to repeat the statement, to write it out freshly again so that Mrs Sinnott wouldn't become irritated at being shown what already she'd been shown. She had all her wits, O'Shea said, only she often couldn't be bothered to give a sign. She understood everything, but, as Mrs Eckdorf could easily see, she needed expert care in many ways. He had spoken to Father Hennessey about that, and Father Hennessey was going to see about getting her a place with the nuns. And Eugene Sinnott would go to a home to be cured.

'What?' said Mrs Eckdorf.

'It is what she wants,' explained O'Shea, 'that the hotel should rise again. It is what she wants only she always keeps quiet.'

Mrs Eckdorf looked away from the eager face of the porter. She could have given herself to this man to make up for her deceiving of him. She could have pressed his face to hers, she could have endured anything.

'It'll be all right,' she whispered to O'Shea. 'In the end it will be all right.'

In the Excelsior Bar Agnes Quin shook hands with Mrs Dargan and Eddie Trump. Early that morning she'd accepted a position, she told them, having come at last to the conclusion that her hand-to-mouth existence was unsatisfactory. She had bidden good-bye to Mrs Sinnott and to Eugene; she'd explained to O'Shea he wouldn't have to worry again. The photographer who was interested in the hotel was sitting in Mrs Sinnott's room, she reported: she was a woman, said Agnes Quin, who gave her the creeps.

'The girl's better off,' Mrs Dargan remarked after Agnes had gone. 'Wouldn't you say so, Eddie?'

Eddie Trump agreed, and soon afterwards Eugene came into the bar. He said that Agnes Quin had taken up a position in a convent and that the woman who wanted to buy the hotel had been sitting all morning in his mother's room. 'She needs a clip on the ear,' he said.

Eugene related his dreams and listened to the dreams of Eddie Trump. Mrs Dargan sighed. At least there'd be more trade about with Agnes Quin gone. Agnes had always been the first choice when Morrissey showed round his photographs, with Beulah Flynn second, herself third and Mrs Kite bringing up the rear. She'd give it another try for a week or so before considering again if she should return to plucking chickens for the butcher.

'Polly Bellino,' said Eugene. 'The first race at Warwick.'

'Or Polly's Prize,' said Eddie Trump. 'Three o'clock in the Park.'

Morrissey came into the bar. He ordered a glass of stout.

'That woman's up with your mother, Eugene,' he said. 'Is Agnes around?'

Eugene said he knew that Mrs Eckdorf was with his mother. Agnes Quin, he stated, had gone off to fresh pastures.

'Pastures? What kind of –'

'She's taken a job in a convent. She said good-bye to all of us.'

'She said nothing to me.'

'She's gone for good,' said Mrs Dargan.

With slow movements, Morrissey drew a two-shilling piece from his trousers and placed it on the counter. Bitterly, he reflected that it was typical she hadn't said a word to him. He had fixed her up with a well-dressed man from Liverpool, making an appointment for four o'clock this afternoon in O'Neill's Hotel, when the place would be quiet owing to O'Shea being engaged with the birthday party in the kitchen. 'Bad luck to her,' muttered Morrissey, crossing the bar to where Mrs Dargan was sitting. Mr Smedley had shown little interest in Beulah Flynn or Mrs Dargan. He had peered closely at the photograph of Mrs Kite, saying she appeared to be deformed.

'I might have something for you,' Morrissey said quietly, 'if I can fix it. Will you be here about four?'

Mrs Dargan nodded.

The rain continued all that morning. It streamed on the windows of the bungalow in which Philomena prepared lunch for her son and herself, while he, at her command, reclined on his bed. In the hall, the crocheted shawl, wrapped now in orange tissue paper, lay beside the tray-cloth he had bought, which was wrapped in tissue paper of the same colour.

Philomena sliced a cabbage, feeling happy because she was able to look after him. She had mixed Disprin with a little water and had watched him drink it. She'd plugged in an electric fire in his room. After he'd had a rest, he'd tell her all about it: how long he'd had to wait with the ache before the dentist attended to him, what the dentist had said, and how severe the pain of the extraction had been. She'd said that perhaps he shouldn't go to O'Neill's this afternoon, but he'd refused even to consider that idea. She smiled, hearing him say that: she liked him best of all when he stood up to her.

In Terenure Mr Gregan regarded the rain morosely, standing at his sitting-room window. His pipe made a noise when he drew on it and he wondered if water had penetrated when he'd been out on his bicycle, riding over to a shoe-shop to buy his new gum-boots. He longed to be standing in his field instead of in the neat sitting-room that his wife had tidied and cleaned with a vacuum-cleaner at a quarter to eight that morning. The rain would be echoing in the two empty glass-houses and running into the big tin tar-drums he'd provided. The rain would be good for the land.

From the kitchen came the spicy smell of curry, which meant she'd be cooking rice instead of potatoes. He sighed, thinking that after he'd swallowed as much of the rice as he could manage he'd have to get the car out in order to drive down to Booterstown to pick up Philomena and Timothy John, and then go on to Thaddeus Street. At breakfast she'd said she was looking forward to the drive, rain or not. She was up and down like a scallion: drooping in the heat, bright as a button when she got a little moisture. He hated driving the car and very rarely took it out of the garage. She'd bought it herself with some money her father had left her, and he had considered at the time that the little vehicle was a better investment than some useless object that was never used. She'd talked about week-end drives into the countryside or maybe to the coast, but when the car arrived he realized that she meant him to drive her out on these excursions, since she said she was too nervous to drive herself. He explained to her that he much preferred his bicycle and had no time whatsoever for gallivanting around the countryside in a motor-car. One of these days he'd take it into a garage and sell it so that he could put the money into something more sensible: what use was a motor-car that came out of its garage only once a year in order to drive four people over to Thaddeus Street?

In O'Neill's Hotel Mrs Sinnott slept, having tired of watching the falling rain. Mrs Eckdorf left the room and returned with her camera. She photographed random pages of the exercise-books.

O'Shea came in with a tray of food. He said that he had prepared chicken and potatoes and parsnips, and that in ten minutes he would serve them to Mrs Eckdorf in the dining-room. In the meantime he was heating up a tin of kidney soup and stewing prunes.

'I'm sorry,' she said. 'I could eat nothing.'

'Little potatoes,' urged O'Shea. 'And the parsnip is tender –'

She shook her head.

She left Mrs Sinnott's room then. She went back to her own, where for several hours she sat smoking and thinking, close to the window that overlooked the street, as Mrs Sinnott's did.

At a quarter to four she heard the voice of O'Shea murmuring to his dog, and then footsteps on the stairs which suggested that O'Shea was escorting Mrs Sinnott on her annual journey to the kitchen. 'Be quiet, can't you?' his voice called out, and she imagined the greyhound whimpering and darting with excitement, affected by the novelty of it.

From the window she noted, after further time had passed, that Eugene Sinnott seemed unaware of the rain that fell upon him in Thaddeus Street. He walked with the same unhurried motion she had seen him employ before. She had thought then that he moved so slowly because he relished the warm sunshine, but it seemed this wasn't so. The water ran from his uncovered head; he wore no overcoat.

Mrs Gregan came in a cloudy blue suit and a hat with flowers on it. She stepped from a small car and stood for a moment with the rain falling on her umbrella, a woman who looked as awkward when viewed from above as she did, Mrs Eckdorf considered, when seen face to face.

Out of the same car emerged Philomena, hatless, in a grey

coat, and then Timothy John, and then Mr Gregan himself. From her window Mrs Eckdorf could hear his voice shouting across the bonnet of the car, laying down the law about some horticultural practice. He was carrying a bunch of mixed flowers; the others bore gaily-coloured packages.

From the first-floor landing, she photographed them as they passed through the hall. 'The stem must be clear of side-shoots,' Mr Gregan was stating. 'You must always remember that, Philomena.'

She returned to her room, thinking she'd give them a little time to get going before she made her entrance. She sat down again, trying to relax. She closed her eyes and actually fell asleep.

Through the open top of the window, the wind having changed direction, raindrops came into the room, falling on to her. She slipped into a deeper sleep; her lower jaw dropped slightly. Occasionally she snored.

'Excuse me,' said a voice, coming to Mrs Eckdorf from what appeared to be the depths of a well. The voice echoed in her sleep. 'Excuse me,' it said, the voice of a man. I've dropped off, she said to herself in her sleep, in a panic: I've dropped off when I shouldn't have.

'Excuse me,' said the voice again, and a rattling or a coughing commenced, she wasn't sure which. She moaned, knowing she must wake herself because in the Lipowskystrasse Hans-Otto was waving his bandaged hand about, saying she had stabbed it with a fork, and laughing at her. She opened her eyes and saw a sandy-haired, balding man, wearing glasses and a brown suit. He was standing close to her, leaning against the window-frame. He had a cigarette in his hand that he appeared to be about to light.

'Excuse me,' he said.

At first she did not know where she was. She remembered, and wished at once to say that this was a private room in an hotel, and then remembered again.

'What do you want?' she asked, pushing herself to her feet. 'This is my room –'

'I know,' said Mr Smedley. 'I know, I know.'

'Who are you, please?'

'I am looking for Agnes Quin. I have an appointment to meet Agnes Quin at four o'clock in this hotel. I was told which room to go to. I thought it was this one.'

'Agnes Quin has gone to work in a convent.'

Mr Smedley laughed, assuming the statement to be a joke. Mrs Eckdorf didn't like him, and in a moment she realized that she was beginning to hate him. He said:

'A man called Morrissey. He tried to make out he was a lung specialist.'

'He is,' said Mrs Eckdorf.

'Oh, now – '

'He made an error due to lack of sleep.'

'But look at him now –'

'It can happen.'

'Blimey,' said Mr Smedley, and then lost interest in the subject. Tapping one of his feet on the floor, he whistled a snatch from *The Mikado*. He broke off to blow his nose.

'D'you know Agnes Quin?' he asked.

Mrs Eckdorf did not reply. Instead she asked him not to go away. She put lipstick on her lips. She brushed her hair and tidied it. She powdered her face.

'I say,' said Mr Smedley softly.

Again she did not acknowledge the comment.

Mr Smedley, still leaning against the window-frame, said he was a salesman of cardboard sheeting. He told her his name. He informed her that he visited many areas of the world, trading in cardboard. He had spent time in the company of West Indian women, he said, as well as Australian women and the women of the Philippine Islands.

'You need a bit of company,' Mr Smedley said, 'when you're in a strange land. Any man of vigour does.'

Mr Smedley laughed and Mrs Eckdorf, glancing at him, noticed that his teeth were set in a particularly small jaw. They were crowded and pointed. Their whiteness shone, as though Mr Smedley used a special kind of toothpaste.

'I was once in the cement business,' said Mr Smedley, while waiting for Mrs Eckdorf to complete her toilet. 'I packed in the job one Friday night. I walked home to the wife and told her. The following Tuesday I went in on the cardboard line.' He said his wife was the daughter of a Presbyterian minister. 'She knows a trick or two,' he added with a laugh.

She experienced disgust at the sight of his small jaw and his shining teeth, and this talk about the daughter of a Presbyterian minister. He was here for lechery, on this particular afternoon, at this chosen time.

'I'm interested in the East,' said Mr Smedley.

Mrs Eckdorf, with the Mamiya hanging from her neck, held the door open. They went downstairs together. She would photograph him in the hall, for it would be necessary to photograph him, since he represented the hotel as it was today.

'The East,' said Mr Smedley, 'has a certain amount to offer a man of vigour.'

'Stand there,' requested Mrs Eckdorf, pointing towards the row of tall chairs. 'Do not sit down, if you don't mind.'

'Am I to wait? Look here, I'd rather you didn't.'

She took a photograph of Mr Smedley looking alarmed. She paid no attention when he said she had no right to do that. He came towards her aggressively, and as he did so Morrissey and Mrs Dargan came into the hall from Thaddeus Street, dripping rain.

'Hi,' said Mrs Dargan, crossing at once to Mr Smedley, so that Mrs Eckdorf was able to catch them together in her lens. Glancing at her, Morrissey seemed nervous again.

'Stop taking those pictures,' shouted Mr Smedley.

'You are a vicious man,' replied Mrs Eckdorf in a voice so low that it only just carried to him.

'Look here, what's going on? Who are you, for God's sake?' demanded Mr Smedley rudely of Mrs Dargan. 'Where's Agnes Quin?'

'In a convent,' said Mrs Dargan.

'It's all right, sir – ' Morrissey began.

'It bloody isn't all right. You made me a guarantee last night – '

'Agnes let me down, sir, at the last minute. I'm sorry about that, sir.'

'Are you spending much?' whispered a voice in Mr Smedley's ear, and he realized to his horror that it came from the throat of the enormous woman.

'I thought you'd be interested in Mrs Dargan,' said Morrissey. 'Mrs Dargan is agreeable, sir –'

'I do not want Mrs Dargan,' cried the cardboard salesman. 'Mrs Dargan is deformed –'

'It's Mrs Kite you said was deformed, sir. That's Mrs Dargan beside you.'

'Hi,' said Mrs Dargan.

'Agnes Quin has made off,' said Mrs Dargan. 'Morrissey thought maybe you'd be interested.'

Mr Smedley, who from the moment of waking that day had been anticipating with keenness the encounter with Agnes Quin, wondered if he had entered an asylum for the crazed. The undersized man whom he had met last night had sniggered when the woman had said in an extraordinary way that he was vicious. It was not usual in a house to be told you were vicious and then to have a woman the size of an elephant foisted on you. He had done what the undersized man had asked him to do: he had reported at the hotel and gone to a certain room, in which he had presumed Agnes Quin would be waiting. Instead he had found a woman asleep with her mouth open, who had woken up and asked him what he wanted. What did they mean that Agnes Quin had gone into a convent?

'You made me a guarantee,' shouted Mr Smedley, trying to catch Morrissey's eye and failing. 'I paid you six shillings in advance. I want that back.'

He reminded her of Hoerschelmann. The unpleasant spectacles he wore rested on his nose in the same manner as Hoerschelmann's had, and his personality featured the same distasteful blend of cockiness and whine. Mrs Eckdorf closed her eyes and heard the salesman's protesting voice and the murmuring of Mrs Dargan, and it came to her abruptly and with clarity that the salesman must mount the stairs. He must mount the stairs, she said to herself, and he must vent his lechery on the flesh of the well-built woman while the birthday party continued below. It was necessary that he should do so: it was part of a pattern of which she herself was another part. She opened her eyes. She said:

'Mrs Dargan has been brought to this hotel at great cost. For the sum of fifteen guineas, Mr Smedley, plus four further shillings for Morrissey here – '

'Now, bloody hell,' roared Mr Smedley.

'Ten if you like, sir,' said Mrs Dargan.

Rage distorted the countenance of Mr Smedley. Obscenities dropped from his lips. He appeared to be about to attack Morrissey, but Mrs Eckdorf and Mrs Dargan stepped between them.

'I'm sorry about Quin,' said Morrissey. 'Mrs Dargan will do the job – '

'For ten,' said Mrs Dargan, nudging Mr Smedley with her elbow. 'You'll never regret it, sir.'

'I came to meet a girl called Agnes Quin, whose snap I was shown – '

'She's saying her prayers,' said Mrs Dargan, simpering at Mr Smedley, her mind excited by the sums of money that were being bandied about. She'd made twelve shillings the night before.

'Do you,' enquired Mrs Eckdorf, 'or do you not wish to pleasure yourself?'

He looked at her. Intimacy developed in his gaze. He moved towards her, opening his mouth to speak.

'No,' said Mrs Eckdorf.

Mrs Dargan was still standing close to him, moving with him when he moved. The calf of her right leg was pressed against his, a liberty which for the last few minutes he had permitted He shifted his leg now; Mrs Dargan shifted hers in the same direction.

'I couldn't pay money like that,' said Mr Smedley.

'Eight pounds ten,' suggested Mrs Dargan quickly, pressing with her knee.

'Five,' offered Mr Smedley, not looking at Mrs Dargan.

'We'll see Paradise for that, sir,' said Mrs Dargan.

'And four shillings for that man there,' insisted Mrs Eckdorf.

Money changed hands in the hall, an activity that, unnoticed by its principals, Mrs Eckdorf recorded.

Morrissey led the way upstairs. 'What kind of a woman was that?' Mrs Eckdorf heard Mr Smedley say when he imagined they were out of earshot. She heard Mrs Dargan issue a throaty laugh; a sound of some kind, probably a laugh also, came from Morrissey. She did not blame either of them for laughing at her.

She waited for Morrissey to return, and when he did she asked him where the couple were. He said they were in the back room on the first floor.

'I'm glad,' she murmured quietly, 'you got the extra four shillings. A man like that has to be watched.'

'He's like them all, missus.'

'No. He's worse, Morrissey. He's like a man I was married to.'

'Dargan will settle him,' promised Morrissey, passing through the glass doors of the hotel.

She would have liked to chat for a while with Morrissey, to have asked him about Miss Lambe of Wigan and the stamp-collector he had once met, and other details she had read about in his conversations with Mrs Sinnott. She would have liked to apologize for her initial rudeness to him in the insurance office. Thinking that, she went swiftly to the doors he had passed through. She called after him, but he did not come back.

Slowly she went upstairs, knowing she should not move slowly because the birthday party was by now under way. Yet it seemed as important that she should allow a degree of progress to be made in the back bedroom before she made her stealthy entrance. Her hatred of the man who had told her that the East had much to offer a man of vigour increased as she advanced. What right had such a creature to quibble over a price or to make any protest whatsoever? What right had he to come here on the birthday of a woman whose goodness had worked a human miracle? Her hatred was like a living thing within her. It tugged at her, like the hatreds she felt for certain other people, and it would increase, she knew, until the moment came when the lecher should be called upon to play another part, until he and she gazed in wonderment at one another, refreshed by understanding.

She turned the handle of the door and found that the blind

had been discreetly drawn. The rain beat noisily on the window behind it. Sounds came from a bed.

She closed the door quietly and when her eyes became used to the dark she saw two piles of clothes on the floor, the salesman's more abandonedly thrown than Mrs Dargan's.

'Lay off that,' the voice of Mrs Dargan was protesting as Mrs Eckdorf crept forward to pick up his clothes: trousers, shirt, tie, a waistcoat with a watch-chain hanging from it, jacket, underclothes, socks, and two black shoes.

She went to the dining-room that had a smell in it and put the clothes and the shoes in a sideboard.

13

In front of her on the table were the presents she had opened: a pencil-sharpener in the shape of the world, a tray-cloth, a shawl in crocheted wool, a small image of the Virgin Mary, a grey knitted cardigan from Mrs Gregan. On her dress was the spider that had caught Morrissey's eye in Woolworth's, in a jug on the table were the mixed blooms of Mr Gregan, on the dresser was the cup that Agnes Quin had obtained in a shop on the Quays.

There were plates of biscuits, and bread that O'Shea had earlier buttered meticulously. There was brack, and a sponge-cake, a jam-roll and two rectangular fruit-cakes. The birthday cake itself was iced in yellow, with orange piping and small edible flowers. It bore no candles.

Mrs Eckdorf, with her camera, came quietly into the midst of all this. Philomena, seated on one side of Mrs Sinnott, looked up and saw her visitor of the previous afternoon, the woman they'd all been talking about: she was wearing the same clothes and the same white hat.

O'Shea, whose face had reddened with pleasure at the sight of Mrs Eckdorf, busied himself with tea and a teapot. Timothy John, who had been saying to his father that he'd had a tooth out that morning, paused when he saw Mrs Eckdorf and did not finish the sentence. Eugene sighing, thinking to himself that this woman was a damn nuisance. Mrs Gregan smiled.

'I'm Ivy Eckdorf,' Mrs Eckdorf said to Mr Gregan. 'How do you do, Mr Gregan?'

She spoke in a whisper. She held out her right hand, and Mr Gregan received it.

'I have been given permission by Mrs Sinnott,' she said in the same quiet way, 'to obtain photographs of this birthday occasion. Please take no notice of me.'

Leo had had a camera, Mrs Sinnott remembered. She had leaned against a tree while he looked into it, signalling at her to smile. She had stood in the Spanish Arch in Galway, on their honeymoon, and another time on Patrick's Hill in Cork. *I have never heard your voice*, she had written on the back of a brown envelope, and then she saw again her father's writing, black on yellow paper. *He was shot*.

In the yard the leaves of the hornbeam tree dripped. It was better like this, Mrs Eckdorf thought, better than sunshine.

Their necks craned this way and that, their eyes following her about as swiftly she worked. Her face, Eugene saw, was almost grim. She held her camera low, angling a shot along the surface of the table; she clambered on a chair and caught them each as they looked up at her in surprise.

Mrs Gregan glanced at her mother and saw that she was wrapped up with her thoughts and appeared to be unaware that a stranger to the family was standing on a chair, frowning into a camera.

'It is something she wants,' Mrs Eckdorf murmured, returning to the ground. 'She'll have a copy of every one.'

She asked that Eugene should rise and stand by Philomena, and when that had happened, and when she had taken the photograph, she asked that Timothy John should join them, which he, with a glance at his grandmother, did. She asked that Eugene should stand by his sister, and that O'Shea should stand beside the two of them.

'Thank you,' she said. 'That's all I'll bother you for.'

She went to a corner of the kitchen to change the film in her camera and they imagined that now she would go away. O'Shea poured boiling water on to the tea in the teapot and placed the teapot on the table. Mrs Gregan said she'd let it wait a bit before dispensing it.

Watch trap one, Eugene thought: Clinker Flash. Watch Clinker Flash, who had beaten Russian Gun by a neck only a week ago and who shouldn't be underestimated any more than It's a Mint, or Drumna Chestnut in trap three. It's a Mint was a flyer on his night, but what dog on that card could hold a candle to the Printer, who had yet to be headed into the back stretch of the Shelbourne track? No dog, as far as he could see, in this race or in any other. No dog under the sun.

Mrs Eckdorf began to take photographs again, moving about unobtrusively in the background, not getting in anyone's way. They were remembering now, she told herself, as they sat there impassive: they were remembering and forgiving too.

Mrs Gregan poured tea from the teapot, cups were handed round. She smiled at her mother, and Philomena smiled too. Timothy John wished that the woman with the camera would go away. Her voice, noisier then, returned to him from her conversation of yesterday, talking about his father. Sometimes when he came to the hotel he met his father on the stairs, or noticed him sitting in the hall. His father was genial on these occasions: he would tell him he was looking well and occasionally offer him a racing tip.

'I think, if you wouldn't mind,' said Mr Gregan, 'you should finish off now.'

He had risen from the table and was standing beside her.

She shook her head. She said he didn't understand, but that soon she'd explain. There was beauty in the kitchen, she said, speaking so softly that Mr Gregan did not hear her.

'What?' said Mr Gregan.

She gently pushed him back towards the chair he'd been sitting on, but Mr Gregan did not sit down.

'Please just continue,' pleaded Mrs Eckdorf.

'It's a family occasion,' Eugene said suddenly and unexpectedly, pulling his head around to look at her. His hands were trembling, she saw. He began to say something else, but changed his mind and lit a cigarette instead.

'It'll be nice to see the photos,' Mrs Gregan said, 'but we'd like to be alone with my mother now.'

The tips of Mrs Sinnott's fingers rapped on the surface of the table; her eyes indicated that Mrs Eckdorf's presence did not offend her.

Something was wrong, Philomena thought. She watched Mrs Eckdorf moving away from the table and again lifting her camera. She heard her sister-in-law say that they'd better take no notice. Opposite her, Eugene was angry.

Mrs Sinnott, having drunk from the birthday present of Agnes Quin, selected a biscuit wrapped in green silver-paper, from which she slowly removed the wrapping and nibbled at the chocolate confection beneath it.

'She's very kind,' Mr Gregan said to Mrs Eckdorf. 'She never turns people away. But this is private, Mrs Eckdorf.'

Remembering the day, Father Hennessey rose from his bureau with a sigh. On a damp afternoon, with the electric fire going, there was nothing he liked better than to sit and write. On his way through the hall he took an umbrella from the hallstand. 'It's Mrs Sinnott's birthday,' he said to his housekeeper. 'I'll not be long.'

On the street he unfolded his umbrella, thinking neither of Mrs Sinnott nor the people associated with O'Neill's Hotel, but of the saint whose day it was. St Laurence remained in his thoughts until he arrived in the kitchen of the hotel and saw that something was wrong.

'I'm Mrs Eckdorf,' a woman with a camera said to him, addressing him in low tones, as a woman might address him in the Confessional.

'Ah, Father Hennessey,' said Mr Gregan.

Mr Gregan, who had not been sitting down when the priest entered the kitchen, came to him now and shook his hand, at the same time whispering.

'We're having trouble with this woman,' he said.

This was the woman that O'Shea had wildly talked about, whom O'Shea had said was going to buy the hotel. She smiled at him, but he took no notice of her, or of Mr Gregan, whose hand was on his arm. He went to Mrs Sinnott and wrote a birthday message in her exercise-book, as he did every year.

'I think she's doing this to get in with Mrs Sinnott,' Mr Gregan said. 'She wants to buy the hotel.'

Father Hennessey looked at O'Shea, who was standing by the range. He would have liked to ask O'Shea's forgiveness for doubting his word, but he thought that this was clearly not the moment for it. He did as well as he could. He said:

'O'Shea told me that.'

Conversation continued while Mrs Eckdorf went on taking photographs. Mrs Gregan talked to Father Hennessey about the work she was engaged on for the Society of St Vincent de Paul, her husband told Eugene that the best fertilizer for tomato plants was slaughter-house blood. Eugene, he urged, must come up and see the field he'd bought, and the two glass-houses. The home-grown tomato could not be beaten: there would always be a steady market for the home-grown tomato because its quality was superior and it could be put up for sale in a fresher condition than tomatoes that had to be imported. It was a ridiculous state of affairs, Mr Gregan said, that a country like this had to import tomatoes in any shape or form. Eugene nodded and Philomena nodded, as did Timothy John. 'You've settled down well in the Department,' Mr Gregan said to Timothy John, and Timothy John, remembering that he had been in the Department for ten years, nodded again.

Eugene wondered if the rumours that had circulated about the Printer's dislike of trap four had any foundation whatsoever. The way people talked you'd think he had never run from any trap but trap six in his life. What trap, for God's sake, was he running from when he broke the record set up by the Prince of Bermuda, and broke two tracks records at the White City?

'We're having a raffle in the autumn,' Mrs Gregan said to Father Hennessey. 'Ten of us are going out on the streets with tickets.'

'A raffle can pull it in. Keep the prizes within reason. Get a grocer to put up a few bottles for you and a nice big box of chocolates.'

'It'll be a break, selling tickets.'

Mrs Sinnott cut her birthday cake and everyone, including O'Shea and Father Hennessey and Mrs Eckdorf, took a piece. O'Shea placed glasses on the table, and the bottle of Gilbey's port that Riordan's had sent up, and nuts and fruit and two packs of cards. He helped Mrs Sinnott to an armchair by the range, knowing what to do because every year after the cutting of the cake, and when the port had been opened, it was her custom to move to the armchair. When she was younger she had remained at the table to play rummy, a game that by tradition had come to be played at all the birthdays in the hotel. Now she was content to drink a glass of port by the range: she would doze until the moment came for her visitors to leave her, until Philomena's hand gently touched her shoulder.

On two other days in the year, in autumn and in December, birthdays were still celebrated in the hotel, but not in the kitchen. Eugene and O'Shea, each on the relevant day, sat down in her room and had tea with her. She gave each of them a pound, which O'Shea had earlier picked up from the bank, with Morrissey's sixpences and Eugene's spending money and his own wages.

Eugene poured the port and Mrs Sinnott's health was drunk. O'Shea had put an extra glass on the table, which Eugene, not bothering to count, had filled as well. From it Mrs Eckdorf now drank. Father Hennessey, who drank also, felt he should be able to say something to the woman in order to make her see that she should not be there. 'It's a family occasion,' he whispered to her. She nodded.

The birthday was the same as all the others that Timothy John remembered, except for the awkwardness caused by the presence of the uninvited guest. His father shuffled together the two packs of cards and then dealt them. Coins of small denomination were placed on the table by all the family, and by Father Hennessey and O'Shea.

As play commenced, there was a silence in the kitchen, except for the sound of the game and the ticking of the clock on the dresser. Red ashes fell silently from the fire in the range. No draught caused a rustle in the paper-chain that stretched from one hook to another, across the length of the huge ceiling. Mrs Sinnott slept. Mrs Eckdorf sat on a chair, far away from the table, near the door. O'Shea's dog lay at his feet.

Mrs Gregan discarded a ten of spades. Eugene picked up a joker. Philomena remembered a birthday of her own in this kitchen, the year after her mother died, when she was sixteen. O'Shea put a seven of clubs beside a seven of hearts. Mr Gregan had a royal sequence in diamonds. Timothy John thought that if what she'd been implying was that he should be living in the hotel with his father, then she didn't know what she was talking about. The gum from which his tooth had been taken throbbed steadily. He needed more Disprin, but he couldn't very well ask for it here. His mother smiled at him, and he could feel her thinking that as soon as they were back in the bungalow she'd insist that he went to bed.

From two different positions Mrs Eckdorf photographed the card-players, working quietly so as not to distract them. Out of the corner of his eye, Father Hennessey noticed her movement, saw also that Eugene was becoming restive. Ten minutes passed before Eugene threw his cards down and stood up.

'Stop taking those photographs,' he ordered in a sober voice.

'Just go on playing,' murmured Mrs Eckdorf, intent on what she was doing.

'It's damn ridiculous,' Eugene protested angrily.

Philomena glanced at Mrs Sinnott, who continued to sleep undisturbed.

'It is ridiculous,' said Mr Gregan.

Father Hennessey rose and went to where Mrs Eckdorf was standing. 'Please now,' he said.

She photographed Mrs Sinnott in the armchair by the range, and then Eugene.

'I'm sorry I upset you,' she said, smiling slightly at them all. 'Thank you for being patient.'

Father Hennessey returned slowly to his chair. Mrs Eckdorf, on her way from the kitchen, paused at the door.

'We concern one another,' she said. 'We are all God's creatures.'

No one present made an effort to reply to this statement, no one denied it.

'Morrissey,' said Mrs Eckdorf, 'and Agnes Quin.'

'Yes,' said Father Hennessey, filling the silence.

Mrs Sinnott continued to sleep. The others, with the exception of O'Shea, regarded Mrs Eckdorf in astonishment and with varying degrees of displeasure. Mrs Gregan and Philomena, who had been friendly yesterday, did not seem friendly now. Timothy John looked as though he didn't care for her. Eugene was still angry. Mr Gregan made an impatient noise. Father Hennessey frowned. Only O'Shea seemed happy.

'You need look no further,' said Mrs Eckdorf, 'than Morrissey and Agnes Quin. We are the victims of other people.'

Mrs Gregan said to herself that she was greatly perplexed. The woman was indeed odd, referring out of the blue to a couple like Morrissey and Agnes Quin, and announcing that you need look no further than them. What did she mean by that? What had Morrissey and Agnes Quin to do with anything, for goodness' sake?

Mrs Gregan had never met Morrissey, but one day she had met Agnes Quin. She knew that a person called Morrissey came to visit her mother and that the man was an orphan and that Agnes Quin was an orphan. Her mother attracted people like that, being a charitable person. When she had seen Agnes Quin, on the landing outside her mother's room, she had wondered about her. She had taken her to be a well-dressed tinker or a tinker who was no longer an itinerant but had settled down in regular work or had married. There wasn't anything out of the way in such a person coming daily to visit her mother, any more than it was unexpected that Morrissey should come and write down prophecies. Her mother's world was private and always had been. No doubt she paid Agnes Quin a little now and again, and Morrissey too: it did her good, Mrs Gregan had concluded, to think that she was still a help to people.

Such thoughts had more than once passed through Mrs Gregan's mind concerning Agnes Quin and Morrissey, and thoughts that were not dissimilar had passed through the minds of Philomena and Timothy John. Mrs Gregan had said to Philomena once that she believed Agnes Quin was or had been a tinker, and Philomena, who had also seen Agnes Quin, had been inclined to agree. She, having met Morrissey as well, suggested that he was or had been a tinker too: he was the same kind of person, she said, a down-and-out. Timothy John, who had never seen either Agnes Quin or Morrissey, had come to believe, because of the descriptions of his mother and his aunt, that the couple were or once had been of the itinerant class. With O'Shea, they were the last of her orphans, and there had never been any question within the family that Mrs Sinnott should be deprived of their company because they were not respectable people.

'Their lives,' Mrs Eckdorf was saying now. 'Morrissey, who will one day forgive his enemies. Agnes Quin who might have been a nun. We must know their lives.'

'Look here, what the heck's all this about?' demanded Mr Gregan.

'And the lives of other people,' said Mrs Eckdorf, 'though some may be distasteful to us. The violent life of Hoerschelmann, and Hans-Otto Eckdorf with his falsely bandaged hand. And Doyle the lemonade clerk, and Miss Lambe in a boarding-house in Wigan. And lives in China and Australia, where Smedley the lecher has travelled after flesh-pots. And the dark lives of Africa. And lives, grey-flannelled, in the United States of America; and lives in Chile, and in India. Do you understand?' asked Mrs Eckdorf.

'No,' said Mr Gregan.

'Father Hennessey understands.'

Father Hennessey said he did not.

'I turned away from a bearded face. I put Elsie Timson's holy book down a lavatory. At St Monica's School for Girls I sat in innocence, drinking cocoa with Miss Tample until Miss Tample became a monster. My father ran away, my mother was disgraceful. God is in this kitchen,' cried Mrs Eckdorf. 'God is revealing Himself through that sleeping woman.'

'Please,' said Father Hennessey, standing up to meet this careless blasphemy. 'Please, Mrs Eckdorf.'

'Even now we should be anointing the feet of persons who are unknown to us, of murderers and those with feet that are diseased. Yet how can we do that without God?' cried Mrs Eckdorf. 'How can I look again at the feet of Hoerschelmann unless God is inside me, as He is in that woman there? How could I touch the feet of Smedley, who even now, a naked lecher – '

'You're upsetting the women,' exclaimed Mr Gregan loudly, his chair scraping on the flagstones as he pushed it back. The greyhound whimpered and ran around. They looked at Mrs Sinnott to see if she'd been disturbed, but she still slept.

'She would bend to anoint the feet of anyone in the world. A man whose feet were eaten up with leprosy would feel the coolness of her fingers. She would anoint the feet of Smedley and

Mrs Dargan, though they lay in sin. She would anoint the sores – '

'Get out of here,' shouted Eugene, and eyes were again turned to where Mrs Sinnott rested. But Mrs Sinnott did not wake.

'Can we only forgive, is there nothing else?' demanded Mrs Eckdorf. 'Your sister cooks food for her husband, Eugene, and does not know him, nor he her. Does Philomena know her son? That gentle porter lives alone, with failing hopes for company. You push all life away, Eugene: you want no part of life now. When you think, Eugene, do you think that we cannot speak to one another, that there is only forgiveness? It's easy to talk in the exercise-books: it's easy to talk to yourself.'

She had read the exercise-books, they individually thought, and their bewilderment increased. O'Shea, who did not share that thought and whose bewilderment did not increase, gazed at Mrs Eckdorf with pleasure.

'Hoerschelmann might lift a table up and strike the life from one of you. He might come into this room, a stranger, and do that. You would not know him and yet in time you could forgive. You could anoint his feet.'

'Go away from us,' ordered Eugene.

'Yes,' said Mrs Eckdorf, and left the kitchen, softly closing the door behind her and causing, after she'd gone, a long silence.

They talked about her then, while Mrs Sinnott slept and O'Shea stared at the scattered cards on the table and did not take part in the conversation. They exchanged again the experiences they had had with Mrs Eckdorf. Eugene told how he had dreamed on the night before her arrival, and how she had seemed to him when he saw her to be a woman who might belong to a circus. Mrs Gregan told of her arrival, unannounced, at the house in Terenure and how she had said immediately that she was keen to buy the hotel and was endeavouring to discover what the members of the family thought about such a proposition. Philomena told of Mrs Eckdorf's visit to the bungalow, how she had seemed quite pleasant and interested. Timothy John said that from the first moment he had seen her he had considered her unusual. He did not, since his father was present, enter into detail about the course of her conversation in the Home and Personal Effects Department, but he managed to convey the impression that the conversation had not been normal.

'She had no intention ever,' said Mr Gregan, 'of buying the property.'

Eugene shook his head. A case like that, he pronounced, couldn't run a tap, let alone an hotel.

'Is she mad, Father?' Philomena asked, and Father Hennessey shrugged his shoulders. You could not be sure, he said, whether a woman who spoke in that way was insane or not.

'Oh, there's madness there,' said Mr Gregan knowledgeably. 'She's up the chute, Father.'

'I thought it quite extraordinary,' his wife said, 'taking photographs like that.'

'We all thought that, Enid,' Mr Gregan reminded her. 'We were sitting here thinking that. The dark lives of Africa,' said Mr Gregan and gave a short laugh.

She had called him gentle, O'Shea remembered. She had spoken quietly about the lives of people in China, she had said that he lived in failing hopes, meaning that he had been faithful not to give up. When she spoke, Mr Gregan had said he didn't understand and Father Hennessey had not understood either. But if she had turned to him and asked him if he understood he would have been able to say that he did. It would be nice for Mrs Sinnott to have photographs of her ninety-second birthday, which was something that Eugene Sinnott could not be expected to appreciate.

'You are never here,' O'Shea cried suddenly and with vehemence. 'You are down in Riordan's, Mr Sinnott, drinking glasses of sherry. The building could fall down into ruins – '

'O'Shea, O'Shea,' murmured Father Hennessey.

'She stood there yesterday, Father, with a light coming out of her clothes. She stood in the attic with a yellow light – '

'You told me, O'Shea.'

'She was sent to this hotel to set it to rights.'

'No, no, O'Shea,' said Mr Gregan.

'It's too much for you to understand. The Queen of Heaven – '

'That'll do now,' commanded Father Hennessey sharply.

'Something has happened here,' insisted O'Shea. 'She came into the hotel singing a hymn. She came a thousand miles.'

'Will we get on with the game?' suggested Eugene.

'She was glowing in the attic,' O'Shea cried shrilly. 'If it was the Queen of Heaven herself you'd say she was a racing tip, Mr Sinnott.'

The cards were dealt again, but O'Shea did not pick up his. They lay before him while the others played, thinking again that the woman who had taken photographs of them and had spoken so oddly had also read their conversations with Mrs Sinnott. She had no right to do that; she had no right to eavesdrop.

'She's a case,' Eugene said, speaking softly so as not to disturb O'Shea in his thoughts.

'She'll go without paying the bill,' warned Mr Gregan.

Eugene shrugged and threw down a three of hearts. Mrs Gregan whispered that no matter what Mrs Eckdorf was or was not, she had upset O'Shea badly.

'She had no intention ever,' repeated Mr Gregan, 'of buying the property.'

The others shook their heads, agreeing easily about that. They all, including Eugene, felt sorry for O'Shea, and they all thought in the same way that it wasn't at all unusual that a person like O'Shea, who was well-known locally for the fruitfulness of his imagination, should have seen an unbalanced woman as a special figure.

'She'll go away,' said Father Hennessey, and thought as he said it that she might stay for ever, that Mrs Sinnott, who was famous for taking pity on people and still made decisions, might decide that the woman should remain in a room in the hotel. He imagined her voice continuing about people he had never heard of, about all the people in the world, about anointing the feet of murderers. It would not be pleasant to have her around.

With her camera ready, Mrs Eckdorf listened outside the room in which Morrissey had placed Mr Smedley and Mrs Dargan. 'I didn't touch your bloody togs,' Mrs Dargan was protesting, laughing her throaty laugh. Mrs Eckdorf opened the door.

The blind was still drawn, but in his search for his clothes Mr Smedley had put the light on. He stood directly beneath the shaded bulb, his face screwed up in perplexity and anger, his pale body naked. Mrs Dargan, seated on the edge of the bed, was drawing on a stocking.

'Hi,' said Mrs Dargan. 'Your man's lost his togs.'

'Get out to hell,' cried Mr Smedley, covering a part of himself with both hands. 'Get away with that camera.'

She closed the door and stood with her back against it.

'Sin has begotten sin,' said Mrs Eckdorf. She photographed the nakedness of Mr Smedley, and when he advanced upon her she said that if he did not behave himself he would not ever receive his clothes. Mrs Dargan attached the top of the stocking to a suspender, and it occurred to Mrs Eckdorf that there could be few women in the world with legs as massive as the legs of this cheerful creature. She looked at the bare white feet of Mr Smedley and knew that she could not yet anoint them. She could not yet bear to touch those feet, or to have them touch her.

'I want to talk to you both,' said Mrs Eckdorf.

'Have you a fag?' enquired Mrs Dargan.

'I demand those clothes,' shouted Mr Smedley. 'There's money in them, there's travellers' cheques and an air ticket – '

'Please don't worry,' said Mrs Eckdorf.

She gave Mrs Dargan a cigarette and offered one to Mr Smedley, who at first refused and then accepted. She lit both cigarettes and then lit one for herself.

'I'll put the police on to you,' threatened Mr Smedley. 'Those clothes were stolen. Someone came into this room – '

'Now listen to me calmly,' said Mrs Eckdorf. 'Do you believe in God?'

'In God? In – '

'In the existence of a Maker.'

Mr Smedley turned away from the two women. There was a small boil on his back that might have been painful. His shoulders were broad and fleshy and excessively white. Dark hair grew along the line of his spine.

'I'm a good Catholic,' said Mrs Dargan.

'In God?' said Mrs Eckdorf, and Mr Smedley, still with his back to her, said that he did not believe in God. He mentioned his clothes again. He said he could not stand here in this condition talking to two women about God. He had a plane to catch.

'An extraordinary thing has happened in this hotel,' said Mrs Eckdorf. 'A family has been cleansed of its crimes by a silent woman, through whom God reached out –'

'I don't care who reached out,' shouted Mr Smedley, turning suddenly and glaring at Mrs Eckdorf. 'It has nothing to do with me what happened in this hotel –'

'In that you are wrong: we are all to do with one another. We must never seek to escape one another. We are here to know one another.'

'Will you shut up that rubbish?' cried Mr Smedley. 'Are you half-witted? Are you mad? My clothes have been stolen and all you can talk about is God reaching out. I don't believe in any God.'

'You have come to mock a woman's goodness,' cried Mrs Eckdorf in sudden fury, glaring at Mr Smedley as he had at her. She felt behind her back and removed from the lock of the door its key. Mr Smedley came towards her. She said that if he advanced another inch his clothes would be set on fire. If she was injured in any way, or if commotion broke out in the room, O'Shea the hall-porter had instructions to burn the purloined garments instantly.

'You have come here with filthy talk and lechery,' Mrs Eckdorf said in calmer tones. 'I looked at you standing before me in my room and I hated the sight of your small mouth and your teeth. Looking at you now, I hate the sight of your body and the boil you have on the flesh of your back. I hate your hands because they are filthy hands. I hate your feet. I could not yet anoint your feet.'

'Please –'

'It is wrong that I cannot do that, and the moment shall come when I will bend to do it. My disgust shall pass away from me and I shall gaze upon a lecher as he shall gaze at me, refreshed by understanding. A lecher has come,' said Mrs

Eckdorf in a poetic way, 'and has entered this holy hotel. A lecher is here, through whom I may offer my forgiveness of other persons, whose victim I have been. Time must pass. I must talk to the priest. I must sit in the azure room before I return to the Lipowskystrasse. I am telling my own story, Mr Smedley, through all these people who have been taught forgiveness. I feel the balm of God.'

Mr Smedley rowdily protested, coming near to Mrs Eckdorf, who gestured him away. His clothes would be burnt, she murmuringly said, and then she added:

'O'Shea will bring you meals to this room. You will remain in humiliation until the moment arrives, until I come to you with a bowl and a towel. You are free to go,' said Mrs Eckdorf to Mrs Dargan, who hurriedly went.

'For God's sake,' shouted Mr Smedley.

'No,' replied Mrs Eckdorf. 'For your sake and for mine.'

She left the first-floor bedroom, locking it behind her, and in her own room she collected together all the film she had used. She placed it in an aluminium container that was already addressed to her, at the apartment in the Lipowskystrasse. She left the hotel and walked swiftly away from it, towards a post office that she'd noticed the day before. She dispatched the film by registered mail, saying to herself that she would be in the Lipowskystrasse to receive it. From past experience, she knew that it was safer to rid oneself of whatever film there was: for one reason or another, it had been demanded before that film should be handed over.

14

The visitors left the hotel: the birthday was over.

The Gregans and Philomena and Timothy John drove away in the car that Mrs Gregan owned and which Mr Gregan planned to sell. They talked of Mrs Eckdorf, repeating that it was extraordinary that a woman who was either permanently or periodically insane had turned up in O'Neill's Hotel. Mr Gregan would look in at the hotel on Monday, he said, to see if she was still there, and if she was still being a nuisance he'd suggest to Eugene that she should be obliged to leave; although after the way he and Eugene had spoken to her he imagined she was packing her bags at this very moment.

Father Hennessey returned to his house, and Eugene made his way through the inclement evening to the Excelsior Bar. She'd gone by now, he hoped, whoever she was and whatever she'd wanted. He forgot about her, and recalled instead that in 1938 humidity in the air had adversely affected the performance of the hitherto imperturbable Skibbereen Hero.

Carrying her presents, O'Shea walked behind Mrs Sinnott as she made her way upstairs. They moved slowly, and in her room she sat down at once. She dismissed O'Shea after he had put her birthday presents on the bedside table. They were kind to bother, she thought: they must find it tedious, having to think of something every year and having to come and sit with her in the kitchen on her birthday. She pulled the china bell-pull, remembering she'd forgotten to make it clear to O'Shea that she wouldn't have anything more to eat, and wished now to wash herself before going to bed.

'There's a woman to see you, Father,' his housekeeper said in the hall.

'Who's that?' he asked, taking off his hat and his mackintosh.

'She's from the hotel. She says you know her, Father.'

He went slowly up the stairs, thinking that the damp affected his joints. He didn't want to see her. He wanted to forget that she had ever come to Thaddeus Street, upsetting O'Shea and gabbling about the feet of murderers.

'I must confess my life to you,' Mrs Eckdorf said in a faint voice. 'I must tell you everything, Father.'

He sat down at his bureau, turning the chair so that he was facing her. He asked her to sit down, too. Even before she spoke he felt frightened. He had his own people to look after, he thought, but he knew as soon as he'd thought it that he shouldn't have. She spoke in the same hushed voice.

Father Hennessey heard how Mrs Eckdorf had been served with cognac by a barman on an ocean liner, and how in the course of conversation, and to Mrs Eckdorf's surprise, the man had told her of his brief sojourn in O'Neill's Hotel. She mentioned her intuitions, which were part of her professional stock-in-trade, and she explained that while the barman told his tale her intuitions had suggested that she must visit this hotel. She described the books that had made her famous, how the pages revealed unvarnished truth, how the lives of people were shown to other people so that people everywhere might be drawn closer through understanding. In cinemas and on television screens, she said, this documentary form was increasingly an accepted mode: he would agree, she slightly urged, that fiction was outclassed by straightforward truth?

Father Hennessey did not particularly agree because he did not at first understand what Mrs Eckdorf was talking about. The coffee-table volumes of which she spoke had never come his way, and it required consideration on his part before he was able to envisage them. They were not books that people read, she said, but rather that people picked up. He imagined people picking them up and turning the pages. They were authentic documents, she said: they made their statements in pictures of actuality and not in words, being concerned with reality. As her voice continued in his study, it seemed that humanity had become a raw material, which was something that Father Hennessey had not known about, any more than he had known about coffee-table volumes. He wondered if there were symphonies composed of real tears and shrieks of anguish, or films which showed how a man continued his life, having destroyed his wife and children. It sounded from what his visitor was saying as if such works might indeed exist, or would soon exist. He shuddered within him, finding the novelty upsetting.

Mrs Eckdorf related how she had walked by the river, arriving in Thaddeus Street by a round-about route, how later she had discovered the tragedy she had professionally sought and had then discovered a greater truth: she told Father Hennessey of what had occurred in O'Neill's Hotel on this day once and of the forgiveness that had developed since. It was of this forgiveness, she explained, that her work would treat; God moving in a mysterious way was what her photographs were about. She spoke at length and slowly. A single action on this birthday twenty-nine years ago had altered the lives of a handful of people. Violence had created the life of a child; it had made the mother what she was today, and the father too. It had driven Enid Gregan from the home she had loved because it was stained with a violence that disgusted her. It had ruined the contentment of O'Shea. And yet there was forgiving now.

Having listened, Father Hennessey's first thought was that speedily he should pray for Mrs Eckdorf. He did not do so. Instead he said:

'Where did you get these facts from?'

She replied that O'Shea had led her into the past and that she had seen what there was to see. The facts were true, she said: she had sensed it in this room. Her eyes fell on the priest's eyes: had not these facts been once confessed to him, a long time ago now? It wasn't difficult, she revealed, for a professional mind to fish out the truth.

'You cannot do a thing like this,' he said with sharpness in his voice.

She looked away from him. She had informed him of all that so that he might understand what next she had to say, which was to do with herself. The photographs would be nicely produced; the volume would be well finished and bound; its price would reflect its quality. They must forget the volume now, since the volume was already a *fait accompli*. She had come to confess her life to him, which was surely more important, a person's life as opposed to a book.

'All you have said is private to that family, Mrs Eckdorf.'

'I had forgotten God, until He was again revealed to me through her. Call it my repayment of that debt, Father: my monument to her, more lasting than brass.'

Father Hennessey pressed with the palms of his hands on the two arms of his chair, raising himself to his feet. He crossed painfully to the window. He parted the lace curtains and looked at the wet evening. He tried to think constructively, but found impatience in the way. He spoke, still looking at the rain. He said again she could not do what she intended to do. He said that a volume such as she proposed would not contain the truth. Quietly, she questioned that. He said:

'These people live ordinary lives. They have a love for that old woman. They come to her birthday, as I do myself. There's nothing more to it.'

'There is all the rest, God working in His way –'

'You are inventing all the rest,' cried Father Hennessey passionately, turning to her. 'You are making an ordinary thing seem dramatic when it is not that at all. The truth is simple and unexciting: you are twisting it with sentiment and false interpretations, so that a book will sell to people.'

'I am not doing anything for mercenary profit.'

His grey face was close to hers. A vein quivered on his forehead.

'You must not do this,' he repeated.

'I wish to show the working of God, Father. I came to your house to tell you that. I came to obtain your blessing, and then to gather strength from you.'

He controlled his anger. She asked if she might smoke a cigarette in his house and he said that she might. She offered him one from her packet, but he said he didn't smoke. He watched her lighting the cigarette and returning the packet to her handbag. As she blew out smoke, he explained that everything was the working of God, that it could not be otherwise. Mrs Sinnott was a kind woman, he said, but she was like any other woman. Her visitors wrote about themselves because she was interested in them. He himself, he pointed out, wrote about his work. There was nothing remarkable in any of it.

'They lay their lives before her,' she said. 'She sees no difference between one person and another, as God does not.'

'They write things about themselves because she likes to hear about them. She likes other people.'

'Timothy is the child of a crime. If a crime had not been committed he would not be there.'

'Will you please stop talking like that? Will you please now?'

'I am speaking the truth, Father.'

'If you read the lives of the saints, Mrs Eckdorf, you'll find that the truth has also been adorned with fancy. Only it is different with you because you have a camera, and people imagine a camera cannot lie. Cameras lie all the time.'

'Why do you hate a stranger?'

'I do not hate you.'

'Then will you listen to me, Father?'

'Yes, Mrs Eckdorf, I will listen to you.'

How could a woman go about invading the privacy of people and then delude herself that it was in a good cause? How could she extract from persons and from families selected elements that put together would make up a story to titillate the interest of others? He imagined the pictures in the book she said she had completed about a priest in Sicily, and he imagined its examination by people who were affluent enough to make such a purchase. They might be moved by the bewilderment of peasants and by the peasants' love of the priest they had always known, but being moved like that was surely a luxury? She was like some awful puzzle, sitting there with her lips moving, talking a kind of gibberish. Her mind was in disarray, yet he believed her when she said that people picked up from their coffee-tables the volumes she composed, and wrote her admiring letters, and even shed tears over the ersatz truth she offered them. It amazed him, but he believed it.

He regarded the powdered face and the teeth that had a slight gap in the centre of them, and her tongue moving swiftly to form the words she spoke. He wanted to stop her flow of speech, to cry out harshly that the currency of her world was all debased, that people were not objects for cameras to look at, nor actors in her documentary form, nor raw material. There was something wrong if living people could be watched and studied so that other living people might somehow benefit. There was something wrong in looking through a keyhole at people being themselves.

'I want to tell you, Father,' she said, 'about my life.'

She told him about her early childhood. She remembered taking her father's hand and walking with him through the streets of Maida Vale, in London. She remembered the smell of her father, an odour of tobacco, and the brownness of his hard fingers, and his mouth smiling at her. He had read to her from books and had told her stories about animals he invented, he had taken her regularly to a waxworks. She remembered walking on Hampstead Heath with him one Sunday morning, an occasion when an Alsatian dog, bounding from its leash, had bounded back upon its master and knocked him to the ground. The man, having dislocated some part of himself in the rough-and-tumble, had been unable to rise. He lay there calling out abuse at his obstreperous pet, while her father ordered a youth who was laughing at the misfortune to telephone for an ambulance. After the incident, when the dog had been punished and its master's injury attended to, she and her father had laughed, too, and had gone on laughing, unable to cease. It had happened so quickly, they said to one another, one moment a cheery Londoner and a dog, and the next a man unable to stand up from the damp ground. She'd been eight at the time.

In their flat in Maida Vale she gave raisins and crumbs of bread to dolls, and her father sat beside them on the floor, receiving raisins and bread as well. There was a doll that always sat on her father's lap, called Janey Rose, whose hair he said he liked because she always kept it brushed. After tea-time with the dolls her father would find that he had sticks of Peggy's Leg in his pocket, or liquorice sweets. 'We'll read the dolls a story,' she would say, listening while he read aloud. And then one day her father wasn't there.

She did not see him ever after that. She asked her mother if he'd died, but her mother replied that he was still very much alive. They had agreed, she said, that none of them should meet again: she had insisted upon that, since she was being left with the burden of the child. He had decided on another wife, she explained, who did not wish to take on another woman's child. They had talked sensibly, her mother told her, the three of them, and had agreed to go their chosen ways. Her mother was glad he'd gone: she hadn't liked him.

And then, said Mrs Eckdorf, the house filled up with one man after another man. In her mother's bed the men lay naked, and her mother laughed, giving them her body like giving a piece of chocolate. On Sunday mornings a man and her mother would sit around in coloured dressing-gowns, drinking coffee and arguing. Sometimes a man would bring her sweets or take her on to his knee. 'She's such a mope,' she heard her mother say. She hated the men, and her mother too, and her father who had betrayed her callously. She went to a boarding-school and found Miss Tample waiting for her.

She walked about his room, smoking and gesturing. Tears fell on to her clothes and sometimes on to his books and papers. He prayed that she would go away. He did not understand, he whispered in his prayer: he begged forgiveness; he was too old to understand this modern woman.

'I sat in a room,' she said, 'in St Monica's School for Girls and could not, after that, bear the thought of other people's flesh. My mother laughed when I told her.'

'Mrs Eckdorf —'

'My heart was full of tears, and all she did was to throw her head back and laugh her horrid laugh. "We all concern one another," I might have said. "A daughter's injury needs a mother's love." Instead I went out for a walk.'

'I'm sorry you have suffered, Mrs Eckdorf.'

'My world today is a different one from yours, Father. You would sit awkwardly in my cinder-grey apartment in the Lipowskystrasse. Hans-Otto would have thought you quaint.'

He nodded, understanding that a man she had been married to should think him quaint.

'My world glitters like glass of different colours, thin and

224

brittle. In my world, Father Hennessey, people dress nicely; they take personal pride. People talk across the length of a room, Bach plays softly, a manservant passes drinks in simply-shaped glasses. On grey walls hang photographs of Mexican peasants, magnified a score of times. The people mention Louis Malle, and a beach in Portugal, and new movements in Dance, and Stan Getz. On a coffee table somewhere there is a volume that tells in candid photographs a human story that's made more beautiful by the beauty of the photographs.'

Father Hennessey, who had not before heard of Louis Malle or Stan Getz, none the less derived from what Mrs Eckdorf had said an intimation of the world she called her own. He saw quite easily people sitting in an elegant room, talking quietly while harpsichord music played as a background to what they said. He imagined a woman moving soundlessly across the floor, and taking from a low table a book that told in photographs a true story.

' "Sugar?" Miss Tample said in a different kind of room. "Sugar in your cocoa, Ivy?" And in my mother's house my mother laughed and lit a tipped cigarette. She said there was someone she wanted me to meet, some small young Frenchman with whom currently she was committing fornication. All that makes up my world, Father Hennessey. My marriages were unconsummated.'

Watching her striding about his room, shedding these facts about herself, Father Hennessey said again that he was sorry.

'Why should you understand? I make no sense to you.'

She went on talking, going into greater detail about all she'd said, going on and on about her life until he thought she'd never cease. In the end she asked him what he thought now. He spoke sympathetically in reply. He would indeed pray for her, he promised. He could offer her only words and prayers, he said, and then he spoke more firmly. He said:

'What concerns me is that you are seeing the lives of people who are strangers to you purely in terms of your own life, Mrs Eckdorf. It is not right that you should do that. It is not right that you should dramatize their lives in a book. It is scandalous to do that, Mrs Eckdorf.'

'The notion of your God was absurd to me until I knew the truth about the people in the hotel and the truth about Mrs Sinnott.'

'Please listen to me, Mrs Eckdorf.'

'I cannot forgive my mother.'

'Many of us cannot forgive.'

'When Hoerschelmann took off his clothes I saw the hirsute face of Miss Tample. I heard my mother's laughter and the laughter of all her lovers. "Give me time," I said to both my husbands, but time was no good either.'

She threw away her cigarette, although it was not used up. He watched her light a new one.

'There is nothing remarkable in O'Neill's Hotel,' he said. 'There is nothing about Mrs Sinnott that should call for a book of photographs.'

'I felt a warmth.'

Again confusion ran through his mind. The feeling of failure that often before had mocked him struck at him less playfully now. Only a few hours ago he had never seen this woman's face.

'It was like being snug in a bed,' she said. 'My father left me in my mother's house, giving raisins to dolls. I've been in need since.'

Father Hennessey talked to her of faith and said that she must pray. She must allow faith to develop within her until it was unshakable. She must be humble.

'I did nothing,' she cried, not listening to him. 'I existed as a child, playing on a nursery floor, and now I am incapable of having a human relationship. I cannot come to terms, as all these people in the kitchen have come to terms in a rough and ready way.'

'They are simple people.'

'They are simple people, which makes it easy for them to accept a myth. Are you saying that to me, Father? Are you denying everything to a stranger you hate and can feel no compassion for?'

'Please, Mrs Eckdorf —'

'Can the needy go mad, Father, for lack of something? Is that what's happening?'

'Please don't distress yourself like this. We'll talk together for as long as you wish. Please don't distress yourself.'

'It is the needy who have made your God.'

The priest's housekeeper tapped on the door and when Father Hennessey bade her to, she came into the room. She whispered to him, saying she'd heard the woman cry out. He said it was all right, and she went away. His mind, unable to grapple, was dazed. He felt hot with a rising desperation; he felt remorse and guilt; he could think of nothing to say to her. If he died in this moment, he feared he would be long in Purgatory.

'Now I think I would do anything,' Mrs Eckdorf said, 'to be no more in need. Father, do you understand?' She cried out loudly that she would lie all day on the hard earth, bitten by maggots, to perish by the sun. It was the needy, she said again, who made his God for him.

'You must not speak like that.'

'I would have given myself to O'Shea, Father. For the first time in my life –'

'I cannot listen to talk like that. I cannot, Mrs Eckdorf –'

'I have told you of my life, I have confessed everything to you. Father, will you help me now?'

He gestured in an anxious way, a motion that suggested his will to help her and simultaneously his own helplessness.

She told him about the arrival of Mr Smedley in the hotel and the later arrival of Mrs Dargan and Morrissey. He was in a locked room now, without his clothes. He was a degenerate: there was wickedness in his eyes, he didn't mind what he said or did.

Father Hennessey moved his head, turning it slightly away. Why had she come to Thaddeus Street?

'I know what I must do,' Mrs Eckdorf said. 'I know it blindly, as I have known everything else about O'Neill's Hotel, as I guessed at tragedy and as the truth came to me. I must anoint the feet of this degenerate.'

He looked beyond her, at the books on his bureau, at his fountain-pen and the white paper beside it. He closed his eyes and shook his head.

'No,' he said.

'It is for courage to do that that I have come to you. I know it in my heart, I know it all over my body and in my brain as well: when I kneel with the bowl and towel my forgiving will begin.'

'Mrs Eckdorf, there is no need to anoint anyone's feet. If you have locked some man into a room –'

'He stood there in the hall, Father, bargaining for his pleasure. I listened to him and looked at him. "There is a reason why this wretch is here," I said to myself. And suddenly I was told. In this holy hotel –'

'The hotel is not holy,' interrupted Father Hennessey mechanically.

'The proud cannot forgive. I felt myself told that I must kneel before him. He shall become my father and my mother, and Miss Tample, and my mother's lovers, and Hoerschelmann and Hans-Otto Eckdorf. And other people.'

'No, Mrs Eckdorf –'

'And yet I seek the strength for that. I am asking you to help me, Father. I am asking to come to your God.'

He repeated that there was no need to anoint a man's feet. That was a nonsensical notion that had accidentally strayed into her mind. She was confused, he pronounced as gently as he could; he asked her to be calm.

'It is not a mistake,' she replied. 'I felt that God speaking to me as He has spoken to Mrs Sinnott in her hotel. He has become used to speaking to people in her hotel –'

'No, Mrs Eckdorf.'

'You said humility. A moment ago you said humility.'

'Humility is a state of mind, Mrs Eckdorf. You are taking too much upon yourself. No one has set you a penance.'

'How do you know?'

'I'm a priest –'

'You're smug,' cried Mrs Eckdorf shrilly. 'You're a smug man sitting there.'

Emotionally, she reminded him that there was a body burning beneath her clothes. She had been a child once, and nothing had given her solace. She came from a world that was strange to him and yet she was a human being: she ate and slept, she washed herself, and sometimes fell ill. She had a human temper, and impatience; she cried salty human tears.

'All I wanted was that you'd give me your blessing. All I wanted was to hear you say I must display my willingness to forgive by performing an action that disgusts me. The man is waiting there.'

He found it hard to imagine her as the child she had described, walking with her father. Whether she was sane or mad didn't seem to matter: he could feel no pity for her because she spoke as she did, and he realized then that she repelled him. If it was true what she said, that other people's treatment of her had turned her into what she was, it wasn't a help to remember it. He thought of the fears and superstitions of O'Shea, and appreciated their simplicity. He was used to such fears and superstitions, and to birth and death and the smell of poverty, but not to this ungodly mess. She was a vandal. She was guilty of pride, presumption, blasphemy, falsehood, heartlessness. She was wrapped up in pretence. She was guilty of inventing a God to suit her own needs, she ordered a God as she might order a dress. She spoke of anointing the feet of some man, her careless language seeming to spit upon the beliefs of other people. He had denied that he hated her: he'd been wrong to do that. He would pray for her when she left him, but he could not do so now: while she was in the room he could not keep revulsion from him. He gave in to it, unable any longer to prevent himself: all charity left him.

'You're saying your God's a bearded face,' she cried out, 'that isn't there at all. You're saying there is nothing but the neediness of the human heart. You're telling me to travail alone. You're telling me to clear off and leave you in whatever peace it is you know.'

'I am saying none of those things, Mrs Eckdorf. I would sincerely like to help you.'

'What good's your God if He's here one minute and gone the next? What good's your God when the breath of a schoolmistress is quickened by passion? What good's your God when a mother laughs and gets into bed with a perfumed Frenchman? I felt a warmth and you have cruelly taken it away. I would have shown my willingness by anointments in a back-street bawdy-house – '

'Anointing feet has nothing to do with it,' shouted Father Hennessey. 'God does not expect you to anoint the feet of anyone.'

'God is a disease in all your minds,' cried Mrs Eckdorf with greater force. 'My photographs will illustrate a myth.'

She turned away again, about to go. With a levelness in his voice, emphasizing each word equally, Father Hennessey spoke to her back.

'O'Neill's Hotel cannot be called a bawdy-house,' he said. 'Nor do those people for a moment believe that God acts particularly and directly through Mrs Sinnott. You are dramatizing everything, including your own state of gracelessness. For me you represent a contemporary decadence. You act in pride and bitterness. You are telling lies.'

'You stupid man,' snapped Mrs Eckdorf in her old, professional manner. Abruptly she left the room.

Having paused in the brushing of the maroon carpet, O'Shea
was imagining a scene in which Mrs Eckdorf was writing out
a cheque. She was blowing in order to dry the ink when he
heard a voice calling him from one of the first-floor bedrooms.
He went to investigate and discovered a locked door. When he
rattled the handle the voice spoke again, asking him who he
was.

'I'm the porter. What are you doing in there? Who are you?'

O'Shea placed an ear against the door and heard that the man
within had been deprived of his clothes, and had been locked
into the room by a lunatic who was coming back in order to
anoint his feet.

'Can you get me out and get my clothes back?' whispered Mr
Smedley. 'I've got a plane to catch.'

At that moment another voice called out in the hotel, that of
Mrs Eckdorf.

'O'Shea!' called Mrs Eckdorf in the hall, and O'Shea left the
locked door and went to where she stood.

'Get a taxi and then carry down my baggage,' she ordered in
a peremptory way.

'You're not going? You're never –'

'Quickly, O'Shea.'

She left him standing there and strode smartly up the stairs.
She was not smiling. He called after her, asking if anything was
the matter. She told him to look slippy.

He carried her suitcases from her room and put them in a
taxi. On four occasions when he spoke to her she didn't reply.
She offered him no payment for her stay in the hotel, she did
not mention that she would be returning in order to make
arrangements for its purchase. She stepped into the car, looking

more severe than he had seen her looking before. He returned to the hall and stood staring ahead of him, not knowing what to think. Five or so minutes later, still confused, and gazing intently at the coloured glass of the hotel doors, he was aware that the glass moved. Eugene Sinnott entered the hotel.

'Where's that woman?' he said.

O'Shea told him, and Eugene nodded with satisfaction. He had come back, he said, to tell her she must go. You couldn't put up with a performer like that about the place, upsetting everybody. In the Excelsior Bar he'd been mentioning the trouble they'd had with her, and Eddie Trump had strongly advised him to give her her marching orders. Falsifying the details, Morrissey had said that she had struck him twice.

'But she's wanting to buy the hotel,' cried O'Shea. 'She'll come back, Mr Sinnott.'

'You're a terrible eejit, O'Shea.'

'Let me out of this bloody room,' demanded the distant voice of Mr Smedley, no longer discreetly muffled but coming as a roar that echoed through the hall, causing Eugene to jump.

'What on earth's that?' he asked.

'She locked a man in a room,' said O'Shea mournfully, 'so that she could wash his feet.'

Mrs Eckdorf returned to the hotel in which originally she had stayed. 'I did not ever say I was not returning,' she protested to the manager. 'I moved out for one night only on business. That was made quite clear to some foolish clerk, who took it upon himself to forward all my luggage and, I ask you, the bill.'

The manager apologized. He thought there'd been something unusual in the manner of Mrs Eckdorf's going: the foolish clerk had in fact been dismissed. Unfortunately, her room had been given to someone else, this being a busy time of year. Hearing that, Mrs Eckdorf shrugged: it was no affair of hers, she sharply said, the internal difficulties of an hotel, and in the end a room was found for her.

Sipping a glass of cognac, she unpacked her belongings. Then she took off her clothes and stepped into a foamy bath.

*

The clothes of Mr Smedley remained in the sideboard in the dining-room and were not discovered for four months. In the meanwhile, Mr Smedley, wearing clothes belonging to Eugene Sinnott, left O'Neill's Hotel. He walked the length of Thaddeus Street with Eugene, relating all that had happened to him, but he noticed that his companion didn't seem to be listening. 'Will you take a drink?' Eugene enquired when they arrived at Riordan's public house, and Mr Smedley said he could do with a drink but had neither money nor cheques. 'Come in anyway,' invited Eugene.

They drank together in the Excelsior Bar and to Mr Smedley's great surprise Eugene offered to supply him with money in return for his permanent address and an I.O.U. They drank some more together. Mr Smedley missed the last air-flight of the night and said it didn't matter. 'I got the wrong end of the stick,' he said. 'I thought at first that woman was the *madame.*'

'There's something up with her,' said Eugene Sinnott.

Later that night, after Eugene had entered a familiar state of inebriation, Mr Smedley walked away from Thaddeus Street to the hotel where his luggage was. It was still raining. The ends of his trousers trailed through puddles; he felt a dampness spreading on his back. In good faith, he thought, he had accepted the word of the man who had shown him photographs the night before. In good faith, he had come to the hotel at the time specified, expecting what had been promised to him, but instead of that his clothes had been stolen and he had been subjected to ridicule. He had been insulted and sworn at by a lunatic, he had been obliged to tie a bedspread about his naked body and then to dress himself in the clothes of another man. The euphoria that his hours in the Excelsior Bar had induced began to evaporate beneath the discomfort caused by the rain. Only the man whose clothes he wore had shown him human decency; a uniformed porter had told him to walk naked through the streets.

As Mr Smedley mulled over his considerable misfortunes, he saw ahead of him, coming towards him with his head down, the undersized man who had instigated everything. He waited in a doorway. When Morrissey was about to pass he drove out an arm to prevent him.

'Good night, sir,' said Morrissey, and then saw that his companion was not one he would himself have chosen.

'You bastard,' said Mr Smedley.

'I'm sorry about that, sir. Agnes was unavailable.'

'You stole my clothes.'

'Ah, no.'

'Where are they?'

'I never touched your clothes, sir.'

'You and the woman between you. You took my money and my clothes.'

'No,' said Morrissey.

Mr Smedley hit his adversary on the neck. He struck him another blow, meaning to land it on the side of the face but striking instead Morrissey's nose. Blood flowed at once.

'Stop it,' pleaded Morrissey, a request that angered Mr Smedley more. He hadn't hit a man for twenty years, he said, and he intended to make up for it.

Morrissey fell to the wet pavement and lay still, hoping that the attack would cease. But Mr Smedley's two hands gripped his shoulders and stood him on his feet again. 'I want to know where my clothes are,' he said. 'Can you hear me?'

'Will you leave me alone? I didn't touch your clothes. I fixed you up with Mrs Dargan –'

Mr Smedley hit him again. He allowed Morrissey to strike the pavement a second time. He rolled the body into the running gutter and then picked it up. He looked into Morrissey's eyes.

'You took my clothes.'

'I did not, sir. I'm bleeding all over me, sir.'

'Where are my clothes?'

'You've nearly killed me, Mr Smedley. I could report this, sir.'

'You sold them. You took the money. There was an air-ticket in the wallet.'

Again Mr Smedley's fist rose and fell. He punched Morrissey in the stomach and then dropped him on to the pavement. He bent down. 'You showed me photographs,' he said. 'You promised me a woman. I came to that hotel in good faith. You took advantage of me because you know I can't go to the police. I'm going to kick your face in.'

In a whisper Morrissey said he was in need of medical and spiritual aid. He reminded Mr Smedley of the presence of Mrs Eckdorf in the hall that afternoon: it was she, he said, who had been up to no good. Still lying on the pavement, he asked for mercy.

Mr Smedley's hands felt in the pockets of the disabled man. They drew out small change and a comb, the paper-backed books on astrology, and the photographs of Agnes Quin, Mrs Dargan, Mrs Kite and Beulah Flynn. He tore these into small pieces, which he allowed to fall on Morrissey's inert body. He would keep the books and read them, he decided. He broke the comb in half; the money, he said, came to three shillings and five pence. He jingled it in his hand.

Morrissey, his eyes closed and running with tears, heard the footsteps of Mr Smedley moving away from him. Why was it he, he wondered, whom men jammed in the stomach with their fingers and other men turned savagely upon, when all he had ever done was to attempt to help such men? Why was it he whom the insane attacked without warning? He rose painfully to his feet. His head felt giddy. His body was wet all over. He felt a gush of fresh warmth on his face as more blood came out of his nose. He had done that man no harm of any kind; he had never done harm to a man or to a woman. Did it harm anyone that occasionally he took stuff out of Woolworth's? Did it harm anyone that occasionally he extracted from strangers small sums of money in return for services?

Wearily, Morrissey walked on, reflecting that once again he had trusted a human being, and as a result had been left for dead on an empty street. He hadn't even his photographs now or books to consult in the presence of Mrs Sinnott, or the small sum of money that he had earned that evening by standing about getting wet. He walked towards O'Neill's Hotel, where in his wet clothes he would lie on the floor of the hall and be wakened in the morning by the boot of a half-wit.

'Extraordinary things have happened to me in this city,' said Mrs Eckdorf in the bar of her hotel at half-past one on the morning of August 11th. 'You would scarce believe,' she said.

She was with people who were talking about an accident to a horse. On Friday afternoon, one of these people said, in full view of all, including the President and the Papal Nuncio, a horse had had to be slaughtered. An Irish horse, another said, a bay gelding called Tubbermac. They appeared to be talking about show jumping: she displayed an interest, liking to have people to talk to.

'On Friday afternoon?' She had been somewhere called Booterstown, she told them, on Friday afternoon, and earlier in Terenure. Before that she'd been relaxing in a cemetery.

'He was approaching the thirteenth fence,' one of her companions said. 'A foreleg snapped with a crack you could hear.'

She nodded.

'I've had a time of it I can tell you,' she confessed a little later. 'I'm a professional photographer. I came here on a story.'

Her companions, whose spirits had all been reduced by the memory of a horse being slaughtered, seemed pleased at the change of subject. 'Photographer?' one of them said. 'I do like this hotel,' another murmured.

After a time, Mrs Eckdorf said to the people around her that the notion of God had recently made sense to her because she had felt a warmth. The people politely paid attention.

'And then,' said Mrs Eckdorf, 'a priest destroyed my God. D'you understand?'

The people said they did not, and were surprised when Mrs Eckdorf did not apparently pursue the subject but spoke instead of an elderly woman whose son had had no alternative but to revolt against the weight of her piety. He had ravaged an orphan girl that his mother had adopted, Mrs Eckdorf in passing said.

The people who had talked about the slaughtered horse left her rather quickly then, all of them yawning and saying they were sleepy. They took their glasses with them and went to another room, where they unanimously decided that Mrs Eckdorf, who in their company had consumed a lot of alcohol, was drunk.

Mrs Eckdorf found the night-porter in a cubby-hole in the hall. She sat down beside him and told him that her mother had taken perfumed Frenchmen into her bed. 'That is my life,' said Mrs Eckdorf, 'if it interests you at all.'

The night-porter, finding it hard to make much of Mrs Eckdorf's conversation, informed her that he had won a sum of money that evening. The unexpected winning of a sum of money, he meditatively argued, made up for many a reversal in life. He had won eight pounds on a dog called Yellow Printer, which had triumphed in the Greyhound Derby by one and a half lengths over Russian Gun.

'That bloody priest was wrong,' cried Mrs Eckdorf. 'What does a priest know, for Christ's sake?'

'What d'you mean, madam?' the night-porter asked, worried because she had raised her voice.

'Tell that priest,' she cried, 'to ask the needy his questions. Tell him to let the needy lead him to a God of their own. Will you do that for me?' she requested. 'Will you go to the priest now?'

Mrs Eckdorf, who had risen to her feet, swayed on them.

'Will you?' she cried again, and since it was apparent to the night-porter that she was not herself and was at last on the way to bed, he said that he would.

'Thaddeus Street,' she said. 'A Father Hennessey, an awful man. Look when you are there at the yellow hotel.'

'I will, of course,' said the night-porter. 'I'll go in five minutes.'

'O'Neill's Hotel.'

'I'll have a look at it.'

'Go now.'

'Yes,' said the night-porter, busying himself with keys and pieces of paper. 'I'll just see to these first.'

'Born of the need within them,' said Mrs Eckdorf. 'Any God they can find will do. Will you remember those words for the priest? Born of desperation?'

'Born of desperation,' repeated the night-porter. 'I'll tell him that, surely.'

He watched while Mrs Eckdorf mounted the stairs, thinking

to himself, as often he had thought during his nightly vigils before, that drink was a curse.

Unable to sleep, Father Hennessey prayed that Mrs Eckdorf might become calm in her mind. He prayed that she would cease to distort the truth with dramatic adornment, as the truth about St Attracta and St Damien and St Cosma had been adorned. He prayed for her happiness, and that she might receive the comfort she sought. He tried to understand the world she occupied and had told him about. He heard again music by Bach played quietly as a background, and saw a silent man-servant passing drinks among elegant people. He imagined the books she composed, all of which appeared to be an invasion of human privacy and were for that reason interesting to some, being perceptive and even charming. A fashion that would pass, he thought: perhaps it didn't matter.

His conscience felt lighter after he had prayed for a time. Towards dawn he slept.

Mrs Sinnott had wakened at midnight and had lain for a while, thinking her familiar thoughts. She had sensed the splattering of rain in Thaddeus Street, which made her feel cosy in her bed, and she remembered a night when she had been awakened by lightning, when the children were small. Eugene had been frightened and Enid had consoled him. She herself had gone to the kitchen to heat some milk. Remembering that, she had dropped off to sleep again.

Hours later she woke with the face of Mrs Eckdorf in her mind. There was a wretchedness in that painted face she thought; there was something the matter with the woman.

She had seen her in Thaddeus Street, a white figure walking towards the hotel. O'Shea had written a message to say that a person from Germany had come to stay. O'Shea had brought her into her room. And later she had sat with her. And then she had taken all those photographs at the birthday tea.

Why had a woman come like that? What was the matter with her? The two questions chased one another in Mrs Sinnott's mind. For a time it seemed that the face of Mrs Eckdorf was weeping, and then that she was screaming out in anguish. These soundless visions frightened Mrs Sinnott. She fell asleep and dreamed that Mrs Eckdorf was pleading with her desperately, unable to understand that she could not hear her. In her dream she made the necessary allowance, knowing that a stranger could not be expected to understand that she was deaf. She saw Mrs Eckdorf in Thaddeus Street and tried to reach her by climbing from the window. She hurt herself. She felt a pain throbbing in her body. Her father shook his head at her. In the yard he gestured at the hornbeam tree, mouthing out words at her, ordering her not to climb it. She ran into the kitchen and sat on a chair, watching her mother and looking up when Leo Sinnott came into the kitchen. She tried to go to him, but the pain in her body held her back. It increased when she moved her legs. She had broken all her ribs, she thought, when she fell from the hornbeam tree; everyone would be cross with her. Mrs Eckdorf came into the kitchen and danced with Leo Sinnott. They waltzed round and round, while her mother and father clapped their hands together and O'Shea stood by the door taking photographs. She had fallen down, trying to cross the kitchen: she pushed her body along the flagstones but found the effort painful. Nobody noticed her as she lay there. Eugene came into the kitchen, and Philomena, and Enid and Timothy John and Desmond Gregan. Agnes Quin looked down at her but did not notice that she was lying in pain. Morrissey sat beside her and wrote prophecies in an exercise-book. She went on making the effort, but the effort tired her and the pain increased. She was dying on the floor, she thought; she was dying while all of them were around her and none of them noticed. And then Mrs Eckdorf's face came to her again, with red marks all over it as if it had been struck, with tears streaming on the cheeks. The lips were drawn back, the mouth was rigidly open, as though a furious grief poured out from it. She tried to speak to Mrs Eckdorf. She tried to explain that she was too tired to move her body, that the pain was numbing her as she died on the floor. The face was full of misery and confusion. She tried to make a gesture but she was too exhausted to raise her arm. She tried to apologize with her eyes but she failed in that too. The face was the face of an orphan who had come to her. The face went on suffering before her, until someone came and gently closed her eyes.

16

Mrs Eckdorf took a knife from the breakfast table and walked with it in her hand across the dining-room of the hotel.

Waiters eyed her, considering it unusual that a guest should openly filch cutlery. The people with whom she had spent some hours the night before observed the knife in her hand and wondered about it too. 'She probably has string on a parcel to cut,' one waiter said to another, and the second waiter agreed that this might be so. The people who had told her about the slaughtered horse didn't form a theory about the knife, and soon forgot about it.

The manager of the hotel, who had the evening before gone to much trouble in order to accommodate Mrs Eckdorf with a room, saw her with the knife in her hand and saw that the knife bore traces of the butter that she had spread on her toast. He memorized the fact that this guest had removed a knife from the dining-room, so that later it could be established that the knife had been returned.

In her room Mrs Eckdorf washed the knife and put it in her handbag. She felt the need of a knife's protection. She felt that when she returned to Thaddeus Street she would be physically attacked: O'Shea and Eugene Sinnott would attack her, and when that happened she would take the knife from her handbag and brandish it. She put the strap of her camera around her neck: in the azure-blue room Mrs Sinnott might like to have her photograph taken again.

In the hall of O'Neill's Hotel Mrs Eckdorf witnessed the figures of Eugene Sinnott and O'Shea coming down the stairs, with the dog trailing behind them. Her hand sought the knife in her bag, but the men seemed not to be aggressive. Eugene said nothing to her. He passed into the passage that led to the kitchen. O'Shea said that Mrs Sinnott was dead.

'Dead?' cried Mrs Eckdorf.

'She is dead now,' said O'Shea.

He followed Eugene, and his dog followed him.

'Dead?' said Mrs Eckdorf again.

The men had not attacked her because the old woman had died. They would not attack her in the house of a dead woman. Voices would be hushed in the house today: there would be neither violence nor unpleasantness, nor horror for Philomena. Slowly, she ascended the stairs.

In her room Mrs Sinnott lay as she had died. Her eyes were closed; there was no suffering in her thin face. O'Shea had lighted two candles and pulled the blinds down. In her room the stillness seemed greater than it had been before.

Mrs Eckdorf looked round. The red exercise-books were stacked as they had been, beneath the deep window-sills. A few were on the table by her chair.

'You have died,' said Mrs Eckdorf, 'and they will bury you in the ground and you will rot.'

Wearily, she prepared the Mamiya, her fingers moving automatically from long practice, her mind elsewhere. She had come back from school at the end of one term and her mother had not been at Paddington. She had taken a taxi, but when she arrived at their house she found her mother was not there either. She had discovered as well that she hadn't enough money to pay the driver. She had never rid herself of the feeling of desperation that had overcome her then, as the taxi-man waited, becoming angry. She'd managed to borrow a pound from the caretaker of a block of flats, and her mother had laughed when she told her, even though she'd been crying. The man with her mother had said a little matter like that shouldn't make a big girl cry. 'Pay back the caretaker,' she had screamed at her mother, who had promised to and then forgotten.

Dutifully, she worked the Mamiya, the professional part of her continuing to operate. The Seikoshna-S shutter flicked, as swift as light in the action. It flicked again, and again and again, in the silent gloom. She took her shoes off and stood on the bed, straddling the body that the bed contained. She changed the

242

lens, thinking of her mother's friend saying that a little matter like that shouldn't make a big girl cry. With skill, she photographed the dead face.

In the hall Eugene Sinnott said to her that she must not again return to the hotel.

'We can't have you here upsetting people,' he said. 'I thought you'd come to get something you'd left. O'Shea says you were in with my mother.'

She took the knife from her handbag and held it before her. Eugene looked at it. She did not say anything.

'We can't be dealing with persons like you,' said Eugene. 'We have a funeral to see to now, Mrs Eckdorf.'

'I'm sorry, Mr Sinnott –'

'You caused an extreme embarrassment for myself and O'Shea yesterday –'

'I only took photographs. I'll explain to you, Mr Sinnott.'

'You locked a man in a room.'

'I'm tired, Mr Sinnott.' She returned the knife to her handbag, realizing again that it was not necessary to protect herself.

'Do not return here, Mrs Eckdorf.'

'There is no need to now.'

She continued to speak to him. She had come that morning to talk to his mother in an exercise-book, as he had and as others had. Yesterday she'd felt a peace in the presence of his mother. She was sorry she'd caused trouble by locking a man in a room: a notion had come to her that she should humiliate herself, but Father Hennessey had said that that was nonsensical and maybe it had been, but how was a person to know, when a person felt something strongly? The God of the needy had spoken through his mother, and now his mother was dead. The God of the needy was a myth, but did that matter? A myth could be potent too, a myth could be a solace and a balm when people failed each other in that respect. His mother, silent in a silent room, surrounded with sacred references and rich in human goodness, made the myth a warm and living thing: you could sit there and give yourself to it, and feel it doing you good. Was there anything wrong in that?

She repeated the question when he didn't reply. He said:

243

'I cannot listen to you, Mrs Eckdorf. No one here can understand you.'

'I shall remain in your city until the time your mother is buried, Mr Sinnott, and then I shall go away from your city for ever.'

She left the hotel, and Eugene shivered. She gave him the creeps, he thought, as Agnes Quin had thought also.

The family came to the hotel. Mr Gregan said he was glad to learn that Mrs Eckdorf had packed her bags. It was an amazing thing that she had turned up in that manner, he said, and Eugene told him how she had returned to the hotel with a knife, although she'd made no attempt to attack him with it. O'Shea was still in the dumps, he said, having seen the error of his ways after Father Hennessey had had another word with him, ordering him to take a hold on himself. Mr Gregan said he'd read in a newspaper one time about a woman of a similar kind who used to go into people's houses on the pretence that she was a saleswoman of bathing costumes. Once she was in she wouldn't go out again. She used to sit down at the kitchen table under the assumption, apparently, that she was one of the family. She'd talk away, twenty-two to the dozen, until policemen were fetched to remove her.

In a lowered voice Eugene related to Mr Gregan the facts of Mr Smedley's captivity. 'A very decent man,' he said, 'that she had imprisoned in an upstairs room.' He related other facts: Morrissey had been making immoral use of the hotel ever since the time he'd given him permission to lie in the hall at night as a temporary arrangement. O'Shea had complained that Agnes Quin had been bringing elderly men into the rooms, but he'd always put it down to O'Shea's imagination. Now, it seemed, it was true. Morrissey and Agnes Quin had abused the hospitality they'd been offered. They'd been turning the joint into a kip while his back was turned. Father Hennessey, who'd had the information from the photographer, had spoken sternly to him about it and he was going to have to give Morrissey the sharp side of his tongue. 'Bedad,' exclaimed Mr Gregan, already fully cognizant of the activities of Morrissey in this respect, 'you'd hardly credit it.'

O'Shea spoke to no one. He made necessary arrangements and went about his ordinary tasks with a mind that was empty of thought. He had found her as he had always known one morning he would find her. She had died peacefully, which was what she had deserved.

The family sat in the kitchen that Sunday morning and drank tea, agreeing about the details of the funeral. After that, Mr Gregan said that Eugene had been telling him that the photographer of yesterday, having left the hotel, had returned that morning with a knife. For the benefit of the others, Eugene repeated much of what he had related to his brother-in-law, but because of the presence of the two women he did not include certain details. The photographer, he told them, had managed to incarcerate an unknown Englishman in one of the hotel rooms for the purpose of washing his feet, although since she had later arrived in the hotel with a weapon he was inclined to wonder if she hadn't had it in her mind to inflict an injury on the man.

Mrs Gregan said she hoped O'Shea had recovered himself, and Eugene passed on the information that Father Hennessey had told O'Shea not to be a damn eejit.

The family sat as they had sat around the birthday table, and the events in the past that had so interested Mrs Eckdorf seemed in no way to concern them. Timothy John was not aware of the circumstance of his conception. Mrs Gregan, although at other times she recalled the occasion, did not recall it now. She had behaved badly that night, and often, when she saw her brother in the kitchen, she hoped he forgave her. Philomena did not think now what sometimes she did think: that she had been the culpable one. In the hotel, before their marriage, Eugene had occasionally sought her out to talk to her and embrace her, and when he had come to her room that night she had not turned him away. She had felt an excitement when she saw him standing there; she had opened the door a little more.

On this Sunday morning Eugene did not remember the occasion either. Long since, he had lived the shame out of his life: he had married the girl at his mother's request, he had witnessed the marriage becoming impossible. Hate would have grown as the child grew, which was what his mother recognized when she admitted her mistake. He felt sorry when Philomena's terror came back to him now, but to have felt that sorrow every day of his life would have been too much for either of them to bear.

The past was tied away. Philomena was a mother, Eugene's sister was another man's wife, Eugene was the inheritor of an hotel he had no interest in. He lived on money accumulated in the past because he preferred to do that rather than have the hotel full of people: he liked an unexacting life.

'Well, she'll hardly trouble us again,' remarked Mrs Gregan.

Philomena agreed, shaking her head. At a time like this in particular, you couldn't put up with a woman who perplexed you.

'I was telling Eugene,' said Mr Gregan, 'of this one I read about. She used to call at houses with a case full of bathing-costumes. For all we know, it could be the same offender.'

Timothy John displayed an interest, and his uncle said you always had to be careful about who you let into a house. With an hotel it was different, but with a private house you could land yourself in trouble. He drew attention to the embarrassment a saleswoman of bathing-costumes could cause to householders by imagining, or pretending to imagine, that she was a member of the family. You had to be very careful.

When they had drunk their tea, they each took their leave of Mrs Sinnott. The exercise-books would now be destroyed. She would remain in each of their memories differently, and she would fade with varying degrees of swiftness. Their conversations with her had been ordinary, only charged with strangeness because she had never learned to read their lips and because she had never imposed her own language on them. She had made her visitors enter her silent world, which now, as each of them regarded her face, seemed only a little more silent than it had been. They prayed for her soul, they wished her well.

Morrissey, who had that morning left the hotel before it was known that Mrs Sinnott had died, was in an ice-cream parlour in O'Connell Street, reading a newspaper he had found in a litter-bin. He had noticed people looking at his bruised face with curiosity rather than with pity or concern. A gang of youths who had been occupying the tables around him had openly referred to his condition, shouting the names of known pugilists, as if to imply that they were in the presence of just such a champion. They had sat with butts of cigarettes in their mouths, at the same time drinking ice-cream sodas through straws. That was the youth of the country, Morrissey thought, on the way home from Mass on a Sunday morning: what kind of a future could any country have with types like that? He watched them leave the ice-cream parlour, pushing their way roughly through the tables, shouting and laughing. Men had gone to their graves so that these fellows could live in idleness and comfort. 'Wouldn't it sicken you?' he remarked to an elderly woman who was sitting at a table next to his. The woman made a non-committal gesture, and when he continued in his castigation she picked up her cup of coffee and moved to a more distant table.

With the newspaper spread out before him, he reflected that Agnes Quin would soon become tired of wiping floors in a convent: one night she would be again there in a doorway and he would welcome her back, not reminding her that she had omitted to say good-bye to him. She was trash, as he had always thought, a woman who would hire her body and had no consideration for anyone. He bet himself a penny that within three months she'd be hearing the call of the pavements and wouldn't have the strength to resist it.

Morrissey sat for two hours, until a waitress approached him and asked him if he required anything else. In order to pass a further period of time, he asked the price of various items that the ice-cream parlour offered. The waitress handed him a menu.

'I was in a train crash,' he said, pointing at the cuts and bruises on his face. 'Did you read about it?' He put the menu on the table without opening it. Hooligans had damaged the rails outside Bray, he said, causing a loss of life.

'D'you want more?'

He'd had nothing so far, he reminded the waitress. He enquired the cost of a cup of tea.

'You had tea already, mister.'

Morrissey shook his head, and when the waitress pointed at the empty cup in front of him he claimed that its contents had been drunk by someone else. The waitress argued, and so did he.

'How could you know what I had,' he demanded, 'since you've only this minute come on duty? D'you deny you've this minute come on duty?'

'The other girl told me –'

'The other girl was talking through her hairpins. D'you deny that you just came up those stairs from the basement?'

'You had a cup of tea two hours ago.'

He shook his head. He'd been up all night, he reminded the waitress, attending to the injured in a train crash. He'd carried stretchers with dead people on them. He'd telephoned for a priest and two doctors. He'd put legs in splints and cleared out cuts that would turn your stomach. After the ordeal he had gone straight to first Mass and then he'd walked about the streets, trying to forget it. He had entered the ice-cream parlour in order to rest his bones, and the next thing was he was being accused of consuming tea that someone else had consumed. He stood up. He said he was leaving behind the newspaper he'd been reading, so that the waitress could read it herself, at her leisure. She protested again: he told her he'd report her to the tourist authorities for inhospitality. He left the ice-cream parlour, hearing the voice of the waitress calling after him and another voice advising her to let him go.

He walked through light rain, considering how he might obtain some money. On O'Connell Bridge he saw the pimpled soldier with whom a few days before he had attempted to be friendly. He was standing with two girls, having his photograph taken by a street photographer. A second soldier was also in the picture, a red-haired youth whose countenance was affected in the same way as his companion's. Morrissey increased his speed, fearing that now, encouraged in the presence of his friends, the soldier he'd been with might seek to extract some kind of revenge for the firm words he'd addressed to him. They were great cowards, he reflected, these soldiers; they always had to have a companion or two before they'd dare to start anything.

Imagine females having their photographs taken with cannon-fodder like that.

Morrissey passed into D'Olier Street and round by the railings of Trinity College, until he found himself in Grafton Street. He followed a well-dressed man and woman, and when they paused outside Switzer's to survey the goods in the windows he approached them. He'd been in a rail crash, he said, and had spent the night attending to those who had been more seriously damaged than himself. He apologized for his clothes and the battered condition of his face. The man and the woman, who were foreigners and did not fully understand what he was saying, smiled and nodded at him. 'Rail crash?' the woman said. He fell into step with them as they walked on from Switzer's. He gestured again at his clothes and his face, deprecating them: he was a lung specialist, he said: hooligans had derailed a train.

Morrissey remained in the company of these people while they walked the length of Grafton Street. As he stood with them at the corner of Stephen's Green he said:

'Since you're strangers in the city, would we have a drink together? I'd like to stand you a drink. A drink,' he repeated, making a drinking motion to his lips. 'Me buy.'

The man and the woman, who had told him that they came from Greece, politely declined.

'Drink,' repeated Morrissey. He pointed at himself. 'Me pay. You strangers.'

'That is kind,' the woman said.

'This way,' said Morrissey.

He led the way into a bar and sat the Greek couple down at a table. They held a brief discussion in their own language, deciding what drinks they would have.

'We like Scotch whisky,' the woman said at last, smiling lavishly. The man smiled also. 'It is kind,' the woman said.

'You can't beat the best Scotch,' said Morrissey.

He went to the bar and ordered large measures of whisky. He carried the three glasses to where he had left the Greeks. He drank his quickly. Then, with a show of embarrassment, he began to pat his clothes in search of a wallet. He ran his hands into his trouser pockets and took from one of them the key to

O'Neill's Hotel, which was his only possession that Mr Smedley had overlooked. He injected his face with a look of horror. In the confusion of the rail crash, he said, his money had become lost. He'd had some change which he must have used up, buying cups of tea for the casualties. His wallet had clearly slipped from his pocket.

The woman nudged her husband, who quickly produced a pound. He would pay for the drinks, he haltingly offered. Morrissey shook his head. He took the pound from the man's hand. He returned to the bar and ordered further whisky for the Greeks and for himself. He drank his own while he stood there. His friend was paying for everything, he said to the barman. In a mirror which stretched the length of the bar he noted that the eyes of the Greeks were not upon him. With the pound-note warm in his hand, he slipped away.

He returned to the O'Connell Street area, his eyes sharply on the look-out for whatever he might profit by. At two o'clock he bought a plate of chips in a café, at half-past three he successfully negotiated an entry to a cinema without paying the admission charge. He enjoyed a programme which consisted of two famed feature films, *Diabolical Dr F* and *The Pit and the Pendulum*. 'Isn't it great entertainment?' he remarked to a child seated next to him. 'Great,' agreed the child. During the interval the child, in the company of other children, ate ice-cream and sweets. 'D'you like sweets?' he asked them. They replied that they did, and he said that he liked sweets too. They offered him a toffee with nuts in it, which he savoured contentedly for as long as he could make it last. He bought an ice-cream, paying for it with a two-shilling piece. 'I gave you a half-crown,' he protested to the girl. 'I had only the half-crown on me.' Suspiciously, she handed him an extra sixpence. He thanked her politely. 'You could have this for threepence,' he offered the children when he returned to his seat. He held up the tub of ice-cream, mentioning that the saving involved was 50 per cent. The children agreed to the purchase. He'd been in a train accident, he told them, which was why he was looking so battered.

Afterwards, as he exercised himself on the streets, he was

watchful again. Men coming from a hurling match wore coloured favours in their lapels, a few carried more elaborate insignia, some wore paper caps. They were provincial men, Morrissey considered as he examined their faces: from experience he knew that they often had little money to spare but were willing, for a time at least, to engage in conversation. He walked to the central bus station, where a number of these men were waiting to travel to their homes in the country. He talked to one who was on his own, who told him that later that night he would cycle nineteen miles from where the bus dropped him. In reply Morrissey said that he was in a terrible way, his wallet having been stolen by hooligans. He drew attention to the condition of his face. The man gave him sixpence. Some of these provincial men, he considered, shouldn't be allowed out.

He laughed to himself as he loitered about the Quays, imagining the barman approaching the Greeks and demanding the price of six double whiskies. He laughed, but he felt as well that something would happen to cancel that moment of good fortune; silver clouds, in the experience of Morrissey, tended to have dirty linings. He tapped on the window of a parked car and when the window was wound down he asked the man within if he was in need of a female. The man looked at him in silence, at length enquiring if the female referred to was Morrissey's mother. Morrissey shook his head: he had never known his mother, he said, having been reared in an institution. While he was still speaking, the man spat through the open window and drove away.

Late that evening Morrissey learnt that Mrs Sinnott had died, and he thought at once that this was the fact that cancelled his good luck with the Greeks. It seemed to him that the death of the old woman had been traded for two drinks of Scotch whisky and a pound; and the only consolation he could discover was that there would be no need now to obtain new books of prophecies. In the Excelsior Bar he reflected that an era of his life, which had commenced with Miss Lambe, had come to a conclusion. He considered that fact and, as if to emphasize it, Eugene Sinnott approached him and upbraided him for his misuse of O'Neill's Hotel. He withdrew the permission that had made the hall of the hotel a nightly resting place for Morrissey and he demanded the return of the key which he knew Morrissey possessed.

'You took a key out of my pocket and had another one cut,' Eugene said, 'so that you could get into the hotel at any hour of the night. Hand it up now.'

At first Morrissey denied possession of this key: he always went to the hotel, he said, before O'Shea closed the door at nine o'clock, unless he happened to be with Eugene, in which case he entered the hotel with him. He'd often helped Eugene up the stairs, he reminded him, when Eugene was incapable.

'You're a bloody liar,' replied Eugene, his hand still held out for the key, which in the end Morrissey gave him.

'I'm sorry about your mother,' he said, but Eugene Sinnott said that he could do without his sympathy.

So that was finished too. He'd return to the hotel tonight with Eugene when Eugene was beyond noticing. He'd spend a last night there, and he'd leave in the morning with his shaving things. As he sat alone in a corner of the pink bar, he knew that, apart from this severance, his future would continue as the past had continued. For a matter of minutes he had indulged in a small dream in the presence of the mad woman, before returning to reality with a floor-cloth on his forehead. Now, he'd find alternative accommodation and he would exist as best he could, wending his way through a world of untrustworthy human beings. After a little time it might be that Eugene Sinnott would be so far taken over by drink that he wouldn't be so mean in himself. After a little time O'Shea might die and he could move in himself to keep Eugene company. As long as the hotel stood in Thaddeus Street and as long as Eugene Sinnott continued to disintegrate, there was hope that something good might happen. O'Shea was a much older man than himself: if O'Shea died when he was in the middle of his sixties, and if Eugene Sinnott remained living for a further five years, there would be a favourable chance of getting back into the hotel. In that case he'd have five years of a permanent home before another change happened. It was possible even that O'Shea, being upset by the passing of the old woman, would die sooner, maybe during the coming winter or in the spring. That could give him a run of up to twelve years, provided Eugene Sinnott himself didn't die. He and Eugene could be good companions to one another in the hotel, even if there were differences between them, even if Eugene was inhuman.

It was a question of waiting, of hanging about for something to happen, which was an activity that Morrissey was well used to. In the meantime, he'd go to her funeral and accept it when the family looked down their noses at him. He had a right to see the last of a woman who'd given him sixpence a day and had never insulted him: he was sorry she was dead.

He crouched over an inch of stout in a glass, waiting for Eugene Sinnott to get into a state in which he didn't know what was happening. It was typical that as soon as a kindly woman died her son should lose the last vestiges of humanity. He had never taken coins from the pockets of Eugene Sinnott before, but there was no reason why he shouldn't remove a good few tonight. He wondered what they'd done with the spider, and he resolved to see if it was still in her room. He didn't want Eugene Sinnott's wife or Gregan's wife going about the town with a spider that wasn't meant for them. He'd get hold of it himself and he'd throw it into the river, or maybe sell it to a child or a poor person.

After ten o'clock Mass on Monday, August 12th, the funeral of Mrs Sinnott left the Pro-Cathedral for the cemetery in which, three days before, Mrs Eckdorf had relaxed among the stones.

By the grave, Eugene Sinnott, neatly clothed, stood beside his sister. Philomena stood by her son. Mr Gregan stood alone.

O'Shea, feeling uncomfortable in clothes that were not his uniform, wept without restraint, while not far away Morrissey and Agnes Quin stood among the crowd of people who had known Mrs Sinnott in her lifetime. Eddie Trump was there with Mr Riordan's daughter, and Keogh the grocer, and people from far beyond Thaddeus Street, people who had read of the death in the newspapers and had made a point of attending. The Society of St Vincent de Paul was represented, as were the Dominican Sisters, the Order of Malta, and various trading concerns. For the intentions of all these people Holy Mass would in time be offered, which was something that Mrs Sinnott had long since requested.

Sunlight spread from behind a cloud; the wreaths were almost gay. I'll miss her in her window, Keogh from the grocery thought, and Eddie Trump's wife remembered her father telling her that Mrs Sinnott had been in her girlhood a lovely thing, made lovelier, he'd said, because of her quiet disability.

She will look down and see, said O'Shea to himself; I will carry out all her wishes. I will see to the needs of her son, I will stand by O'Neill's Hotel no matter what it becomes or how much deeper it sinks. I betrayed her in her last days, saying she should go to the nuns. I will absolve my betrayal. I will suffer if she sends me that.

The family wore mourning, Mrs Eckdorf saw: the women's faces were hardly visible behind veils, O'Shea looked like an undertaker. She moved gently through the people until she came to where he was.

'I'm sorry,' she said. 'I'm sorry I was like that to you. I'm sorry she's dead, O'Shea.'

He turned his damp face towards her. He wiped his mouth with the back of a hand. He shook his head, and then looked away again.

'Oh God, by whose mercy the souls of the faithful have rest . . . ' intoned Father Hennessey. 'Release from all bondage of sin . . . '

'O'Shea,' she said. She sought his hand, thinking to stand there with him, together at the funeral of the good woman. But his hand was clenched and he did not release it. 'It's all right,' she said. 'It's all right, O'Shea.'

She felt tears on her cheeks and she wanted O'Shea to see them. She wanted to make it plain to O'Shea that she was the last of Mrs Sinnott's visitors, that if Mrs Sinnott hadn't died she would have come to her room as all the other visitors had, until she felt at peace with the people who had made her a victim, until she felt she could forgive. O'Shea was the only person by the graveside who would understand her, because he had understood her once before. The priest had taken against her, as

Eugene Sinnott and all the others had, as Miss Tample had when she would not allow Miss Tample to take her hand, as her mother had because she was a nuisance in the house when her mother wished for privacy with a friend.

The coffin had been wheeled on a barrow from the little chapel in the older part of the cemetery, where it had rested for a brief time. She had walked at the end of the procession, following the wheeled coffin, behind the priest who had been no help to her, behind all the people who had respected Mrs Sinnott in life and continued to do so now. Motor-cars had halted while they crossed a main road to the newer part of the cemetery, where white marble tombstones gleamed harshly and in thousands on a windswept plain. On other barrows other coffins moved slowly towards open graves. 'Is this the Kinsella funeral?' a man with a woman and two children had asked her, and she had said it was, anxious that there should be as large a crowd as possible at Mrs Sinnott's burial. People came away from burials that had taken place, chattering and sometimes smoking. 'Well, that's that,' a man had remarked, stepping briskly by.

'O'Shea,' she said, seeking his hand again. 'I'm sorry for my lies, O'Shea. I'm crying too, O'Shea.'

But O'Shea moved slightly away, his attention on the coffin that was now being lowered.

'Our Father who art in Heaven,' said Father Hennessey.

'I loved her too,' she said to O'Shea, touching him again. 'I would have loved her more than anyone.'

She sobbed more noisily, and then her sobs became hysterical. She pushed through the people and clambered on to the dug soil and into the grave itself.

With her head bowed, feeling cool in the fresh morning air, Agnes Quin heard a woman screaming and looked up to see that Mrs Eckdorf was being pulled out of the grave of Mrs Sinnott by two grave-diggers. People edged forward, trying to see. Mr Gregan's voice rang loudly out in protest. Father Hennessey seemed uncertain about procedure. One of the children whom Mrs Eckdorf had enticed to the graveside screamed also.

Typical, thought Morrissey, that a scene should take place, a woman screeching and fighting. He watched while, her clothes dirtied with clay, she was led away by the two grave-diggers. Tears were streaming from her eyes, her body was quivering, she appeared to be unable to stand properly It pleased Morrissey to witness this because he knew that, as well as the blows she had struck him, he owed his treatment at the hands of Mr Smedley to her. He followed the grave-diggers, one of whom was murmuring to Mrs Eckdorf in a consoling voice.

'Don't waste your time with that one,' he said.

'What's the matter with her?' one of the grave-diggers quietly enquired, and Morrissey replied that Mrs Eckdorf was keen on methylated spirits.

'Is she a member of the family?' the grave-digger asked, still marching Mrs Eckdorf along with the aid of his colleague. Morrissey laughed.

She heard the laughter, having previously heard Morrissey saying that she was keen on methylated spirits: she did not mind. Both her stockings were torn, she was filthy with dirt from an open grave. In a strange city, her own voice said to her, she had fallen upon a coffin in a grave. Her finger-nails had broken, scratching at the varnished wood. I am dying too, her voice cried out to her, but she knew that was not so.

'She wanted to speak to the woman,' she heard one of the grave-diggers say to Morrissey. 'She kept screaming she wanted a word with her.'

'She was screaming for her mother,' the other man contradicted.

'She didn't know who she was screaming for,' said Morrissey.

'She mentioned God,' said the grave-digger who had spoken first.

She did not remember screaming. She remembered, the day before, taking the knife from the breakfast table in the hotel and going to the other hotel with it. She remembered taking it from her handbag and holding it in front of her. She didn't know why she had done that. She remembered photographing Mrs Sinnott when she was dead: she had done that because the photograph might be useful in a book that had to do with forgiveness and the myth of God. The potency of the myth was what she had to show, how good could come out of people's delusions.

'I'm all right now,' she said. 'I'm quite O.K. again.'

The grave-diggers cautiously released her. The left side of her body was sore with bruising. She said she had a car waiting for her.

'Typical,' said Morrissey, as she walked away, 'a female like that to spoil a funeral.'

On Tuesday afternoons, which was the time he regularly visited her, she was not the same as she had been. Her hair did not gleam like pale gold, but seemed to be a shade of grey. It was tired hair that she'd asked should be cut off short to save her the bother of attention. Her finger-nails were cut back too, and were not brightly red; her lips were as bloodless as any human lips he'd ever seen. A fieriness that had often flashed in her eyes was there no more, and tears belonged to the past. She sat in the clothes they had given her, a grey dress that hung about her like an overall and the black laced shoes of a woman who had not long ago died. She could have new clothes, they'd said to her, now that her money had come through, but she said she didn't want new clothes. Her lips were drawn back crookedly from her teeth in a smile that never left her face – not even, he was told, in sleep. 'Tell me about them,' was what she said, first of all, when he came to her on Tuesday afternoons. 'And the yellow hotel, Father, which has a hornbeam tree outside its kitchen windows. Tell me.'

She talked only about the hotel and the people whose lives she had advanced upon, arriving in an aeroplane. She did not ever again mention her mother or her father, or her mother's lovers, or the schoolmistress at St Monica's School for Girls, or her two German husbands. 'I am sorry about that man I locked up,' she always said at some point during his visits, adding that she knew she had been silly to go on about anointing a stranger's feet: it made no sense to her now, the notion of doing that. Her mind retained only the events of a few days in her life. Her childhood and her marriages were gone from her for ever. 'Tell me,' she said on Tuesday afternoons, and then she would talk herself.

An officer of the gardai had come to his house on the afternoon of Mrs Sinnott's funeral to say that a woman had created a scene in a children's playground on the south side of the city. She had been playing with the children, running about with them as though she were a child herself, and then she had frightened them by screaming. She had taken a knife from her handbag, appearing to imagine that she must protect herself against attack. She had called out his name and the name of Thaddeus Street, she had talked about O'Neill's Hotel and a tragedy there. Then she had calmed down and had gone away, and the children had reported the matter: it would be as well, the officer pointed out, to know something about this woman. The address of the hotel to which she had returned after leaving O'Neill's was ascertained from O'Shea, but when the officer went in search of her there he was informed that she had already left. Father Hennessey and O'Shea had said she came from Munich, but in the hotel register her address was given as Maida Vale, London.

People that night, the night of Mrs Sinnott's funeral, saw Mrs Eckdorf looking into the river from Usher's Quay. She had requested a taxi-driver to drop her at a certain spot, a request the man had questioned, because the hour was late and there was nothing in the way of an hotel or a lodging house near the spot she indicated. People saw her, after the taxi had driven away, opening her white suitcases and emptying their contents into the water below her. They saw her drop the suitcases into the river too, and then she took from her neck a camera and threw it far away. The people watching heard the splash and then, worried about her, began to move to where she stood. As they advanced they saw her take off her hat and then her shoes and then her clothing. She was a naked woman when they arrived at her side. She was as she came into the world, she told them. The world had distressed her, she complained. She said she was happy now.

After she had been admitted to the asylum the same police officer had come again to Thaddeus Street, to tell Father Hennessey all that. They would keep her in the asylum, he said, unless it was the wish of someone that she should be moved to another place. It might be better, he suggested, if she could be returned to Munich or to Maida Vale, or wherever it was she had come from, so that family and friends could visit her on visiting days. 'I think it's Munich,' Father Hennessey said. 'A street called the Lipowskystrasse.'

The officer went away and returned a few weeks later to say that that was correct. The cinder-grey apartment had been discovered; there was quite a lot of money in the bank account of Ivy Eckdorf. She was, or had been, a photographer of some kind, apparently. 'Of some kind,' Father Hennessey repeated. 'She certainly took pictures here.'

In the asylum they suggested to her that perhaps she'd like to return to Munich, but she replied that she had never heard of Munich and would not go there. She asked that Father Hennessey should visit her and when he came the first time she told him that there was something like a night in her mind, a blackness she could not penetrate and must not ever again attempt to penetrate. It was lovely, she said, being where she was. She told him how she felt for the people of O'Neill's Hotel the love that Mrs Sinnott had felt for them, and when he asked her if she would like one or two of them to visit her, Mrs Gregan and Philomena perhaps, she replied that they all did visit her. 'Tell me about them,' she would say then, always in the same way, and he would pause and she would tell him.

'I was a stranger to them and yet they took me in. They made me one of the family, they gave me birthday tea. When they are not here I think of them the whole day long. Father, can you understand a thing like that?'

He had never told them that she was still in the city, in a room in an asylum, and that their faces and their bodies were all she knew now. He saw Eugene in Thaddeus Street and O'Shea in his uniform, occasionally on the streets he caught a glimpse of Morrissey. The others, he imagined, continued as they had continued before, while occupying, for her, a heaven.

On Tuesday afternoons Father Hennessey left behind him the lives of the saints and made his way across the city, on a pilgrimage that was a penance. Always at the same time, at half-past four, he visited the woman who once had been a stranger to him, a woman who in her madness confused all the facts of living, who saw things as they were not and people as they were not, who turned everything upside down and inside out. Often he asked her to pray, but she would not pray, saying that to pray was to address absurdly a bearded face. Her God was different, she said: the God that had been in the azure room, the balm that had reached out from an old, dead woman.

'How could your God create that life for Morrissey or have the parents of Agnes Quin throw her away? How could your God give that life to O'Shea or that one to Eugene Sinnott? We arrive alone in the world, Father: your God's another word for human comfort, and maybe it's enough. But don't be silly, Father: no God created a world like this one.'

In late September, on the last day of that summer, she told him that morning O'Shea had visited her. 'He came with his greyhound,' she said, 'and we lay together, O'Shea and I.'

For a moment he thought she spoke in reality, so matter-of-fact her voice was. 'He thought I was your holy Virgin,' she said. 'O'Shea forgives me.'

She sat in the plain room that she wished to be in and for which her money paid, a room with a bed on a stained floor, two chairs and a cupboard. Through stout green bars she looked out on trees and the gardens of the asylum, in which on warm days she walked herself with other lunatics. She was a good patient.

'When do people die?' she asked Father Hennessey on the day she told him that O'Shea had come with his greyhound.

'At different times,' he answered. 'Sometimes a child dies. People live to be a hundred.'

She shook her head. 'Mrs Sinnott was dead already when I met her in that hotel. She had been dead for years and years, sitting at her window, looking into Thaddeus Street. And Eugene had the smell of death about him too. Her goodness killed some spirit in him, as perhaps his act of violence had killed her. People do kill one another, Father.' He listened while she drifted into muddled talk, about the Gregans and Philomena's love for her son. 'I am dead myself,' she said. 'I am in my heaven.'

She told him about walking in the sunshine through the gardens and the conversations she had, sometimes while she walked and sometimes in her room, with the people of the hotel. 'It is risen like a phoenix-bird,' she said. 'O'Shea was measured today for two new uniforms. O'Shea carries suitcases up and down the stairs, and people come from the Far and the Near East, from Europe and Australia and the two Americas. Eugene Sinnott presides like a king, sharing with favoured guests a bottle of old claret, smoking rich panatellas. There's a red rose in the button-hole of his blue-striped business suit, bonhomie bursts from him, he gives to charity. His wife bustles through the bedrooms, keeping an eye on all her maids, his son draws up accounts and corresponds with foreigners, his sister cooks rare dishes in the kitchen. Timothy John brings a wife to this family hotel, and Philomena kisses her with pleasure because her son is happy. Her son will remain for ever in the prosperous hotel and Philomena is pleased for that, and then forgets about her son, for she has much to do. In the dining-room Agnes Quin, in the black and white habit of her calling, serves the food of Mrs Gregan. Three other maids hurry beneath her scrutiny, carrying plates of soup and oysters and peppery moussaka. In a field some miles away Mr Gregan toils beneath the kindly sun, urging lettuces and tomatoes from the fertile soil. He grows all vegetables, and flowers as well. The little fruit trees he planted will yield, he says, next summer. Youths labour all around him, and Morrissey, his friend and foreman, is always near his side. On two bicycles these friends convey to the hotel the bounty they have grown, wheeling the bicycles over the cobbled yard to the kitchen door. Mrs Gregan smiles, and the two companions return to the good earth, pausing on the way only to savour a little refreshment, for cycling is thirsty work. O'Shea and Morrissey, who occasionally meet, respect one another and have come to admire the qualities that each possesses.

'In turn throughout the year everyone's birthday is celebrated, with paper-chains hanging in the kitchen and nuts and fruit and a specially baked cake, and the favourite sandwiches of the birthday person, and biscuits wrapped in silver paper. Eugene claps his hands at the head of the table. O'Shea pours port. The air is pleasant with the smell of Eugene's cigar. Morrissey reads out the birthday person's luck for the year ahead, Mr Gregan tells a joke or two, his wife touches him affectionately with her hand. Eugene, a heavy drinker, dreams profitably by night and gambles by day, but such play does not affect his proprietorship of O'Neill's Hotel. He has grown a moustache and wears a watch-chain now. In the autumn of last year, when the seasonal pressure had ended, he brought Philomena to Venice, for Eugene is proud of his Venetian blood. He is proud of Philomena too, and who can blame him? Philomena has aged so gracefully. They sat together in the Piazza San Marco listening to the café orchestras, Eugene beating time with a thin walking-stick. One night just after dinner, Philomena wept with happiness. Do you believe me, Father?'

He nodded. 'Of course,' he said.

'On August 11th every year they do not fail to remember specially the old woman who died. She is a legend now in the hotel, among the new people who have come there and among guests who happen to be staying. Those who did not know her see in their mind's eye a woman in an azure room with children's exercise-books all around her, a woman who had never heard the human voice and who had never spoken. In all the bustle of the hotel she is not forgotten, just as she in her time ordained that her husband who was shot, and her own parents, were not forgotten either. A family is a lovely thing, a family stretches back with memories, and reaches to the future. They live the lives they were born to live; there is happiness everywhere in O'Neill's Hotel, and warmth among its people.'

He left her on that September Tuesday, knowing that for the remainder of his life he would hear her speaking as she had spoken now. In the asylum they said she was the happiest woman they had ever admitted, and he remembered her distraught face and her more wretched craziness when first he had met her. In the bus that carried him away he thought again that it was a strange thing to have happened, a woman to have gone mad in a city that was unknown to her, who believed now that she was dead and in a heaven. Was it, as she had once suggested, the emptiness in her life that had bred a desperation which in the end had maddened her? Would she be a normal woman now, living some normal life, married and with children, if once in her distressful need she hadn't thought that the notion of God was absurd? He could offer himself no answer to such questions.

'We concern one another,' she had said in the kitchen of the hotel, and had said it again and repeatedly. She had whispered in the kitchen of people in distant parts of the world, and people in her own life, and people in the lives of Agnes Quin and Morrissey, people who were unknown to those who were present. Strangers were the concern of strangers, she had repeatedly said, and she had proved it in a kind of way, for she, like an itching conscience, was his concern, in her asylum room. She would take a toll of him, he knew that well, for sometimes her madness was knitted into sense. His voice might continue for ever in her ears yet she would not hear it, and all the pillars of the Church could not stifle her private, poor man's God. She had spoken so often of victims that he wondered if, without her knowing it or willing it, he had become hers: a cross to bear at the end of his life. And yet it was not entirely so: when she talked about the hotel as it might have been he sometimes felt that he could listen to her for ever.

He left the bus and walked towards Thaddeus Street, past wastelands and houses boarded up. Such happiness he had never seen before, and he thought of the strangers who had by chance made it for her, whose lives went ordinarily on. That story, he imagined, might indeed make a coffee-table volume that people could pick up in a room where Bach played as a background to their conversation. She had come a long way since the Sunday morning when the cheery Londoner had been felled by his dog. She had lived in bitterness, and with her camera she had taken some kind of revenge even without wishing to. In her beautiful documentary form she had shown the ugliness of people, their violence and their weakness, their viciousness, their agonies and their fears. All that, he guessed, didn't matter much one way or the other: what mattered more was herself, and her fingers gripping a camera like a weapon, her mind respecting no privacy, cruelty coming from cruelty. She had caused revulsion in him once, as a bird of prey might cause revulsion. He had been unable to imagine her as a child, yet being with her now was like being with a child.

On the last day of that summer Father Hennessey entered Thaddeus Street and looked towards the mouldering yellow edifice that was O'Neill's Hotel. The evening sun softly lit it, picking out the letters of its title that were strung in white between rows of windows. For a moment he imagined that painters had come to paint the walls and shine the decorations, that inside there throbbed the life she'd lingered over, that the happiness in her voice ran about among the people, up and down the stairs and into all the rooms. It would be a good thing to happen, he thought, and yet too strange for any world but that of make-believe or madness. Slowly he turned his head and walked the last few paces to his house.

'I'm back,' he called, from habit, in the hall.

He mounted the stairs, his thoughts the same as always they were now at this time on Tuesdays. He wondered and sought to understand, and came to few conclusions. In the mood that possessed him the single certainty he felt was that on her behalf there was something he had to render thanks for. For her at least there was a happy ending.

Penguinews *and* Penguins in Print

Every month we issue an illustrated magazine, *Penguinews*. It's a lively guide to all the latest Penguins, Pelicans and Puffins, and always contains an article on a major Penguin author, plus other features of contemporary interest.

Penguinews is supplemented by *Penguins in Print*, a complete list of all the available Penguin titles – there are now over four thousand!

The cost is no more than the postage; so why not write for a free copy of this month's *Penguinews*? And if you'd like both publications sent for a year, just send us a cheque or a postal order for 30p (if you live in the United Kingdom) or 60p (if you live elsewhere), and we'll put you on our mailing list.

Dept EP, Penguin Books Ltd,
Harmondsworth, Middlesex

Note: *Penguinews* and *Penguins in Print* are not available in the U.S.A. or Canada

Also by William Trevor

The Boarding House

The Boarding House is about a man who tried to build
his own memorial . . . with people.
By selecting carefully, William Wagner Bird filled his
boarding house with people that society would never
miss – even if it noticed they were around.

There was Nurse Clock – ugly without enough
consideration to have a nice personality. Studdy – a
petty thief who could never find anything petty enough.
And Miss Clerricot who wanted someone to make
indecent suggestions, so she could refuse.

With misshapen bricks, like these, William Wagner Bird
built a unique atmosphere. But then he made a fatal
mistake.

He died.

Not for sale in the U.S.A.

The Love Department

William Trevor

Irresistible to all women was Septimus Tuam, especially women aged fifty in and around Wimbledon. He lay in wait for them and with the aid of a rolled umbrella made them fall in love with him, and some of them died of it.

That is why Edward Blakeston-Smith – who knew nothing of love – was sent by Lady Dolores's love department to track Tuam down and discover the secrets of his ensnarements. He couldn't put a stop to it but he found out all about the friends and enemies of love.

'A fantasy which proliferates entertainingly from a germ of reality – the reality of boredom felt by comfortably-off suburban wives . . . Mr Trevor's scenes range from the near-realistic to the completely fantastic, while his tone blends the humorous, the satirical, and the sympathetic with a touch of the sinister.' – *The*

Listener

Not for sale in the U.S.A.

The Old Boys

William Trevor

'Uncommonly well-written, gruesome, funny and original' – Evelyn Waugh

The little world of a public school, with its grudges and rivalries, reaches out into the little world of the aged, as the Old Boys grimly battle over the post of President of the Association.

'Mr Trevor has written a book in which no phrase seems superfluous or wrong. It is as perfect in every part as it perfectly executes its theme' – *The Times Literary Supplement*

Not for sale in the U.S.A.

The Day We Got Drunk On Cake and Other Stories

William Trevor

In this collection of short stories William Trevor takes a look at a wide range of people. Amongst them Mr Jeffs; his 'penny wise' philosophy works because most of his customers are 'pound foolish'. Then there's Miss Efoss, who baby-sits for a couple who refuse to let her see the baby. And General Suffolk; being an octogenarian doesn't stop him going on a drunken rampage in search of sex.

William Trevor doesn't treat these people as weirdies . . . more as the people next door.

That, alone, should make you take another look at your neighbours.